Killing SUKI FLOOD

Killing SUKI FLOOD

Robert Leininger

ST. MARTIN'S PRESS • NEW YORK

Library of Congress Cataloging-in-Publication Data

Leininger, Robert
    Killing Suki Flood / Robert Leininger.
        p. cm.
    "A Thomas Dunne book."
    ISBN 0-312-05453-X
    I. Title.
PS3562.E488K5 1991
813'.54—dc20   90-48354
                                              CIP

First Edition: February 1991
10 9 8 7 6 5 4 3 2 1

For my wife, Pat, with love

Acknowledgments

I would like to thank Antoinette Leonard Matlins for sharing with me her wonderful knowledge of large gemstones.

Special thanks to my agent and friend, Marcia Amsterdam, for all her hard work on behalf of this novel.

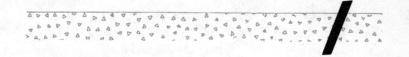

T rouble. The feeling struck Frank Limosin the instant he saw the girl. She was sitting on the rear deck of a fiery red Trans Am that was slumped at the side of the road in the hot empty desert. The feeling persisted, which told him more than he wanted to know about how old and fusty he'd become, but also had something to do with the $77,000 in unmarked bills he had stashed behind a false panel in one of the camper's cabinets.

The past few days had been interesting enough; what Frank didn't need now was a big change of plans.

The girl was leaning back comfortably on her arms, legs dangling, high-heeled sandals swinging from her toes, not a worry in the world. Young—too young. Nineteen, give or take. When they got that young, Frank couldn't figure ages worth a shit. Worse, she was wearing short shorts and one of those tiny strapless tops that Frank had always thought of as "tuck and roll"—the way it looped over and under her breasts without any visible means of support. Frank stared as he drew near, not so distracted that he didn't slow for that big sudden dip that could bust an axle if you took it fast enough. She was one of those unreal Pepsi girls, every rib and tendon visible, belly tight, hips slender, not a gram out of place.

"Aw, shit," Frank said.

Hot-pink shorts, Day-Glo lemon top: the girl was a real piece of work.

And right in his path, that was the cherry on this sundae; her car was partly blocking *his* goddamn road. Not his road, really, couldn't call it that. It wasn't his, and it certainly wasn't a road, just a dirt and gravel washboard that rambled up into the De Baca Mountains of New Mexico off Highway 401, nine miles southwest of Quiode. Out where vultures glide the empty blue sky and sometimes strip the carcass of a cow, or of a person who'd run completely out of luck.

Dust swirled past the hood of Frank's truck as he slowed. The girl—smooth young skin tanned a dark honey color, sleek young muscles making the honey skin ripple as she moved—slid off the Trans Am and stood with her thumb stuck out comically, smiling. Her other hand clutched a map.

Funny.

Dust coated the Trans Am. Its left rear tire was flat. Frank checked it out as he pulled up: new car, not a ding in it, fancy wire wheels. The tableau had a distinctly surreal aspect to it—one that stank of trouble.

He looked around, saw nothing threatening in the emptiness around them, and it *was* empty. No trees or scrub within five hundred yards, just dry needlegrass, knotweed and rocks. Bad place to stage an ambush. He decided his paranoia was showing; the melodrama of the past few days had worked on him too long, addled his brain. He needed a rest. Still, he couldn't shake that brooding sense of trouble.

2

He leaned across the seat, rolled down the passenger-side window, and spoke to the girl through the width of the cab.

"Trouble?" Might as well find out.

She blew a bubble. Late afternoon sun blazed off her pale corn-silk hair, almost a glossy, translucent vanilla, tied back in a ponytail to keep it off her shoulders. Big green guileless eyes the color of old Coke bottles. Small, upturned nose. A shiner mottled her left eye, a ripe bruise the color of mustard and mud.

"What I did was I turned left instead of right," she said.

"Huh?"

"Sixteen miles from Imogene, except it was supposed to be sixteen miles the *other* side of Imogene, not this side."

"Try to make sense."

"I am." She blew another bubble. "Hell, I was tired and it was dark and I don't read maps real good."

"You're lost."

Her eyes narrowed. "I am *not* lost. I'm just not where I expected to be."

"Which is?"

"Santa Verti."

"Christ, you're lost."

"Lost means you don't know where you are, right?"

"Right."

She stuck the map through the window and pointed to an emptiness northeast of Quiode. "Well, I figured it out and I'm right here, right?"

"Nope. Other side of the highway. Over here." He pulled her finger over and down a few inches.

"Well, hell," she said, pouting. "Which way's north?"

Frank pointed over his left shoulder. "That way."

"Dammit. Sun sets in the east, right?"

"West."

"Did I say east? I meant west."

Frank sighed. "How long've you been here, anyway?"

"Since morning, just before dawn. Tire's flat."

"I see that. Got a spare?"

"Sure. In the trunk."

"Why don't you change it?" Hell, why bother asking? He knew why. The silver dangly earrings she wore spoke volumes. She wouldn't know a carburetor from a tin whistle.

"I don't know how. I figured somebody'd come along in a while, so I waited."

"No one comes this way more'n once every couple of weeks, maybe not even that."

"Guess I got lucky, huh?"

"That's no way to stay alive out here."

She gave him a blank look. "You gonna help me with this tire or what?"

Reluctantly he switched off the engine and climbed out. His back felt slow, tight. He'd been driving half the morning and most of the afternoon, mile after mile running beneath his wheels. Putting distance between himself and the police.

He came around the front of the truck.

She took one look at him and backed away a step. Frank was used to it, half expected it, especially out here where if she screamed no one would hear a thing. He weighed two hundred forty-five pounds and stood five foot eight, shoulders as wide as a door. She was two inches taller than he was, wearing two-inch heels, so they were of a size. Except that she'd be lucky to tip the scales at more than a hundred sixteen pounds. Frank's neck and her waist had roughly the same circumference.

His face was craggy, unshaven, eyes dark beneath a heavy brow. His hair was graying, lopped off in a bristly crew cut that left the bumps of his skull visible, and his left index finger was just a stub, the first two phalanges sheared off.

She sized him up, evidently wondering if she could outrun him if she had to. Not in those heels, Frank decided, but she had long, lean thighs, and her calves were hard. Nice ankles; slender, like a deer's. Frank was fifty-four years old, not as nimble as he'd once been. In good shoes she could probably

4

leave him in the dust, sad to say. In those dumb-ass heels it would be an interesting scramble.

"Peace," he said. "I'm a tank, I know, but I'm a friendly tank."

"God, I hope so."

"You thirsty?"

"Yeah." Still wary.

Frank went around to the back of the camper, a ten-year-old Caveman he'd picked up for eight hundred bucks and loaded on a used Ford pickup he'd bought in Palmdale, California, two days ago. He'd used the name Steve Hayden for both transactions, paid cash, drove off with temporary plates. Using one alias or another was already becoming a habit.

He swung open the camper's door. "Beer okay?"

"Anything. I'm dry."

He dug a Budweiser out of an ice chest and handed it to her. She popped the top, spit her gum out on the ground, threw her head back and drank like a construction worker. Frank took the opportunity to look. Firm breasts; nicely rounded globes, a good handful each. No sign of a tan line, and about a hectare of cleavage visible where the material of her top was gathered at the midplane of her body, so it was likely she was the same color all over up there. Took her just thirty seconds to empty the can.

It was mid July. Even though they were over four thousand feet above sea level in the De Baca foothills, the temperature must have topped out at over a hundred that day. Not much breeze either. Frank squinted at the mountains across the valley, tinged blue in the hazy distance, far beyond Highway 401.

It was still hot. She'd been here over twelve hours. If he'd come this way three days later he might've come across a Trans Am and a corpse.

"Another?" Frank asked.

She nodded.

Took her a few seconds longer to empty this one, throat

working, neck arched. He watched a bead of sweat roll down her neck, over her collarbone, disappear between her breasts.

"Again?"

She shook her head. "Better not. Another of those and I'd be on my butt. You got anything else?"

"Coke."

She nodded. "Thanks, if it's not too much bother."

"No bother." He rooted around in the ice chest, hauled out a dripping can of Coke and handed it to her, suppressed a frown. He'd brought along three cases of beer and a couple six-packs of Coke. Girl kept on like this, though, she was going to punch a serious hole in his drinking plans. She'd already cramped his schedule. He wanted to reach camp before it got all the way dark, and it was still way the hell up in the De Bacas over a road—hard to call it that—that was only going to get worse, a whole lot worse, which was why he'd picked up a truck with four-wheel drive.

She spent a full minute downing the Coke, beginning to slow.

"Another?"

"Thanks, not right now. You must think I'm a pig, huh?"

"Nope, just parched. Let's see about that tire."

She wobbled across the broken ground to the Trans Am and popped the trunk. Bright yellow flames were painted down both sides of the car's body. Twin mufflers stuck out the back, one of them dragging on the ground.

"How fast you come up this road, anyway?" Frank asked. She had pink sparkly polish on her toenails. Cute.

"I dunno. Thirty, maybe thirty-five."

At least. And hit that bad dip and launched herself, came down hard and ripped out a muffler, blew a tire. Way far out in the hot summer desert. Stupid. Frank peered into the trunk.

Spare tire. Jack. Lug wrench. Two plastic bottles of 10-40 Pennzoil. A gallon of gas. Couple of rags. Duffel bag in a corner. Everything she'd needed to get moving again, but she was too dumb to figure out how. Frank didn't like dumb.

"Spare looks okay."

"Uh-huh," she said, arms folded across her chest.

"You want to haul it outta there?"

She frowned. "Me?"

"Yeah, you."

"It's dirty. You got a bad back, mister?"

"Frank. Frank Wiley."

She smiled. "Like the coyote, huh?"

"Kinda. Just one word, though. W-I-L-E-Y."

"Oh."

"You got a name, or should I just call you hey you?"

"Suki."

"Come again?"

"Suki. S-U-K-I. Erickson."

Jesus. Bubblegum name for a bubblegum girl.

"Well, Suki, my back's fine, thanks. Now, if you'll haul that tire outta there, you can get started."

She gave him an odd look. "*Me?*"

"That's right."

"You're not going to . . . to help me?"

"I'm gonna give you all the help you need. Which is to say I'm gonna tell you how to change a tire."

"Christ!"

He got himself a beer and went over to a large flat rock, sat down on it with a sigh.

"The tire," he said, wagging a finger.

She banged the trunk lid down and climbed up on it. Frank watched appreciatively as her muscles flexed. No Einstein, but she was sure a work of art. In those shorts he could just see the tendons of her inner thighs, up near her crotch.

"See," Frank said, "if I changed that tire for you—"

"I don't wanna hear it."

"—next time this happened you'd be just as helpless as you are now."

"Be prepared, all that crap?"

"Being prepared never hurt anyone yet."

"Think I'll just wait for the next Good Sami . . . Samarian to come along. Thanks anyway."

"That's Samaritan."

"Whatever."

"Could be a while." Frank stood up.

"C'mon, Frank," she said, sliding off the car. "Be nice, huh? All it is is a tire."

It was more than that, a hell of a lot more, but all the finer points of the situation were sailing right over her head. "Pretty doesn't pay the bills, Suki."

"Huh?" Her eyes widened.

"And pretty doesn't get your tire changed when you're all alone in the desert, either."

She stamped a foot. "I'm *not* alone, you jerk."

"Take a look around. Imagine how it'll look after I'm gone." He trudged back to his truck and opened the door.

"Hey!"

"What?"

"You can't just leave me here." She came lurching toward him in her heels. He decided he could probably catch her, if he wanted to. Which he didn't.

He said, "You don't want help, that's your business."

"I want *help*, not instructions."

"Give a man a fish and he'll eat today. Teach him to fish and he'll eat for the rest of his life."

"*What?*"

"Nothing. Forget it. See you around." He got behind the wheel and banged the door shut.

She stared at him.

He started the engine, put it in gear.

"Okay!" she cried. "*Okay*, dammit, tell me what to do."

Frank switched off the engine and pocketed the key. "What you do first is get out the spare."

She lurched back to the Trans Am and opened the trunk. She glared at him, then wrestled with the tire while Frank Limosin made himself comfortable on the rock again.

"Oh! Dammit!" She clutched her hand.

"What?"

"I broke a nail, that's what."

"Life's rough."

She gave him a baleful look. "You're a dear. Now what?" She stuck the wounded nail in her mouth.

"Get the jack out."

"That's this, right?" She pulled out the jack, frowning. "It's dirty too." She shoved a wisp of hair out of her eyes, leaving a nice grease mark on her forehead. Frank smiled.

"That's it. Better set your emergency brake."

She did. He squatted beside the car and pointed to the place underneath where the jack should go. It was a scissors jack, with a threaded shaft that ran through the center.

He stood back, arms folded, and watched her butt wriggle as she planted her elbows in the dirt, back arched, and positioned the jack. Very nice. The movement pulled her shorts way up, exposing a rounded haunch the same golden shade as the rest of her. Frank wondered if she had any tan lines on her at all.

"This all right?" she asked.

He crouched beside her. "Little to the left. You got to catch that heavy lip of metal there."

"Now what?"

"Now you stick the handle on this shaft here and turn it. Clockwise."

She sat on her heels, knees splayed out wide, and cranked the handle around a few times. The car groaned, began to lift.

"It's working," she said, surprised.

"Incredible." Frank sat on the rock again. "That's enough. Too much and you'll have trouble getting the lug nuts off. Where'd you get the shiner?"

"None of your business. What's a lug nut?"

"Under the hub cap."

She pried it off.

"Those." He pointed. "Holding the tire on. Maybe you walked into a door."

"Maybe I did. How'd you lose the finger?"

9

He held up the stub, examined it. "Had it resting in a hydraulic lift when my partner hit the switch."

"Smart. Hurt much?"

"Not a bit. Felt terrific."

She stood up. "Now what?"

"There's a wrench in back. You'll need it to get the lug nuts off the wheel."

She peered into the trunk. "What's it look like?"

"There's not much left in there. Take a wild guess."

"This?" She held up a heavy chrome object, shaped like a cross.

"Bingo."

She pursed her lips. "Thank you so much."

"See, what we're doing here is we're trying to get the bad tire off and put the good tire on."

"No shit. What do you mean *we*, anyway?"

He ignored her. "What you do is think of it as a bunch of little tasks. You just have to know what they are. Do 'em all in the right order without skipping any and you've changed a tire. It's a lot like life."

"What're you? Like a poet or a phili . . . philot . . . philozer or something?" She whipped her ponytail back in an angry gesture.

The modern high school education in action. *Philosopher* had one too many syllables in it, wouldn't fit in her mouth.

"There's a bunch of different-sized sockets on that wrench there. See which one fits the lugs holding the wheel on."

She crouched down. Frank admired the long, lean stretch of her thighs. She tried a few sockets, found the proper one. She pushed it on a lug and gave it an experimental twist, the wrong way.

"Counterclockwise," Frank said. "In America, off is just about always counterclockwise, except for water faucets."

She gave him a furious look, then returned to her task. She twisted the wrench. Nothing happened. Harder, the muscles in her arms and shoulders beginning to stand out.

Though her arms were slender, he could see they had strength in them.

"Shit," she said.

"Trouble?"

"I can't turn it." Frustration filled her voice; a heated kettle, beginning to steam. "You want to fucking help out here a minute?"

"You pick up that language at home or at church?"

"I'm old enough to say whatever I want."

"How old's that?"

"None of your business."

He shrugged. "Fine. Nineteen?"

"You gonna help or what?"

"See, I do that and you're right back where you started. You get a flat out somewhere all alone and can't get the lug nuts off, you're in the same fix as you are right now."

"I can't turn the sonofabitch!" she yelled. She looked good, mad. Corded and wiry, sort of like a cat.

"Relax," he said. "We'll figure something out."

Her eyes glittered. "All those muscles you got, you won't goddamn help or nuthin'?"

"What you need is more leverage. You might try lashing a stick to the crossbar, that'd do it."

"God, I don't believe this shit!"

"Not many of 'em around, though. Another thing you could try is sticking a rock under one end of the crossbar and sort of hopping up and down on the other. Use your weight to better advantage."

"Hell," she muttered.

"It's a bit tricky, though. Unless you rotate the wheel as you go, you'll need different-sized rocks for each nut. The good news is, there are lots of those around."

He pointed out a likely specimen, watched with interest as she squatted next to it, lifted it, hugged it to her belly, staggered over to the Trans Am and let it drop.

Frank stood a few feet away. He told her how to place the

rock, describing its purpose. She put her hands on one end of the wrench and pushed down on it tentatively.

"Harder."

She glared at him and then lunged on the wrench, grunting, hair dancing, and the lug nut racked over a few degrees.

"That might do it," Frank said. "Grease monkeys grind those bastards on with pneumatic wrenches, using twice the foot-pounds they need."

"Tell me somethin' I don't know."

"Anyway, you might be able to get it now without the rock. Give it a try."

She crouched over the lug wrench, lifting on one side as she pushed down on the other. Cords stood out in her neck. Looked good like that, too, Frank reflected. She looked good in almost any position, but she looked best with her muscles drawn tight, standing out.

Lord, she made him feel old.

The nut spun a quarter turn. "Got it," she said.

"Another Coke?"

She nodded.

"Keep at it," he said encouragingly. "Try the next one."

Inside the camper he looked out and watched her for a while. She was getting the hang of it, lean torso bent over, straining, and he heard the squeal of metal as another lug nut came loose.

His schedule, such as it was, was dying. At the rate she was going, it'd take her another half hour to get it done, but at least she was doing it. Frank didn't like helpless, and he didn't like dumb. Which was a riot, what with half the highway patrol in California looking for him—wrong state, which wasn't *too* bad—and maybe the FBI as well—which wasn't too good. Hard to get much dumber than that, he supposed, except by letting a cute little number like Suki walk all over him in jackboots just because she looked like somebody's wet dream.

Hell with it. He had thirty-five years on her and it'd been

a long time since his palms had gotten sweaty over some girl, no matter how finely tuned she was. A very long time . . . since long before Fanny had died. Fanny and Frank; he still liked the sound of that.

He came back out, handed her a Coke. "Tell me again how you ended up here."

"I already said."

"I'm not all that bright. Run it by me again."

She swept her hair out of her eyes again. Doing a pretty good job of greasing her face.

"I was headed for my cousin's place, out near Santa Verti. Cora told me to turn left off the highway when I got sixteen miles from Imogene. That's what I goddamn did, and here I am."

"Where'd you come from?"

"Shreveport . . . Louisiana."

"You get the black eye there?"

"I told you, that's none of your damn business."

"Touchy subject, huh?"

She hunched over the last lug and leaned into it. Getting better at it too, Frank noted with satisfaction.

"So, what she meant was the *other* side of Imogene," Suki said. "Which means I turned in the wrong direction as well as the wrong place. Left instead of right. Got it?"

"Not entirely. Anyway, left and right are kinda relative. Better if you used north and south, east and west."

"It was dark out."

"Right. Good thing Columbus sailed in the morning. Where would we be now if he hadn't?"

"Very funny. Now what?"

She had the nuts off, scattered in the dirt. Messy. It grated on Frank's nerves.

"Looks like that tire might come off now."

She crouched down, tugged on it. "Nope."

"Maybe if you jacked the car up a little higher, get the weight off that tire. I saw that done in a movie once."

She glowered at him, squatted by the jack again and began cranking. Slowly, the Trans Am lifted. The tire tottered and fell off; Suki jumped back with a squawk and fell on her rump.

"Guess that's probably high enough," Frank said.

"You're really enjoying this, aren't you?" She stood up, slapping dust off her seat.

"Beats TV."

"Now what?"

"The bad tire's off. What d'you think?"

"Put the good tire on?"

"Bingo. See, you can do this."

She struggled with the spare, a wide, heavy Goodyear VR50, grunting, puffing, arms trembling with the effort.

"After you get it settled on the lugs, put a nut on partway to hold it while you find the other nuts you've scattered all over hell and gone in the dirt."

While she did this, Frank observed—in what he hoped was a suitably detached and clinical manner—the way in which her nipples pocked the fabric of her thin cotton top. She had to know. Probably knew what effect she had on men and counted on it, had used it a thousand times. Wasn't working out this time, and she was angry, mouth tight as she spun lug nuts on with her fingers. Which was fine.

Thirty years ago Frank's heart would've lurched into arrhythmia just looking at her. Thirty years ago he would've given her the world for a smile. Now . . . now she was good to look at, gave him pretty good range for his fantasies, which weren't all that heated these days anyway, but he couldn't imagine things getting past the fantasy stage. That's how old he'd gotten, and he supposed it was a goddamned shame.

He explained how to tighten the lugs to seat the wheel properly. She cranked them on tight, then lowered the car onto its new tire. Old tire in the trunk, along with the jack and the wrench. She banged the lid down.

"Done." She dusted her hands, a smug, satisfied look on her streaky, glistening face.

14

"Good." Frank was almost sorry the show was over, but he had to get on the road. The sun was behind a western projection of the De Bacas now, a ridge known as the Devil's Spine, spreading a ruddy glow over the mountains to the northeast.

"Another one for the road? How 'bout an apple?"

"Thanks." She came around the rear of the camper and accepted a Granny Smith and another Coke, then trailed along behind as he ambled to the cab of the truck. He slid in behind the wheel.

"Just want you to know you're a real creep, Frank," she said. "But thanks anyway."

"Anytime."

He started the engine and she stepped back. He gave her a last look, smiled, and said, "See you."

She lifted her Coke in farewell and he took off, past the fiery Trans Am, up into the darkening foothills of the De Baca Mountains.

Terrific opening chapter

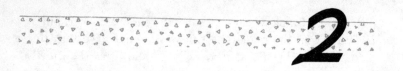

The plan was off schedule, not that the schedule meant a damn thing or that the plan itself was all that great. It wasn't. But Suki'd seen him, and that wasn't good. She'd sure as hell recognize him if she saw his face on television, and she knew he was headed up into the De Baca Mountains.

All he'd meant to do was fade into the landscape with five bottles of Jack Daniel's, three cases of beer, enough steak and chicken, corn, fruit, and canned goods to outlast the booze, and five or six Stephen King novels, which he intended to read fast and loose and partly drunk. Only way to read King.

Lay low for a week or two, as they say.

Maybe by then he'd come up with another plan. Like maybe a way to get to Rio, something like that. Seventy-

16

seven thousand dollars might last quite a while in Rio, if he lived like a native and not like some hotshot who thought he was big time now and could afford a girl for each arm. The pot wasn't all *that* sweet, and he couldn't afford to blow much of it on the ladies, or anything else, for that matter.

Right now, though, all he wanted was to get up to that spot between Cable Peak and that other mountain—its name had somehow slipped through the cracks of his memory; happened a lot lately—where a natural spring bubbled up year round. Hell to get to, but that made it all the more likely he'd have the place all to himself the whole two weeks, or however long it took him to work his way through five liters of good sour mash without regretting the experience too much.

The road angled left, climbed steeply, and Frank Limosin looked out over the valley, where long dark shadows now covered the land. He'd gained considerable altitude in the mile since he'd left Suki. Down there, looking small, he saw her open the door to the Trans Am and get in. He stopped the truck, watching, racing the engine a bit to let it cool.

Damn good-looking gal, Suki. But dumb.

Well, maybe not dumb, but goddamned inexperienced, like so many were these days. Unprepared. Tearing around without any comprehension of reality. They watched television and then got their toy cars stuck way out in the hot summer desert.

What the country needed was a good war, not like Vietnam, but a good one, like World War II. Shake these spoiled brats up, give them some direction. Except that he had the feeling that kids with blue mohawks and earrings would roll over and die before they marched willingly off to war to protect their freedom.

The Trans Am went crossways in the road, backed up, moved forward again. Even this far away he heard the deep-throated beat of its engine. It crawled forward, stopped. He heard a roar as Suki gunned the engine. And then it died.

He waited. Shit.

Waited, and then she got out, slammed the door, kicked the fenders, pounded the hood, and walked away a few steps.

"Shit," Frank said. "Shit and more shit."

And there she was again, sitting on the rear deck of the Tranny, legs drawn up, head resting on her knees.

"I will be," Frank said, enunciating each word with terrible precision, "a miserable . . . son . . . of . . . a . . . *bitch.*"

He jammed the truck into reverse and backed to a wide spot he'd just passed, got it turned around, and began rumbling back down the trail.

She looked up as he approached. Slid off the car and stood there, waiting.

"What's the deal?" he asked.

"Son of a bitch is dead."

He switched off the engine and got out. "Dead how?"

"Dead dead. How the hell would I know?"

How indeed?

He went over to the Trans Am, opened the door. Glanced up and saw a dark sheen covering the road fifty feet away. Oil. Lots of it.

Shit again.

Frank walked up the road, Suki trailing awkwardly in her desert survival gear. He crouched down and dipped a finger into a smear of oil. It was fresh.

"What do you know about this?" he asked.

"It's oil, huh?"

"Yeah. Same stuff they sometimes dump in Prince William Sound. In Alaska."

"Well, I don't know." She stood there, biting her lip. "It's from my car, you think?"

He walked back, took a look underneath. Yep; pan was torn all to shit under there. His fault, of course. He should've known she would figure out a way to do a lot more damage than just to blow a tire and rip off a muffler.

She'd frozen the engine. Gunned it just as it was dying

18

and turned forty-five hundred dollars' worth of fine machinery into scrap metal.

But what did you expect? She was a golden, glorious girl with brains of sawdust and air. An oil pressure light blazing red on her instrument panel didn't mean squat to her.

He tried the ignition, just in case. Starter motor had a go at it but couldn't budge it. Nice.

The sky was clear, not a cloud anywhere. When night came the temperature was going to drop into the low fifties, maybe lower; not enough to kill her, dressed the way she was, but enough to make her pretty uncomfortable. And that wasn't the point, really. The problem was, she was going to die out here if he left her, period, like a poodle with a rhinestone collar lost in the Everglades. When he came back this way a few weeks from now he would find her lying on the trunk of her petrified toy car with vultures standing on her chest, eyes gone, tongue ripped out.

So what he had to do was drive her to the nearest town—Quiode, almost twenty miles away.

"It's bad, huh?" she asked.

"It's terminal." He got out, slammed the door.

"Yeah, well, now what, Mr. Frank Wiley?" The sun was all the way down now, temperature already into the seventies. She shivered slightly, more from her predicament than the cold.

"Now I drive you into town."

"What town?"

"Quiode."

"Sounds charming."

"They all are, out here. Grab your stuff and let's go."

She opened the trunk of the Trans Am, took out a duffel bag. Black nylon with maroon trim, REEBOK on the side. Not a large bag, but it looked full.

"You want to change into something a little less obvious?" Frank asked.

She shook her head.

"Might turn a few heads where we're going, you dressed like that. Place isn't much."

"That's life. Bet they're just sick, the Charleston going out of style like it did."

He shrugged. "That all you're bringing?"

"Yeah."

"Okay, let's move it."

She climbed up into the cab of his truck and sat near the door on the passenger's side with her legs stretched out, the duffel bag on the floor under her knees. Frank eased the truck around the Trans Am and bumped across the small gorge in the road that had killed it.

"Wait!" Suki yelped.

He slammed on the brakes, skidded the truck on the loose dirt. "What?"

"I forgot something. Just a sec." She grabbed her bag and scrambled out the door. Gone.

"Aw, shit," Frank said.

He watched her in the side mirror as she made her way back to the car in the twilight, lifted the trunk, hauled something out. Opened a door, leaned in. Came back out, backed toward him for a distance of about twenty feet. Stood and fumbled a few seconds with something.

A lighter flared. She dropped it. Flames leapt up, gold, hot, running swiftly for the car. Frank's jaw dropped. Suki came toward him, hurrying.

The atmosphere was mildly explosive in the Trans Am when the flames hit it. The windows blew out and it jumped a few inches off the ground, then began burning merrily, rosy flames spewing out the windows, black smoke curling into the sky.

Suki opened the door and climbed in. "Ready."

"Sweet Jesus, wha'd you do *that* for?"

"I believe in cremation."

"Sonofabitch." He stared at the flames in the mirror a moment longer, then looked at her. Her face was dark in the gloom, unreadable. "Sonofabitch," he said again.

"We gonna go, or what?"

What else? Piss on the flames? He pulled away. A few minutes later the gas tank blew, the sound rolling over them and across the valley.

She was quiet. Maybe pensive, but Frank didn't want to give her too much credit. Might not be much of anything going on upstairs in that sawdust mill of hers.

"Married?" he asked.

"Hell no."

"Boyfriend give you that shiner?"

"Who says I got a boyfriend?"

"That his car back there?"

She stared at him. "Maybe."

"Gives you a black eye, gets his car thoroughly trashed, something like that?"

"Full of questions, aren't you?"

"Just trying to figure out what happened back there."

"Well, don't."

"Want to at least tell me how old you are?"

"What's it matter? You worried I'm jailbait?"

"Maybe." Frank picked up a tennis ball on the seat beside him and began to squeeze it slowly and rhythmically, muscles flexing in his right forearm.

She stared at his fist. "I'll be nineteen first week in October. Happy now?"

"Relieved."

She fell silent and he just drove, down the rocky slope with its endless loops and rises and dips, feeling the weight of the camper in the bed of the truck, wondering if Suki was crazy or what. Somewhere below in the gathering darkness was Route 401. Behind them lay a smoking ruin.

"You got a heater in this thing?" she asked.

"Yeah. You got any useful clothing in that bag of yours?"

"It's fulla toys."

"Huh?"

"For my cousin's kids, Cody and Gretchen. Toys. Teddy bears, stuff like that."

"Christ, that all? You don't have any other clothes with you?"

"No."

"Really came prepared, didn't you?"

"Don't start with me again. I didn't plan on getting stuck out there and—"

"Left Shreveport in a hell of a hurry, didn't you?"

"Who says?"

"Just figures. You grabbed a duffel bag full of toys and hauled ass, not bothering to pack when Mr. Clean got in a shot at your eye. Makes sense."

"Smart-ass. I didn't grab the bag and run. It was in the trunk for a week. And if it makes you feel any smarter, yes he hit me. Asshole son of a bitch."

"Now we're getting somewhere."

"Where?"

He stared at her. "Where what?"

"Where're we getting? What's it to you, anyway?"

"Hell, I don't know. Christ, you always this hard to get along with?"

"Mostly."

"Figures. So what you're wearing is all you've got?"

"This's it."

"Fantastic. Hope they let you on the bus."

They reached the highway. Frank turned right and drove fifty-five all the way to Quiode. A sign marked the limits of the town:

Quiode
pop. 41 el. 3973

The place was quiet. A one-pump Texaco station built in the fifties; two bars: the Blue Bottle Bar and Ernie's Tavern. Some sort of all-purpose drugstore cum hardware store cum food market standing next to a laundromat that had been

22

boarded up with weathered plywood. And Belinda's Café.

At the far end of town was a motel of cracked adobe, six tiny, faceless units featuring queen-size beds and TV. The Siesta Motel. Near the street, a vacancy sign was illuminated by a dirt-encrusted bulb.

Belinda's was blue and red neon, a blaze of fluorescent lighting that punched a glaring hole in the night. The bars sported Coors, Budweiser, and Miller signs; a couple of rangy-looking trucks languished in front of each. The remainder of the town was dark. A dog crossed the street and disappeared down an alley between Ernie's Tavern and Mason's all-purpose whatever. Suspended from overhead wires in the middle of the street, a melancholy yellow light winked on and off.

"Lovely," Suki said.

Frank drove past Belinda's Café and pulled up in front of the Siesta. A car with a big V-8 engine rumbled slowly by on the street behind them.

"Guess this'll have to do," Frank said.

Suki opened her door. "I hope this place doesn't have too many roaches. I hate roaches."

The motel was squat, umber, dark; gloomy beneath rustling cottonwoods and mulberrys. Tangled shrubs, malign and shaggy, crowded the concrete walkways in front. Frank pressed a button on the office doorframe. Inside, a distant buzzer sounded.

"I'm hungry," Suki said, gazing at Belinda's with drooping eyelids.

"Let's get you a place to stay first."

A light came on. Frank felt eyes staring from somewhere inside. Ten or fifteen seconds later the door opened and a man with hunched shoulders and hanging jowls peered out. Six foot two. Endless liver spots. At least eighty-five years old.

"Room?"

"Yeah," Frank said.

"Single bed do ya?" He had a smoker's voice, phlegmy. An eye-watering garlicky aura filled the air around him.

"It's for her, not us."

The man looked Suki up and down, slowly. "You alone?"

"Yeah."

Another look, gaunt, fixed mostly on her breasts. A gray tongue licked cyanotic lips. He blinked. "C'mon in, then."

Frank turned to Suki. Under his breath, he said, "You got money?"

"Some."

"What I mean is, enough?"

"I guess so, sure."

"Want me to stick around a while?"

"Maybe a few minutes. My skin's crawling."

"Okay."

They went inside. The proprietor—Mr. Drummond he told them his name was, Earl Drummond—was on his last legs. Suki was probably the best thing he'd seen in twenty years. While she signed the register he leaned partway over the counter, trying to peer down her top, eyes fluttering in their leaky old sockets, drinking so deeply of the vision of her that Frank was sure Drummond's skull would split wide open. At any moment his heart would cough out an embolus that would drift up into his brain, and that'd be that. Frank had come across Suki and saved her, more or less, and already another old buzzard was pecking away at her.

Drummond's eyes wandered, took in Frank's finger. "Used to live on a farm," Frank offered. "Sonofabitchin' pig bit it off, big six-hundred-pound sow." Suki looked up at him.

"That'll be fifteen dollar," Earl Drummond said when she was finished, and went immediately into a coughing fit that sounded as if it might be his last.

Suki produced a twenty-dollar bill from the waistband of her shorts, handed it to him, got change and a key.

"Room one-oh-five," Drummond said, eyes suddenly sly.

Suki did a double take. "One-oh-five?" The place only had six units.

"First floor, room five," Drummond said, and went into a wheezing fit that sent him reeling through the door behind the counter and into the next room where a television was playing, some used-car dealer trying to make an honest buck. Drummond hawked, spat into something.

"Unbelievable," Suki said, rolling her eyes. "Let's get outta here."

They stepped out into the night. The temperature was down to about sixty-five now. A couple of cats screeched nearby. Suki shivered.

Frank pushed three wadded twenties into her hand.

She shook her head. "No, I'm okay."

"Take it."

She looked into his eyes. "Yeah, thanks."

"You gonna be all right now?"

"I guess, when I get a little food in me."

"Okay." He didn't know what else to say. Belinda's was just a hundred feet away. He didn't want to see Suki's room, a naked twenty-five-watt bulb illuminating the saggy bed and peeling wallpaper. "See you around, huh?"

"Sure."

"Try not to blow anything else up, okay?"

"Yeah, okay. Frank?"

"What?"

"You hungry?"

"Not very."

She gave him a look, almost hurt, then turned away. "See you." She began walking toward Belinda's.

He watched her go, hips swaying in silhouette against the glowing backdrop of the café. Nice walk. Gorgeous calves.

He shook his head and climbed back into his truck.

Now what?

Back up into the hills? He didn't relish the thought of trying to reach camp in the dark. Couple of serious slopes on the way up that'd be bad enough in daylight. What he could do was drive back to where Suki's Trans Am was probably still smoking and crash for the night in the camper, way off the highway.

And what he could do before that, come to think of it, is get a start on the booze in one of the bars in Quiode, just to take the edge off the evening. All the unexpected changes in his plans had wound him up pretty tight.

He drove the two hundred feet to the Blue Bottle Bar, glanced at Suki at the counter in the café as he went past, parked his rig beside the building, off the street. No one would be looking for him here, this far from L.A.—at least, not for a very long time—but why take chances?

In the Siesta Motel, Earl Drummond squinted at what the girl with the city hooters had inscribed in his register:

> s. arksun
> 60 gan stret
> srepot, lu

He shook his head at this ciphertext, rubbed his grizzled old cheeks, and clumped back to his bathroom to spit.

Frank locked up tight. Quiode didn't look like a big crime area, but with all that money back there he wanted to play it safe. The two pickup trucks still stood out front, and a muscle car—a dark Oldsmobile Toronado with a custom-mounted air scoop on the hood, vinyl roof ripped all to hell, scabrous gray primer. Brutish machinery. A Bad Boy's car. The sound of the throbbing, slow-moving horsepower that Frank had heard as he pulled up in front of the Siesta Motel passed through his mind again. Might've been the Olds.

The Blue Bottle was saving a fortune in electricity. Coming in from the night outside, Frank almost felt it necessary to let his eyes adjust to the gloom. A glowing Heineken sign the size of a license plate was perched atop the cash register. At the end of the bar, a blue and yellow neon sign on the wall read HIRAM WALKER *SCHNAPPS*. A poisonous blue-green phosphorescence emanated from the well beneath the bar. The jukebox was inky glass, its cord trailing cobralike on the floor. The place was like a crypt in the Caverns of the Dead.

A couple of cowboy-looking types with mustaches and dark inhospitable faces sat at a table against a back wall, nursing beers. Belonged to the trucks outside, Frank guessed. At the bar sat two hard cases who were probably with the muscle car.

Frank ordered a double Daniel's and took it to a dim corner—which was dumb, he thought: he was wide and ugly, as memorable as an earthquake. It wasn't as if the barkeep or Drummond couldn't finger him if anyone came by asking. Have to catch Drummond pretty quick though; he wouldn't be around much longer. It wasn't terribly smart, sitting here. Running into Suki had already done enough damage to his plans, and here he was, doing more.

The bartender was fortyish, balding, dozing off and jerking awake; ticking, it seemed, like some strange clock. The two old ranchers were downing their beers quietly, sullen and serious.

The Bad Boys had their heads together at the bar, talking in low voices. Suddenly they stood up, one of them tossing a handful of change onto the bar. They came drifting over in Frank's direction.

Uh-oh.

One skinny, the other with muscles; both in jeans, dirty T-shirts, tattoos, even. The big one sported a buzz cut that gave him a dangerous, retarded look.

The skinny one's dark eyes reflected points of light. He held out a lighter and a picture. Flicked his Bic and said, "Seen this girl around anywhere in the last day or two, dude?"

It was Suki.

Shit.

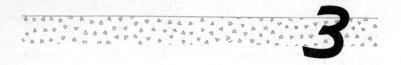

Nope," Frank said.

The skinny one snapped the lighter off. "Let's split."

They walked out, both wearing boots, looking like fun-house images of each other. In her high-heeled sandals, Suki wouldn't be able to outrun either one.

"Son of a bitch," Frank said.

There were more vultures hunting her than flies circling horse turds. Wasn't his fight, though. Wasn't any goddamn reason at all why he couldn't just sit right here, drink his drink, let the world do whatever the hell it was destined to do without his interference. People were starving in Ethiopia and he had a bunch of steaks on ice in his truck outside and there wasn't a damn way he could make those two facts come out right either. Suki had her problems; Frank had plenty of his own. His plate was full as it was, and besides, he didn't owe her a thing. Not one damn thing.

Bloody hell.

He stood up, gulped his drink and went out into the night. The two hardcases were halfway to Belinda's. They hadn't spotted Suki yet, but Frank thought things would liven up any moment now. That pair wasn't tracking her down to tell her she'd won the California lottery.

He crouched behind the muscle car, still figuring it for the one the toughs were driving, and peered over its flaking, air-scooped hood at Belinda's. He didn't want to make some sort of a big deal out of this, but he wasn't sure how to avoid it. What he didn't need was a big scene. On general principles, he began letting air out of the Toronado's tires. He crouched at the driver's side, where the two thugs couldn't see him. He'd feel pretty dumb if it turned out not to be theirs, but if it was, it seemed only prudent to limit their mobility.

Yep, they'd made her. They drew back into the shadows by the door, partly hidden by a truck that looked like some kind of local fuel-oil hauler. Skinny had a few words with Muscles and then he trotted around back.

Under normal conditions, it'd be smart to split up: Belinda's had two entrances, one on either side. No way to tell which door Suki'd come out, and if they took her quick, before she could holler, they might make a clean job of it.

Frank started shuffling toward the café, hands stuffed in his pockets, head down. The town was quiet, no wind. Gravel crunched beneath his shoes. Wasn't his fight and here he was, playing Sir Galahad like some twenty-two-year-old feebleminded schmuck.

He went around the front of the stubby oil truck. GUMP'S FUEL & HEATING was printed on the doors of the cab in bold black letters. Muscles was hanging around by the door of the café.

"Got the time?" Frank asked, slurring his speech.

Muscles shook his head. "Ain't got no watch."

"That your buddy comin'?" Frank pointed.

Muscles turned to look. Frank kicked him in the groin. Muscles staggered back, doubled over. Frank dropped him with a fist to the side of the head.

Rubbed his knuckles. Been a while since he'd last used them that way, twenty years at least. Hurt like hell. Maybe he'd busted one, or at least sprained something in there.

Muscles was sprawled in a heap on his side, legs loose. The town was quiet. An owl hooted in a tree behind Belinda's. The highway was empty; the yellow glow of the caution light pulsed in the trees. Frank took a ten-dollar bill from his wallet and went into the café. Four people were inside: an old man and his wife picking at their food, sour-faced and silent; the Gump's oil man in greasy blue coveralls; and Suki, midriff bare, legs lanky and tan, wearing those dumb-ass shoes. Frank dropped the bill on the counter next to her plate and grabbed her arm.

"C'mon."

"What?"

He hauled her to her feet, pulled her toward the door he'd just come in. She grabbed her bag as she went.

"What're you *doin'*, Frank?" she asked around a big bite of hamburger. "I didn't hardly get started yet."

"Don't talk with your mouth full."

His hand was big on her arm. No arguing with that. She went outside with him.

Frank rolled Muscles over with his toe. "Know this guy?"

She paled.

"C'mon. Let's move it. His pal's on the other side of the building." Frank drew her toward the Blue Bottle at a half run.

She trotted along—and broke a heel.

Of course.

Hobbled around looking for the useless sonofabitch until

Frank pushed her into the shadows behind the Blue Bottle and told her to get lost.

Frank looked back. Skinny was coming fast, arms pumping. Frank glanced around, saw an old push broom leaning against the building by a box of trash. He grabbed it.

Skinny had a knife. He'd seen Suki run behind the Blue Bottle and he wanted to go after her, but Frank was in the way.

"Move it, fucker," Skinny snarled.

Frank held the broom in both hands, the handle pointed at the skinny shit.

"Who the fuck're you?" Skinny said.

"Ed Sullivan. Who're you?"

Skinny smiled. Missing a few teeth, mostly in front. He tossed the knife from one hand to the other, showing Frank he knew what he was doing, feet kicking up a pale mist of dust as his legs scissored black shadows over the ground. The blade wasn't real long, but it looked long enough. Sharp enough, too.

"How 'bout I whittle some of that beef off you, old man?" Skinny said.

"How about I ram this poker up your kazoo till your ears ring?"

"Give it your best shot." Skinny danced from one foot to the other, swinging the blade. Frank drove the broom handle straight out several times, short hard jabs; connected with Skinny's belly on the fifth try. Skinny went down hard and fell to one side, retching. Might've been good with a knife, given a log to whittle, but he wasn't all that great with his feet.

Frank grabbed Skinny's knife and jogged cautiously around the rear of the bar, calling Suki's name.

"Over here."

"C'mon, let's get outta here."

She came hopping out of the darkness, yellow Day-Glo tits bobbing up and down, side to side. Jesus H. Christ.

He unlocked the truck and she piled in, scooting over. He started the engine and backed out into the street. Muscles was up, lumbering toward them, hunched partway over his nuts.

Frank roared off. A minute later the truck topped a rise and the lights of Quiode disappeared behind them.

"Spill it," Frank said.

"Spill what?"

"What the hell you think? Those two were looking for you, showing your picture around. What was that all about? You knew the big one. Small one, too, I'll bet."

She was silent. "Mote and Jersey," she said after they'd gone about a mile.

"Huh?"

"Those two. Big one was Mote, small one was Jersey."

He waited.

She sighed. "They're friends of Mink's."

Like that explained it; like he knew who the hell Mink was. Real good name for some dumb-shit hoodlum though. No lights behind them, so maybe he'd flattened the tires on the right vehicle after all. He kept it at fifty-five and waited for her to talk.

Kept on waiting.

Nope, she just sat there, sunk into a tangible cloud of silence. "Who the hell's Mink?" Frank finally asked.

"Mink's the guy whose car had a real bummer of a day today."

"Same guy that gave you that shiner?"

"Yeah."

"Mink a nickname or what?"

"Yeah."

He waited. Nothing. He pulled the truck to the side of the road, turned around, started back toward Quiode.

"What're you *doing*?" Suki yelped.

"Maybe Mutt and Jeff'll talk to me."

"Mote and Jersey. Don't be a jerk, Frank." She reached over and switched off the ignition.

32

The truck lunged. Frank stomped on the clutch and they coasted to a stop in the middle of the empty road.

He doused the headlights. The night suddenly got big around them, full of stars. He left the parking lights on, dash lights glowing in the cab. "You got guys chasing you, showing your picture around, carrying knives. All the way from goddamn Louisiana. What's the story?"

She bit her lip.

"C'mon."

"Nobody drives Mink's car," she said in a low voice. "Nobody *touches* Mink's goddamn car except Mink, understand? He's nuts about that stupid car. He hit me and I grabbed his car, because nobody touches *me*, either."

"All this is about a car?"

"Yeah."

"A stupid goddamn *car*?"

"And a black eye, Frank. Don't forget the eye."

In the glow of the dash lights Frank stared at her. "So who're Mutt and Jeff?"

"Mink's . . . friends."

"Must be a real prince, friends like that."

"Can we get goin' now?"

"In a minute. So, this Mutt and Jeff were chasing around the whole damn country, looking for you. Right?"

"I guess."

"You didn't know they were after you?"

"No."

"Those two must be bloodhounds, trailing after you six or seven hundred miles like they did."

"This is a very stupid place to sit around and talk. Turn around and let's get moving and I'll tell you what I know."

Made sense. He got them rolling away from Quiode again, still doing fifty-five.

"There might be more than just Mote and Jersy after me," she said.

"That right?"

"Mink's got lotsa friends."

"So what you're saying is Mutt and Jeff just got lucky, that there's a whole army of Mink's buddies out looking for you?"

"Could be. I don't know how many and I don't know how hard it'd be to keep on my trail. Car like that, hair like this."

"Girl like you, dressed in an outfit like that."

She looked at him. "Guess so. And I'd told him about my cousin here in New Mexico. Maybe he remembered."

"Maybe he did."

She was silent a minute. "We were gonna get married."

"Who? You and this Mink guy?"

She nodded. "Back in March we set the date for September. The eighth, it was gonna be."

"How old's this guy?"

"Thirty-four."

"Like 'em older, huh?"

"Yeah. That all the hell right with you?"

"Fine. So what we've got here is your basic domestic squabble, right? Guy pops you in the eye and you take off in his car. Gears of love all filled with grit."

"Mink loves his car, not me. Mink doesn't love anybody. I don't think he can."

"Nice. And you were gonna marry this guy?"

"I didn't know him then like I do now. The marriage was off, as far as I was concerned."

They rode in silence for a few more miles and then Frank slowed at the place where they'd come out of the hills just an hour or so earlier. Paved road for a quarter mile, leading up to an old gravel pit, then dirt and rocks after that, a track winding up into the hills that eventually faded into the kind of disuse only the most rabid of outdoorsmen ever bother with.

He pulled to the side of the road, stopped the truck and switched off the lights.

"Now what?"

She looked at him. "Hell, I don't know."

"Next town up is Imogene. Sixteen miles. Guess you'd know that, though."

"They'd find me there too." Fear was back in her voice. "I suppose."

"Where were you goin' up there?" She gestured at the De Bacas. The hills were dark now; no moon was out.

"Place I know. I was hoping to have it all to myself."

Softly, she said, "I wouldn't be any trouble, Frank."

"You gotta be kidding. You've already been a bad year's worth."

"I mean now . . . anymore." Her voice was pleading. "If we go up there, that'll be the end of these guys."

"How about you go back to whatzizname. Mink. Straighten things out. Christ, what kind of a name is Mink, anyway?"

"I killed his car, Frank. He'd kill me."

Knowledge of the inevitable filled Frank, but he fought it anyway. Not his problem, this business with Mink. None of it had anything to do with him. He could just take her back to Quiode, dump her off in Imogene, boot her ass out right here.

Sure he could—like pigs could fly. "Shit," he said.

"That mean yes?"

"It means shit, exactly like it sounds. Don't try to read between the lines when someone says shit."

"Lights coming, Frank. Behind us."

Yep. Mile, mile and a half back. Could be the muscle car. Shit again. He turned the engine over, kicked up gravel pulling onto the side road, lights off, and banged over potholes and broken asphalt. Hard to move fast in the dark, but Frank pushed it. They were maybe an eighth of a mile up the road, partly hidden by a gravel pile, when the car tore on by on the highway. Doing a hundred miles an hour, easy.

"That's gotta be them," Suki said.

"Which means they're not in Quiode anymore, right?" He looked at her.

"Thanks a lot, Frank."

"Shit," he said.

Forty minutes later they passed the Trans Am, still smoldering in the lights of the pickup.

"Nice work," Frank said.

"Thank you."

Then up the hillside, grinding over rocks, spinning tires on loose gravel, up into the switchbacks that took them high enough to see where the highway lay dark and empty below. This was a part of the world that not many people had any use for. No wonder they exploded the first atomic bomb out here.

"Mind if I look in that bag of yours?" Frank asked.

"I already told you what's in it."

"Humor me. I've got a problem with the way things've gone this evening. I'm getting tired of surprises."

She picked the bag up, unzipped it, pulled out a stuffed rabbit and shoved it into his arms.

"Here. Just don't get it pregnant, okay?" She held up a rubber duck, squeezed it, quacked it in his face.

He shoved the rabbit back at her. "Who the hell's Mink? And don't tell me he's the guy that owns the car, either. I mean, what's this guy do? What is he?"

"He's an asshole."

He gave her a quick look and she said, "He's just some . . . I dunno. Corporate executive kind of guy, I guess. Owns his own company. Some kinda telecommunications or marketing thing, something like that."

"Guy like that'd have insurance on his car, right?"

"Might, yeah."

"So when his car is found, the insurance company'll pay up and he'll just buy another one and that'll be that. You'll be off the hook with this guy, right?"

"Mink isn't like that."

"Like what?"

"Reasonable. He's a son of a bitch. Keeps coming at you, like the Terminator or something. I've seen him do it before. Nobody gets the best of Mink."

"Terminator? What the hell's a terminator?"

"You didn't see the movie? Arnold Schwarzenegger?"

"Arnold who? I haven't been to a movie in twenty years."

"Figures. You're into what? Baseball? Boxing? Cockfights maybe?"

"Reading. Keeping life simple." Riding around with almost eighty thousand bucks squirreled away in my camper and a bunch of cops trying to figure out where I've gone. Getting into knife fights while trying to lay the hell low. Stuff like that. Just your basic shit.

"Reading?" Amazement in her voice.

"Yeah, as in books. You've heard about books?"

"Jesus." She shook her head. "Go figure. You really look like some kinda big-time reader to me."

"So we've got this CEO called Mink who's maybe psychotic, has a lousy temper, and has a whole bunch of friends out looking for you."

"Yeah." Defiantly.

"That your story?"

"Yeah. Like it?"

"Shit," Frank said.

She hadn't wanted to tell him the rest of it, get him any more riled than he already was. If she'd told Frank what Mink was really all about and what she'd done to him, Frank might've just dumped her at the highway and taken off. Hard to tell.

So she kept her bag tucked carefully under her legs and went over her story, searching for holes. It had plenty, but nothing she couldn't patch up, or so she hoped. Frank wasn't dumb.

Her eyes burned, but she was still too wired about everything that had happened that evening to think about sleep yet. She hadn't slept much in the past two days. She'd driven Mink's Trans Am across Texas the previous day and much of the night, catching a few cramped hours of sleep at rest stops along the highway. Her sleep had been disturbed by the windy snarl of passing trucks and by dreams of Mink—Mink coming for her, smiling, his eyes glowing like angry coals. By the time she'd reached New Mexico her eyelids were heavy, her mind numbed by fatigue. She'd crash-landed the car just before daybreak, and then dozed a few minutes at a time during the day, waiting for someone to come along, until Frank had.

"What d'you do?" she asked. If she got him talking about himself, maybe he wouldn't pester her with so many questions about her past, questions for which she might not have ready answers. "For work, I mean."

"Drive a truck," he said.

"Yeah? What kind?"

"Big rig. Standard eighteen-wheeler."

"Fun?"

"Lotta laughs, sure."

"I mean really."

"Twenty-five, thirty years ago it was a kick; now it's just a way to make a buck. I guess you get tired of anything you do that long, except maybe for habits you oughta give up. Like drinking."

"Yeah? You drink a lot?"

"I've done my share. Still do, I guess."

"Married?"

He shook his head. "Used to be. My wife passed away four years ago. Her name was Fanny."

"I'm sorry. Miss her?"

"Yeah."

"Where're you from?"

"California."

"This a vacation, or what?"

He wasn't used to anyone asking so many questions. "No, I'm meeting these guys up here in this garden spot to cut some big business deal. I've got this Eye-talian suit back in the camper and—"

"Hey, you don't have to get nasty. I was just askin'."

"Yeah, a vacation." His voice was tight. "Sometimes I just want to be alone. Been that way a lot since Fanny died."

"How'd you find out about this place up here?"

He shifted into low, four-wheel drive, and took a creek bed at one mile an hour. The creek was bone dry. "I stumbled across it a couple of years ago, just out looking. These days if you want to get away, I mean really get the hell away, you have to go out looking in places you can't hardly get to."

"Like this?" She gripped the seat as the truck heeled over sharply, engine racing, wheels spewing dust that turned to bloody mist in the taillights.

"Like this."

The headlights played over a rocky moonscape tilted at a dangerous angle, darkness and big boulders all around, stars bright in the black night sky.

"How much farther we going?" Suki asked.

"Six, seven miles."

"Jesus. Like this?"

"You ain't seen nothin' yet."

"Super. How 'bout we stop somewhere, go the rest of the way when it gets light?"

He sucked on a knuckle. "Naw. That's what I was gonna do after I left you at the motel, but the hell with it. Now I just wanta get there."

"Hurt your hand?"

"Maybe popped a knuckle against Mutt's head back there in Quiode."

She laughed. "Mote."

"What's it matter?"

"Guess it doesn't, really."

He was pretty rough around the edges. A good man behind that crusty facade of his, and dangerously savvy. What she'd told him was mostly true, just that she'd left out the two best parts, which left her story kinda thin. He probably wasn't buying the whole thing, but she couldn't think of any way to

40

flesh it out without risking getting caught in a lie, so she just left it alone. So far they'd been mostly lies of omission, which was bad enough, but manageable.

He was strangely attractive. She tried to figure out why, big wide moose that he was. She didn't come up with much. He'd saved her, twice, but that didn't seem to have anything to do with it. He'd looked her over pretty well, but hadn't come on to her. Aware, but polite; that was nice. She felt good about the way she looked; it turned her off, though, when guys, even nice-looking guys, started panting and trying to talk her into bed five minutes after they'd met her. That'd happened a lot. Until Mink came along.

So here she was, bouncing along in this truck, feeling a little something for Frank, a looseness in her loins. Crazy. He was maybe ten years older than her father. . . .

Dear old Dad. She wondered if her mother was still pushing the ineffectual little shit around like she'd always done. Big brassy bitch married to this bony little twerp way out in Des Moines, where in the best of all possible worlds a nuclear warhead would wipe it all away so people could start over, or walk away from it and just let it be.

Suki shook her head. She couldn't imagine anyone pushing Frank Wiley around, and that included Mote and Jersey. She'd seen what he'd done to Jersey. Very quick, very neat. Whatever he'd done to Mote must've been quick too.

Mink could take him down, though. Jesus, wasn't Mink one of the world's all-time horrors? She could just see him in that big old house in Shreveport where they'd set up the last operation, silhouetted against the misty morning light coming through those tall French doors, performing those exotic moves of his in a deadly kind of slow motion, all controlled and silent. Like he wasn't really real, like he was on film or something, with the sound turned off. Like Bruce Lee, in the movies—

"You hungry?"

His voice startled her. "Huh?"

"Hungry?"

"Oh. Yeah, a little. Didn't get much dinner, did I?"

"Want another apple?"

"Maybe when we get to where we're going."

"Be another couple of hours yet."

"That's all right."

He shrugged, shifted into second as they rolled over the crest of a hill and down into the blackest kind of black she'd ever seen in her life. End-of-the-world black.

Not even Mink could find her here. She hoped.

They got there at one twenty in the morning. Half a dozen cottonwoods grew on a low rise fifty yards away, pale rustling ghosts in the glare of the headlights. Dark mountains blotted out the stars all around. Frank found a level spot and parked. When he doused the lights, colored spots floated in the emptiness before her eyes.

"Dark," she said quietly.

"Camper's got lights." The dome light blazed as he opened his door and climbed out. Cold air swirled into the cab; high mountain air.

She climbed out. Frank opened the camper and went inside. A few seconds later an overhead light came on. He straddled a big pair of Igloo ninety-four-quart ice chests that must have weighed two hundred pounds each.

Suki shivered. "Got a shirt I can borrow?"

"Just a sec."

He backed out, dragging the first chest with him, and set it in the darkness beside the camper with a grunt. After he'd done the same with the second, he went back inside and pulled a neatly folded flannel shirt out of a drawer.

She stepped up into the camper and put the shirt on. The sleeves weren't too bad, just needed a little rolling, but the rest of it was a joke, like some kind of a tent.

"Thanks." She gazed around. "This thing got a bathroom, by the way?"

42

He opened a cabinet, handed her a roll of toilet paper and a flashlight. "Out there. Just keep away from the trees."

"Wonderful."

She went outside, hobbled thirty yards in her broken heels before saying, "Screw it," in a low voice and squatting in the cold amid a pile of rocks. Dry grass brushed her thighs.

"Remind me never to do this again," she said softly. The camper glowed like a jack-o'-lantern in the night, Frank in there, banging things around. The winking red and green lights of a distant airliner passed soundlessly overhead. Something howled in the hills—dog, coyote, werewolf. Something.

Goose bumps stood out on her arms.

She got to her feet, staggered back, found Frank staring uncertainly at the bed he'd made up, above the cab.

"Problem?" she asked.

"You tell me."

"Only got that one bed, huh?"

"I wasn't expecting company."

"Got room up there for two?"

He met her gaze. "I'm not sure that's a good idea, Suki."

"Fine. Got another?"

He stared at the bed a while longer with the corner of his mouth sucked in thoughtfully. "It's a double. I'm a bit on the large side, though."

"Hell with it," she said, extricating herself from his shirt and kicking off her shoes. "I'm not. Anyway, it's all we've got and I trust you. And I'm exhausted; I wouldn't be a whole lot of fun anyway."

She climbed up in her shorts and top and slid into the coolness of heavy flannel sheets, felt the camper jostle as Frank went out into the night.

When he came back she was almost asleep. She heard the soft rustle of clothing, felt him struggle into the bed beside her and knew he was doing his best not to touch her accidentally. The old sweetheart.

And then she was asleep.

5

Jersey spat on the floor of the car between his feet, a thin mixture of puke and blood. He'd discovered that at a hundred and fifteen miles an hour it wasn't real smart to spit out the roaring darkness of a window. His gut throbbed where Suki's gorilla had rammed the broom handle into it.

Son of a bitch had stole his knife, too. Black Mantis butterfly knife with a four-inch blade. Fuck. It'd been his favorite. Patches of hair were missing from his forearms where he'd tested the keenness of its edge.

Mote was still complaining about his balls, telling Jersey his head was sort of ringing.

"Shut up," Jersey said.

"I got this headache, Jers."

"Just shut the fuck up." Jersey leaned over and let more

watery gruel dribble from his lips to the floor. The ache in his belly wasn't going to go away anytime soon.

The lights of Imogene showed ahead, maybe half a mile.

"Shit," Jersey said. "Missed 'em."

"Couldn'ta," Mote said. "They couldn'ta made it here that fast in that big old camper."

"Slow the fuck down. You sure it was a camper they took off in, Mote? You *sure*?"

"Sure, I'm sure, Jers. I seen it."

Jersey wasn't sure, couldn't really trust Mote, whose name he figured derived from the size of his brain. But Jersey had been curled up on the ground when the girl and the gorilla had taken off, losing his dinner and three dollars' worth of rye. He hadn't seen a thing, which he sure as shit didn't ever want to have to explain to Mink.

If Suki and this guy she was with were in a truck with a camper—and even Mote could probably identify a camper—then it was likely that they couldn't have reached Imogene ahead of the Toronado, even though that sort of analysis wasn't something Mote was noted for. This time he might be right, though. It'd taken them only five minutes to get the Olds over to the Texaco station not a hundred feet away and fill its tires with air. Good thing it was one of those old places where you could still do that.

Five minutes. Jersey wasn't much on math, but it stood to reason that at about a hundred and fifteen miles an hour over a twenty-five-mile stretch they'd have caught up to a god-damn camper sooner or later.

Jesus, would Mink ever be pissed. And getting Mink pissed was something you just never wanted to do.

Imogene was bigger than Quiode: maybe a hundred and fifty people, two gas stations, two restaurants, one of those Sears catalogue stores, grain and hardware store, Gump's Fuel with a couple of big black tanks out back, a fair-sized market, sheriff's substation, post office, houses scattered up and down the street among the business establishments. It didn't have a traffic light, Jersey saw, but what'd you expect? Like Quiode, it was dark and empty, just a few bright blots of neon and another flashing yellow caution light.

Mote cruised the main drag slowly, Jersey looking everywhere for the camper.

"What color you say it was again?"

"Kinda white," Mote said. "Bluish stripes, I think."

Kinda. Blu-*ish*. Shit. "You think?"

"It was dark, Jers."

Jersey looked at Mote. Great big anaconda arms, not two grams of brain. Like one of those brontosaurs in those books his grandpa used to read to him when he was just a kid.

At least Mote's description of the truck hadn't changed. When Mote's descriptions got to wandering, you knew you were in deep shit.

Nothing in Imogene. Couple of old campers off a few side streets, but the colors were wrong and the hoods of the trucks they were on were cold. Jersey went into the two restaurants and showed the girl's picture around. Nothing. But if they'd come through, they would've been idiots to stop.

Still, Jersey was feeling fairly comfortable with the idea that they'd never made it as far as Imogene. What he wasn't comfortable with was the idea that they might've let the Toronado go wailing on by on the highway, then doubled on back to Quiode and headed out east, maybe gone on down to Roswell.

Either way, it was time to report in. Past time, he saw nervously. Should have done it before leaving Quiode, but if he'd done that, the girl and the gorilla might've made it to Imogene before them, and then where would they be?

He found a pay phone, made the collect call to Shreveport.

The Bitch, Mrs. Voorhees, answered the phone. She was coordinating the search. Mink's mother, Charlotte Voorhees, was a tummy-tucked, chin-lifted, nose-jobbed cunt. It hadn't helped any either—she still looked like a disease. He could just see her there at the big rosewood desk, light shadowing her small, deep-set eyes, lips tightly puckered around a Vantage cigarette like the asshole of a pig.

"Tell me," she said.

Tell me. Not hello or Mrs. Voorhees, or even yeah; but *Tell me*, like she was flying on coke or something, even though she'd put a rat up her nose before she vacuumed a line of nose candy. A real space case, but dangerous as quicksand—like her boy. If the pay wasn't so damned good, Jersey'd go find something else to do. But where else could a guy with an eighth-grade education make $52,000 a year, tax free, and have a nice expense account?

"This's Jersey, ma'am," he said. "We found her."

"You *did*?" The sound of a tarantula. "Where? *Where?*"

"Quiode."

"Where's *that*?" She made it sound like where the fuck's that, but Charlotte Voorhees would never let so foul a word slip past her lips. She was much too much a lady for that.

"Twenty-five miles northeast of Imogene."

Paper rustled. "Okay, okay, I've got it."

Jersey closed his eyes. "Mote and me're in Imogene now."

"Why? You've got her, haven't you?"

"Not exactly."

Cold silence. "What do you mean by that, Jersey?"

God, he hated it when she spoke his name. She rarely did so when she was happy, and when Charlotte Voorhees was unhappy you could taste her bile in your throat.

"She's with some great big guy now. Must weigh over two hundred and fifty pounds. Old guy, probably about fifty. They . . . uh, they got away, ma'am."

More silence. Then her voice, like embers snapping in a fire: "Mink's not going to like—"

"We've got 'em boxed, Mrs. Voorhees. At least, we will if you can get Benny and Isaac to cover the road from Quiode out to Highway Two-eighty-five. We chased 'em from Quiode

47

to Imogene and didn't see 'em, so they gotta be somewhere back along the road. We get Four-oh-one north outta Quiode cut off real quick and we've got 'em. Ma'am," he added respectfully.

"Elaborate," she said.

He did, editing madly as he went. Mote had been sucker-punched by this big dude and Suki'd run off with the guy. Jersey'd seen 'em take off in a white camper with blue stripes.

"Truck color?" Mrs. Voorhees snapped.

"Uh, kinda beige, maybe cream." At least that's what Mote had told him. Jersey's breath came a little faster.

"What make?"

"Chevy, I think." This was pure fiction, but necessary.

"You think?"

"It was dark, ma'am."

"No license number, I suppose."

"No, ma'am."

"Okay, Jersey. Now listen carefully to me. Are you listening very carefully, Jersey?"

"Yes, ma'am."

"I want you and Mote to stay right there in Imogene and watch the road from Quiode. I want you to do nothing but watch the road, do you understand?"

"Yes, ma—"

"If you see them, call me. Then follow them, and if you can, I want you to capture the girl. If you can't, then I want you to continue tailing her. If you let her slip through your fingers again, Jersey, I'll have your feet flayed and soaked in alcohol. Do you understand?"

Jersey trembled. "Yes, Mrs. Voorhees."

"Can you see the road from where you're standing now?"

"Yes, ma'am."

"What's the number of the phone you're calling from?" He read it off to her.

"Be watchful," Charlotte said. "Be sure to answer if I call." She hung up.

Jersey wiped sweat from his upper lip with the shoulder of his shirt. "Motherfucker," he whispered.

"Simon?"

"Yes, Mother." It was late, late and quiet, but Simon had been awake, imagining. His imagination was well developed, and it often gave him great pleasure. As now.

"Can you talk, dear?"

Simon Voorhees, alias Mink, alias forty-three other names at last count and increasing at the rate of roughly eight or ten a year, looked around his private room in Stanford Medical Center's dermatology unit.

"I'm alone."

"Jersey found her, but he let her slip away."

Mink sat up straighter in his bed. "Where? When?"

"Southeastern part of New Mexico, maybe an hour ago. In the region around the towns of Quiode and Imogene." She told Simon what Jersey had told her, and what she had told Jersey, including the business about flaying his feet. Already Benny and Isaac were moving.

"I want that bitch alive, Mother." His voice was calm, almost conversational. What he felt was less human than rage. Enraged, a person's thoughts are impaired, but Simon Voorhees was never, never impaired.

"I know, darling. You'll have her."

Mink wanted to tear the bandage off his forehead and rub madly, but he let the itching continue. As he suffered, so would that vile little whore suffer, but exponentially. And when he could do nothing to increase her suffering, she would die.

Charlotte Voorhees said, "How's the graft taking, dear?"

"It's too early to tell yet."

"Dr. Pinnell is one of the best in the country."

"*Find* her, Mother."

"We will, darling. We will."

"How are things coming along in Reno?" He didn't really

care, not with Suki still free, but it seemed as if he should ask.

"Very well. Daniel's got the usual paperwork completed. We're fully licensed now. Banks are being most cooperative, as always."

"Good." He didn't care.

"Sleep now, dear. We'll have her soon."

Mink hung up, gazed around the room with its private bath, curtains, IV stand, colorless decor, medical stink and sterile hush.

Suki'd put him here, he thought. Amazement fed the fires of his hatred. She'd taken him by surprise, and Simon Voorhees didn't like surprises. They shook that sense of invulnerability he'd thought was inseparable from the rest of him.

Steamy little sugar-candy bitch from Des Moines. He closed his eyes and visualized her, stretched out naked, immobilized, a single glowing coal lying on that tight little tummy of hers in a place where the light was dim and he could see the fever of its fire. Screams, flesh searing as it slowly ate its way down into her guts. In a place where no one could hear her agonized shrieks. He wanted to *hear* her die.

One single coal. He would give her one place on which to focus all her pain. Such a wonderfully Oriental way to die, so very Zen.

The image soothed him, made him hard, but he didn't think she would die in quite that way. It would be too fast.

Much too fast for Suki Flood.

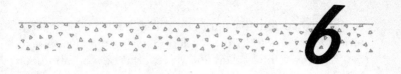

6

Sleep wouldn't come. Frank stared up at the darkness; pure, clean, interstellar black. Could be a zillion miles up there instead of ending only a foot above his head.

Suki breathed slowly, deeply. Just like Fanny had, years ago.

Frank had wanted Fanny to quit smoking; he just hadn't been able to really get on her case about it. Nagging would have only made their time together unbearable, and he hadn't wanted that. He wasn't too smart about relationships, but he'd known that much.

So she'd just killed herself, or so it seemed. Frank had no idea why. Smoking was an addiction he didn't understand, particularly in doctors, nurses, even chemotherapists. People who knew the risks, saw what terrible damage smoking caused to—hell, to *other* people's lungs.

Until you'd felt that on-again, off-again pain—and let it settle a few years to be certain it'd metastasized nicely—and then had the X rays taken and discovered beyond all doubt that those coffin nails—SURGEON GENERAL'S WARNING:—had finally taken hold, cancer was something that Wouldn't Happen to You.

No way, José. That professional knowledge of what happened to other people made you immune, somehow. You were different, special. Cancer sticks might kill those other poor bastards out there who didn't have that rabbit's foot of Special Knowledge, but for you those butts were just like candy. Yessiree. Just like chocolate, and they didn't even make you fat.

The depth of his bitterness was a stake through his heart, and he rolled over on his side to dislodge it, away from Suki.

Seventy-seven thousand dollars. What would Fanny have thought?

He slept.

He came awake with sunshine boring straight through a window into his left eye. Better than coffee, that blood-red haze filling his entire brain. His hand throbbed.

He'd slept fewer than four goddamn hours, but he was up. He turned his head; Suki's fluorescent yellow top was hanging from a vent handle over the bed.

Jesus.

He got up stealthily, still dressed in jeans, and pushed his feet into his shoes. Went outside carrying his shirt, socks, the roll of TP, a book, and a toilet seat on a sturdy aluminum frame. He set the seat up out of sight of the camper, over a hole from which he'd removed a good-size rock, and began the day's business with a Stephen King novel cradled in his hands, morning sun already warm on his shoulders. *

Halfway through chapter three he packed it in, replaced the rock, checked back in the camper. Suki was still flaked out, glossy hair spread over her duffel, which she was using

* Even I don't read 3 chapters **52** sitting on the toilet!

as a pillow, same as when he'd left. Only six thirty; she hadn't even slept five hours yet.

So he made breakfast: eggs and bacon, even coffee. If the noise and the smells didn't wake her, nothing would.

But they didn't, so he figured her for dead, except that the blankets were lifting at slow, regular intervals.

He stared at her top, hanging where she'd left it. When the hell'd she do that?

He opened windows in the camper, got a breeze moving through, and left the door open while he went outside and set up a folding chair in the sun on the east side. He got an apple from one of the ice chests and sat down with the King novel as the day heated up. It was too early to be hitting the sour mash; he would have to read sober for a while.

Three hours went by. Suki was still dead to the world.

The sun was beginning to cook. Frank climbed on top of the camper and unfurled the big roll of canvas he'd stowed away up there, hung it off the rails on either side. He staked it to the ground, shading the camper from the heavy beat of the sun. If the pounding of the hammer didn't wake her, nothing would.

But it didn't, so Frank said the hell with it and grabbed a towel and his book and marched off toward the smilax shrubs and cottonwoods in the distance, to the place where the spring burbled out of the ground, cool and eternal.

Suki stretched. She rolled onto her side and looked around at the empty camper.

Swinging her legs over the side of the bunk, she clambered down and stood rubbing her breasts absently, scratching underside itches. She didn't hear Frank anywhere around, but even so she reached up and grabbed her tube top from where it was hanging.

He must have seen it. What had he thought? She smiled, imagining his consternation.

She slipped the top on, staring in surprise at the breakfast things lying where he'd left them. She hadn't heard a thing. She glanced at the stove, her eyes passing over the printed operating instructions without really coming to rest. She couldn't figure out how to use it, so she went outside.

Frank wasn't in sight, but he had to be around somewhere. He'd spread a big canvas tarp over the camper to keep it cool. Crude, but effective. She found an apple in one of the ice chests and took it inside.

A radio was mounted in a nook. Car radio: AM-FM, tape deck. She turned it on, got a roar of static. FM was useless out here, so she switched to AM, found a station playing some old Ventures tune: "Walk, Don't Run."

It made her feel less like she was out in the wilderness, which gave her the eerie feeling that Mink was closer too, but she left it on anyway and began checking out the digs.

Wasn't much to see. Tiny refrigerator, which didn't work and was packed with warm cans of Budweiser. Bed over the cab. Small booth with green seats and a white Formica table. Stove. Counters. Cabinets all over hell and gone, scarred and gouged. Tiny wardrobe. A stainless steel sink, stained.

She felt suddenly jumpy, wondering where Frank was. She switched off the radio, grabbed the apple, and went outside to look for him.

He'd stuck King face down on a rock and was sitting there with his eyes closed, the sun on his shoulders, and the cool water of the spring up to about his armpits.

Ninety minutes he'd been there. Keep this up and he'd shrivel up like a prune, but it felt good on his hemorrhoids.

They weren't all that bad—yet. And now that he was out of the trucking business for good, maybe they wouldn't get any worse. Doc Schneider, the old shit, had told him last year he'd ream him a new asshole in another ten years. "Right about here, Frank," he'd said, grinning that hideous nicotine grin of his, pressing a cold, probing finger into a spot on Frank's left side. Another unfathomable smoker; it wasn't

54

likely he'd last long enough to ream a new exit hole in Frank's side, even if Frank needed one.

In Rio, if Frank made it that far, he wouldn't be burning diesel, jamming gears. And if he got caught, he wouldn't have to worry about hemorrhoids, either. The warden would no doubt have a fit if Frank even went nosing around a truck.

"Hi."

He opened his eyes, felt a fluttery feeling around his testicles. Suki was standing on the bank, smiling, chomping on an apple, dressed in that skimpy top she hadn't been wearing in bed this morning. Good legs, rising up into hot-pink shorts. Even had her silver dangly earrings on, and here he was, wearing nothing but this cool, crystaline pool of water.

"Hi yourself." He crossed his legs and created a bit of turbulence to ripple the water's surface.

She gazed down at the pool. Six feet wide, maybe twelve long, jammed in among granite boulders. Nearly five feet deep at its deepest point. Undisturbed, you could see the bottom like you were looking through glass.

She'd let her hair down, and it spilled over her shoulders and halfway down her back in a cascade of sunlit silver. Hell of a sight.

"Nice," she said. "Last place the circus out there hasn't found yet, huh?"

"People've been here. Not many, but a few. I've seen signs. Most people who come out here don't leave much behind, though."

"Good place for skinny-dipping." Her eyes took in his jeans and underwear and shirt, drying on a rock where he'd laid them out after washing.

"Uh, yeah," Frank said uncomfortably. "Look—"

Suki dipped a toe. The flex of her calf gave her leg an exquisite look. "Not bad. Thought it'd be colder."

"What I maybe oughta do is slip into something—"

She stepped down gracefully into the pool, from one rock to another until she reached the sandy bottom. Six feet from him she sat on a ledge with the water just lapping the top of her shoulders. She shucked off her top.

Frank swallowed.

She leaned back, eyes closed, face turned up to the sun, and sighed. Her dark areolas moved beneath the surface.

Frank wasn't sure what to say, so he didn't say anything. Every so often Suki took a bite of the apple, eyes closed, as if this were the kind of thing she did every day.

Frank had trouble filling his lungs. The day felt quieter than before, his breathing louder.

"What's with the tennis ball?" Suki asked, setting the apple core on a rock. She began washing her top, scrubbing it beneath the water.

"Huh?"

"In the truck. Last night. You were squeezing a tennis ball most of the way into that town. Quiode. And then after we left."

"Oh. I dunno. Habit, I guess."

"Habit?"

"Ten or twelve years back I started losing strength in my right hand. Doc gave me a bunch of shots, vitamins or something, said it was something to do with my nerves and told me to exercise the grip and get more sleep. Whatever it was got better. Now it's just something I do. Here, have a look."

He held up his arms.

She stared at them. "Yeah. So what?"

"Right forearm's bigger than the left, see? Not a lot, but a little."

"Yeah, I guess." She put her top on a rock. "How'd Fanny die? If it's none of my business, just say and I'll shut up."

"Lung cancer. Cigarettes."

Suki stripped off her shorts and underwear, began rubbing them together in the water. Hot pink flashing against creamy ribbed cotton. "What'd she do?"

"Hah?" His response was airless; not real swift, either.

"For work. Housewife, or did she work?"

"She was a nurse."

"Yeah? That's good."

"It was, yeah."

"How's the knuckle this morning?"

"Better."

"You planning on shaving today?"

He rubbed the heavy stubble on his face, more salt than pepper now. "I didn't bring a razor."

"Figures. Got any soap?"

"What kind?"

"Like for washing clothes." She gestured at his, drying on the rock.

"This here's our drinking water. Get it soapy and it'd be two days before we could drink it again."

"Oh."

Just as he was beginning to feel almost comfortable with her, sitting there chatting in the nude, she stood up and laid her things out on a rock, water just at her knees. His breath caught at the sight of her. Her nipples were standing out from the cold of the water. Thatch of pale golden hair. Not a tan line on her. It seemed like he ought to look away, but he couldn't.

"Where're you from?" he asked, his voice unsteady.

She sank back into the water. "You mean originally? Like where I grew up?"

He nodded.

"Des Moines," she said.

"Yeah. Been there lotsa times."

"Driving a truck?"

"Uh-huh."

"Ugly, ain't it?"

He gave her a look. "Depends on your point of view."

"Like if you've been driving a long time and hafta take a leak, it looks pretty good. Otherwise not, right?"

"I take it you don't care much for Des Moines."

57

"Place sucks, Frank. I couldn't get out fast enough."

"So you hitched up with this guy, Mink."

Her eyes lit on his face, green, flashing. "Got it all figured out now, don'tcha?"

"I've been around."

She closed her eyes, leaned her head back, face to the sun. In the light, Frank could see the tiniest of cracks in her skin, mostly around her eyes. Too much sun, but she was still young and like all kids her age she was never going to grow old, never going to get wrinkled, never going to die.

Had he ever been that young, that certain of his immortality? Not since his football days. He'd been an all-state tackle on the Webber High football team in Northern California where he'd grown up. Sometimes a center. He'd been big then, too; two hundred fourteen solid pounds as a senior, seventeen years old. He'd run over a lot of guys in his day. Back then, he couldn't imagine someday growing old, dying.

Dying? Christ, he was going to be seventeen forever, and with a perpetual hard-on, too.

But life didn't give a shit if you dealt with reality or not. The years passed and you learned that the mountains were going to outlive you by about ten million years and grass was going to flourish on your grave.

Tell that to a kid, though. Like Suki—a flower, just beginning to bloom. She'd probably look at him like his skull was full of oat bran.

He glanced at his watch, a big waterproof Casio Fanny had given him one Christmas. It was a few minutes past noon, time to begin drinking, which was one reason he'd come up here in the first place. That, and to figure out what he was going to do when he left. Two of those mutually exclusive objectives that make life so interesting.

"I've got a stack of books in the camper," he said. "If you want something to read. Stephen King."

"No, thanks." She ducked her head under, came out with hair plastered to her head, dripping.

"Rather watch television?"

58

Her eyes grew wary.

It seemed to be a closed subject, so he dropped it. "You hungry?"

"Yeah."

"Turn your back and I'll get up outta here, go make us a couple of sandwiches."

"You're a hell of a prude, Frank."

"I know. Turn."

She smiled. Turned slowly and gazed off toward the west where a gap in the mountains showed a blue expanse of space, a wedge-shaped view of blue-gray peaks in the far distance.

He got up, dripping, his back turned to her, and reached for his shorts.

"That a bullet hole?" she asked.

She was looking at him. He'd never felt so naked in his life—or so old and fat.

"Thought I told you to keep your head turned."

"Nope. You said turn, didn't say anything about keepin' turned."

Jesus. He hurried into his shorts.

She climbed out of the water, shook water from her arms and legs. "That a bullet hole?" she asked again, slinging her hair from side to side, staring at the cicatrix on his shoulder.

"Bullet wound, yeah."

"Where'd you get it? I never saw one before."

"Korea."

"Korea?"

"Yeah, Korea. Ever heard of it?"

"Sure. How'd you get shot over *there*?"

"We fought a war there, remember? Long time ago."

"We did?" Giving him an incredulous look.

Christ. He was into his jeans now, feeling a little more comfortable. They'd dried hot and stiff under the sun. Suki stepped into her panties, facing him, as unconcerned with her nakedness as a child of two, breasts perched high on her chest, hair spread over her shoulders in ropy tangles. ✳

"Tell me about it," she said.

& I think I'm in love! **59**

"What? The Korean War or the bullet wound?"

"Both."

"Maybe later sometime."

By the time he'd put on his shirt, socks, and shoes, Suki was in her shorts and top again.

What struck Frank as funny, just before they went back to the camper, was that neither he nor Suki had mentioned the big Ruger .357 Magnum he'd left flying on a rock within easy reach the entire time they'd been there.

A how about "lying"?

he phone rang. It was the Bitch.

"Yes, ma'am," Jersey said. A couple of hayseed kids went by on the far side of the highway, one on a bicycle, the other walking. A blond cocker trotted along behind, tongue lolling.

"Have you been watching the highway, Jersey?" Charlotte Voorhees asked.

"Yes, ma'am."

"You haven't seen the girl?"

If I had, I would've phoned, you skinny old fuck, Jersey thought. "No, ma'am," he said, standing in the ungodly heat near a Conoco station at the east end of town, sweat trickling down his back. Rory's Conoco. Mote sat in the Olds, sucking on a bottle of Orange Crush, feet up on the dash. The radio was playing hillbilly music. On the rear bumper was a faded sticker that Jersey thought was a kick: HERE'S HOPE! JESUS CARES FOR YOU. Bugs chirred hotly in the weeds. In the distance, the highway quivered beneath the blazing sun.

"Listen to me, Jersey," she said. "Are you listening very carefully, Jersey?"

"Yes, ma'am." Like talking to a leech or something, he thought. Bitch could suck your soul right through the wires.

"You'll need two cars. Possibly a truck. I want one of you to stay in Imogene and continue to watch the highway for the girl. The other, preferably you, Jersey, must search for her between Imogene and Quiode."

"Where we gonna get a truck?" Silence. "Uh, ma'am."

"*Rent* one, Jersey."

"I don't think this place's got anyplace to rent a truck, Mrs. Voorhees. Ma'am. I didn't see nothing like that around here. Place ain't all that big, an—"

"Maybe from one of the locals, Jersey? A private transaction, perhaps?"

"Oh. I guess. Yeah."

"Do you suppose you could manage that, Jersey?"

"Yeah, sure. Ma'am. I kin try."

"You've got enough money?"

One thing they had was plenty of money. Hang around Mink and one thing you had was plenty of the green.

"Yes, ma'am."

"Then why don't you ask around, Jersey? See what you can find. People in small towns often jump at the chance to pick up a little extra money."

She was so deadly patient, like she was talking to a kid or something. A retarded kid. Her and Mink, so fucking superior, like no one else didn't know shit.

"Yes, ma'am."

"Let me know."

"Yes, ma'am."

She hung up. Didn't even say good-bye.

Bitch.

Simon Voorhees practiced killing Suki Flood, over and over and over, experimenting with one idea and another, filling himself with her richly imagined suffering. He lay perfectly still on his bed, a tiny smile lifting the edges of his thin lips. Not a cruel smile though, but one that reassured the nurses drifting in and out of his room on silent, crepe-soled shoes. When Simon was amused, his smile was quite pleasant. He was thought to be one of the better patients at SMC.

Dr. Ernest Pinnell came in, pale blue eyes questing.

"How's the patient?"

"Bored." He wasn't, really, but under the circumstances it would be expected.

"There's television."

"Television is for children, Doctor."

"Children?"

Simon's empty gray eyes locked on Pinnell's. "Children of the mind, Doctor. Children of the soul. Television is the womb of strangling mediocrity."

Pinnell's eyebrows lifted. "Something from the library, then?"

"Spinoza, if you have anything. If not, then Kafka might be an interesting diversion."

Pinnell's eyebrows lifted another improbable notch. "I'll tell a nurse to look into it. Perhaps we can locate something suitably enriching."

Pinnell changed Mink's bandage himself this time. "Looking good," he said, eyes never shifting down to look directly into Simon's. He stared only at the place on Simon's forehead where the graft had removed Suki's vile word:

CROK

"Terrific," Mink said. He'd tell his mother.

Pinnell's eyes crinkled in a smile. "No more wild parties after this, eh, Mr. Voorhees?"

"No. How long before I can leave, Doctor?"

"Well, we want to be sure the graft takes, don't we? A few more days should do it. If everything looks good, we'll try for Saturday. How's that?"

"Good."

"Fine." Pinnell scribbled something on Simon's chart and then left the room, humming something that sounded suspiciously like an old Sousa march. His stride was a march, too, the corridors of the hospital his parade ground.

Mink returned to Suki's pain.

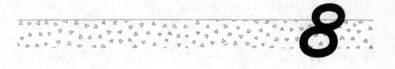

8

Darkness came to the hills. Frank was pleasantly lit, but he hadn't gotten as far into the booze as he'd intended back when he'd been motoring through Arizona. Suki had distracted him, puttering around all afternoon in that skimpy outfit of hers.

Frank hadn't got much thinking done about his situation, either. He still wasn't sure if Rio was the place to go, or if maybe he should try someplace that didn't sound quite so full of bugs. He didn't know why he thought Rio was infested, but the image refused to go away. Brazil was jungle, maybe that was it; jungle implied bugs. He'd never been to South America, never even been south of Corpus Christi, Texas. Rio was probably too exotic for him. What the hell would he do in Rio anyway?

He hadn't gotten much further with the book, Suki prancing around just inside his field of vision. Not prancing, really, but there, moving around. His mind was active, conjuring up images of her tits, the way they'd looked with water sparkling on them in the sun.

Young tits, nicely sized, perfectly formed.

Jesus.

So he'd pissed away the day; taken a dip in the afternoon—alone—that'd removed whatever buzz he'd managed to acquire to that point, napped a couple of hours, went over in his mind the things that had happened that had brought Suki up into the mountains with him, said "shit" fifty or so times just to keep it fluid, and now the sun was just a dying purple glow through that low place in the mountains to the west.

They sat out in the gathering gloom, Suki on the big red cooler, leaning back against the side of the camper, Frank comfortably hunkered in a folding nylon chair, letting the night slip down around them. Not saying much.

"Nice," she said.

"What?"

"This. Up here. It's so quiet."

"Ain't it, though."

"I've never seen anything like it. I've only been up here one day, and I think I could stay forever."

"Without television?"

A bristly little pause, then, "Yeah, I might last a week or two without the tube, Frank. You never know."

"Sorry. Cheap shot."

"So I'd rather watch TV than read; so what?"

"So nothing. I didn't mean anything. Forget it."

She didn't reply, but he could feel her sitting there in the dark, steaming. Funny how you could feel another person's anger, like heat. Fanny had been like that. Every once in a while she'd get worked up over something and bang pans around in the kitchen, radiating her displeasure like an oven.

Suki cooled off after a few minutes. "You hungry?" she asked.

66

He was. It was almost nine thirty and they hadn't gotten around to eating yet. "Yeah. You feeling domestic?"

"What's that mean?"

"Can you cook?"

"Sure—if you teach me how to use that stove in there. I never used one like that before."

"Nothing to it. But I think tonight we oughta barbecue. I've got steaks that need eating."

"Barbecue? You better do it then, Frank. All I ever do is catch things on fire."

"Like cars?"

She laughed, a bright, happy sound in the night. She was still pleased with the way she'd fried Mink's car.

Frank lit a Coleman lantern and hung it from a bracket just outside the open door of the camper. Suki unwrapped a couple of steaks from one of the coolers while Frank squirted starter fluid on some charcoal briquettes and set them ablaze.

"Got some fresh corn we can cook, too," he said.

"I'll do it, if—"

"Yeah, yeah. If I show you how to use the stove, right?"

"Right."

Fifty minutes later they were sitting under the stars in the quiet of the night, eating, each with a beer. Frank had turned the lantern low and put it in the camper. Only a dim glow spilled outside. Overhead, the Milky Way blazed.

"Tell me about Korea," she said.

"Not much to tell."

"Getting shot isn't much, huh?"

"I was walking along and suddenly I was lying in a rice paddy with mud in my mouth. One moment you're all right, the next hundredth of a second you're down, numb, not really even wondering what the hell happened. Just there."

She absorbed this in silence for a while. "How old were you?"

"Nineteen."

"Almost like me now," she said quietly.

"Almost like you now."

"What happened then?"

"Took them two days to get me to a hospital. Medic kept me pumped so full of morphine I hardly knew my name."

"Freaky," she said.

Freaky. Yeah, freaky. Thought he was going to die; that's freaky, in the parlance of the young. During moments of painful consciousness, he'd had words with a God he'd barely known existed.

Please, God, don't let it be over yet.

Freaky. At nineteen he'd lost his immortality.

"It's getting cold out here," she said.

"You could put on that shirt I gave you last night."

"Think I'll just turn in instead. I'm beat."

"Suit yourself."

"I don't guess you'd have toothpaste and a toothbrush anywhere around, huh?"

"Try the drawer next to the sink."

"Mind if I use 'em?"

"Nope."

She tramped out into the night, tramped back, got herself ready for bed while he watched a couple of shooting stars die way up overhead. Last few seconds of a four-billion-year journey. That was freaky too.

"Night," she called.

"Night."

Frank sat alone with his thoughts, but now everything was wandering, nothing sitting still inside his skull. Suki, Mutt and Jeff, some guy called Mink. Seventy-seven thousand dollars hidden away in the camper. Fanny gone. Bullet wound he hadn't given much thought to in ten or fifteen years that'd earned him a Purple Heart.

What you gonna do, Frank?

Christ, I dunno.

How 'bout Rio? Thought you said Rio was the place.

It's fulla bugs.

You don't know squat, Frank. Stick you in Madrid instead

of Rio and you wouldn't know the difference for a month.

I know. That's the problem.

How'd you get yourself into this mess, anyway?

Long story.

He got up, went inside. Bright lemon boob-holder slung over the vent handle. He stared at it, turned the valve on the Coleman lantern. It sputtered and slowly went out.

Life just never was what he thought it'd be.

He wore his shorts to bed; taste of Colgate in his mouth. He felt cumbersome, working his way under the covers, trying not to touch her.

Fanny, up there in the darkness, smoking, wanting to talk, waiting to see how close he'll get to this girl.

Forgive me, Fanny, not tonight. I'm all talked out.

Okay, Frank. Whatever you say.

He closed his eyes, tried not to think of the young girl lying topless next to him, tried not to think of money or the FBI or pictures of himself in the L.A. *Times* or on TV. Tried not to think of anything.

Might as well try to turn a hurricane by spitting into the wind.

She was eighteen years old. Eighteen. He had a daughter in Spokane nine years older than that. Fairly worthless kid of twenty-seven with three spoiled screamers of her own and a pudgy husband who managed a 7-Eleven. Debra Limosin, now Debra Speth. Never even graduated from high school because she knew so goddamned much more than her old man.

And Robert Limosin. Bobby. Twenty-five now, couple years of college at U.C. Davis, and still the kid couldn't find his ass with both hands and a candle. A clerk at some men's store in San Francisco; Frank couldn't even remember the name of the place. Gerardo's or Gregorio's or some such shit.

Suki's hand found his arm, slipped down and took his hand, placed it on her breast.

69

Soft, but firm. Warm. He could feel the nipple pressing against his palm. Good handful, just like he'd thought.

Jesus.

"Suki, I don't—"

Her lips sealed his. He was startled, surprised that her face had been so close.

She backed away a few inches and her voice came at him, kind of husky in the dark. "What you're gonna do now is give me a big lecture of some kind, right? Talk me to death?"

She still held his hand to her breast. In spite of himself, he felt himself respond. No stopping it.

"I just don't . . . You don't have to do this." He was having trouble getting air into his lungs.

"No shit, Frank."

"I'm old enough—"

"To be my father, that what you're gonna say? Think that matters?"

"Christ, I'm three *times* your age, Suki."

"So what?"

So what? He wasn't sure what. Just seemed as if it oughta what, that was all. She should be with a kid her own age.

"It doesn't mean anything, Frank. Here, look at you for chrissake. You're all tensed up."

She tugged his hand down to the flat of her belly, held it lightly against her while moving it around. God, she was soft, hard too; a medley of textures. Up across her rib cage, down past her navel. Pubic hair lightly brushed his fingertips.

Jesus Christ, she didn't have a stitch on.

"You gettin' the idea, Frank? Touch me." She turned loose of his hand.

No way. He couldn't do this.

Her hands found him, gently. He shuddered.

"Christ, Suki . . ."

"Don't tell me you don't want to," she whispered.

In his state, that would have been too obvious a lie. It was just as well he didn't have enough air left in him to say much of anything at all.

Her hand guided his again. Down between her legs, into a silky wetness.

"Leave your hand right there," she said. She began to tug off his undershorts.

Oh, Christ, Fanny! Please understand. I don't want you to think that I—

Shut up, Frank, you silly old foof!

He smiled then, for just an instant. She'd called him an old foof a million times. Which meant old fart and they both knew it, and it was true, too, but foof was Fanny's word, and her saying it meant everything was all right.

Jesus. Thank you, Fanny.

Suki pressed herself against him.

"Frank?"

"Yeah?" Frank lifted his head an inch. Suki'd been quiet, lying on her side, one leg thrown over his thigh. He'd thought she was asleep.

"That gun you got . . ."

"What about it?"

"What's it for?" Drowsily.

"A guy'd have to be nuts to come all the way up to a place like this without some kind of protection."

"I thought so. You sure got a lot of booze up here with you."

"I'd planned on doing some drinking."

"Figured that, too. Frank?"

"Yeah?"

"I think I broke a nail on your back."

He smiled, waited half a minute. "Go to sleep, Suki."

But she already was, too warm and soft and young to really be lying next to this run-down old foof in the starlit darkness of the De Baca Mountains in southeastern New Mexico. But she was.

She was.

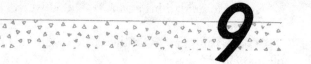

9

Darkness flowed sluggishly around Jersey's truck, a rattly old Dodge he'd picked up for twenty-five dollars a day from an old geezer of seventy who'd farted loudly and moistly maybe ten or twelve times while Jersey'd been negotiating with him.

Ed Farley, widower, and his dog Belle. Jersey'd found the bucolic duo sitting out on a screened-in porch watching Imogene's sparse traffic churn up short-lived dust devils in the street.

The truck didn't have a clock. It didn't even have dash or dome lights that worked, so Jersey didn't know what time it was and couldn't tell how fast he was going.

He guessed it was maybe midnight, maybe a little after, and he thought he was doing about forty-five. When the truck got moving much faster than that it had one hell of a shimmy.

Jersey's head nodded. The Dodge's right wheels went off the road, onto the gravelly shoulder, and Jersey snapped his head around, eyes burning, got the truck back on the road.

Fuck this.

He'd been up how many hours now? Since the morning of the day that big dude had dropped him in Quiode. His fogged brain added it up: thirty-eight hours. He was running on fear—which he'd managed to sublimate into dedication to his employers. Fear of Charlotte Voorhees, which was really fear of Mink, Charlotte's baby boy; but even Jersey's fear was beginning to wear a bit thin as fatigue set in.

He'd been up every little dirt track and side trail from Imogene most of the way to Quiode; Benny and Isaac were doing the same from Quiode all the way out to Highway 285. The task was just about hopeless, but they were keeping at it anyway.

He wondered if Mote was awake in Imogene. Probably not. He and Mote should get a room at Imogene and trade off watching the road, catch up on some sleep. But that'd cost them a whole day and the Bitch wouldn't go for that; the Bitch was rabid about catching Suki Flood.

For the thousandth time he wondered exactly what Mink and Charlotte did to get so much money, but in his exhausted state the thought wouldn't stick. Something illegal, he was sure of that. He was just one of Mink's messenger boys. He and the others followed orders, which were always simple and specific, part of some larger scheme. But he didn't know what it was, why Mink and the Bitch had so much money to burn.

A paved road appeared off to the right. Jersey slammed on the brakes and still had to back up a ways to make the turn. His lights swept over a gravel pit that looked as if it hadn't been used in years. He went slowly, almost letting the old truck idle along, peering into shadows.

Nothing.

The asphalt was cracked, chunks of it scattered around, and even that gave out after a quarter mile. Beyond, a dirt road of sorts ran out past the reach of his lights.

Nope. Wasn't gonna go out there. Not tonight.

He thought about going back to Imogene and trying to get a room. Probably too late for that, though. Anyway, it was fifteen, sixteen miles from here, and he was bone tired.

Jersey switched off the engine, parked right there in the middle of the road where the asphalt left off. He curled up on the seat of Ed Farley's truck with his greasy denim jacket pulled over his shoulders, knees cramped into the gear shift, and was dead asleep in seven seconds.

World-record time.

Jersey came awake when a hawk landed on the hood of Farley's truck and flapped its wings. Christ, maybe it was an eagle. Whatever it was, it was a big sonofabitch. Sounded like a fucking helicopter.

Jersey pounded the horn and the sonofabitch flew off like he'd shot it in the ass with rock salt.

Nine fifteen, sun already high in the east. Jersey got out of the truck with a groan, legs stiff, and took a lengthy leak against a rotting fence post, eyes following the scrabbly dirt road he'd seen the night before. It looped over a rise and disappeared. The foothills beyond rose up into barren, rocky mountains.

Beautiful New Mexico. All tarantulas and dust.

He walked a short way up the road, looking around like an Apache or something, checking out the dirt, and found the tracks of some rig that'd been through since at least the last rain. Christ only knew how long ago that'd been; probably sometime in the early fifties.

Now what?

He saw Charlotte Voorhees's face, black-widow eyes staring at him like shiny agates. *Go up the road, Jersey,* she said.

Yeah, he'd go up the road. If for no other reason than to say he'd done it.

He got in the truck and started out, pounding the rusty old Dodge over bumps and through washes, up the sides of hills covered with hackberry shrubs, needlegrass and sand-bur. He was miles from the highway and just about to hang it up when something ahead caught his eye. He roared around a curve and over the crest of a hill and was staring at a burned-out wreck in the road ahead when a bump launched him into the air, engine whining. When he came down, two of Farley's balding Firestones blew out with the sound of farting elephants. Jersey's head slammed into the roof.

"Sonofabitch!" he yelled.

The Dodge slewed sideways in the road, came to rest canted like a leaking sloop. Jersey hopped out, kicked the door shut, and examined the truck's tires.

"Mother*fucker!*" he said, drawing air from deep in his diaphragm, letting the curse resonate, rubbing his head.

It took him five minutes to get around to looking at the wreck in the road. Farley's truck didn't have a spare, not that one would have done him any good when what he needed now was two.

Jersey stared at the burned-out ruin. A Trans Am. With Louisiana plates on it. Mink's plates.

Oh, Christ, Jersey thought.

Not that it meant Suki and the guy she was with were up in the hills ahead, or that they were even in goddamn New Mexico any longer. Mink's Trans Am wasn't even warm, at least not from the fire that'd destroyed it.

Not much left to see. Just an ashy ruin, seats burned up, dashboard mostly gone, glass blown out. Tires were burned up too—which figured.

The day was heating up nicely.

Not a goddamn thing he could do here, so he began walk-ing back down the road, the way he'd come. Ten or twelve miles to the highway, and his stomach was already beginning to rumble. Fourteen hundred and seventy-three dollars in his pockets, and not a HoJo in sight.

This wasn't going to be his best day ever.

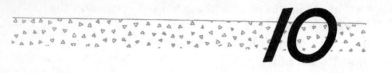

Frank was gone. Again.

He couldn't relax, just cuddle up with her and sleep an extra hour. He wasn't the cuddly type. Well, he was and he wasn't; just wasn't the type to think he was. And he wasn't the type to sleep in either, had to be up and doing something. Probably still a little shook up about last night, too. Her and him; her so much younger. Suki knew it bothered him.

She stretched, feeling the good tightness of muscles that had been properly used, legs a tiny bit rubbery.

She got out of bed, went outside naked and looked around, didn't see Frank anywhere. Probably at the spring, soaking. After what they'd done last night, he probably needed it, the sweet old thing.

She smiled, felt deliciously naughty.

Inside, she turned on the radio. It was 10:02; she'd slept pretty late. Keep this up and Frank would think she was a pig for sure. The news was on, some story about disarmament talks in Geneva with the Soviet Union. She turned it down low so it wouldn't bother Frank if he was out there somewhere reading.

She put on underwear and slipped her feet into the thongs he'd given her yesterday. Better than her busted sandals, but not much. Size eleven men's on her size seven feet.

"... *still searching for Frank Limosin, who left his partner stranded at a truck stop at the outskirts of Bakersfield Monday morning and disappeared with a load of ball bearings valued at over half a million dollars. Limosin is described as five feet eight inches tall, two hundred forty pounds. As yet, the truck he was driving has not been found, and the search has been expanded to include ten counties in central and southern California. The highway patrol has—"*

Suki went outside to pee, thongs flapping, shivers running through her as the morning sun caressed her body.

Came back. Still no Frank, so she rummaged through the shelves, looking for something to eat. The Byrds were singing "Mr. Tambourine Man." Old music, but it had a nice sound.

She had a good eye for checking things out; living with Mink had given her that. Mink was good at stashing things in weird places. Charlotte too. Even so, Suki almost missed the fake ash cabinet up over the sink where Frank kept the hard stuff, five bottles of Jack Daniel's.

It was rather crude, but, hell, she hadn't been expecting anything like it.

The cabinet wasn't quite as deep as the one right next to it. Curious. It took her a while to figure out that the vertical brace to the left wasn't really a brace. She pried it out, slid the rear panel to the left, reached in and took out a small navy blue nylon bag.

She unzipped it, looked inside. Stared, mouth open at the sight of all the money.

Beneath the money was a driver's license and several other wallet-sized items. Gun permit, Sears credit card, Texaco and Chevron and Visa. The license had Frank's picture on it.

Frank, she thought. You sneaky old son of a bitch!

All the cards were made out in the name of Frank Somebody. Not Wiley, though.

L-I-M-O . . . She pieced it out painfully, straining to understand the letters, say them aloud.

Li-MO-sin. Li-mo-SIN. LIM-o-sin.

Not Wiley.

Limosin. She'd heard a name like that before, somewhere. Not long ago, either.

Something clicked in her memory and she stared at the radio in surprise, where Frank Zappa and the Mothers of Invention were singing "Jelly Roll Gum Drop." Right there. Something about a Frank Limosin. Something about truck stops and money. Lots of money.

Jesus. Frank'd said he drove a truck.

Heart pounding, she zipped the bag shut and shoved it back where she'd found it, slid the panel back in place, and returned the vertical brace to its original position. And the booze.

She hurried outside and looked around. No Frank. Good.

Went back inside, tried to think. No wonder he'd wanted to be alone, and to drink. He didn't seem the criminal type. She knew criminals, and he wasn't one.

She didn't feel unsafe, way out here in the middle of nowhere with Frank. Not after being around Mink a while, and not after finding all that money, either. Frank wouldn't hurt her. Frank and Mink—Christ, there was no comparison.

This was weird, really weird.

At 11:00 A.M. the newscast was repeated, word for word, and this time Suki heard the whole thing.

He'd never get used to this. Never. Suki gliding up to him in the pool like an otter, wrapping her arms around his neck,

78

letting her breasts slide teasingly over his chest. Him just sitting there stupidly in his Levi's; Suki laughing at him with her eyes.

He still felt too old for this, still didn't know what to do with his hands when she was around.

Last night already had a dreamlike quality to it, and this afternoon felt about as unreal—Suki showing up in thongs and that cream-colored cotton bikini underwear that emphasized the slender firmness of her hips. No top, skin glowing, a perky little grin on her face. She'd handed him a beer and stepped into the water, sank in up to her chin, flipped her underwear up on a rock, closed her eyes and sighed. After a while she'd glided over, wrapped her arms around his neck and said, "So, Frank, what's new?"

Never get used to that. Not in a million years.

She slid away, climbed out onto a rock, and began to comb out her hair with her fingers.

Water glistened on her skin. Frank couldn't keep his eyes off her, couldn't believe he'd made love to this young beauty the night before.

"What're you gonna do?" she asked. "After this vacation of yours is over, I mean?"

Frank shrugged. "Go back to driving a rig, I guess. It's what I do." Which, of course, he could never do again, but he wasn't about to get her tangled up in his affairs.

"Ever think about doin' something else?"

"Like what?"

"Like anything. You said drivin' a truck was just a way to make money. That all you want?"

"What else is there?"

"I don't know. Bein' happy."

"Driving trucks is all I know, Suki," he said uncomfortably, wondering at the turn the conversation had taken. "Tell me, that your real name? Suki?"

"Why?"

"Just sounds . . . I don't know, unusual."

Her emerald eyes watched him. "My real name is Anne. So what?"

"So nothing." Anne.

"After I left home, I called myself Suki. I didn't want to be Anne anymore. I'd had enough of bein' Anne."

"You ran away from home?"

"Sorta. I left when Mink came along."

"Looking for a thrill?"

"Looking not to die. Looking not to wake up some day and find myself old and fat and shrill like my ma, married to some scaredy-cat wimp who'd kiss my feet just to avoid a fight."

Lot of bitterness there, Frank thought, not just in her words but in the way she said them. Under that sunny hide was a toughness that had come from doing something more than watching television, baking herself at the beach, teasing the boys with her body while numbing her brain with rock music.

Some kind of semiarticulate common sense operating there, even if she couldn't change a tire or read a map.

"Why'd you go with him?" Frank asked.

"Mink? He was . . . I dunno. Fun, I guess. Flashy, exciting. He treated me real nice, at first. Seemed to care how I was feeling. Talked to me. Mink can be pretty much whatever he wants—but mostly what he wants, I found out, is to hurt people, just as much as he can."

Her head was thrown back, face catching the sun, nipples standing up like tiny pebbles. She could easily be a Playmate, wouldn't even need an airbrush. An easy awareness of her body showed in her movements.

It was almighty damn confusing.

"You change your name legally?" he asked.

"Uh-uh."

"So your driver's license still has you as Anne?"

"I don't have a license, never did. Forget about Anne; my name's Suki, period. Anne is someone who died."

"You drove all the way from Shreveport in a red Trans Am without a license?"

"Yeah." She grinned at him. "In those shorts and that top, I was pretty safe. I know how to smile and act ditzy, Frank. If some cop pulled me over I'd just look for my purse and then start cryin' when I couldn't find it. I'd tell him I must've lost it at the last place I stopped to eat. Just look kinda dumb and sexy and lost, and sniffle a lot. I can cry real good. Anyway, after the first hour I wasn't driving all that fast. Maybe sixty, sixty-five."

And it'd work, too. Suki could melt hearts like chocolate on a tin roof in August. Unless she got herself stopped by a woman cop whose reaction, when presented with so fluffy a confection, might be rather less sympathetic than a man's.

"These guys, Mutt and Jeff—"

She grinned. "Mote an' Jersey."

"Whatever. Names like that, who can remember. Anyway, it still seems pretty crazy. Them out chasing you like that."

"That's Mink for you. Son of a bitch is worse than crazy, he's goddamn insane. Really."

"Even so," he said. "All the way from Louisiana?"

She sat up. "You're pretty smart, Frank. Been around and seen a lot, but there's something you've never seen yet, I can tell: you haven't never seen anyone like Mink."

"I've known some fairly rotten bastards in my day." He wondered why he felt so defensive about it.

A strange look was in her eyes, something that gave Frank an uneasy feeling. "Not like Mink," she said softly.

"Christ, all this over a goddamn car."

She stared into his eyes, chewing on her lower lip. "Can I trust you, Frank?"

"What d'you think?"

"Tell you what. Maybe we could trade . . . I dunno. Secrets, maybe. You tell me one of yours, I'll tell you one of mine."

"What makes you think I've got any secrets?"

"*Every*body's got secrets, Frank."

"Got something you want to get off your chest?" He spoke without thinking, then grimaced at his words. Too late.

She glanced down at herself. "Nope. Can't spare it." She smiled at him.

"Like hell."

She wrinkled her nose and climbed down off the rock, sliding back into the water. "Mink's got another reason for chasing me. More than just the car."

"Yeah? What's that?"

"I left real early in the morning." She paused, thinking. "Last Tuesday; like about three o'clock, before it got light. Mink and me were up late the night before. I made dinner for just the two of us." She gave Frank a searching look. "I can cook, really. Not just corn, either."

"I believe you."

"Anyway, it was some kind of Cajun casserole thing Mink likes. Catfish, lotsa spices. I didn't really wanna do it, and I was pissed off at Mink for some reason, so I told him I wasn't his slave and I wasn't gonna make it for him. So he hit me— the son of a bitch. Gave me this eye. So what I did was I put some of Mink's mother's Sec—"

"Mink's mother?"

"I didn't mention her? Charlotte Voorhees? That's Mink's real name, Voorhees. Two of them are real close. I mean *real* close. Simon's his real name, but he likes people callin' him Mink."

"Dandy."

"Mink's mother is a bitch like you wouldn't believe."

"It happens."

"Actually, she's his stepmother, ever since he was like two years old. His real mother died when he was born. His father ran away when Mink was five. Just took off—not that I blame him any. Charlotte raised Mink after that.

"Anyway, I put some of Charlotte's Seconal in Mink's food. She can't hardly sleep without it. The two of us were alone 'cause Charlotte had a headache and went to bed early. Didn't even watch Johnny Carson like she usually does. So I emptied six or seven pills into Mink's plate and stirred it up, along with extra pepper an' stuff. It really knocked him out."

"I'll bet."

She looked pleased with herself. Frank waited, gazing at her as this new image of Suki-Anne Erickson unfolded.

Suki shrugged. "Before I took off, I got this bottle of India ink and a needle and I tattooed his forehead. Guess he didn't like that very much."

"You did *what?*"

"Tattooed his forehead. He steals from old people, Frank, that's how he makes money. So I tattooed 'crook' on his forehead. C-R-O-K, crook. That's right, right? And then I took his goddamn car and split."

Frank just stared at her.

"Now you," Suki said.

"Now me what?" Frank asked, a little dazed.

"Your turn. Tell me a secret."

Frank rummaged through his memory, sorting, discarding, searching for something with some bite to it that didn't give away too much.

"Back about twenty years ago in El Paso, I came out of a bar, I don't remember what it was called, and this guy was across the street, knocking some woman around in a parking lot. So I ran over and slapped him."

"Slapped him?" Her lips screwed up in a frown.

"Yeah. Openhanded, real hard. Guy landed on the ground, eyes rolled up in his head like I'd hit him with a billy club or something."

"Hmmph," she said, disappointed.

"I took off. Didn't know how bad I'd hurt him, but I go kinda crazy when I see guys beating up on women. No one ever found out it was me. Next morning I was on my way up to Albuquerque with a load of roofing shingles."

She didn't say big deal, Frank, but it was in her eyes. She climbed out onto her rock and sat there a while, quiet. Finally she looked at him and said, "I think my secret's a lot better'n yours, Frank. Maybe you don't trust me enough to tell me anything really interesting."

Then she put on her underwear and the thongs and clumped off in the direction of the camper.

"Shit," Frank said. "What'd she want, anyway? Murder?"

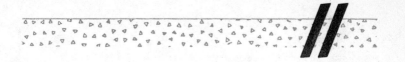

By the time Jersey pulled in to Quiode he was all money and no smile, not even a remnant—which, however, didn't keep him from being civil to Mrs. Voorhees, the Bitch of Shreveport. He was sweat-sticky, ripe as a Hell's Angel's T-shirt, and his booted feet hurt like blazes.

It had taken him nearly five hours to hike out to Route 401, another two hours to hitch a ride with a pair of Mexicans who'd tried to sell him some grass—successfully, too; screw Mrs. Voorhees and her boy. What they didn't know wouldn't hurt them, or Jersey.

Jersey's stomach was just a scrap of shriveled flesh inside him. His mouth felt like an acre of prime Oklahoma dust bowl. The first thing he did when he reached Quiode was to chug three beers at the Blue Bottle Bar, one right after the other. By the time Jersey picked up the phone and made the call, it was five in the afternoon.

"Tell me."

Jersey gripped the phone tighter, like it was her skinny fucking neck.

"It's Jersey. I found Mink's car."

"You *did*? Where?"

He described the place. Wanted to tell her it was about six thousand miles from nowhere, but instead managed to pinpoint it within some kind of reason.

"It doesn't appear on my map, Jersey."

"It isn't much of a road, ma'am."

"You say it goes up into some mountains?"

"Yes, ma'am. There's sure a lot of empty territory up there, though. No tellin' how many places it branches off or if there're other ways out or anything. Shitty—uh, real bad road, ma'am. Truly."

A moment of silence. The Bitch was thinking. Finally she said, "Can you rent a plane somewhere around there, Jersey?"

"A plane, ma'am?"

"You know. Those things with propellers and wings? That kind of plane."

God, he wanted to kill her. "To search the hills, ma'am?"

"Yes, Jersey; to search the hills. Something quite small. I'm really not pleased with how long it's taking you to find the girl, Jersey."

"I . . . dunno. Probably nothing like that in Quiode or Imogene. I could maybe ask around, though."

"Why don't you do that, Jersey?"

Something in the ensuing silence made him ask, "Uh, *now*, ma'am?"

"Yes, Jersey. Now."

Christ. "Just a minute. Ma'am."

He let the phone hang from its cord. Before he left it he gave it a violent twist so it banged against the wall, *whack, whack, whack.* Muzak.

86

Jersey went to the bar, waved the bartender over.

"Yeah? Whatcha need?"

"Look, I want to rent an airplane. And a pilot," he added hastily. "You know of anything like that around here?"

The bartender grinned. "You mean like with a propeller and wings, that kinda plane?"

Jersey almost substituted the Asshole for the Bitch, but he held himself back.

"Yeah, that kinda plane."

"Naw. Not round these parts."

"Someplace else maybe?"

"Chicago. O'Hare."

"Very funny," Jersey said, still keeping it in. Maybe he would burn the place down before he and Mote left for good. "I mean around here; Imogene, or someplace else nearby."

The bartender, swarthy, wearing a mustache long enough to chew thoughtfully against his upper lip, said, "Just a minute, Mac," and disappeared into a back room.

Jersey went back to the phone, gave it another spin.

Whack, whack, whack.

The bartender returned.

"Roswell," he said. "Got a place in Roswell for sure, but you might give Cap Streeter a try first."

"Streeter? Who's that?"

The bartender grinned. "Cap's got a kind of chicken farm off four-oh-one. You go up north about ten miles, turn left off the highway, go another five, six miles out. He's got this place back in the hills. Can't miss it."

"This Streeter guy's got a plane?"

"Be pretty funny, wouldn't it, me tellin' you t' go all the way out there if he didn't."

"Figure he'd take us up?"

The bartender's grin widened. "Us? You got crabs, Mac?"

Jersey almost killed him, right there. "I got a friend wants to go up too. Think this Cap fellow'd do it, pay him enough?"

"Christ only knows what Cap'd do for money."

Jersey didn't like the sound of that, but he went back to the phone where Charlotte Voorhees was still hanging.

"Ma'am?"

"Yes, Jersey."

"We could rent a plane for sure in Roswell, but there's a guy here who thinks maybe some guy called Streeter might take us up. Cap Streeter, local dude."

"Check it out, Jersey. Get back to me." She hung up.

"Sonofabitch," Jersey snarled. He dialed the Bitch's number again.

"Tell me."

"This's Jersey. Uh, look, Mrs. Voorhees; I'm in Quiode. That truck I rented blew two tires way up in the hills, so I had to walk out. I don't have any wheels. You want to maybe send Benny or Isaac over to pick me up?"

She didn't; he could hear it in her silence. "What I think I'll do, Jersey, is send Benny to Imogene to relieve Mote and then have Mote drive on up to Quiode. That way we'll keep the road covered at both ends, and you and Mote can go up in the plane first thing in the morning."

Assuming we can goddamn rent one, Jersey thought. "Yes, ma'am," he said.

"Wait where Benny can't miss you, Jersey. When he comes through, tell him where he can find Mote in Imogene. See if you can locate this Streeter person before dark."

"Yes, ma'am."

"I'll be in Reno by three o'clock tomorrow afternoon. Phone me there after that time. Daniel will coordinate the search while I'm en route."

"Yes, ma'am."

She hung up.

"Up your wazoo, Bitch," Jersey said, gesturing vulgarly. Oh, but the money was too good to even think about quitting; just too damned good. And he'd never been to Reno before. Twenty-four-hour town, Reno. Could be fun. Be even more fun if he just had the money, none of this aggravation.

* * *

88

The road to Streeter's ranch shot arrow-straight through a flatland of sage, giant hyssop, and senecio toward the southwest end of a rounded knob of rock that looked just like the tit on that old one-tit whore Jersey'd known back in Memphis. The one who'd still had a pretty face and good legs and who'd discovered she could charge a kinky clientele a lot more after the operation. Pretty soon she'd gotten so expensive Jersey'd had to take his business elsewhere.

The road wound past the base of the tit and up into the cleavage, if a single tit can be said to have cleavage. Streeter's ranch lay nestled like a mole against the far side of the hill, out of sight of Route 401. Not many chickens, but the whole yard was covered with chicken shit.

The sun was already behind the hills when they got there, the day vaguely purplish. A decrepit-looking Cessna 172 stood in a field of scrabbly hardpan, a quarter mile from the house.

Cap Streeter was fifty-five years old, but a touch of Alzheimer's and thirty-odd years of cigarettes and booze had left him looking at least seventy. When he gazed at Mote and Jersey through watery eyes and said he'd gladly take them up in his Cessna for ninety bucks a day and gas, Jersey wished he'd never asked. But it was exactly like Charlotte Voorhees to get hold of Streeter's number and find out if they'd been there. If she found that he and Mote had gone tearing off to Roswell to find a plane after Streeter'd agreed to take them up, she'd flay his goddamn feet for sure.

He was stuck with it.

"Sure you boys don't wanna drink?" Streeter asked as they were leaving.

"Well, yeah, sure," Mote said. "I'd kinda like—"

"No thanks," Jersey said curtly. All he wanted was to get some kind of room in Quiode, inhale the half lid of Mexicali Gold, and crash—all night long.

"See you boys tomorrah then," Streeter said, rubbing three days' worth of snow-white stubble on his chin.

"Can't wait," Jersey mumbled, turning away. ""Simply can't goddamn wait."

One more day. Mink worked on maintaining his inner calm. He closed his eyes and found that deep place of utter darkness in which Suki screamed. If you lacked such a place, a place over which you were absolute master, you had nothing.

One more day, then he would leave the hospital.

. . . Suki, screaming . . .

And now Mink knew how she would die. Not in the seething, restless maw of fire, but beneath the deliberate, dispassionate, hammering thud of water. And in the end, he would combine the two. Fire and water . . .

The phone rang. It was his mother, and she had a surprise for him. Two surprises.

"What, Mother?"

"Jersey found your car. The girl left it in the hills in New Mexico. She burned it. It can't be traced, of course, but at least it's a sign that she was there."

Was there. "And the other?"

"You'll see when you arrive in Reno, darling. Daniel has arranged it. I'm still in Shreveport of course, but the operation is completely shut down here. We're no longer checking post office boxes, and all the accounts have been emptied."

"That's good."

"I'm only here to coordinate the search. I expect to be in Reno tomorrow." She gave him the number of the new Citadel Daniel had set up for them in Reno.

Simon didn't even write it down. He had that kind of a memory. Charlotte spoke a while longer and then hung up.

Mink went back inside his head, back to where Suki still lay screaming.

He smiled.

12

It hadn't started out like much, Suki practically sulking in fact, but whatever funk she'd slipped into that afternoon had all but disappeared by nine that evening. The whiskey she'd put down had probably helped. Lots. In no time at all, everything was dandy; maybe a little too dandy, Frank thought, but after Suki's immodesty at the pool earlier that day—not to mention what'd happened the night before—any prudishness he was still harboring seemed both false and a little too damned late.

After downing her fourth whiskey—which was by no means a precise measure of her blood alcohol level—Suki'd removed her top and gone wheeling around like a minx, not quite making herself obnoxious but nonchalantly flaunting herself, showing herself off, posing in small ways.

Looking good, too, even if her hair was beginning to get a bit ratty. She'd smiled at Frank's discomfiture.

Later, when the sun had gone down and the chill had driven her into one of his shirts and a pair of faded Levi's, she'd hit the bottle even harder. While she drank, he'd fixed up a dinner of chicken and beans to help counteract the booze.

His Levi's looked ridiculous on her. Snockered, she'd tried to prove that she could get both her legs down one leg of his pants and still pull them up to her waist. Damn near made it too, giggling furiously, golden thighs wedged together.

She was drinking Jacky Dee straight now, eyes blurry, a funny little smile on her lips.

"You believe that?" she asked, running her words together like a painter mixing watercolors. "My ma was third runner-up in the Miss Iowa contess back in, shit, I dunno, sixty-eight, sixty-nine. Sumpin' like that."

"I believe it," Frank said, not even feeling a buzz. One of them had to stay sober; looked like it was going to be him. The damage being done to his drinking schedule was incredible.

"Five four, hunnerd an' ninety pounds now. Looks like a schmoo. You know what a schmoo is, Frank?"

"Yeah."

"Guess you'd know my ma, then, if you saw her." She drank half an ounce of amber liquid and poured herself another.

"You're gonna get sick."

"No way, Frank. You never saw me drink, didja?"

"I've got an idea how it'll go."

"I kin hol' my liquor."

"Let's hope."

But for the long sweep of her neck and a glimpse of perfectly formed collarbone, the clothes hid every lovely curve of her body. The two of them sat inside, the heater turned down low, just enough to keep things comfortable. Overhead, the Coleman lantern hissed, giving off a pale yellow glow. The world outside was part of a different universe.

She wagged a finger at him. "You know the def'nishun of a wimp, Frank?"

"Sure."

"My ol' man. That's a wimp. Right there in the dick-sherry."

He wasn't going to tell her not to talk about her father that way. Guy sounded like a wimp to Frank. Just because he was her father didn't mean he wasn't a wimp, and she was old enough by now to know.

"Get this," Suki said. "One day my ol' man comes home from the store, middle of the day. My ma said she was sick, so she stayed home. Usu'ly worked down at the store with Pa. Pa came home, check an' see she's all right. She's all right, all right—fuckin' one of the Miller boys right there on the couch. Kid was like, I don' know, seventeen. Sumpin' like that. Mike Miller. Had pimples an' this big cowlick. Tried t' feel me up a coupla times. I wouldn' let him, so then he's over't the house, bangin' Ma.

"Think my pa did anything? Fuck no. Miller kid jumps up with these big scared eyes an' Ma grabs his arm, throws the phone at Pa, almos' hits him in the face, tells him to get the hell outta there. He got out an' Ma just kep' on doing it with Mike. Pa tol' me 'bout it later, whinin' like he always does, cryin' an' callin' me his li'l baby, over an' over, his hands kinda on my boobs. I pushed him away and went out walkin'. Guess how old I was, Frank?"

"I don't know. Fifteen?"

"Twelve. Didn' hardly have any boobs for him t' grab. How's that for fam'ly?" She grabbed the bottle and poured herself another.

"Better take it easy with that stuff."

"Chill out, Frank. I kin han'le it. Ma knows Pa'd never leave her, no matter what. She *knows*, know what I mean? Pa owns a feed an' grain store out on Southeas' Fourth, up near

Saylorville. What I did growin' up was I cleaned out chick pens an' swep' the floors out back, carried sacks of feed."

"And went to school."

She gave him a funny look. "Las' year I was Miss Tractor Pull, down at the fairgroun'. All those bozos, whistlin' an' shoutin' when we came out wearin' our bikinis. I hated it, but Ma said do it. Firs' prize was three hunnerd bucks. She said I could win easy, an' I did. So guess what I did?"

"What?"

"I was suppos' t' give a trophy to this sweaty guy in bib overalls just won some event. So I gave it t' some old lady in a suit, some kinda judge or somethin', tol' her t' do it—kiss the sweaty sonofabitch for me, I tol' her, an' I grabbed some guy's arm and made him take me on the Ferris wheel 'bout ten times. Thought fuck'em, they can't take a joke. That was that for Missy Miss Tractor Pull. Had'ta give back mos'a the prize money too. Boy, was Ma ever pissed!"

"Then Mink came along."

"Mink." She sneered. "Yeah, Mink. The son'vabish. He knows how t' dress, though. Nice car, too." She gave Frank a cloudy look and then began to laugh. "BOOM! You see the windows come outta that thing, Frank?"

"I saw. Why'd you leave him, Suki?"

"Who?"

"Mink."

"He's crazy, thass why. Din' I tell you that?"

"You did, often. Didn't say how, though."

She poured another slug of whiskey into her glass, a big one, spilling half. Frank winced, took the bottle away.

She leaned forward. "Din' never make love t' me, how's that for crazy?" She downed her drink like it was water.

Frank swirled his drink, same one he'd been nursing for the last two hours. His drinking wasn't making any headway at all. Not a goddamned inch.

"So I ast him why we never made love. 'We gonna get married, Minky. Why'd you never take me t' bed?' Shit, he don' like me callin' him Minky. All he ever done is get me all dolled up and we'd go out t' dinner in these fancy-ass places. Sometimes I'd cook, but mos'ly we'd go out an' he'd show me off. At home, too. He'd get me wearin' these li'l skimpy outfits. Guess lookin's all he really wannid."

She reached for the bottle, found it gone.

"Gimme li'l bit more, Frank."

"I think you've had enough, Suki."

"Uh-uh. C'mon."

"Nope. Bar's closed."

She looked at him. "Hell, I gotta pee, don' I?"

"Bathroom's outside."

She tried to get up, slipped back down, began to giggle. Frank got behind her. He grabbed her under the armpits and hauled her to her feet.

"Jeez, you stron', Fran'."

"Yeah."

"I gotta pee."

He helped her outside. She clung to things—the refrigerator handle, cabinets, the doorframe, Frank—as she wobbled along in his oversize thongs, clothes flapping.

"This's far enough," he said when they were a little way from the camper. "You gonna be all right here alone?"

She fumbled at her waist. "Where's the butt'ns on this son'vabish?"

No buttons. He untied the length of nylon cord she'd been using as a belt. His pants dropped suddenly to her knees, his shirt hitting her at mid thigh.

"You gonna be all right?" he asked again.

She stood there, swaying in his grasp.

"Why don't you pee here?" he suggested patiently.

She nodded. "Yeah. Gotta pee." She seemed confused, didn't quite know what to do next.

"Hell," Frank breathed. He put an arm around her waist and helped her free herself from his pants.

"Col'," she said.

"Yeah, cold. Let's hurry, huh?" He worked her underwear off with his left hand, holding her upright with his right.

"Now squat," he said. He lowered her to the ground, heard a sudden rush of liquid and looked away, into the night. She was beautiful, but human. Probably wouldn't want to go over the details of this glorious evening when she was sober again.

He gathered up her clothes and walked her back to the camper, taking most of her weight. She began to struggle weakly, making noises, and he let her down gently, knowing what was coming next. She threw up suddenly, a lot of the alcohol she'd recently consumed. Do her good. Keep her from getting even sicker. Might even keep her from upchucking in bed, although Frank didn't want to hope for too much.

He let her go dry, then carried her into the camper, wet a rag and wiped her face. She had a tangly, wretched look, still moving feebly, beginning to go entirely incoherent. He undid the buttons of her shirt, speckled with vomit, got it off her, wiped her down again and lifted her naked into bed.

He'd never seen her look so vulnerable.

He pulled the blankets over her. In seconds she began to snore. He rolled her onto her side, which helped.

"Beautiful," he said softly. Now he'd seen her drink. She wasn't very good at it. He hoped she wouldn't get any worse. Or better, whichever. Girl like that shouldn't ruin her life with alcohol. No one should.

He capped the whiskey, put it back in the cabinet. Got King off the counter and began to read. Couldn't quite remember who'd been killed and how, so he backtracked four or five pages* and caught up on the gore, read straight through for a few hours in the light of the Coleman lantern while the night deepened and Suki slept, snoring gently.

He felt very protective. It was a feeling he hadn't had in a long time.

Mink. Someone named Simon Voorhees, but who pre-

*the correct procedure! **96**

ferred the name Mink. Real sweetheart of a guy, sounded like.

How Suki'd gotten mixed up with a shithead like that was beyond Frank, but she was young, and kids got themselves mixed up in all kinds of things these days. Got in over their heads before they knew what they were doing. From the sounds of it, Suki'd escaped just in time.

Mink and Charlotte Voorhees.

Left Mink with a tattoo, too. Not real smart, but she'd explained her reason for doing so with all the maturity of her years: she'd been pissed at him for hitting her. Enough said?

C-R-O-K. Couldn't say much for her spelling. You couldn't hardly guess what she was trying to write.

Suki's parents sounded like real winners too. But, Frank reflected, not all that goddamned unusual, really. Just your usual screwups. He'd known a few people in his day who'd give the Ericksons a run for their money in the asshole department. He'd even once met a supposed former beauty queen who'd gone to seed early, down in Phoenix, and the world was awash with losers and wimps.

Even had a few people on the run from the law, too.

Jesus.

Thing of it was, he wasn't real sorry he'd done it—at least, not yet. It'd been just four days now; five, since it was after midnight. Two-ten in the morning, in fact.

Suki groaned, rolled over. Her duffel bag slid off the bed, landed on Frank's shoulder, and tumbled to his feet. She was quiet again.

He picked it up, looked at it a moment, then unzipped it, feeling a bit crawly inside at the invasion of her privacy.

Took out the stuffed rabbit, the duck, a plastic B-52, a goddamn Rubik's Cube, three twenty-dollar bills—the ones he'd given her. Underneath was a towel. He took it out and stared into the bag at all the money, a great huge wad of it. He blinked.

Ho-ly *shit*.

13

Loose bills lay piled in the bottom of Suki's bag like lettuce in a chef's salad.

Frank's first thought was that she'd found his stash and ripped him off.

He emptied the cabinet over the sink and shoved the false panel aside. His bag was still there. He got it out, opened it, found his money and his papers, just like he'd left them.

He sat down, hard.

Jesus Christ.

Jesus *H*. Christ.

He tried to think, but his brain had turned to chowder. Dazed, he carefully returned his bankroll to its hidey-hole, put the Jack Daniel's back in the cabinet, and sat down again.

Mostly fifties and hundreds in her bag, a few twenties and a scattering of tens.

Used money.

Suddenly he wasn't a bit tired. Suki was asleep, breathing heavily, out of it.

He upended the bag over the table. The musty, unique odor of money filled the air. A few big wads slithered to the floor, *plop*. Money even had its own sound. Lord, there was a lot of it. He felt a chill creep up his spine.

He started gathering up the hundreds first, because there seemed to be more of them than anything else. Ten bills to a thousand, a hundred bills makes ten thousand.

He found some string and began tying it up in bundles of ten thousand. He gathered more of it from the floor where it had fallen.

It was a task of no little magnitude. Twenty-two bundles, sixty-four bills left over. Whatever she'd done, she'd scored big. Bigger than he had. Suddenly Mink's interest in her made a lot more sense.

Then the fifties. A hundred bills makes five grand. He made up five bundles before he realized it was getting light outside. Another seven bundles, twenty-six bills left over, and then he didn't need the lantern any longer. Dawn light tinged the hilltops orange.

Twenties: ten bundles, fifty-seven extra. Tens: two bundles, six extra. Even had seventeen fives thrown in. No ones. Frank totaled it up: $310,985.

If that don't beat all, he thought, using another of Fanny's favorite expressions.

"Sheee-*it*," he said softly.

The Cessna lifted off like an albatross on methamphetamine. Jersey stared at the ground below with glazed eyes, wondering if the last thing he would see would be rocks coming at him at a hundred and forty miles an hour. The possibility didn't seem remote enough to suit him.

Mote and Jersey sat in back, Cap Streeter in the pilot's seat up front, his dog, Woozer, sitting copilot.

Woozer, a baggy-eyed basset hound with wet, drooly flews, was stolidly indifferent to anything going on around him. He'd got his name from his bark, a soggy chuff that was half bark, half howl. Streeter'd told them that Woozer was hell on prairie dogs, but Jersey believed that like he believed Manson would one day be president. The mutt wouldn't give a merry fuck if prairie dogs did laps around him on the front porch, goosed him, and stole his Purina. Sorta liked to fly, though. Every few minutes he'd look outside, blink wetly, and *whoof* a bit, or *wooz*, like he was happy, or maybe he'd inhaled a jowl.

"Okay, now't we's up, what wuzit you boys wanted t' see?" Streeter asked. Stale booze rode his breath.

"Mountains up over there." Jersey pointed.

The Cessna went into a sudden rolling turn and Mote's eyes bugged from his head. Jersey's stomach reached his testicles before crawling back up. Woozer howled.

"Wooz likes that," Streeter called back over the unsteady throb of the engine.

"Great," Jersey replied, bile flooding his throat, wondering how Wooz would taste, skinned and deep-fried, served on a stick.

They'd got off fairly late, a little after two. Which wasn't late enough, Jersey thought, looking distrustfully at the crate Streeter'd said he'd take them up in. The plane looked like it was missing parts. He'd said as much to Streeter, trying to sound like he was kidding around, and Streeter'd said it was, "quite a few of 'em, which makes the ol' kite lighter." Jersey couldn't tell if the son of a bitch was joking or not.

As they passed over Quiode, Jersey picked out the Siesta Motel where he and Mote had spent the night last night. They crossed Route 401 at an angle, and a few minutes later Jersey spotted the wreck of the Trans Am six hundred feet below.

"There," he said. "There's the car."

Streeter stood the plane on its left wing and roared in a circle above the blackened hulk, banking at a forty-five-degree angle.

Woozer howled.

She came awake like a carp on a riverbank, ninety-five percent dead. Not even the smell of coffee helped. One eyelid rolled up, exposing a bloodshot eye, slid shut again with a quiver.

"Morning," Frank said amiably. Beneath the canvas awning, the interior of the camper was dim. Warm, but not unbearably so. Frank kept on cooking.

Suki moaned.

"Four-ten in the afternoon, actually. You've been asleep for something like seventeen hours. Must have a bladder like a ballast tank."

She made another little sound of pain, almost a whimper, and turned toward the wall with the blankets pulled up around her head, bare feet hanging out.

"Want a beer?" Frank asked.

"Ugh!" She shuddered under the blankets.

"At least you're alive."

"Who says?" She rolled over, moaned again. "Hurts."

"What, your head?"

"Yeah."

"That surprise you?"

She wiped a dewy line of sweat off her upper lip. "Jesus, what're you cookin'?"

"Eggs. Got to use 'em up or they'll go bad. Want some?"

"Don't be disgus—" She saw the money, stacked neatly on the counter. She lunged for her duffel bag, but it wasn't there. Her face, already pale, went white. She propped herself up on an elbow. "What's goin' on?"

He gave her a direct look. "It appears you haven't been entirely honest with me, Miss Suki-Anne."

She got out of bed, still looking drawn, but awake now. She put on Frank's thongs and went outside, moving unsteadily, muscles working in her honey-colored rump.

She came back a few minutes later, pushed past him without a word, and began searching for her underwear. She found them and slipped them on, climbed into her pink shorts and shrugged on the bright yellow top.

Still not a word, which Frank found rather amusing. He'd grown accustomed to her wicked comments, but this had stopped her cold. The eggs were done, so he turned off the stove, got a fork, and began to eat right out of the pan, egg and catsup stew. He waited for her to make the first move.

She opened the cabinet over the sink and set bottles of Jack Daniel's down on the table, hard, right next to his eggs. His heart began to beat heavier, faster. Christ, what was *this*?

She slid the panel aside and took out his blue nylon bag, tossed it in his lap.

"Guess you haven't been entirely, wonderfully honest with me, either. Frank Goddamn Liar Limosin-Wiley." Her eyes gave off sparks. She turned and stormed outside.

Limosin. Even knew his goddamned name.

Shit.

He sat there a while with the bag in his hands, wondering how long she'd known.

He took another bite, sighed, got up and went outside. "Now what?" he asked, trying to figure her mood. She was angry, sure, but what else? And how much more did she know?

Her arms were folded, back turned, afternoon sun blazing on her hair.

She spun around, bleary eyes level with his. "How much was there?"

"Where?"

"My bag."

"Three hundred thousand and change."

Her eyes flickered. "Jesus. How much change?"

"Eleven thousand, give or take. You didn't know how much you were carrying around?"

"I left in kind of a hurry. I didn't bother counting it."

"Looks like we both left out a few details when we were trading stories."

"Looks like."

"How long have you known?" he asked. "My name, I mean. And the money."

"Since yesterday, a little before noon. I found the money kinda by accident, and there was something on the radio about you. I didn't know it was you they were talking about, till I found your license."

On the radio—way out here. That wasn't good. And now she knew he was wanted. More trouble.

"Hungry?"

She shook her head. "Not very. You got any aspirin?"

"Tylenol. How about some toast? Dry."

"Maybe. Lemme try the pills first."

They went inside. Suki hefted a few bundles of hundreds—$40,000 worth. She saw his .357 lying on the counter, and he saw her looking at it.

She glanced at him, took the Tylenol he was offering and a cup of water. "I was drunk," she said. "You could've just taken off with all of it."

"Could've, yeah. Still could."

She blinked. "So? Why don't you?"

"Because I'm basically an honest person, Suki. I want you to understand that."

"That's why the cops're after you?"

"It's a long story."

"Usually are, aren't they?"

"Yours too?"

She thought a moment. "Not really. What I did, before giving Mink that tattoo, was I got that week's take out of a

103

small safe Mink kept around. Business Mink's in, ripping off old folks, he likes to deal in cash so he can clear out quick if he has to. The safe was the same kind my dad had at the store, a Fidelity model 40 combination safe. Took me a year to figure out how to pick the lock on my dad's safe, but then it wasn't all that hard, even when he took to changing the combination." She held up her hands. "I've got good fingers. Probably make a good burglar, maybe."

"So you picked Mink's safe, took the money, tattooed his forehead, and split?"

"Yeah."

"Anything else?"

"Uh-uh. That's it."

"Gave him another reason for hunting you down, don't you think? Over three hundred thousand reasons."

"You don't know Mink, Frank. Losing that money'd bother him, sure—but not as much as you'd think. The tattoo's what'd made him go really crazy. Maybe I shouldn't have done the tattoo."

"Maybe not. Too late now. Toast?"

She shook her head. "Uh-uh. Think maybe I'll just go to the pool and soak instead. Try to keep from dying. I still don't feel all that wonderful."

"Suit yourself."

She went outside. He had an oblique view of her through the window and beyond the canvas awning as she walked away.

He heard the sound a minute later: an engine laboring in the high mountain air. Went outside to take a look. Saw an old Cessna, a mottled dusty yellow, coming in at an angle not three hundred feet off the ground, wingtips swaying.

Oh, Jesus.

"There!" Jersey shouted, pointing. "What's that?"

Streeter hung a breathtaking turn so close to the ground that Jersey could see every rock and wildflower below, saw

104

where and how he was going to die, big seventy-foot cotton-woods reaching up for him.

Woozer howled with pleasure. Shit-for-brains mutt.

Jersey saw a man below, standing next to a dark green trapezoid that soon resolved itself into some kind of a tent. The hood of a truck stuck out from beneath one end of the tent.

"That it?" Jersey yelled at Mote. "That the guy's truck?"

"I dunno," Mote said.

Jersey hardly heard him. "That's him, that's the son of a bitch that—" He stopped abruptly.

"That what?" Streeter asked, ears twitching.

"Never mind," Jersey said. "That's him."

"There's the girl," Mote said phlegmatically, like he was pointing out the dairy section in a supermarket.

Jersey grabbed his shoulder. "Where?"

"There, kinda under them trees."

He saw her then, white platinum hair in shadow but still blazing away. Yellow top, pink shorts. Looking up.

"That's her, all right." To Cap Streeter he said, "How the hell do we get up to this place?"

"Truck, I reckon."

"Shit, I know that. I mean where's the *road*? How're we supposed to get up here?"

"Beats me."

"Can we follow it out, see where it goes?"

"Yuh. Give it a try. We're gettin' a mite low on juice, though."

"Let's do it."

The plane straightened out, moving northeast into a high gap where the road, such as it was, came over a ridge. Just about impossible to see where the truck had come in from up here. An all but invisible double track snaked through the rocks. They lost sight of it repeatedly as it switchbacked down the mountain. They circled, picked it up again, lost it a dozen times more. It was tedious, stomach-wrenching work, but Woozer loved it.

"We don't go back pretty soon," Streeter said after forty minutes of aerial artistry, "an' you kin pick out which rock you want t' kiss when we come down. Course, by then your asshole'd be puck'rin' up a sight more'n your lips." He grinned, chortling muddily at his wit.

"Shit," Jersey said. In the hazy distance he could see Mink's fire-gutted Trans Am. He'd only gotten a rough idea of how the trail crawled up into the hills: a big loop to the left as you went up past the Tranny, then right, over a ridge, down through a washboard canyon. Up again, southwest. Something like that. Mostly what he'd learned was that the girl was up there. El hombre, too.

"I've seen all I need to," Jersey said. Which wasn't entirely true, but he was starting to feel he'd already used up too many years' worth of luck in Streeter's crappy old plane.

Streeter jinked the plane like he was dodging SAMs. Woozer howled. The plane rumbled toward Quiode, engine coughing every so often, which didn't faze Streeter a bit.

The time was five-twenty.

Frank Limosin watched the plane disappear over a ridge. The pilot was a crazy son of a bitch; that much was evident, but not much else. He couldn't see who was up there. The plane had circled one and a half times, sunlight glinting off its windows, before flying off more or less back the way it had come. That seemed ominous.

Suki came hobbling over the rocky ground, pinwheeling her arms for balance.

"What was that all about?" she asked.

He stared at the now empty horizon, shading his eyes. "Your guess is as good as mine."

"Someone looking for us?"

"Could be."

"Mote an' Jersey?"

"Or maybe just a pilot out having fun, showing off."

"You think?" she said hopefully.

"I dunno."

He went into the camper and Suki followed. He said, "If it was those two friends of yours, then—"

"Those two ass-wipes aren't friends of mine, Frank."

"Sorry. Ass-wipes, then. Anyway, if that was them, we'd be smart to get the hell out of here, and soon. On the other hand, if we leave and it wasn't them, we'd be clearing out of a damn nice place to hole up for no reason at all."

She bit a knuckle. "So, what're we gonna do?"

Frank sighed. "Only thing we can, I guess. Clear out, at least for a couple of days."

"I'm making trouble for you, aren't I?"

"That's one way of looking at it, yeah."

"What's another?"

"I don't know." Frank looked at his watch. "If we left now, it'd be about dark by the time we reached the highway."

"I got time for a quick soak before we go? I still feel like hell."

"Few minutes wouldn't hurt."

"Wonderful." She squirmed out of her top and handed it to him. "Put this someplace safe for me, huh?"

She gave him a quick kiss on the cheek and then went out the door.

He stuck his head out. "Hey!"

She turned, striking a nice hipshot pose. "What?"

"Why the hell you do this kind of thing, anyway?" He held out her top, dangling it from his hand.

"A present. You like to look, Frank. Don't tell me you don't. Anything else I gave you right now would slow us down too much."

He stared at her. "Go soak yourself. And don't forget to include your head. It needs it."

"Yeah, yeah, yeah. Hey, Frank."

"What?"

"Are the cops really looking for you, like they said?"

"Must be."

"I'm sorry then. About all this."

"Yeah, yeah, yeah."

He ducked back inside, looped her tiny yellow top over the vent handle, and began thrashing about, putting things away.

14

The plane came sideslipping into the weedy field where they'd taken off, engine throttled back, coughing, and Jersey knew he was going to die. They'd made it this far, found the girl, and now they were going to smear themselves like cheese pizza over a little nothing patch of New Mexico. The landing gear wasn't aligned with the runway, the plane was crabbing awkwardly into a side breeze, and Jersey saw that they were going to flip at fifty-odd miles an hour, wrap themselves into a noxious wad of blood and bone and aluminum that would make a page-three item for a few local newspapers.

At the last instant, Streeter did something with his feet. The Cessna slewed to the left, and settled into a bumpy roll over the field.

"Shit-fire," Jersey breathed.

Woozer howled. Liked landings too, fuckin' retard.

They paid Streeter in cash, didn't bother thanking him, and roared back to Quiode, Jersey liking the proximity of the ground. In the darkness of the Blue Bottle he dialed the Reno number.

"Tell me," she said.

"It's Jersey, ma—"

"Where have you *been*, Jersey? Do you have any idea how late it is?"

"We saw her," Jersey said quickly. "Ma'am."

"*Where?*"

"Way up on a mountain, southwest of Quiode."

"Is she still up there, Jersey?"

"I think so. It's a bad fuck—uh, real bad road, Mrs. Voorhees. That guy's up there with her. Probably take them at least a coupla hours to reach the highway from way up there."

"Is there any other way out?"

"I didn't see one, ma'am." And I wouldn't have if there was anyway, and up yours very much ma'am. He felt goddamn lucky just to still be alive.

"Okay. Listen carefully now, Jersey."

Jersey closed his eyes, waiting for the rest of it. "Yes, ma'am."

"Are you listening very carefully, Jersey?"

Red lights shot like tracers through the darkened interior of his brain. "Yes, ma'am."

"What I want you to do, you and Mote and Isaac, is to go up into the mountains, find the girl and bring her out. Have Benny stay at the road near the highway in case they manage to get by you. Is that perfectly clear, Jersey?"

"Yes, ma'am."

"Don't hurt the girl."

"No, ma'am. How 'bout the guy? Want him messed up any?"

"If you must. Not too much, Jersey. He's not important. Don't do anything that would make it anything but a strictly local matter for the police."

"Yes, ma'am."

"Don't fail us this time, Jersey."

"No, ma'am."

"Call when you've got her."

"Yes, ma—" But the line was already dead.

"Fuck you and all your kin, ma'am," he said softly. "And your dogs and cats and all their fleas."

A rock clanged against the wheel well, making the cab of the truck ring like a bell.

"Jeez," Suki said.

The truck heaved, tossing them both several inches in the air, slammed back down. Frank jammed in the clutch.

"Was it this bad coming up?" Suki asked.

"Yup."

"I didn't notice. Must've had something on my mind."

"Must have."

Afternoon sun slanted into the hills, giving the canyons a gloomy look. Lengthening shadows crawled over the land below, out where Route 401 arrowed through the valley.

"Be dark in another hour or so," Frank said.

"Yeah." She gave him a sidelong glance. "Where'd the name Wiley come from, Frank?"

He didn't look at her; he felt uncomfortable with the lies he'd told. "Wiley's my mother's maiden name."

"Why'd you do it?"

"Do what?" But he knew what she meant.

"Take that truck. What kind was it? What'd you do with it, anyway?"

"You writing a book?"

"Just I'd like to know. That so bad?"

He spun the wheel, narrowly avoiding boulders as the truck ground up a twisty slope of loose rock. "Guess not."

"Well?"

"I drove a truck for this company, J. K. Lomax. They make bearings; one of the bigger bearing manufacturers on the West Coast."

"Bearings?"

"Ball bearings. Roller bearings, needle, lot of special-order stuff. Do a good business in turbine and pump bearings for power plants all over the western United States."

"Guess there's money in that, huh?"

He gave her a wry look. "Yeah, there's money in it. You take a case of quarter-inch ID ball bearings, thousand bearings to a case, weighs twenty-nine point three pounds and takes up about as much room as your average bowling bag. Guess what that box retails for."

"I dunno. Couple thousand bucks?"

"Not bad. Try seventy-five hundred. Hundred cases'd run you seven hundred fifty thousand dollars and weigh about the same as an eighty-two Cadillac."

"Jesus, Frank. You stole that much?"

"More. Hundred and twelve cases of assorted-size general-purpose needle and roller bearings, a few dozen big turbine bearings, a couple thousand special-order rollers for some big farm equipment outfit out in Iowa. Manifest put the shipment at six hundred twenty thousand dollars, but that was just the wholesale price. Retail, it'd go for something like one point two million, give or take."

"How much you get for it?"

"Eighty-four thousand seven hundred."

"That all?"

"I got the price I'd negotiated. Ten cents on the dollar, retail, for the stuff they could unload fairly easy. Less on the special-order stuff. Fairly typical black market."

"Why'd you do it?"

He glanced at her. "That's enough about me. These sons-a-bitches of Mink's are out looking for you, not me, and I want to know why. I want to know what this's really all about."

"I already tole you, Fr—"

The right rear tire blew out with a sharp report.

"Dirtysonofawhore!" Frank yelped.

The truck, which wasn't going very fast, thunked down on its rim and heeled over hard to starboard in a dry wash that descended steeply into a dark saddle of the hills.

Frank got out, glared at the tire, kicked it. "Shit," he said.

"Flat, huh?"

"Just look at the sonofabitch. Ever seen one flatter?"

"Once. Got a spare?"

He nodded. "Two. One underneath, the other on top of the camper."

"Okay, lemme help."

He stared at her.

She sat on a nearby rock. "First thing you do," she said, "is haul out the spare and the jack. Probably oughta set the emergency brake too."

"Christ," he growled. "Thanks."

"No problem, Frank. I'm pretty good with tires. Give you all the help you need."

Jersey'd rented the truck for eighty dollars from some old Indian with the crotch of his jeans sagging down around his knees. A four-wheel-drive, three-quarter-ton Ford pickup. On the radio, Slim Whitman was singing "Blues Eyes Crying in the Rain" at nearly full volume.

Jersey'd wanted two trucks, but Quiode was a dry well and in Imogene he'd only found the one before he noticed that the sun was getting low in the sky. Real low.

So he and Mote and Isaac had piled in the Ford and taken off, meeting Benny a little after six-thirty at the gravel pit where the road went up into the hills. Benny in the souped-up Chevy Malibu he and Isaac had been driving, cheese-burger juice dribbling from his chin. Benny was a class act all the way, just one rung up the evolutionary scale from Mote. A pterodactyl, bony, with pale skin and protruding blue eyes.

"Seen anything?" Jersey asked.

Benny shook his head. "Nope."

"Keep looking." Jersey gunned the engine and roared off toward the hills.

Mote sat in the middle, with his big arms and Neanderthal brain, playing pretend cowboy with his snub-nose .38, spinning the cylinder, flipping it in and out, peering down the barrel, snapping it shut with a twist of his wrist. Isaac, a slender black from Detroit, whose palms were as pink as Jersey's ex-wife's ass, sat nursing a beer in silence.

Jersey imagined that Isaac's silence was a sign of satisfaction. Whatever happened, Isaac couldn't lose. Isaac was the one who'd gotten them this far, and it wasn't likely that Mink or Charlotte would forget that, even if the girl managed to get away. Isaac had been standing guard over the house in Shreveport when the girl ran. He'd tailed her in the Malibu as she left town and followed her all the way to the west side of Dallas before she stopped and he finally had a chance to phone in.

What a commotion then! Everyone scrambling, Charlotte giving orders, Mink out cold, Jersey and Mote and Benny taking off in the Toronado, headed for Dallas like they were sitting astride a bomb.

Isaac had lost the girl somewhere east of Abilene, and for a while it looked as if he'd lost her for good, since she didn't show up for over four hours. But he'd waited just outside Sweetwater and, Jersey thought, gotten lucky as shit, because she'd finally come rolling along, just about dusk. She'd turned up Highway 84, headed for Lubbock, surprising the hell out of everyone. That night she'd disappeared somewhere around Fort Sumner, New Mexico, sixty miles west of Clovis.

By then the Toronado wasn't far behind, so Isaac had waited around and Benny had piled into the Malibu and the two had roared up north on 84 to Santa Rosa, then down 54 to Vaughn, while Mote and Jersey had gone south on 20.

114

For a while it looked as if she'd gotten away clean, but then Mote and Jersey had gotten lucky themselves and stumbled across her in Quiode. Just about had her, too—would have, if that big sonofabitch hadn't come along and interfered.

Jersey wanted the sonofabitch, wanted him real bad. He still felt the ache in his gut where the bastard had rammed him with the broom handle.

Dust piled up on the corners of the windshield, billowed out behind the truck in a vast reddish-brown rooster tail.

"Put that sonofabitch away," Jersey said to Mote. It made him nervous, Mote whipping his gun around like that.

"When you gonna gimme my bullets?" Mote asked.

"When hell freezes over, or when we see this guy Suki's with, that's when."

"Jeez, Jers."

Isaac snickered.

Jersey looked over at him. "You got your piece, Izzy?"

"Yeah."

"Loaded?"

"What d'you think?"

Mote said, "How come he gets bullets an' I don't?"

"Cause you'd blow your nuts off, fucking around like that, that's why. Izzy's got brains; what you got is wood shavings and liberry paste."

"Goddammit, Jers—"

"Christ, cool it, you two," Isaac said. "Jersey didn't mean nothing, Mote. Listen, tell me whatcha think: suppose this big airliner took off from somewheres in Ohio and crashed in Canada. Where d'you think they'd bury the survivors, back in the U.S. or right up there in Canada?"

Mote gave him a perplexed look. "How come you're always askin' me questions like that, Iz, huh?"

"No reason. Just passin' the time, bro."

"Shit, I dunno. Canada?"

Jersey laughed.

(the joke, you see, is that the "survivors" are

115

alive, so they wouldn't be buried. Get it?)

The truck was nosed downhill, leaning. The slope made changing the tire a much more difficult task. It had taken Frank nearly fifteen minutes to block the front wheels with boulders so the truck wouldn't roll downhill and to dig out a place for the jack so the truck wouldn't slip off and crush him to jelly. Suki sat on her rock, watching.

"So," Frank said, "tell me about Mink's operation."

"Whatcha want to know?"

"Everything. We've got these guys after us, I'd like to know what we're up against."

"Scuzzballs, that's what we're up against."

"That's not very helpful, Suki. Tell me about Mink."

"He's the head scuzzball."

He glared at her in the failing light.

"Okay," she said. "All right. What Mink does is he's got this scam worked out where he sells phony shares or something to old people. Mostly in phony mutual funds."

"It's been done before." Frank put the wrench over a nut, tensed, and spun it a quarter turn—*rak*—as easily as if someone had put it on with his fingers.

Suki stared. "Shit—how'd you . . ."

"Huh?"

"Nothin'," she said. "Mink and Charlotte've got a bunch of people who talk on the phone, ten hours a day. Six of 'em, usually."

"Standard boiler-room operation, sounds like." *Rak.*

"Yeah. I heard someone call it that once; boiler room."

"So what's so special about this one?"

"I don't know, maybe nothing. They make a pile of money, though."

Rak. Another nut spun loose. "What do you think?"

"Maybe the psykill . . . psycolol—"

"Psychology?"

"Yeah. Psy-*chol*ogy. What he does is he scares old folks, but he does it real nice, without scaring them about *him*. He

116

makes 'em wonder if they're doin' the right thing with their money, makes 'em wonder if their money is really safe where it is. Gets 'em worried sick about inflation."

"Charming." *Rak.*

"Listen to this. I heard this kinda thing so many times I sometimes hear it in my sleep." Her voice changed, becoming more confident, more soothing, and, Frank thought, subtly sly, although she probably wasn't aware of it.

" 'Lord, isn't inflation awful, Caroline?' " she said. " 'May I call you Caroline? You sound so much like my own mother, it makes me kinda homesick. Seems like every time you go to the store these days, things cost a little bit more, don't they? Shame, isn't it? . . . Yes, thank God it isn't as bad as it once was, but what with the government printing money like it was going out of style, now that we're not on the gold standard anymore—well, how long can it last? You'd think Congress would *do* something, but it just keeps getting worse. It makes me feel terrible to think that some day innocent people like yourself might not be able to afford to keep living in their own homes, inflation and taxes eating them up like they are. That's why it's so important for your money to not only be absolutely safe, but to *grow*, Caroline. If the interest on your savings doesn't keep pace with inflation, you'll find that as time goes by—what's that? . . . Your son said the same thing just last week? There, you see. Inflation hurts us all, doesn't it? Why, just last month the power company turned off the electricity to my grandma's house when she couldn't pay her bill. She didn't tell us she was having trouble. . . . Yes, we got the power back on, thank God, me and my brother, but we wouldn't want anything like that to happen to you, would we?' " She uttered a faint, sad little laugh, perfectly sympathetic, perfectly cold underneath.

Frank stared at her.

In a normal voice she said, "They get to that part of the speech about ten minutes into the call. Before that it's all nice and chatty, talking about this lady's grandchildren and how they like to come visit, how her son is a big shot in some company, or maybe a doctor, and the name of her cat. No talk at all about money in the first five minutes. What they look for is someone who's kinda lonely and has a little money, but not enough to feel real comfortable with what they've got.

"After a while, if this person's still listening, they get something like this: " 'I'm lucky, Caroline. I've got a really good job with a really good company—good benefits too, which is nice. V. R. Gibbs and Associates. We mostly handle investments for banks and industry, but we have a division that sets up accounts for people just like yourself, too; people who want a good return on their money and have to have absolute safety too.

" 'You're getting how much from your bank? Maybe six percent, six and a half? Well, V. R. Gibbs and Associates—' " She looked at Frank and said, "That's what Mink called this phony company he set up in Shreveport. He was good at inventing phony names. In Wichita we were the Cheney Investment Group."

"Uh-huh," Frank said, pulling off the flat, lifting the spare into place and pushing it onto the lugs.

"Anyway. 'Caroline, V. R. Gibbs and Associates pools its investors' money and invests in mutual funds. Surely you've heard about mutual funds? . . . Yes, I thought so. Last year the fund earned twenty-six point three percent interest. . . . Yes, that's right. Isn't it wonderful? I had two thousand dollars in it myself. I wish I had more, but, well, my mother was kinda sick last year and I helped her out with the bills. And the year before that the fund earned twenty-four point five percent, so it's up a little. This year it's doing about the same, maybe a tiny bit better.

" 'But what's really special about V. R. Gibbs, Caroline, is that money invested with us is backed by U.S. Treasury notes earning ten point five percent. What that means is that no matter *what*, you can't earn any less than ten and a half percent, and your money is absolutely safe, because treasury

118

notes are absolutely safe, backed by the U.S. Government.' "

"Bullshit," Frank said. "They can't invest X dollars in X amount of mutual funds, *and* X amount of treasury notes."

"Jesus, Frank, they weren't doing *either*. But that isn't the point. The point is, most of these old fogies don't know treasury notes from toilet paper. It sounds good, that's all. That's all Mink wants, and that's all an awful lot of old people want too. They want so much to believe that nothing bad can ever happen to them. Caroline is told that her money is absolutely safe, making twenty-six percent interest, and that she can have it back in her own bank with just a single phone call anytime she wants, day or night."

"And that crap works?" He began to tighten the lug nuts on the new tire.

She laughed, a soft, clean sound in the twilight. "Yeah, that crap works. Ask me how well."

"How well?"

"I heard Mink and Charlotte talking one day, maybe three weeks ago. In Shreveport they had six operators bringing in a little over twelve thousand dollars a day. Each. Not all that much, Frank, considering. An operator'd talk to seventy or eighty people for every one that sent in money. Sometimes they'd talk to two hundred people and get nothing, and then hit two in a row. They had little contests, see who had the best day, best week, that kinda thing."

He paused. "Six operators, twelve grand a day. Christ, that's about three-fifty, three-sixty grand a week." He gave the nuts a final twist, then lowered the truck on to its new tire.

"Mink told me they'd made over two million in Shreveport in just six weeks."

"He told you that?"

"He trusted me, sort of. Mink doesn't really trust anyone but Charlotte. But he told me how much they'd made. Bragging, kinda."

"Want a beer?"

119

"Oh, please." She made a puking gesture.

Frank opened an ice chest, dug a Budweiser out of floating ice. "FBI never caught on to these assholes?"

"There was a close call once, before I came along. They move around fairly often now. They were in Des Moines, then Seattle, Pittsburgh, Wichita, and Shreveport. After Shreveport was gonna be Reno. They were about half packed up and ready to move when I split. Operators were all off on vacation, like they do between moves; supposed to get to Reno sometime next week, Monday or Tuesday. Daniel Turpin was out in Reno, getting things set up. Danny's this kinda moonfaced guy, about forty years old, wears glasses. Some sort of business manager or something for Mink. I guess Mink trusts Danny too, sort of."

"I've been to Reno," Frank said.

"Yeah? Anyplace you haven't been?"

"Rio."

"Where's that?"

"Rio? You know, Rio. Rio de Janeiro. Brazil."

"Oh, sure. I meant in the United States."

"Lotsa places."

"Name one."

"New York City. Believe it or not, I've never made it to the Big Apple."

"The big what?"

"Forget it. So what you did was you grabbed Mink's money before they all took off for Reno, huh?"

"Just the last week's take."

"What happened to the rest of it, that two million?"

"Mink takes the week's take and puts it somewhere, I don't know where. I think only Charlotte knows."

Frank frowned. "Then he's gotta have what? Ten, maybe twenty million dollars floating around somewhere. Maybe more."

"It's in diamonds."

"Diamonds?"

"Danny told me. Way back in Seattle, last year. Mink goes to New York, Manhattan, and buys a bunch of diamonds when they move from one place to the next. Doesn't ever keep them on him, just keeps them in some kind of a safe-deposit box in some big bank—hey, what's that?"

"What's what?"

She stood, pointing. "Down there. Lights."

Frank saw the tiny flash and sweep of headlights over the land below, between them and Route 401, moving slowly over the rough, broken country.

"Shit," he said.

"Think maybe it's Mote and Jersey?"

"I'd say it's a possibility we can't ignore." He finished stowing the jack, shoved the flat in the back of the camper. They got back in the truck and Frank started the engine.

"Now what?" Suki asked.

He stared straight ahead out the windshield for a moment. "Now I don't know what. Now we wing it, kid."

"Wonderful."

"Yeah, ain't it though?"

15

Frank drove at a crawl in the direction of Route 401. Darkness descended in the De Baca Mountains; a burnt orange glow lay dying across the far horizon as if all of Southern California were ablaze seven hundred miles to the west.

Frank wanted to avoid these guys altogether. If they could get past them somehow, that'd be the end of it, no big confrontation, no muss no fuss, no nasty little knife fights or shots fired in the night. He had to figure on the worst: that Mutt and Jeff had guns and that they would come straight up the trail without getting sidetracked or lost.

The blackness of the night was a mixed blessing. A puny silver crescent hung over the western mountains, illuminating nothing, including the trail they were trying to follow. Frank didn't want to use his headlights and possibly give away their position, and the fact that he and Suki were on the move. The trail was a rocky blackness, all but impossible to follow. Frank couldn't see much of anything to either side. If they stayed on the trail, however, Mutt and Jeff would eventually run across them, assuming they were the ones winding through the foothills below. Every so often the lights were visible, drawing closer.

"Stay here," Frank said. Letting the truck idle, he climbed out and walked ahead with the flashlight, searching for a place where he could pull the truck far enough off the trail to conceal it.

He went a hundred feet, two hundred, found nothing that looked promising. The seconds seemed to tick by faster, and he felt a sense of urgency begin to build. They were in a box, and its stony walls were closing in on them.

"Nothing?" Suki asked when he got back.

"Nope."

The darkness was all but complete, smothering.

"Couldn't we use the lights?" Suki asked. "Just long enough to find a place to hide?"

Six of one, half a dozen of another. Without headlights, they were trading speed for stealth; the Defense Department thought that was a hell of a fine idea. Frank put the truck in gear, inching forward. "Let's go up a ways farther and try the flashlight again."

She didn't say anything. She wiped her palms on her jeans.

"Know why the moon shines?" Isaac asked Mote.

"Jesus, Iz, c'mon."

"Know why?"

"Sure, the sun, right?" Mote's voice was a whine.

"Yeah. Okay, now suppose it's night and there's a full moon out and there's an eclipse of the sun over in China, where the sun's shining. What color's the moon then, over here?"

"I dunno. Kinda black or somethin'?"

Jersey cackled.

Mote said, "What's so funny, Jers?"

"Nothing." He slowed the truck, stopped, flicked off the lights and killed the engine.

"What're we doin'?" Isaac asked.

"Piss break," Jersey said. "Looks like we're gonna be up in these friggin' hills all night."

All three piled out into the night's deep silence.

Jersey said, "There were these two guys crossing a bridge, see, had to take a leak one night." He unzipped his own fly.

"Yeah?" Isaac said.

"Yeah. Coupla black dudes, how's that? Bridge wasn't very high, so these guys pull out their dicks, toss 'em over the side and there're these two splashes in the darkness. One guy turns to the other and says, 'Cold sonofabitch, ain't it?' and the other guy says, 'Yeah. Deep too.' " *(funny)*

Isaac laughed softly.

Mote said, "What's that suppos' t' mean, Jers?"

Jersey shook his head. "Christ."

"Listen," Isaac said.

"What?"

"Just listen, you two."

They listened. Quiet. A soft susurration of air moving over the land, through the weeds. Rhythmic ticking of the truck's cooling engine. Hiss of white noise in ears deprived of all but the remotest of vibrations.

Mote began to hum.

"What're you, a kazoo?" Jersey said. "Shut up."

Far away, a faint, faint purring noise.

"There," Isaac said.

"Shush."

Again. In the distance, an engine revved up, faded.

"Sounds like they're movin'," Jersey said.

"Maybe they seen our lights," Isaac suggested.

"Maybe."

"You know where we're going?"

"Yeah, sure."

124

"Sure is a dark sonofabitch out here."

"Let's get movin'," Jersey said, touching the grip of the Llama Comanche .38 special he had jammed between his belt and belly. If he'd had it with him back in Quiode that night, the big old bastard with Suki'd be worm chow right now and they wouldn't be way up here in the dark, making like Daniel fucking Boone.

The truck crept down a long rock-strewn slope into a saddle between two hills. The oppressive blackness grew deeper once the fingernail wedge of moon slipped below the hills.

At the bottom, Frank got out and scouted around, played the dimming beam of the flashlight over the road.

"Maybe found us a place," he said, climbing back in.

They went forward slowly, stopped after forty yards or so. Frank risked turning on the parking lights, and a surprisingly bright orange glow revealed a rocky but navigable region to the right of the trail. Frank gunned the engine and the truck lurched up a barely visible shoulder, weaving past boulders and weedy hummocks and depressions.

"Don't know if this is smart or not," Frank said. "If this doesn't work out, we could get trapped in here."

"Anything else we can do?"

Frank tapped the gas gauge. "What we can't do is wander around these hills all night, trying to keep one step ahead of them. I would've got gas in Quiode that night, but we left in kind of a hurry."

"Got an extra gun?"

"Nope."

"Figures," she said.

"Why? You know how to use one?"

"More or less."

The truck pounded down a slope, surging over loose rocks, wheels spinning. A low ridge of black basalt forced Frank to the left, where they reached a rocky formation fifty yards from the road.

"End of the line," Frank said. He switched off the parking lights and killed the engine.

"Think we're far enough off the trail?"

"Wouldn't be far enough in daylight, but now . . . Who knows? We'll just have to wait and see." He climbed out.

Some of the day's warmth still lingered in the air. Frank listened intently to the night. He heard a distant chirr of crickets, nothing more. Hills rose up around them, black and craggy, limned against the stars.

Suki came up beside him. "What about the money?"

"What about it?"

"Maybe we should like, I dunno, hide it somewhere. Just in case."

"Maybe." Hell, there wasn't much else they could do. It was better than letting Mutt and Jeff get their paws on nearly four hundred thousand dollars if things didn't work out. Might even give them some bargaining power if they were caught.

Frank slung the canvas tarp over the side of the camper facing the trail, trying to cover its chromed surfaces. Might help, might not. He retrieved his money from the camper. In the dying glow of the flashlight, they tramped into the darkness beyond the truck. Suki's thongs flapped; Frank's clothes billowed on her, shirt sleeves rolled up to her elbows. She carried her duffel bag. Frank had given her a dark-colored knit cap and told her to tuck her hair into it. Even in that darkness he'd been able to make out the platinum ghost of her hair.

Fifty feet from the truck he pried a large rock partway out of the ground, jammed his bag into the depression and shoved the rock back in place. Ten paces away they hid Suki's bag, piling a low cairn of rocks over it.

Back at the truck, Frank checked his revolver in the glow of the dome light. He stuffed the gun in a jacket pocket and extinguished the light again.

"Now what?" Suki asked.

126

Frank shrugged, a useless gesture in the darkness. "Now we wait, see what happens."

"That offer of a beer still stand?"

"Water'd be better."

"Anything. I feel like I swallowed talcum."

With water and a bag of cookies, they sat on a rocky outcrop ten yards from the camper, partly hidden from the road.

"What's Mink look like?" Frank asked, biting into an Oreo.

"Kinda thin," she said. "About five ten, hundred and forty pounds is all. Spooky gray eyes: like smoke. Nice smile—one he can turn off like a light. I never saw anybody who could do that before. At least, not like Mink. If he wants, he can be the scariest sonofabitch I ever saw. Most of the time he's just this good-looking guy, nice face, nice clothes. If you didn't look at his eyes, you'd trust him with anything. Then, all of a sudden—*boom*, he's a devil or something."

"His eyes and his smile. That's what makes him so scary?"

For a moment she was silent. "It's more than that. Maybe it's his attitude, how he thinks. And the way he knows how to fight."

"Fight, how?"

"I dunno. Something Chinese, like in a movie. There was this guy working for Mink back in March, Jimmy Lynch. Like Mote an' Jersey. Jimmy stole some of Mink's money just before we left Pittsburgh. So in the house we'd rented—Mink always stays in some kinda big old house wherever we go, usually in a neighborhood where lawyers and types like that fix up places for offices. In Pittsburgh we had this big white house with green trim, two stories. Klein and Penrod Investment Group, that's what Mink's company was called there.

"Anyway, in the basement of this house, Mink and Jimmy had a fight. Mink told all the guys to come and watch—ordered them to, really. I had to go down too; Mink wanted me to, and you got to do what Mink says. His mother came down, but she likes that kind of thing, I could tell. She thinks her boy's really something. Jimmy was tall, like six foot four. Maybe weighed two hundred and twenty pounds. Real mean, but you could tell he was awful nervous anyway, the way his eyes kept looking all around.

"So Mink strips to the waist and takes off his shoes and asks if Jimmy's ready. Jimmy nods his head yes, sorta slow, and puts up his hands like a boxer. Then Mink comes in, kinda gliding, and hits him the face so fast I didn't hardly even see it. Broke Jimmy's nose, I guess. There was blood all over, and Jimmy wipes his face and just stares at the blood on his hands. Mink backs away, tells Jimmy now he's gonna break his leg. I mean, he just *tells* him what he's gonna do, like Jimmy can't do nothing to stop him, and then he comes in close and falls on his side real sudden and kicks Jimmy's knee. It sounded like someone breaking chicken bones. Jimmy fell on the floor, screaming. Mink kicked him in the head, kind of a funny kick with his heel, and Jimmy got real quiet. Mink told a couple of the guys to carry Jimmy out of there, and then he took me back upstairs. Told me that's what happens when the hired help does him wrong."

"Very nice," Frank said, listening to the deep quiet of the night. "This Jimmy fellow . . . he die, or what?"

"I dunno. Want another cookie?"

"Uh-uh."

"So anyway, that's Mink. Jimmy was eighty pounds heavier than him, pretty tough too, and still Mink knew he could take him easy. *Knew* it."

"That's confidence for you."

"Mink's got plenty of that, all right."

"And you went and tattooed that snake's forehead."

"Pretty dumb, huh?"

"It's beginning to look that way." He mixed up some dirt and water and smeared mud over his face. He put some on hers, too.

They were quiet a while, and then she said, "Last night when I was kinda drunk, I told you Mink never made love to me, didn't I?"

"Yeah. I'm surprised you remember."

"I tell you any more than that?"

"You said you called him Minky."

"Yeah, he doesn't like that. I didn't do it very much. That all?"

"You didn't get around to telling me why he didn't make the effort, if that's what you're wondering. Why? Did you want him to?"

"I couldn't of stopped him if he wanted to, but he never did. But you want to hear something freaky?"

"Go ahead, shock me."

"You're making fun. So, okay, get this, you want to hear crazy. We'd been sleeping together in the same bed ever since this . . . gang of his, or whatever you call it, left Des Moines. We had this really weird relationship. We never did nothing, and I never, you know, saw him hard or anything. Like I was just some kind of . . . *jewelry* or something when we'd go out to dinner, him showing me off. You wouldn't believe some of the outfits I wore.

"So in Wichita we had this place and I woke up one night. It was real late and Mink wasn't there with me, so I got up, kinda hungry, wondering where he was. He wasn't in the bathroom we had, so I—"

"You saw Mink break some guy's leg," Frank said, "might've even killed him, and still you stuck around?"

"I never heard what happened to Jimmy. Mink was treating me all right, buying me all these expensive clothes—"

"You knew he was a crook by then, didn't you?" There was an edge in Frank's voice.

"Yeah, and I know you're a crook, too. Looks like my life is connected to crooks everywhere I go."

Frank said nothing for ten or fifteen seconds. "Guess I deserved that. Sorry."

"Look, I never said I was real smart or wise or anything. I made a lot of mistakes, okay? Sometimes you just do something and it takes a while to know how bad it is and to figure out what you're gonna do about it. I was seventeen when I met Simon Voorhees, Frank. He was like some kind of a god or something to me for a long time."

"Okay, I understand."

"Take your time, Frank. Don't bust nothing, okay?" She drew in a breath, let it out. "Anyway, our room was on the second floor of this big house. Mink likes places with lotsa rooms and more than one story; in Seattle we had three floors and a basement. So like I said, Mink was gone, and I went out into the hall. It was dark. I heard noises coming from Charlotte's room, voices, and breathing, like someone was doing exercises."

"Guess what that was," Frank said.

"Yeah, guess. Go ahead an' try."

"Mink and Charlotte?"

"Nope. The door wasn't locked, so I pushed it open a few inches and in a mirror I saw Mink without any clothes on, and these two naked girls, twelve, thirteen years old, hardly had any boobs. Mink was tied with big silk scarves to two hooks in the ceiling and a couple in the floor, kinda spread-eagled, and these two girls were all over him, touching and licking."

"Sounds like the man's got a problem."

"I guess, but get this. Charlotte was in a chair, watching the whole thing."

"Watching?"

"Yeah, just watching. Had all her clothes on and everything. She's thin as a stick, no boobs or ass, flaming red hair that's dyed, has a cigarette in her hand all the time. She was just watching, smoking, eyes like some kinda bird."

"Jesus."

"I figure Charlotte goes out and finds these super-young girls somewhere for Mink, brings 'em back, then ties Mink up like that and turns the girls loose on him. And then she just sits there and watches. I don't guess it happens very often though. Otherwise I'd've found out a lot sooner."

"After that, why'd you stick around?"

"Think I *wanted* to? I didn't, believe me, but Mink or

130

Mote was always around. Mote was sorta my bodyguard or something, but I think he was really supposed to make sure I didn't run off. Sometimes Jersey'd look after me too, and there was this jerk called Benny. So I never acted like I wanted to. I was pretty sure Mink'd hurt me if he caught me trying to run off, and besides, I never had any money of my own."

"So when the opportunity came up, you flew?"

"You bet. Took a while, but I finally got the hell out. For a couple of months, I was scared for my life, sleeping in the same bed with Mink like that. It made my skin crawl, but I never said anything. I'd rather die than have him—"

Frank touched her arm. "Quiet."

A new sound in the night. An engine, laboring uphill. A few minutes later headlights threw shifting shadows over the rocks out by the trail, where Frank and Suki had turned off.

Slowly, the sound of the engine grew louder.

16

O kay," Isaac said to Mote, "say you're in this rowboat that's floating in a swimming pool an'—"

"Christ up a rope, Iz!"

"—an' in the boat you've got this big rock. So then you drop the rock into the water. What happens to the water level in the *pool*? Does it go up or down or stay the same?"

"Howthefuck'dIknow?"

"You got to *think*, that's how."

"With what?" Jersey said, eyes searching the darkness to either side. "C'mon, Izzy, leave'm—hey!"

"Hey what?"

Jersey hit the brakes. "I just seen something."

"What? Where?"

"Back there." Jersey began to bounce the truck backward in reverse. "Something didn't look right."

"I didn't see nothing."

"That's 'cause you had your gums flappin', that's why. See?" He stopped and pointed. "Over there."

"I still don't see nothing," Mote said.

Jersey put the truck in gear and swung it around, lights glaring into the darkness off the trail.

"Look," Isaac said. "What's that over there?"

Blinding lights swung almost directly at them. Frank pulled Suki down behind the rocks and the two of them waited, barely breathing. The glare shone on the canvas-draped camper; stark black shadows writhed across the ground.

The engine noise drew closer and then stopped. The lights went out and doors opened, slammed shut.

"Christ!" Frank exclaimed softly. "Here we go."

"What d'you want me to do?" Suki said in a frightened whisper.

"Stay here, keep down, and keep quiet. Make yourself small and don't move."

"What're you gonna do?"

"Hell, I don't know. Just stay put." He crept off into the darkness.

"Super," she breathed.

Blackness was a substance that coated the night like tar.

"Shit, this ain't no good," Isaac whispered.

"Maybe, but it's all we got," Jersey responded, crouched down by the side of the truck.

"Gimme my bullets, Jers," Mote whined.

"I'd rather stomp rattlesnakes barefoot."

"*Jers!*"

Jersey ignored him. In a low voice he said, "What we'll do is me an' Mote'll go down there to the right of the camper, real slow and quiet. What you do, Izzy, is hang back a minute or two and then come in quiet, keepin' off to the left. You got that natural midnight color, might come in handy."

"What about my bullets?" Mote said.

"Shut up!" Jersey hissed. He grabbed the front of Mote's shirt. "Find a stick or throw rocks, Mote. If someone comes near you, you kin deck 'em, okay? But I don't want you using that goddamn gun. It's too fuckin' dark out here."

Jersey pulled his own gun and Isaac did the same. "Just be sure of what you're shootin' at," Isaac warned softly.

"Yeah, you too. Stay wide left, huh?"

Mote and Jersey crept off in the direction of the camper.

Frank crouched by the right front wheel of the truck, listening to the soft breath of the night.

Too late now to tell anyone, himself included, that this wasn't his fight. It'd become his fight the moment he'd followed those two clowns out of that bar in Quiode, and maybe even before that, back when he'd come across Suki sitting on the Trans Am in the desert, lost. He'd figured her for trouble then, and trouble she was—trouble was dogging her heels like a shadow. Dumb shit like him'd get involved in it as natural as a giant sloth'd wander off and get stuck in a tar pit.

What would Fanny say about *this*?

He had his .357 out, uncocked. Stars blazed overhead. Frank couldn't make out anything where the sound of the engine had stopped, not even moving shadows.

He thought there ought to be something clever he could do in a situation like this, but nothing came to him. He didn't have much information. He couldn't hear or see anything, and there were an unknown number of guys out there armed with unknown weapons.

He and Suki could've just abandoned the truck and taken off cross-country with the money, hiked on down to Route 401 in maybe a day or so—if she'd had decent shoes, and if they could've been guaranteed that the first car or truck to come along wouldn't be Mote and Jersey's.

If, if, if. What was happening now was the result of all those ifs that hadn't panned out.

He could crawl under the truck. Be harder to spot under there, but then he'd lose most of his mobility. If he nailed one of them from under there with the gun, the other might do the same to him.

He had on blue jeans and a blue denim jacket, which made him all but invisible in the night. The darkness was filled with an electric tension. The thing to do, of course, was to wait it out, not move at all, let it all come to him. In the absence of light, sound or movement were the only things that might give away his position, or that of his enemies.

So he waited.

Crouched low, Jersey stuck out a foot, transferred his weight to it slowly, pulled his trailing foot after. His legs burned with the effort. Sweat made the grip of his gun slippery. He wiped his hand on his shirt.

Mote was somewhere off to his right—making a ton of noise, but Mote was a fucking moose. Whether he knew it or not, he was acting as a decoy for Jersey. Trouble was, he was moving too fast for Jersey to keep up and still be quiet as those goddamn Ninja books'd said you could.

Jersey'd pored through some of the magazines Mink'd left lying around. Karate tournaments, uniforms, Tae Kwon Do (*Tae*: feet; *Kwon*: hands; *Do*: mind), kung fu and Ninja shit, lotsa Ninja shit. Tell you how to crawl up someone's asshole, light a candle and have a look around, leave without the guy's ever knowing. Jersey'd thumbed through a coupla articles like that, hadn't quite understood what the hell he'd seen, but it didn't look to him as if it'd work very well. Even so, he'd read a few articles, and it had to've done him some good, right?

Something scraped in the darkness, and suddenly Jersey was aware that he had no way of knowing if it was Mote or that big sonofabitch who'd saved Suki. Or even Suki herself, who they weren't supposed to hurt.

"Shit," he breathed. This wasn't working out the way he'd

thought it would. A bead of sweat rolled into his eye, and he wiped it away.

Maybe what they should've done, just to keep it simple, was spread out in the darkness around the camper, keep Suki and this guy boxed in, and wait till morning, take them then.

Too late now, though.

Frank heard a noise, a scrape of leather on rock, off to his right. He remained perfectly still. He saw a shift of blackness in the night, darkness moving, gliding closer.

He could shoot, but then what? In Korea he'd maybe killed a guy or two, he didn't know. He'd sprayed a bunch of bamboo one morning with a machine gun while his company had scrambled for cover across a road that'd been churned to mud, but he'd never found out if he'd punched anyone's clock with it. War was like that. Imprecise, messy.

Now he could take a shot, but if he killed some guy he would probably regret it the rest of his life. And if he took the shot, would the guy's buddy see the muzzle flash and drop him? Worse, he didn't know for certain that this was really Mutt or Jeff. It could be some guy out camping. Frank didn't think so, but it could be, and he sure as shit didn't want to kill some sorry bastard who'd taken off from behind his desk in some accounting office in Albuquerque and was acting like a complete idiot up here in the hills.

Too much was going on inside his head. Frank waited. The shadow drew closer, and Frank wound himself up slowly, tensing every muscle. Whoever it was, the guy was a fool, standing up most of the way as he crept closer, hugging the side of the truck. Too bad if this was some dipshit accountant. His face was a pale luminosity. Frank squatted by the truck, a compact ball, waiting. Good thing he'd smeared his own face with mud.

If the guy kept on like he was, he'd run right into Frank. Five feet away. Now three. Still hadn't seen him.

Two feet. Frank twisted and drove his right hand into the

guy's midsection with all this strength. Air *woof*ed out of the fellow's lungs, and he doubled over, sinking to his knees. Frank slammed the barrel of his gun against the side of the man's head, and he crumpled to the ground.

A voice came out of the darkness. "Mote, that you?"

Frank grunted. "Yuh." Trying to imitate the voice of that big guy he'd decked outside the café in Quiode. Also trying to get a fix on this genius who was out there calling for Mote.

"Where are you?" Whispering hoarsely, as if Mote could hear him and Frank couldn't. As if Mote would answer, too. Hell, maybe the dumb sonofabitch would.

Frank grunted again and began edging cautiously around the front of the truck to the driver's side, then down to the rear of the camper where the roll of canvas hung from the roof. He peered around the corner. His hands had started to shake.

More silence. Then a scuffle of dirt, a moving darkness just ten feet away, crouched low.

Frank cocked his gun and said, "Hold it!" His aim seemed unsteady. Suddenly, ten feet looked like a mile.

The shadow froze for an instant, began to twist.

"You're one second from dying, friend," Frank said. "Drop the gun, *now*." He didn't know for certain if the guy even had a gun, but it seemed a likely thing to say.

Something heavy clunked to the ground.

"Don't move," Frank said. "Don't even twitch." He crept out from behind the camper toward the shadowy form.

"Face down, and spread'em," Frank ordered. *"Move!"*

The guy flopped down, still not saying anything. Frank put his knee in the small of the guy's back, let the hammer down on his gun and then cocked it again, right behind the guy's ear so he'd know where it was and where it was aimed.

"Call your friend in," he said softly. He groped around in the blackness, found the gun the guy had dropped, and flung it out into the night.

"What friend? Thought you already got'm."

"Not him, the other one." He was fishing, but, hell, it might give him something.

"What other one?"

Frank considered this. "What I'm going to do is turn some lights on here. If I see anyone out there, you're dead, understand? If I see anyone, and I mean anyone at all, your brains are gonna splatter all over the dirt. Now, one more time: is anyone else out there?"

A pause. "No, man. There was just us two."

"Okay, make like a crab. Scoot on over this way, on your belly. Keep your arms and legs spread wide." He tugged the collar of the man's T-shirt, guiding him.

"Watch that gun, huh?"

"Just don't forget where it's pointed, ace."

They inched forward over weeds and rocks, the guy grunting, working hard.

Frank opened the door of the cab and the dome light came on. Lying on the ground at his feet was Skinny: Jersey. In the cone of light Frank saw Muscles, out cold on the ground with his face in the dirt.

"Suki," Frank called.

Nothing.

"What're you doin' this for?" Jersey asked. "I got money. How 'bout I give you some money?"

"Shut up. Suki, it's Frank. C'mon over here."

He heard a scuffling sound in the night: her thongs flapping as she drew nearer on the opposite side of the truck.

"Suki?"

Light spilled out the windows of the truck's cab all around, illuminating the ground dimly for fifty feet to either side. Frank kept his gun on Jersey, muzzle pressed against the back of Jersey's head.

Suki came around the rear of the camper. A black guy with a gun jammed behind her ear was right behind her, his left arm hooked around her neck.

138

"She dies if you even blink, hero," the black man said. "Your move. What's it gonna be?"

Frank stared, frozen in a crouch over Jersey. The man's eyes were on his. Cold eyes.

"What's it gonna be?" the guy said again. "She dies, then I got this corpse to hide behind while I send you home to Jesus."

Frank stood slowly, letting the gun hang down at his side.

"Drop it."

Frank dropped it, feeling empty. Hell with it, he'd lived a lot of years already. Maybe Suki would survive this. If he shot Jersey, both he and Suki would probably wind up dead.

Suki's eyes were wide, frightened.

"Step back," the black man said. "Slowly. Keep your hands out where I kin see 'em."

Frank moved away from Jersey.

Jersey bounded to his feet, snatched up Frank's .357 from the dirt.

"Sit," the black man ordered, his gun still pressed against Suki's head.

Frank sat.

Jersey kicked him in the head and Frank went over on his side, a sudden roaring in his ears. The toe of Jersey's boot caught him on the cheek and he felt the bones in his neck creak. Dirt filled his mouth. Lights and shadows whirled. A foot slammed into his ribs. Frank rolled, trying to get away, and again the boot hammered him, and again, and again. Frank tried to roll out of it, tried to cover up, and again the boot slammed into his side, Jersey breathing hard.

"That's enough, Jers," a voice said. "Remember what Mrs. Voorhees said."

"Fuck that bitch."

The boot slammed into Frank's ribs again, and he felt something give. Pain shot through his body. From a distance, he heard Suki scream. The boot caught him full in the face, and all the lights went out.

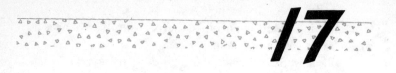

Half a dozen ants roamed the slopes and canyons of his face, feasting where blood hadn't yet dried. Another experimented with the dark cavern of his nose, clinging precariously to the rim where the moist, warm wind shuttled softly in and out; yet another explored the tunnel of his left ear, biting intermittantly.

Frank snorted, then gasped at the pain that tore through his side. The ants began to scurry for cover.

He opened his eyes and stared out at the bright yellow sun, just beginning its climb into the morning sky. The gray silhouettes of mountains rose up high on either side. Pebbles and weeds bit into his cheek.

He struggled to sit up, found that he could move but that movement was accompanied by pain. Something moved in his ear. He dug it out with a finger, dragging out tattered pieces of the explorer. Grit filled his mouth, and he leaned over and spat feebly. The effort unleashed new pain in his mouth and ribs.

Suki.

He looked around. The world spun and wobbled softly, as if it were imprinted on a soap bubble.

"Suki?" The word was just a whisper.

"*Suki?*" Pain blazed through his torso at the increased effort. No one answered.

His truck and camper were still there, but something was wrong with the way they were sitting. He wasn't sure what it was, but it wasn't right.

His head was a bell, ringing, aching savagely. He got to his feet, breathing slowly. He prodded his ribs and winced. His face felt huge, raw. One eye, the left, was swollen shut.

But his legs seemed all right. He could walk. Each step sent needles of pain shooting through his side as he shuffled toward the camper.

"Suki?"

The silence of the mountains was unbroken. No voices; no distant sound of engines. Nothing.

Open cans of beer lay strewn about; the two coolers were on their sides, empty. Bottles of Jack Daniel's had been smashed against the side of the truck.

He reached up to open the camper door before realizing it was six or eight inches too low. He walked around the truck like an octogenarian, hugging his left side, staring at the four flat tires.

"Shit," he said weakly, wincing at the flare of pain the word caused him. He probed his ribs gently again, deciding they probably weren't broken, just tender as hell. Maybe a little sprung.

He opened the camper door and stared at the mess inside. Mutt and Jeff and the black guy had trashed it, torn out the radio and ripped doors off cabinets, shredded his clothes and slung catsup and flour and Quaker State motor oil over the debris.

Suki was gone.

Unless they'd killed her and left her outside somewhere, but that seemed unlikely. Mink would have reserved that sort of pleasure for himself.

Even so, Frank walked around, looking. This was a good place for murder, although they hadn't bothered to kill him. He didn't find Suki, but the remains of the cairn of stones they'd piled over her duffel bag were strewn about, the bag and money gone.

Frank hunted for the place where his own money lay hidden. The hillside looked different in the daylight, but in time he located the rock. He grabbed it and tried to move it, but the effort made his ribs sing. Sitting behind the rock, he pushed with his feet until it shifted. He peered into the gap, feeling a flood of relief at the sight of blue nylon. He pulled the bag out. All his money was there.

She hadn't sold him out in the hope that his money would make a difference; she'd managed to keep some presence of mind during her ordeal, whatever it had been.

If even part of what she'd told Frank about Simon Voorhees was true, though, Suki was in for a very, very bad time.

"Shit," Frank said, and this time he hardly noticed the wicked jolt of pain that accompanied the oath.

He would've thought that his body would eventually get tired and just shut down those nerves that were sending the endless messages to his brain. What was the point? He knew he'd been trashed, for chrissake, but it just kept on and on and on, no sign of letting up. Every step was agony, every mile an encyclopedia of hurt. He sucked in air in shallow gasps.

The foothills of the De Bacas went on forever. Except for needlegrass and occasional tufts of hackberry and sandbur, the country seemed as empty and inhospitable as the far side of the moon. The sun rose high in the sky, baking the land. Frank walked through the brassy, shimmering heat, hunched into his pain. The torment of each plodding step was penance for all the mistakes he'd made the night before.

Not penance enough, however. Simon and Charlotte Voorhees had their hands on Suki again. Nothing could make that right.

He'd wrapped a strip of canvas around his ribs. The bag of money hung from his right shoulder. A torn sheet over his head and shoulders, held in place by a California Angels cap, gave him a dusky Arabic look. With every step he took, a can of beer thumped at his hip, riding in a pocket of his jacket, which was tied by its arms around his waist. The can was one of two he'd found that hadn't been emptied; he'd downed one early on in his walk and was hoarding the second.

Sweat had already removed most of the mud he'd smeared on his face the night before. His sleeves were grimy where he'd wiped his face with them.

Frank estimated that he and Suki had been caught roughly eighteen to twenty miles from Route 401. By ten o'clock that morning, three hours after he'd started out, he'd covered five of those miles. At least he'd had the sense not to set out cross-country, trying to reach the highway just ten miles away as the crow flies: the rocks and ravines would've eaten him up. In the next few hours the day would heat up another ten or fifteen degrees, probably peak out somewhere around a hundred. Ground temperature might reach a hundred fifty.

Dust devils spun in the distance. Carrion eaters wheeled overhead in the bright blue sky.

Simon Voorhees. The name came swirling out of the mist of pain that clouded his mind. Age, thirty-four. Called himself Mink and made up names for himself and his "investment companies" like other people put on clothes. Liked little girls. Frank realized he knew a surprising amount about the man.

Five ten, hundred and forty pounds. Rented older two- or three-story houses in the sort of neighborhoods inhabited by lawyers and other professionals.

And the Shreveport operation was folding. Mink was setting up next in Reno.

Frank slowed.

Reno. Christ, Reno wasn't all that big a place. Maybe a quarter the size of Pittsburgh or Seattle, half as large as Shreveport.

A long shot all the same, not much chance he could—hell, who was he kidding? Walking along, hurting, he'd known what he was going to do from the moment he'd discovered that Suki was gone. Known what he had to do. If Mink preferred run-down tenements and was headed for Harlem or the Bronx, Frank would still try to find Suki.

He owed her that, for some goddamned reason.

Frank had one slim hope: Mutt and Jeff couldn't take Suki on a plane. They'd probably drive her to Reno, and it was likely they'd hold their speed down to keep from attracting the attention of the highway patrol.

Frank calculated distance and velocity. Five hundred miles to Flagstaff, two hundred more to Vegas, four hundred to Reno. Eleven hundred miles altogether at, say, sixty miles an hour. Assuming they'd reached the highway between Quiode and Imogene by one o'clock, they could be in Reno by seven that evening. Not likely they'd get there that fast, though. With stops for food and gas and all the thirty-five-mile-per-hour towns along the way, they'd more likely get there between nine and midnight, possibly later.

But all these calculations assumed that they'd headed for Reno instead of Shreveport. He picked up a little speed, trying to ignore the pain in his ribs.

A sense of helplessness filled him, crawled around in his belly. He had no way of knowing for certain which place they would head to, and if he picked the wrong one, Suki'd be dead. Very likely she'd be dead *either* way: his chances of finding her were slim and none. That goddamned tattoo. If Suki was right about Simon, the demented son of a bitch'd kill her for that alone, never mind the money.

But Frank had to pick one place or the other, and from what Suki'd told him, the Shreveport operation was pretty well shut down, the Reno operation just about ready to roll.

So, Reno. If he was wrong. . . .

Jesus, a pair of sociopaths like Simon and Charlotte Voorhees with their hands on Suki. No telling what they'd do. Frank didn't even want to guess. But if Suki disappeared from the face of the earth, so would this Simon character, guaranteed. In a week, a month, a year. Longer, if it took longer. Sometime.

He could at least promise Suki that.

Suki said, "There's over three hundred thousand bucks in that bag, Jersey. You take me back to Mink and you've got to hand over all that money, too, but if you let me go you could take the money and live real nice somewheres."

The air conditioner wasn't working. Jersey sat slumped in the passenger's seat while Mote drove. Suki sat between them in the sweltering heat, barefoot, wearing her shorts and top. Benny and Isaac followed in the Malibu.

"Shut up," Jersey said.

"It's not like stealin'. No cop'd ever come after you, you take that money."

"Shut up."

"You scared, Jersey? Must be, 'cause I know you're not honest. Jesus, think what you could do with that much money. Never have to work again in your life. You won't ever get a chance like this again. Not ever."

"I said shut up."

"Christ, so scared of Mink you'd rather kiss Charlotte's wrinkled old butt and be poor all your life, right?"

"Keep talking an' you're gonna get gagged, sweetmeat," he warned.

"That'd look nice, wouldn't it? Some cop passes us and there I am, wearing this gag."

"Tied up on the floor in back, there wouldn't be much for a cop to see," Jersey replied.

"Christ, over three hundred thousand goddamn dollars, Jersey. You know how much that *is*?"

"Shut *up*."

Frank came across the burned-out ruin of Mink's Trans Am at a quarter past one that afternoon. Another truck was there, both rear tires blown. Frank didn't mess with it, just kept on walking, past the little gully that murdered cars and trucks, down the trail that wound through the stifling kiln of the valley, toward the highway.

He drank the second beer at three o'clock. Maybe six miles left to go. He'd picked up a little speed, worrying about Suki. Fifteen feet away an anthill swarmed red, like a tiny volcano. A good-sized hill. Die here, and a man would disappear into that nest with its myriad tiny rooms, bit by infinitesimal bit, until nothing was left but bones and patches of hair.

In the distance, blue and gray mountains danced in the heat, hazy and insubstantial.

He trudged on, ribs aching bitterly. A piece of cartilage felt loose in his nose, and a place inside his cheek was raw. Several teeth were loose in their sockets; he could wiggle one with his tongue.

Insects buzzed in the weeds.

This was a land that could kill you, eat you whole, bleach your bones, and forget you'd ever walked the earth.

They passed a sign on Interstate 40:

WINONA 12
FLAGSTAFF 28

"I gotta go," Suki said. "Bad."

Jersey was driving, Mote dozing, Suki wedged between them. Jersey didn't say anything, just kept on driving.

"I said, I gotta—"

"I heard what you said."

"Well?"

"Well what?"

"We gonna stop or what?"

"Sure. That'd be smart, wouldn't it? You yelling your head off, locked in a toilet somewhere."

"We're gonna drive another six hundred goddamn miles and no one's gonna pee? That's intelligent. How 'bout I go right here?"

"Yeah," Jersey said. "How 'bout you do that?" He slowed, turned the Olds onto a rough dirt road that angled northward off the interstate. The Malibu followed. Mote stirred.

"Where're we going?" Suki asked.

"Find you a patch of ground t' squirt."

"Out here?"

"Out here or you hold it, sweetmeat. Take your pick."

"Stop calling me sweetmeat."

"You look like sweetmeat to me. What d'you think, Mote?"

"Yuh, sweetmeat."

Suki looked at him. "What've you got, Mote, like one brain to move the lips, another to wag the tail?"

He gave her a sullen look. "What d'you mean?"

"Nothing; forget it."

Ten minutes later they were back on the interstate, headed west. The men had pissed all over the place, like cattle. Suki had secured the barest shred of privacy by asking them how they thought Mink'd like it, them staring at his girl without her bottoms on. They hadn't known for sure if she was still his girl or not, so they'd turned, reluctantly. Even so she'd hurried, almost couldn't pee at all, and there'd been no chance of escape, not out there.

She hoped Frank would be all right. He'd have been fine

147

if she hadn't come along, bringing all this trouble. Before they'd left the hills she'd knelt beside him and checked his breathing. He was pretty beat up, but at least he was still alive.

Before she was handed over to Mink, she might try to do Jersey some damage, payback for what he'd done to Frank. She hoped the opportunity would come up.

Mink. And Charlotte. Even in this sweltering heat the thought of seeing those two again—after what she'd done to Mink—made goose bumps stand out on her arms.

he world began to blur and spin. Frank squinted, trying to make out the numerals on his watch. Five forty-one. The hot air scorched his throat as he clumped wearily past the gravel pit and out to the highway.

It was empty. Some-alien-plague-had-wiped-out-humanity-and-he-was-the-last-one-left kind of empty.

He opened his bag, took out five twenties, and stuck them in a pocket. He ran a tongue over his parched lips.

He removed the piece of bedsheet that had protected his head and stood at the roadside, waiting, feeling the heat.

Five minutes . . . ten. . . .

Fifteen.

The sun seemed to halo in the sky, growing larger. Dark spots floated in Frank's vision.

One of the spots drew nearer, missing every so often on one cylinder, coming up the road toward him. Frank blinked, squinted, made out a rust-red pickup doing maybe fifty miles an hour.

He held out the bills as it went past, showing green.

The truck rattled on by, dragging dust, then went into a skid as the driver locked up its tires. It backed up, weaving, engine whining. Frank shuffled forward to meet it.

"Ride?" asked the driver.

"Yeah." Frank's voice was little more than a croak.

"That yer thumb you had out?" He was completely bald, in his fifties, face and scalp burned to the same bronze color by the sun. Pale bushy eyebrows, nicotine-stained teeth. A small ice chest sat on the seat beside him.

Frank held up the five twenties.

"Climb on in."

Frank's ribs spat fire as he opened the door and got in. Without a word, the man took the money and shoved it into a pocket. The truck started up, accelerating lethargically in the direction of Quiode, its one bad cylinder making the cab shudder.

The driver glanced curiously at Frank. "Hot, ain't it?"

"Yeah."

"Too hot for bein' out here."

"My truck broke down, up in the hills."

"Yeah? Lucky I came along, huh? The name's Hew. Hewitt Hooker."

"Frank."

"Y'look a sight," Hew said. "Had some kinda accident too, didja?"

"Some trouble, yeah."

"Look like ya could use a drink. Hep y'self." He indicated the ice chest.

"Thanks." Frank opened the cooler, found three cans of 7-Up swimming in half melted ice, one can of Mr. Pibb.

He took a 7-Up, popped the top. The liquid was cool fire

in his throat, swelling his parched tissues. He sipped it slowly, trying to keep it down. From time to time Hew Hooker cut a glance at him.

"Know where I can charter a plane?" Frank asked.

Hooker stared at him. "Nowhere round here."

"I figured. Where's the nearest place?"

"I dunno. Reckon Roswell'd be it."

"How far's that?"

"From Quiode? Sixty-eight mile."

Frank sipped from the can. "Fast road, here to there?"

"Pretty fast, yeah. Ain't a lot of traffic round these parts."

"You live in Quiode?"

"More'n twenty years. Evenin' cook over t' Belinda's."

"Tell you what, Hew. You let me phone the airport at Roswell from your place and wash up a bit, and then figure out a way to get me to Roswell in an hour from Quiode, and I'll give you three hundred bucks. Ten more for every minute you shave off that hour."

Hooker eyed him. "Had your fill of this dry son'vabitchin' country, huh?"

"That offer includes you not asking a lot of questions."

"If that's how you want it. I know how t' zip my mouth."

"That's good, 'cause I got another question for you."

"Yeah? Whazzat?"

"Know where I can get a gun?"

Mutt and Jeff hadn't killed him, so all that was left now was borrowed time. Hooker was using that up at a hundred and five miles an hour, hunched over the steering wheel of Belinda Maxwell's son's kelly green '72 Camaro with the 350-cubic-inch engine and gray primer spots, sheepskin seat covers and fuzzy dice swaying from the rearview mirror.

"Quentin Maxwell's doin' ninety days over at the county jail at Carrizozo," Hooker said. "Good name for a jailbird, huh? Quentin. Reckon he won't mind we borra his wheels, blow the engine out a mite." He patted the dash as they chased the Camaro's shadow eastward on Route 401.

Frank turned the German Astra M600 pistol over in his hands and stared at the Waffenamt acceptance stamp, a small seal that also bore the date of manufacture: 1939. He had no idea what the relic was actually worth, but Hooker had parted with it for six hundred fifty dollars. It came with six nine-millimeter rounds in the magazine from a box Hooker had bought over in Socorro way back in '76.

From Hooker's trailer, Frank had gotten through to Castledyne Aviation at Industrial Air Center in Roswell. A secretary by the name of Rose acted as an intermediary on an intercom between the office and the hangar where Chase Castledyne himself was servicing the landing gear of an old Beechcraft.

"You wanna go where?" Rose had asked.

"Reno. Leave in about an hour. Something fast."

"Yeah, hang on."

He'd hung on. Rose came back on the line, saying, "This just a drop?"

"A what?"

"One way?" she asked with a kind of weary patience. "No hold at the other end, or are you comin' back?"

"One way."

"Hang on." Pause. "Mr. Castledyne's got a Seneca three, get you there in about five an' a half hours for thirty-two hundred bucks. He's got a Lear twenty-five waitin' on some guy wants to go to Chicago tomorrow morning; says you can have that for fifty-four fifty, get you there in maybe two, two an' a half hours."

"I'll take the Lear."

"Yeah, waitaminute." Pause. "Mr. Castledyne says that'd be cash only on the Lear. No checks, no cards."

The Lear wasn't going to leave a paper trail. "I'll take it."

"Uh, okay. What's the name on this?"

"Wiley. Frank Wiley."

*   *   *

Through the double-paned windows of Castledyne Aviation, the little Lear 25 looked like a ballerina at an Arkansas square dance, pale blue elegance sitting on the cracked concrete in the heat outside, twin turbines already spooling up.

"Who's in her now?" Frank asked, hunched over slightly. He'd started to stiffen up on the drive from Quiode, but the pain in his ribs was easing some. The walk out of the hills had hurt, but it'd kept him loosened up for most of the day.

Chase Castledyne was a likely enough specimen in his blue flight suit, fortyish, a hank of ginger-colored hair falling across his forehead. He examined Frank's ruined face without comment. "Copilot," he said. "FAA regs."

"Okay," Frank replied. "How soon can we get going?"

"Soon's you show me fifty-four hundred and fifty dollars."

"Got a bathroom I can use?"

Castledyne pointed. Rose was looking at Frank too, not saying a word, paperwork piled high on a cluttered desk, green pencil stuck behind her ear, poking out of frizzy black hair.

"Back in a minute."

In the bathroom Frank peeled fifty-five bills off a stack of hundreds, splashed water on his face, stared at the damage in the mirror. Left eye puffed almost shut, a raw cut on his right cheek, a week's worth of gray stubble on his cheeks and chin. General blackguardly dishevelment. Nice.

Back in the office he handed the wad to Castledyne. The pilot quickly counted it out in the airy rumble of the room's air-conditioning. Frank didn't blame him for being careful.

"Okay, Mr. Wiley. This business or pleasure?"

"Pleasure."

Castledyne gave him a look and then said, "Let's do it."

They crossed the scalded tarmac, heat waves boiling up off the weedy flatness of taxiways and runways, and climbed a little ramp into the plane.

153

Castledyne lifted the ramp, seated the door. "Way it works," he said, smiling easier now, "is this little baby'll eat your money about as fast as you could comfortably peel dollar bills off a roll and stuff 'em into a mason jar."

"Get us to Reno pretty quick though, huh?"

Castledyne's eyes met Frank's. "I got the message, Mr. Wiley. You're a man who takes his pleasure pretty serious. Get yourself comfortable; we'll be up in a few minutes. There's a bar in back that covers the basics."

"Thanks."

Frank poured himself a straight Coke, lowered himself with a groan into a seat of maroon crushed velvet, strapped himself in, leaned back, and closed his eyes.

Christ, this was crazy.

He tried to still his thoughts. Inside, a river moved deep and quiet, sluggishly churning up a load of debris: she was just eighteen, he was fifty-four . . . they had shared a bed . . . Fanny was gone . . . he hadn't been to Reno in ten years . . . Rio was fulla bugs.

Four minutes later they shot down the runway and lifted off at a hundred and fifteen miles an hour, climbing steeply toward the north into the hazy heat. Frank looked down; a green Camaro rolled northward along U.S. 285. Hooker was down there, pockets stuffed with the four hundred and twenty dollars Frank had handed him for getting him to Roswell in just forty-eight minutes.

They banked left, climbing, the De Baca Mountains already coming up ahead, sere and empty. Place was hell on tires.

The time was 7:28.

Three Big Macs," Mote said. "Two large fries—"

Jersey stared at him. "Christ, we could buy a condo in Hawaii for what this's gonna fuckin' cost!"

"I'm *hungry*, Jers."

"Yeah, Christ, what else?" Jersey had parked in a remote

unshaded corner of a McDonald's in Las Vegas. Benny and Isaac had pulled up alongside in the Malibu. Isaac stood beside the Chevy, arms folded.

"You got the two fries?" Mote asked. "Two *large* fries?"

"Yeah, yeah, c'mon."

"Okay. Couple choc'lit shakes, large Coke, and a coupla those pie things."

"Jesus H. Christ." Jersey glared at Suki. "How 'bout you?"

"Whopper with cheese, small Coke."

"That all?"

"Yeah."

Jersey started off, came back a few seconds later, face red, fists clenched. "This's a goddamn *McDonald's*, sweetmeat. What the fuck you askin' for a goddamn *Whopper* for?"

She smiled at him. "You upset, Jersey?"

"Yeah, I'm upse—"

"Guy's gonna throw away three hundred thousand dollars," she said, glancing over at Mote. "Guess he's got a right to be upset. Ain't that right?"

Mote said, "I dunno—"

"Shut up," Jersey snarled.

"I'll have what Mote has," Suki said.

Jersey's face turned a fiercer shade of red. "Do that, sweetmeat, I'll cram every fucking pickle and sesame seed down your throat, you don't eat it."

"So get me one of those McTunas or McWhales or whatever a fish thing is called. A McFishwich maybe, and a small Coke."

Grumbling under his breath, Jersey strode off, Isaac in his wake, grinning. Benny, already beginning to thin on top at the age of twenty-four, hung around near the driver's side door of the Toronado, helping make sure Suki stayed put, doing deep knee bends to limber up his legs.

Suki turned to Mote, who smelled like a locker room. "What would *you* do with three hundred thousand dollars, oaf?"

"I'm not supposta listen t' you."

"Three hundred *thousand*."

"You heard what Jers tole me. You talk t' me or scream or somethin', I got to shut you up."

"You wouldn't hit a girl, would you?"

"Yeah." He nodded. "Jers said do it, so I'd do it. You jest set still there an' be quiet, okay?"

Jersey dialed the Reno number, got through on the fifth ring.

"Tell me," the viper's voice answered.

Maybe he *would* take the three hundred grand and split. "We're in Vegas," he said. "Everything's cool."

"The girl's still with you?"

Wouldn't be very cool if she wasn't, would it, Bitch? "Yeah. They been doing a lotta work on the highway between here an' Flagstaff, Mrs. Voorhees, an'—"

"*What* did you call me, Jersey?"

Jersey closed his eyes. *Shit*. "Uh, Mrs. Garrett—"

"Garrick, Jersey. Gar-*rick*. Is the name too long or too complex for you, Jersey?"

"No, ma'am."

"Is there any hope you might remember it in the future?"

"Yes, ma'am."

"Say it, Jersey. *Garrick*."

"Garrick."

"Wonderful, very nice, Jersey. I know this is a bit challenging for you, but do you suppose it's possible we could use the name Garrick from this point forward?"

"Yes, ma'am."

"Okay, continue."

"Uh, that's all, ma'am. I was just reporting in, like you said."

"When do you think you'll arrive?"

"We're gonna leave Vegas soon." He checked his watch. "We oughta be up there maybe one, two in the morning."

"Fine. Now listen to me, Jersey. Are you listening very carefully, Jersey?"

He ground his teeth. "Yes, ma'am."

"When you get to Reno, phone me. I'll have instructions for you on how to deliver the girl. Do you understand?"

"Yes, ma'am."

"Very well, Jersey."

The phone went dead in Jersey's hand. He slammed Ma Bell's equipment into its cradle, ignoring the scowl being given to him by a monstrously obese woman in her twenties with buttocks the size of beachballs and thighs thicker than his chest. The bitch probably hadn't got change back from her dollar in over twenty fucking years.

Simon sat in the darkness of his room, eyes closed, resting, waiting. The door snicked open; Charlotte entered in a spill of light from the hallway. She shut the door quietly, crossed to the window overlooking Flint Street, and nudged the heavy curtain aside with a bony finger. A needle ray of late afternoon sunlight fell on the crimson spread of Simon's bed like the eye of some malevolent god.

"Please don't smoke in here."

"Sorry." She went into the adjoining bathroom and threw her cigarette into the toilet bowl. Returning, she said, "It's a good house, isn't it, dear?"

"Yes, very good. Daniel did well this time." His voice was flat, however, betraying a certain lack of enthusiasm.

She sat in an armchair opposite him. "The advertisement was placed two days ago. On Friday."

"Which one?"

"For the new girl. Already there have been responses."

"I don't want another girl yet." A hard edge was in his voice. "I want Suki."

"I understand. Jersey says they'll be here sometime after midnight, darling, but we *must* look ahead. Suki will be but a fleeting thing."

157

His eyes glittered. "Not so fleeting, Mother."

She shivered, enjoying the sensation. "No, darling. Perhaps fleeting was not the appropriate word. Still, we must prepare. You'll be wanting a proper escort sometime."

"With this?" he replied harshly. The shadow of his hand moved over the shadow of his face, where the pale rectangle of his bandage hovered in the dimness of the room. "How can I go out with this?"

"It will mend."

"The scar will be visible six months from now. That quack, Pinnell, assured me of that."

"Only to those who know where to look. And Dr. Pinnell is anything but a quack, Simon," she admonished. Into his silence she added, "Do you like your present, darling?"

"Present?"

"The car," she said, piqued. "It was meant to be a surprise. Daniel found one of the same color and everything."

"You should have asked. I'm tired of the Trans Am. I want a Ferrari, black with blue striping, dark plum interior. Something with a little class this time, not just heat."

She raised an eyebrow. "If you like, of course."

"Soon. Tomorrow."

She sighed, stood up. "Perhaps what you need is a little diversion. The hooks were installed yesterday. Would you like that, darling? I'm sure something could be arranged in the next day or two."

"It's too soon since the last time, and anyway, not until after Suki, Mother."

"Well, it's up to you, dear. I just hate to see you like this."

"All I need is Suki. Everything will be fine when Suki's here."

"A few more hours. Just a few more hours, sweetheart." She slipped out the door with a soft rustle of silk.

19

The Lear jet banked left, bleeding off altitude; Frank Limosin peered out the window at the Sierra Nevadas. Even in mid July, the higher peaks were sparsely capped with snow. The sun dropped behind the mountains, backlighting the reddish-umber haze of forest fires burning in the west. The plane banked right as Castledyne held the tiny jet in a descending turn, flaps down.

Houses below, a vast shopping mall, roads crawling with toy cars, and then a field of scraggly weeds, a gray blur of concrete and the plane was down, rolling past a green-glassed flight operations tower that seemed to ripple in the desert heat.

They halted on an apron in front of a low building with a sign that read RENO FLYING SERVICE on the front.

Local time was 8:22: they'd crossed a time zone, gained an hour chasing the sun.

Castledyne came through the cockpit door and cranked open the hatch of the fuselage while the copilot made last-minute additions to the flight log. Castledyne stepped out into the heat and Frank followed. The two men hiked fifty yards to the building as a sleek National Guard F-4, vaguely sharklike in appearance, thundered down onto the runway.

The Reno Flying Service night staff stared curiously at Frank; he could only hope that his too memorable face hadn't made the television news up here. It didn't seem likely that a truck robbery in L.A. would stir up much interest in Reno, but you could never tell. Six hundred grand was a lot of money. During the flight, Frank had done what he could with his face, which wasn't much. His left eye was still caught in a puffy wink, and his white-stubbled cheeks gave him the look of an aging derelict. The Lear jet was an inexplicable contradiction.

"Mr. Wiley?" Frank turned. A secretary in a green dress was standing behind a counter, frowning. She said, "There's a taxi waiting outside for you, sir."

"Yeah, thanks."

Frank shook Castledyne's hand. "Good service, thanks."

"Anytime."

Frank went outside. A Whittlesea cab was parked crossways in the parking lot, engine running. He opened the front door.

The driver was a middle-aged woman with drab brown hair, a mustache, big misshapen breasts on a heavy frame. "You Wiley?" she asked.

"Yeah." He got in next to her.

Her name was Shirley Budd. Her eyes fixed briefly on his face; she decided she'd seen worse. "Okay, where to?"

"You got someplace in town where lawyers hang out? What I mean is—"

"Lawyers, huh? You looking to get divorced?"

"No, what I want—"

"Can't say you look a whole lot like a legal corporation yourself. You aren't, are ya?"

"No."

"Good. Board of Trade'd be the place to go, if it wasn't Sunday."

"What's that?"

"Mouthpiece hangout. Fancy-ass waterin' hole."

"What I want," he said, "is to go to where lawyers have offices. Someplace with old refurbished houses, two or three stories, lots of rooms."

"Think you'll catch one of 'em workin'?" Shirley gave him an astonished look.

"No." He offered no explanation. "This town got a place like that? Big houses, older?"

She pursed her lips and thought a moment. "Okay, that'd be up around the courthouse. Hill Street, Flint, Court, Clay. Parts of Arlington and California. You wanna go up there?"

"Guess so. I'm in kind of a hurry though."

"Yah, sure." She put the car in drive and roared off. "How'd you lose the finger?"

"Korea," Frank said. "Commie machine gun bullet tore it clean off back in 'fifty-two."

"Shame."

"Ruined a promising career as a concert pianist."

She stared at him and then laughed.

They reached streets that grew progressively more crowded with traffic, hot streets with drivers that swerved and honked and sat impatiently at lights that took forever to change.

"Nice, huh?" Shirley Budd said. "All this mess."

"You oughta give L.A. a try."

"Yeah? That where you're from?"

A mistake; he'd have to watch it. "Nope. Albuquerque. Been to L.A. a couple of times though."

"It's comin'," she said.

"What?"

"L.A.'s problems," she replied, a certain ferocity in her voice. "Traffic, drugs, crime, water shortage, street gangs, smog. You name it, it's comin'. Lot of it's here already."

He didn't respond, not wanting to encourage her. Woe and damnation was evidently this woman's forte. A little push and the conversation could turn into an avalanche.

Too late.

"This's a desert, right?" She gave him a quick glance. "Right. You think the goddamn planning commission's figured that out yet? *Hah!*" Her laugh was a derisive bray. "Not on your life! I've unplugged drain clogs with more intelligence than our planning commission. Or the goddamned city council. Developers've got the whole lot of 'em in their pockets. You get to talkin' water storage an' water rights with those snakes an' you learn the meaning of double-talk and bullshit, Mr. Wiley, you'll pardon my French. What's gonna happen is we're gonna have a five-year drought sometime and then the fur's gonna fly. Mark my words, people'll lose their jobs an' their homes an' there'll be graft-eaten officials hangin' from the trees in their own front yards. Serve 'em the hell right, too."

Her words washed over Frank. There wasn't much he could do but tune her out and keep his eyes open for something familiar on the streets. Maybe that big ugly Toronado Mutt and Jeff had been driving in Quiode. Already the hopelessness of the task was beginning to sink in; all these nameless streets, all this hustle and bustle in the gathering dark. And somewhere, perhaps not even in Reno, Suki might already have been delivered into Mink's hands.

Frank's chest felt tight at the thought.

". . . goddamn sticky fingers takin' money under the table while they smile an' tell you they're working like slaves in the public interest. Tell you what, Mr. Wiley, words is the devil's tool. Clever man kin say any damn thing he wants an' you can't never pin him down. Lies, half truths, blather an' triple-talk; these people are experts. They want something, nothin' like the will of the voters or the reality of livin' in the desert'll get in their way. They're like bulldozers. Get between them and the smell of money an' you better . . ."

Frank tried to visualize Mink, remembering what Suki'd said about him. And Charlotte Voorhees. There was that guy Mote, big stupid-looking oaf, and Jersey, skinny fellow with longish hair, small eyes. Both with tattoos. And that black dude, and someone called Danny.

If Mink was here, he'd have a new company with a new name, but Frank still wasn't sure how the operation worked. It was unlikely that Mink would rent a big house somewhere and hang a sign out front that said G. F. LAYTON, INVEST-MENTS, or whatever their name was this time.

". . . kickbacks, bribes, campaign contributions. Every-one runnin' around with their fingers twitchin' like maître d's in some snotty hotel, smilin' out one side of their mouths while lyin' and sayin', 'Up yours, buddy,' out the other. So anyway, here we are. You want lawyers, tomorrow this place'll be crawlin' with 'em."

She pulled to the curb at the corner of a quiet street lined with two- and three-story houses. Tall trees stood dark and shaggy against the reddening sky. Beyond a leafy veil, the luminous crystalline psychedelic glitter of casinos in the nearby gaming district was a visual roar: the Flamingo Hil-ton, Circus Circus, the Virginian, Harrah's, Eldorado, half a dozen others.

Frank felt disoriented. How was he supposed to find Suki in all of this?

"Drive me around," he said. "Slowly. Just wherever law-yers've got offices."

"It's your nickel. Really got a bug about lawyers, don't you?"

"Guess so."

Gables, angles, cornices, columns; dense foliage and un-kempt privet hedges; wrought iron, shingled roofs. All the accoutrements of small-city barristry. Lights glowed dimly behind a few windows. Shirley took him up one street, down another, circled slowly in the darkness. The effect was one of general rattiness: too many run-down one-story shacks and weedy rubble-strewn lots standing side by side with brooding monstrosities that needed paint. Daylight was certain to reveal further shortcomings. Numerous signs out near the sidewalks announced the law offices of such-and-such and thus-and-so, along with those of CPAs, realty firms, marriage counselors, architects. For those who thought pain to be an essential ingredient in their "structural integration," there was even a certified rolfer. Not many people out walking. Frank didn't know if it was the day's residual heat or the neighborhood.

"That's it," Shirley said.

"One more time," Frank said. "I'd like to get to know the area better."

"Say, if you're a burglar, I could point out a couple of commissioners' homes to ya."

"Sorry."

She shrugged, took him around again. This time he paid attention to street names, trying to define the extent of the neighborhood in his mind.

"Again?" she asked, pulling over outside an elderly lilac mansion with royal blue trim. It housed a graphic artist, a software designer, and a trio of attorneys-at-law.

"No, that'll do it."

"Comes to thirteen eighty-five altogether," she said.

He handed her a twenty. "Keep it."

"Thanks. You wanna watch yourself in this neighborhood, Mr. Wiley. Specially in the daytime." She cackled.

He got out and watched as she pulled away, turned right at the corner, disappeared.

Ribs aching, Frank stood on the sidewalk and considered his situation. He was armed with an old German pistol and he had about seventy thousand dollars tucked in his small travel bag. He hadn't eaten in over twenty-four hours. He had no wheels, no place to stay, and he was in a city he didn't know particularly well except for having been given an account of its corrupt officials and traffic snarls, courtesy of Shirley Budd. Not far away, police were uprooting entire counties, trying to find him. He looked like a recently rolled wino desperately in need of a bath, and Suki could be either practically under his nose in one of these old peeling monoliths or two thousand miles away. He had no way of knowing.

But he couldn't do anything now except keep his eyes open and walk around, see what he could see. He toyed briefly with the idea of placing an anonymous call to the cops, seeing what he could stir up that way, but the only story he could tell was a lunatic's tale. He'd sound like a goddamn kook. Worse, the cops might send a few extra patrol cars into this district and end up hassling him, possibly finding his gun and picking him up. That wouldn't do Suki any damn good at all.

He began taking halting steps up Court Street, looking at every car and person in sight, trying to spot any subtle something that might ring bells in his subconscious. Court Street crossed Arlington and climbed a low hill above the Truckee River. Frank walked past Clay to Lee and then over to Ridge and back down to Arlington. Across Arlington to Flint and Hill, up Hill to Liberty.

Hopeless.

The thread leading eleven hundred miles from the De Baca Mountains of New Mexico to this relatively seedy neighborhood in Nevada was simply too tenuous, too ethereal. Not a waste of money, because Suki was worth it, but a depressing, wrenching, futile expenditure of hope.

But because Suki was worth it, and because hope was all he had left, Frank walked, keeping his eyes open, trying to stay alert, searching for that elusive gossamer filament that could be spun into thread and then into rope.

Just a filament would do. Anything at all.

But there was nothing.

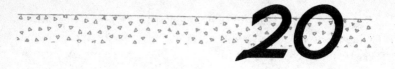

20

"Yes?"

Not, *Tell me*? Jersey blinked; for an instant he thought he'd dialed the wrong number. The long drive had left his eyes grainy and red, his senses dulled.

"Mrs. Voor—Mrs. Gar . . . *rick*? That you?"

"Where *are* you, Jersey? Do you realize it's nearly two in the morning?"

"Yes, ma'am. We're in Reno, at some all-night place on, um, Wells Avenue, a couple blocks off the interstate."

"The girl is still with you, Jersey?"

Jesus Christ. "Yes, ma'am."

"Fine. Wait a moment."

Jersey heard paper rustling; she was probably reading a map. In the Toronado, Mote was a hulking shadow behind the reflection of lights in the windshield, Suki sitting beside him. Benny was off taking a leak somewhere; Isaac half asleep in the Malibu.

"Are you there, Jersey?"

"Yes, ma'am."

"Okay. What you do is come south on Wells. Turn right on Fourth Street, then left on Arlington Avenue. Come across the river, turn left on Court Street then right on Flint. We're in the big off-white clapboard house on the left. It has third-story gabled attic windows and columns by the front doors."

"Yes, ma'am."

"Do you think you can find the house?"

"Yes, ma'am."

"Fine. Now I want you to listen carefully to me, Jersey." Jersey picked his nose. "Are you listening very carefully to me?"

"Oh, yes, Mrs. Garrick."

She hesitated at the tone of his voice. "I want you to bind and gag the girl before you bring her here, Jersey. Do you understand?"

Christ on a Moped. Right here in the parking lot of an AM-PM Mini-Market and all-night gas station? "Yes, ma'am. Feet too?"

"Yes, Jersey. Bind her feet too."

"Yes, ma'am."

"Do it now."

The line went dead. Jersey went into the store, looked around, bought some nylon-filament strapping tape. It would have to do.

Back at the car, he told Mote to take off his undershirt.

"What for?" Mote asked.

"Just do it, huh?"

"Yeah, sure, Jers."

He took it off, revealing a chest like Arnold Schwarzenegger's. Son of a bitch'd been coldcocked twice in less than a

167

week, so it was likely that all that muscle was somehow feeding off what little there was of his brain.

Jersey tore the shirt in half.

"Hey!" Mote cried.

"Hey what?" Jersey tossed the remnant in Mote's lap.

Mote picked it up. "Goddamn, Jers. That was my fav'rit."

Jersey folded the rag several times. "Open wide," he said to Suki.

"Shit, Jersey, I won't scream, I promise. You don't gotta do that."

"I said open up, sweetmeat."

Suki screamed. Jersey'd been expecting it. He drove a fist into her belly, just enough to double her over and keep the scream from building. She gasped for air and he waited, watching, seeing if she was going to puke. When he saw that she wasn't, he forced the filthy rag into her mouth, wrapping tape across it and around her head several times.

He wrapped a few more sticky coils around her wrists and ankles, and then backed the Olds out of the lot and turned left on Wells, the Malibu trailing. Mote kept Suki's head down in his lap, stroking her hair as if she were a kitten.

Frank walked up Court Street to Clay, up Clay to Ridge. The muscle cars turned the other way up Court Street, right on Flint, stopped in front of an oyster clapboard mansion that squatted in darkness, framed by half a dozen blighted elms.

Jersey got out, pushed open a raspy iron gate and went up the path to the front door. It opened before he got there. Mink stood beneath the heavy oak lintel, eyes bright. "Where is she?"

"In the car. Gagged and tied like Mrs. Voor—Garrick said we should."

"Good. Excellent. Drive around back, to the left there. You and Mote carry her in through the kitchen door. Keep your lights off."

"Sure thing, Mink."

168

"Tell Benny and Isaac to stay put out there a while. I don't want a carnival in here."

"Yeah, okay."

Jersey guided the Olds up twin ribbons of cracked concrete to the rear of the house, deep in shadow beneath the trees. A garage stood apart from the house, double-hinged doors closed.

"Take her shoulders," Jersey said. "I got her feet."

Suki squirmed as Mote, bare-chested, hauled her headfirst out of the car. Jersey caught her feet. They clambered up three steps and through a door into the kitchen of the house.

Yellow light leaked into the room from a hallway that ran into the depths of the house. Charlote stood limned in its glow. Mink smiled at Suki as Jersey stood her on her feet.

"Welcome home, Suki," he said. "We're going to have some fun, you and I. I think you'll find it interesting."

Frank hiked up the buckled sidewalks of Ridge Street to Lee, then over to Court and down Court to Clay, where he stood on the corner debating which way to turn. Not that it mattered; he was shuffling down streets at random. It was all a crapshoot in a game that might've never come to town. He turned on Clay and drifted back up to Ridge, thereby missing the pair of cars that rumbled down Court Street and swung right on Arlington, headed for the Rancho Sierra Motel on Fourth Street, where a couple of rooms had been paid for by the week. Frank heard the heavy beat of horsepower, however, and he broke into a crippled run down Ridge, reaching Arlington as the two loud cars crossed the bridge spanning the Truckee River and passed through a green light at First Street.

Not even much of a glimpse, really. Just a couple of muscle cars, out cruising. Even so, it had been a tantalizing moment. Frank breathed deeply, ribs throbbing, heart pounding, staring at the empty street that looped downward toward the western edge of the gaming district glittering in the night.

This just wasn't any fucking use.

God, Suki, I'm so damn sorry.

Mink was crazy, insane, yet possessed of some sort of unimaginable control. Cold sweat formed at Suki's armpits. It would be better, she thought, just to die, now, this instant.

The basement air was unpleasantly cool against her naked body. The only light came from a single bulb screwed into a fixture in the ceiling. Except for cardboard cartons stacked against one wall, the room was empty. Cobwebs fluttered in the corners.

"Knowledge, as they say, is power," Simon said, standing on a chair as he dumped crushed ice into a gallon bucket that hung from the old joists of the mansion. "But certainly it's very much more than that. It's also the wellspring of imagination, wouldn't you agree?" He smiled emptily down at her.

She lay spread-eagled on a mattress in the middle of the floor, wrists and ankles securely bound with silk bands. Jersey's gag had been replaced with one that was more effective, and more hygenic. With the new gag in place she could barely grunt, much less respond to so philosophical a question. Several other silk bands had been looped around her hips and rib cage, preventing all lateral movement of her abdomen.

"And," Mink continued, "imagination is the basis of fear, and fear is the primary source of the sort of unbounded agony of which the human mind is capable."

Suki stared at him, eyes wide. His bandage was off, exposing the still-angry wound of the graft on his forehead. Charlotte sat in an overstuffed easy chair, smoking silently, watching with grackle's eyes as her adopted son made his preparations.

Simon stepped off the chair and crouched next to Suki. "Wouldn't you therefore agree that knowledge is an essential ingredient of agony? Yes, I thought you might. For that reason I will explain what is about to happen to you, and I will tell you how you will react to it. I will give you all the *knowl-edge* you need to make this a most rewarding experience."

The bucket hung directly over Suki's midsection. A short length of glass tubing hung from an inch-long piece of rubber hose that protruded from the bottom of the bucket. A stopcock of the sort used in chemical laboratories was fitted to the glass tube.

"The Chinese were masters at inducing agony," Simon said. "The so-called Chinese water torture is a case in point. Few of those raised in the West truly comprehend its power." He gazed upward, and Suki's eyes followed. "The bucket contains ice water. Soon, drops will fall from the tiny spigot you see beneath it. Each drop will fall at a fixed rate at a specific location. In years past, this has generally been on a person's forehead, but to reflexively do what has been done before is to miss the point entirely. Perhaps," Simon said, standing, "you will soon be able to tell me what that point is, Suki."

He reached up and turned the stopcock, catching the drip in a washcloth while he adjusted the flow to about four drops per minute.

"There," he said. "Shall we begin?"

He stood back. The next drop slowly formed at the end of the glass tube, growing round and fat, catching the light. She watched it, mesmerized. It fell, landing with a hollow *thip* in the middle of her naked belly, two inches below her navel.

She blinked. A blood vessel in her neck began to throb.

"Cold, isn't it?" Simon asked. "And the height from which it falls increases one's awareness of it quite substantially, don't you think?" He watched as the next drop slowly filled, grew round and fat, trembling in a hidden current of air. It fell, splatting against Suki's belly with that same tiny, hollow *thip*.

"Notice how slowly each drop forms," Simon said, crouching beside her again. "If they come too often, one's mind tends to integrate the impact of each individual drop into a continuous experience. But if the drip is made sufficiently slow, the mind reaches a state of equilibirum between each drop in which each can be fully *anticipated*."

Thip.

"The brain then becomes a most active participant in the process. A state of denial is achieved, continually disrupted. Like the very best sex, Suki dear, the very best pain occurs within the dark, uncharted pathways of the mind.

"On the other hand, too slow a drip would lack significance. Frequency is therefore important; moreover, the drip is ice water and falls from a good height, giving it an impact that the mind finds meaningful. Observe. . . ."

Thip.

He smiled at her, the smile of a cobra watching its poison working in its victim. "It *is* unpleasant, isn't it? Very cold and, as you will soon discover, very hard. Does that surprise you, Suki? That water can be hard, harder than stone, harder than diamond, harder than *life*?" He glanced upward, waited.

Thip.

For a moment, his eyes got bright. "One is incapable of fully comprehending this sort of torment without actually experiencing it for oneself. Intellectualizing is wholly ineffective, while observation is just an abstraction of a different sort. Would it surprise you to learn that a little less than twenty-four hours ago I was lying where you are now?"

Her eyes widened.

Thip.

"It's true," Mink said. His voice was soothing, almost dreamy, but his eyes had the empty, distant stare of bullet holes in sheet metal. Charlotte's eyes were even worse; her face pale and featureless behind a veil of smoke. Mink said, "Your suffering will in a sense be real to me, Suki, as real as my own, because we will have shared this incredible experience. In less than ten hours I felt a scream building inside of me that I knew I would soon be unable to contain. I would have screamed, Suki, nor am I the least bit ashamed to admit it. I watched with horror as that unyielding—"

Thip.

"—globule formed above me, knowing, as few men on this earth know, how it would explode upon me when it dropped. But think, Suki, it was not at the moment the droplet landed on my flesh that I felt the scream well up inside, but as it *formed*. Not at the moment of pain, but at the *anticipation* of pain. I think that's significant. Watch."

Above, the crystalline orb swelled, swelled . . .

Thip.

A tremor ran through her. A coolness touched her belly. Mink's face hovered near, pale madness in his eyes.

"Do you regret marking me, Suki? No? Yes? Wait and see? Oh, but I promise you that you shall, Suki. Whatever regrets you have at this moment are nothing compared to those you'll experience, say, eight hours from now."

Thip.

He stood. "I almost envy you," he said. "You will pass beyond even the distant shores that I have reached. You will know pain, Suki Flood, as few have ever known it. I don't particularly envy you the pain, but I do envy you the knowledge." He looked up at the droplet forming. "Would you like me to catch it for you, Suki?"

No . . . yes.

Thip.

Mink turned toward Charlotte. "Will you turn the music on upstairs, Mother? I think it's time."

"Of course." She stood and went up the stairs without a glance at Suki, shoes tocking loudly on the old wooden risers.

Thip.

Simon waited. Seconds passed.

Thip.

From upstairs came the faint sounds of music, jazz, Bix Beiderbecke and Paul Whiteman's Orchestra. "These old houses were built like fortresses," Simon said. "Screams down here are all but inaudible on the street outside, I know. With the stereo—"

173

Thip.

"—playing upstairs, it's quite impossible to hear anything that might take place down here. When you scream, Suki, I want to hear it, I want you to give full vent to your agony. I know you won't want to give me that, and I know you will do everything in your power not to, but you will do so, all the same." He bent down and removed her gag.

Thip.

She tried to spit in his face, but her mouth was dry.

He smiled at her. "When you've had enough of the cold, my pet, you will ask me for the heat."

"Motherfucker." She spat at him again, still unable to work up any moisture. Her tongue was dry, slightly swollen; even her teeth felt dry, like chips of porcelain.

Thip.

Charlotte appeared on the stairs, a wraith in dark silk. She stopped partway down.

"You will ask for the heat," Mink said. "I promise. And when you ask, I will replace the ice water with boiling oil. Oil, Suki. Have you ever been spattered by hot grease? Sure you have. Each drop will destroy a hundred cells, eating into your guts in precisely the same place as the cold is now. The oil will drip upon you until you die. You might—"

Thip.

"—think you'll never ask for the scalding oil, Suki, but that's only because you lack the imagination to know how the cold will affect you. You *will* ask. That's what's truly incredible about this . . . process. Inevitably, a time will come when you will scream out for change, *any* kind of change—"

"I saw you with those girls, Mink. You're sick, and so's your crazy fucking mother." She shot a look at Charlotte and said to her, "I saw you watching—"

Thip.

"—Mink and those young girls." She stared into Mink's dead eyes. "You two sick, disgusting perverts."

Simon raised an eyebrow at her.

174

"How old were they?" she asked. "Thirteen? Twelve?"

He said, "Do you understand how old *you* are, Suki? How jaded and ancient you've become? Do you realize how quickly innocence is corrupted on this vile planet, how quickly it is reduced to numbing, sexless cynicism?"

Thip.

She felt suddenly sickened by his presence, as if she would soon vomit. "You're a monster," she said, turning her head away so she wouldn't have to look at him.

He walked to the base of the stairs. "You *will* beg me for the oil, Suki. But first you will scream."

Thip.

"Concentrate now on just one thing, Suki. I won't return to distract you for a while. Your mind must attune itself to the rhythm of the water. Good-bye."

Footsteps sounded hollowly on the stairs. A door snicked shut above.

Thip.

Silence filled the room, a deathlike silence, full of dust and dark and age and rot. She would never scream. She would die before she gave Mink that awful joy.

Overhead, the next drop grew swollen. Larger, larger . . .

Thip.

21

A purple glow revealed the contours of the mountains to the east. Stars faded overhead as royal blue brightened into day. Sunlight crept from the peaks of the Sierra Nevadas into the irregular bowl of the valley in which "the Biggest Little City in the World" sprawled funguslike over the land.

The night's chill began to burn off.

Frank's stomach growled. His mouth was dry and his ribs ached. He looked like a bum and he felt like a bum, and like a bum he roamed the neighborhood restlessly, as if hoping for a handout or seeking a likely house to rob. One eye was still puffed to a slit. Still, he wouldn't give up, wouldn't even stray a few blocks outside his self-assigned beat to an all-night liquor store where he might get a can of Coke or a container of orange juice. If he did, he might miss something, and the thought of allowing the slightest opportunity to slip by was intolerable. He didn't expect a parade of Voorheeses to come marching by.

Up Lee to Ridge, across Arlington to Hill, down to Court and then up Flint Street.

Music came from the big mansion to his left. Cab Calloway or Duke Ellington. One of those.

Up Flint to California Avenue, up California to Arlington; a brief tour of the immediate neighborhood south of California Avenue, where he'd found a few more law offices, then back to Ridge.

A time would come when he would have to make a decision: continue the search, or quit. He didn't want to quit, but he realized the impossibility and futility of keeping this up indefinitely. He'd find her soon or not at all, and as the hours passed, the odds increased that Mutt and Jeff had taken her to Shreveport instead of Reno.

Pain welled up inside him at the thought, filling him with despair. He would continue his vigil at least another twenty-four hours before considering a search of Shreveport; perhaps Suki would survive that long in Mink's hands.

He would never forget Suki, and he would never allow Simon Voorhees to slip from his memory either. He was amazed at how quickly and thoroughly Suki's little war had become his own.

Her breath came in short gasps. She closed her eyes, but saw the hated globule forming anyway, growing fatter, heavier, an evil thing ripening, near critical, falling . . .

Thip.

Her belly trembled under the impact. Her skin felt raw, half frozen, and it seemed as if each drop were penetrating an inch into her skin. Her sides heaved. Her muscles stood out as she tried desperately to twist her body out from under the hideous drop, to make the the next drop fall at a slightly different location, but the silken web held her firmly in place.

She opened her eyes. The next drop was half-formed, just as she'd known it would be, catching the light of that single bulb in a way that never varied. It swelled . . . grew larger . . .

A scream built up within her; with effort, she forced it down. She'd never give him that. Never.

Thip.

She groaned, a low sound, full of agony.

"Yes."

The word was a mere breath, a sigh. She twisted her head, seeking its source. Simon stood in the shadows to her right. She hadn't heard him come down. Or perhaps another staircase led into the basement; the chamber was certainly large enough. Her mind seized upon these meaningless thoughts like a drowning woman clawing at flotsam.

Simon took a step forward. He was naked, hard.

"Your first groan, Suki," he said. "Four hours, twenty minutes. You're—"

Thip.

"—doing very well, darling."

"Mink . . ." His name was airless on her lips.

He cocked his head, smiled. "What's that I hear in your voice, Suki? Could it be remorse?"

"Fuck you," she said, hating the clogged sound that issued from her throat.

"Really? We will see if you're still capable of uttering so tiresome a sentiment in a few more hours, Suki Flood."

Thip.

He stood over her, turgid, wiry; eyes glowing, yet oddly moribund, the sort of contradiction he delighted in. "If you will take back those unkind words, darling, I will catch the next drop for you. Would you like that, dearest?"

Yes, yes, yes, yes, yes—

"No, you asshole motherfucker," she hissed. "I love this."

He gazed fondly down at her. "My, aren't you tough? That is very good. This . . . experience works best on the tough ones. When they break, and they *always* do, they break—"

178

Thip.

"—so *completely*, my love. When hammered, tough rocks often shatter. You will do everything I have said you will do, and more."

She stared at him, numbed with pain and hatred. Overhead, the next drop swelled. She realized that talking with anyone, even Simon Voorhees, was an enormous relief, diversion from the relentless, battering plunge of the achingly frigid drops.

Simon turned away. At the base of the stairs he stopped. "Perhaps, Suki, you are beginning to understand the wonderful, terrible patience of water." He began to climb.

"Mink . . ."

He looked down at her. "Yes, Suki?"

"Don't go," she whispered. Tears formed in her eyes.

Thip.

"What did you say, dearest?"

Her lips trembled. "Nothing."

"Until later, then." He went up; the door closed.

Silence.

The next drop filled. It grew fatter, fatter . . .

She felt the scream, way down inside, wanting to come out, wanting to shatter the terrible thing to atoms.

Thip.

Frank Limosin bought three prepackaged sandwiches and a couple of cans of Coke at Dumar's Liquor Store on Center Street, three blocks east of Hill. If he collapsed from dehydration or hunger, he wouldn't be of any use to anyone. Wolfing a stale tuna sandwich, he hurried back as fast as his hurting ribs would allow.

A glitzy parade of money cars began to arrive at a little before eight that morning, Audis and Porsches, Mercedes and Cadillacs. A quiet influx of status machinery. Lawyers and other professionals emerged from these glossy, purring shells in business suits, carrying attaché cases.

The day heated up; the sidewalks began to bake under the

bright morning sun. A few cicadas sang their crazed electric song in the straw-colored weeds.

Frank stood on the corner of Court and Arlington. A red Trans Am rolled toward him along Court Street. Frank stared, a roast beef sandwich held motionless before his open mouth. A pudgy, baby-faced man sat behind the wheel, wearing wire-rimmed glasses and a dark suit. Suddenly Frank didn't know what to do. His vision seemed to dim. He froze, trying to absorb every detail, madly evaluating his options, most of which were insane, beyond reason. The car was new, a temporary license taped to the window.

The car turned left at the corner, rumbled up Arlington.

Danny. Suki'd said there was a guy called Daniel, Danny something, who was some sort of a business manager for Simon Voorhees. Kinda moonfaced, wore glasses.

Oh, Jesus.

His mind spun as he watched the Trans Am wind up Arlington away from him, toward California Avenue.

Couldn't chase it. Guy might see him, and that would give the game away. And what the hell would he do if he caught it, even at the light? Which was damned unlikely in his present condition. Might be any of a million other moonfaced guys in North America.

But in a brand new red Trans Am, in Reno, in the kind of neighborhood Mink was partial to? And about forty years old. Suki had said Danny was about forty. Mink had lost one Trans Am; maybe he'd bought another. He was the sort who might.

Frank mopped sweat from his brow with his sleeve. He gazed up Court Street. The car had come from that direction. But from where, exactly? Some guy cruising through, or had this Mink character really rented some kind of a house up that way?

Frank knew the streets by heart. Court and Ridge and Liberty, with Flint and Hill running between them. Pickard was just a block-long alley.

The guy had come down Court. When he returned,

chances were he'd come back the same way. Frank tried to remember exactly where he'd first seen the Trans Am. Not far up the street; the image was engraved in his mind. He hadn't seen it turn onto Court from one of the side streets.

He walked up Court Street and stood at the first intersection, looking up Flint Street. It was quiet, dozy, hot. Same general shabby look as the rest of the neighborhood. Big off-white, dingy clapboard mansion in the middle of the block with gables, columns, casement windows, ivy climbing the first foot of a wrought-iron fence set between brick posts. A collection of lilac trees and catalpa in the front yard, tall elms at the sides and back, steeply pitched roof. Jazz music had been coming from the place since a little before dawn. Did that mean anything? To the left of the mansion was a low, single-story structure with scaled paint, broken windows, and other signs of abandonment. To the right was a two-story house of blond brick, the offices of a pair of attorneys and some kind of a paralegal outfit. As he watched, a woman in a pale green summer suit came out, eased into a little Toyota MR2, drove off.

Frank hiked down to the next corner, Hill Street, and scrutinized the street carefully. Same hot, afflicted look. Peeling paint, lawns drying out, a ground-in patina of dust turning everything a tiresome shade of gray.

The thing to do, Frank thought, was position himself somewhere between Flint Street and Hill, wait for the Trans Am to return, see which street it turned up, or if it pulled into a place on Court Street itself.

He couldn't think of any other way to handle it.

Thip.
Thip.
Thip.
The next horrible drop grew bloated, hung, fell.
Thip.
Her groan was a watery gurgle of raw agony, shattering

181

nerves. The long lean muscles of her legs stood out as she writhed helplessly in her bonds.

"Yes," Simon whispered.

"Mink?" her eyes fluttered, trying to find him.

"I'm here, Suki. Over here."

"I'm . . . I'm s-sorry, Mink," she said, voice wrenched, cords standing out in her neck.

Thip.

"Aaa-agg."

"Are you *really* sorry, Suki? Truly?"

"Aaagh . . . Yes, yes." Tears rolled from her eyes. "Please, no more. Please, I can't . . ."

"It's been nine hours and ten minutes. You're amazingly strong. Isn't she strong, Mother?"

Suki's eyes shifted. Wreathed in cigarette smoke, Charlotte sat in the chair, silent, intense, watching with her empty grackle's eyes. The chair had been pulled back into the shadows. Suki, lost in pain, hadn't even smelled the smoke.

"Why don't you scream, Suki?" Simon suggested.

No.

Thip.

Her belly rippled under the impact of the falling glacier, muscles spasming.

"Oh, God!" she breathed, body arched. "Oh, my *Gooooood!*"

"Yes," Simon said. "Yessss. Pain has stripped away your cynicism, has it not? Do you feel the innocence of your agony, the childlike purity to which you have returned?"

Her eyes refused to focus. Above her, he was a fractured figure, gently stroking himself. Charlotte watched. Insane.

"S-Simon—"

"What is it, Suki?"

Thip.

Her mind clenched. Agony reverberated within the ragged fabric of her brain. "Aaaa . . . aaaagh."

"Scream, Suki," he whispered.

182

Something was already screaming inside her, had been screaming throughout eternity, an insane shriek that threatened to shatter all the world. Spittle ran from the corners of her mouth and down her jaw.

"Shall I catch the next drop, Suki?"

"Yes. Oh, God, *yes!*"

"Here it comes, Suki. I'll get it, I'll—"

Thip.

"I'm sorry," he said. "I missed."

"You . . . bastard," she hissed weakly. And then she began to cry, wet sobbing gasps that wracked her body.

"Do you want the heat?" he asked softly. "Do you want the boiling oil, Suki darling? Wouldn't the heat feel nice?"

Yes.

No. Oh, God, *no!*

Thip.

She bit back a soul-rending shriek, gagging.

"It will take a while to set up. Fifteen minutes, perhaps. Would you like that, Suki? Fifteen minutes in which the drops will cease?"

Yes. Yes, yes, yes, yes.

"Scream for me, Suki. Scream for me and then you may have the heat."

Thip.

"Aaanaaghhh." Her eyes bulged, the whites bloodshot.

"So close," he whispered soothingly. "So close. Soon you can have the heat. Soon. And then the torture will begin in earnest. Boiling oil will hurt so very much more, Suki, but even so, you will ask for it, *beg* for it, I promise."

The next drop swelled.

"Can you stand this for—"

Thip.

"—another hour, my love? Another day, another *week?*"

His words were bullets, ripping bloody tunnels through her brain. Another hour? The next few drops would surely destroy her, but another day, another *week?*

Thip.

She screamed, a tremendous blood-curdling shriek of utter agony, and Simon stroked harder, spurting warm semen over her belly as she writhed. The next cruel drop began to expand.

Charlotte watched a minute longer, then went upstairs to change the compact disc on the stereo. She was growing weary of Cootie Williams and his "growling" trumpet.

A midnight blue Ferrari rolled up Court Street, turned onto Flint. For a moment Frank didn't react. All his concentration was on the reappearance of the red Trans Am.

Suddenly he broke into a lurching run.

Jesus.

By the time he reached the corner, the Ferrari had pulled into the crumbling driveway beside the mansion from which the weak sounds of jazz still issued. A man with a round face and wire-rimmed glasses got out and, without knocking, used a key to enter the house through the front door.

Indecison was a bloated monster in Frank's head. What was this? What had he seen? Just a harmless-looking guy who drove off in a Trans Am, came back in a Ferrari. Right city, right neighborhood. An implied scent of money with a capital *M*. No lawyer's shingle hung in front of the mansion, no sign of any kind.

An inexorable logic took over, logic with its own truth, its own unyielding call to action, its own dark gravity existing far outside any code of law. He couldn't afford the time it would take to gather a greater preponderance of evidence. If it was the right place, then either it was already too late or Suki needed him *now*. And if it wasn't; then it wasn't, as best he could, Frank would extricate himself from the brouhaha that must inevitably follow and try to make his way to Shreveport, see what he could turn up there.

It was all he had left.

He reached into his bag and pulled out the nine-

184

millimeter German Astra, tucked it into the waistband of his jeans where it was concealed by the denim jacket but where he could reach it easily. Perhaps the pistol would actually fire if he had to use it. The night before, he'd built a packet of money, a brick of twenties and fifties with a couple of hundreds on the outside. It looked worth having. He slipped it partway up his right sleeve.

He wandered down Flint Street, same side of the street as the mansion, eyes wary, heart beginning to pound as if he were seventeen and out on his first date with a busty blonde who'd given vague signals that she might be willing.

Had Mutt and Jeff told Mink what he looked like? Perhaps Mutt and Jeff were inside the house now, watching from one of those curtained windows as Frank ambled foolishly up the sidewalk. No muscle cars were in sight. Did that mean anything?

His palms were damp. Traffic sounds were light on neighboring streets; nothing moved on Flint.

He reached the iron fence that separated the mansion from the moldering bungalow next to it, plodded along for another fifty feet and then stopped by the mansion's gate. He opened it, stooped as if to pick up something from the ground, and let the money brick slip down into his hand. He stared at it. He gazed doubtfully up the street, then at the house. Without further delay he trudged up the flagstone path to the porch steps, climbed stolidly, leaned on the doorbell.

His breath came in short tense puffs through parted lips. He waited, rang the bell again, keeping the bad side of his face turned from the peephole in the door.

A bolt was thrown from within. A two-inch gap appeared between the door and the frame.

"Yes?" a woman asked. She had a smoker's gravelly voice. Frank caught a glimpse of red hair, a wizened face.

Charlotte Voorhees had red hair. Frank tried not to stare. Was it her? *Was it?* Coincidences were beginning to pile up.

185

"Uh, yuh," Frank said. "I found this in your front yard, ma'am. Didn't know whose it was." He held up the money brick, fanned its leaves. "Thought maybe I oughta ask."

The woman pulled the door open a few more inches, gave his whiskers a fierce frown, reached out for the money. Her hair was definitely red. A dead look was in her faded blue eyes.

Frank pulled the money away. "Is this yours, ma'am?"

"Yes, thank you, very much. You want a reward?" The door opened wider, the sounds of Thelonious Monk and his jazz piano leaking out in greater volume.

Frank grabbed the old crone by the throat with his left hand and stepped swiftly through the door, pulling his gun. She scrabbled at him, reaching for his eyes, and he spun her around, his arm clamped around her spindly neck.

"Simon!" she shrieked. Frank tightened his arm against her windpipe.

Simon! Frank's heart leapt. He crouched, dragging the writhing witch down with him.

Too many coincidences. One too many.

The woman kicked at the floor; her arms flailed as she struggled for air, bony blue-veined fingers shaped into claws.

"Where's the girl?" Frank hissed in her ear. He eased up on her throat. "Where's Suki?"

Charlotte attempted to scream.

"Christ!" Frank choked off her squawk and rapped the back of her head with the butt of the Astra. She went limp in his arms.

The moonfaced man came into the room. Frank leveled the gun at him from a distance of fifteen feet. "C'mere, sport."

The man hesitated, about to run.

"Run or yell, you're dead," Frank said. "Get over here."

The man took a few hesitant steps toward him. A faint scream came from somewhere in the house.

Suki!

Frank tossed Charlotte's limp body aside, tore across the

intervening space in a lineman's rush, slammed the man up against a doorjamb, and jammed the muzzle of the gun into his soft manager's belly.

"Where's the girl?"

"Downstairs," Danny gasped, blinking. "In the basement." The impact had thrown his glasses from his face; his myopic eyes were wide with fear.

"Show me."

The sound of "Light Blue" filled the room, Thelonious ripping up the keyboard as Danny led Frank from the room and down a dim hallway. He stopped before a heavy oak door with raised panels.

"Down there," Danny said.

A muffled scream came from behind the door, full-throated and raw, barely recognizable as human. The hair on the back of Frank's head stood up.

He slammed the butt of the gun against Daniel's head and lowered him to the floor. A moment of sudden silence came over the house, then Chick Corea took his turn at the ivories, hammering out "Sundance."

Frank opened the door. Wooden steps led down into gloom. The stairs reached a landing at the midway point, the second set of steps descending from the landing at a right angle to the first. Frank went down quickly, heart pounding in his throat.

When he reached the landing he was momentarily stunned by what he saw: Suki, naked, tied to the floor, writhing, breath coming in hoarse gasps. A naked man stood at her side, turning slowly.

"Mother?" the man said. Whipcord muscles stood out on his body. His buttocks were pale, hard, hairless.

Frank aimed the gun at him, came down a few more steps, crouched. He used the railing to steady his hands.

"Don't even breathe, asshole," he said.

With shocking swiftness, the man leapt at Suki, placed a hand on her throat.

"Hold it," he said. "Believe it or not, I can kill her even if you pull that trigger."

Frank kept the gun trained on the man's chest. "I believe it."

"Well, then. Look's like we've got us a standoff here."

"Frank?" The word was half cry, half groan. It sounded bubbly, as if she were drowning.

"I'm here, Suki."

Thip.

Suki screamed again. *"Fraaaaaaaank! Oh, God, oh, Jesus, make it stop, Frank! Please make it STOP!"*

Frank's blood went cold. He came down the remaining steps to the basement floor, hands trembling violently.

"No closer," Mink warned.

Frank stopped. "You call this a standoff?" What in the name of Christ was going on?

"Looks like it, doesn't it?"

Thip.

Suki gasped. Spittle bubbled at her lips. Her eyes were like frosted glass, staring blindly up at Frank. "God, Frank, *please!*"

"I'm not leaving," Frank said.

"Then she's dead, old man."

"What's her life worth, like that? I don't have a fucking thing to lose, you slimy bastard. She's all that's keeping you alive right now. She dies, you die. That's a fact."

Simon's eyebrows raised. "Who *are* you?"

Thip.

Suki's entire body shuddered. She moaned, thick and low.

"Question is, do *you* want to live, motherfucker?" Frank's voice shook. "If you're not face down on the floor by the time the next drop falls, you're worm food, cocksucker, and that's a promise." He aimed the gun squarely at the livid red scar on Simon's forehead, using a two-handed combat grip. Suddenly his hands were like rocks.

Something in his voice got through. Or perhaps it was the

gun's implacable dead eye gaping at Simon, as implacable and dead as Simon's own. Or Frank's finger, white on the trigger.

For an instant Simon hesitated. He glanced up at the drop forming above Suki's belly, smiled uncertainly. "Okay." He lowered himself quickly to the floor by Suki's head, just inches from the rear wall.

Frank caught the next drop in his hand.

Suki began to cry, a wet blubbering sound filled with madness. Frank reached up and hammered the bucket from the ceiling with a fist. Icy slush sprayed the floor as the bucket crashed against a wall and clattered into a dark corner.

Simon twitched.

"Uh-uh," Frank said. He reached down, pressed the barrel of the gun into Mink's ear. "Put your nose against the floor, asshole. Eyes front."

Suki sobbed weakly.

Mink slowly turned his head until his nose just touched the cold gray concrete. Frank carefully transferred the gun to his left hand and pressed the muzzle into Mink's neck. He pounded a fist into the back of Mink's head, slamming his face into the concrete. Stunned, Mink tried to come off the floor at him, still snakelike and wiry. Frank caught Mink's face in his open hand and slammed the back of his head into the nearby stone wall. The sound was that of coconut on marble. Mink's eyes rolled up in his head and he slumped to the floor on his side.

Frank spoke to Suki as he untied her. She cried, a bitter, aching sound that wrenched his heart. An angry red spot low on her belly showed where the water had dripped. With the bonds free, she curled up into a ball, folded over the wound. For a moment he held her, his hands and heart clumsy, breathing unevenly. She was a rag doll.

Frank stared at Mink, trying to understand what kind of a mad dog the man was. How could evil come to so sharp a focus? The world did not deserve this.

189

He wanted to kill him but knew that he could not. Logic demanded it, but logic was insufficient and, amazingly, so was the sick rage that burned within him. He simply wasn't capable of cold-blooded murder.

Suddenly all he wanted was to get Suki and himself out of that house, away from the evil slimy creatures that inhabited it. The gray walls were like the lining of a demon's stomach, trying to digest them, even now sucking them inch by inch down some unimaginable maw into blackness.

"Can you walk?" Frank asked.

She was barely conscious, jackknifed on her side, moaning, still in the grip of the horror she'd endured.

Grating agony shot through Frank's ribs as he lifted Suki and climbed the stairs. Beads of sweat stood out on his brow. He stooped momentarily over Danny's inert form and fumbled in the man's pockets for the Ferrari's keys. Charlotte was lying in the living room where Frank had left her. He kicked her in the face as he stepped over her slack body because he simply could not help himself, and because her evil was as inexplicable and vile as that of her stepson. He tore a curtain from one of the front windows, bundled Suki in it and carried her out the door.

Coleman Hawkins's lively tenor sax followed them out into the hot afternoon sunshine.

22

Suki mumbled something.

Frank barely heard the papery sound of her voice in the rush of air over the Ferrari's hull.

"What?" He leaned closer.

"Did you kill him?" Her eyes were closed, face pale. Her voice was a tattered wisp from all the screaming she'd done.

"No."

"Why not?"

"Christ, Suki. I couldn't."

Translucent flakes of spittle encrusted her lips and chin. Her head lolled against the headrest. "I could've."

"I know."

She was silent a moment. "That me I smell?"

"Us, I believe."

A spasm of some kind seized her, doubled her over. She groaned miserably, teeth gritted.

"You gonna be all right?" Frank asked.

"I look all right?"

"Gorgeous." Cocooned in mauve polyester and cotton with ruffles all over and a tieback dragging on the floor. Tangled strands of hair covered her streaky face.

She didn't look at him. "If I die, my name's Flood. Suki Flood."

"You're not gonna die."

"Flood, as in too much water. That's my real name, Frank, I just want you to know."

"Anne Flood?"

"Used to be, yeah. Suki, now."

"You're not gonna die," he repeated.

Her eyes remained shut. They weren't up to focusing yet. "I wanted to," she said. "He isn't human."

"I know."

"If you'd killed him, it wouldn't've been murder. It would've been like . . ." She paused, groping for an elusive idea. "Like public service or something."

They passed the Mount Rose turnoff and cruised down U.S. 395 toward Carson City, capital of Nevada, now twenty miles away. Frank didn't want to head west, into California; anyway, Auburn or Sacramento were too far to go with Suki in the condition she was in. North and east of Reno was wasteland, hopeless.

He wasn't yet sure what he was doing, driving around in a stolen car worth as much as a house, with a more or less naked teenage girl beside him who looked as if she'd barely survived the wreck of the *Titanic*. He wasn't likely to be mistaken for the Prince of Wales himself. They had to get cleaned up before any major moves could be contemplated, and he wanted to ditch the Ferrari as quickly as possible. Suki needed a place to lie down and rest, soon, but first there were these technical difficulties to be taken care of.

"I want to kill him, Frank."

"I know."

"I'm serious."

"Oh, Christ, Vi, what'd he do to you?"

In his pain, Mink had inadvertently called his stepmother by her real name, Violet, breaking the one cardinal rule they had agreed upon right from the beginning. Violet and De Witt Schlenker had become Charlotte and Simon Voorhees five years ago, Paul Schlenker having had the sense to run, years before that, and in that time neither of them had once slipped and called the other by his or her real name, until this moment.

But no harm came of it, since no one was around to hear. Danny was still out cold in the hallway. The house was empty, quiet but for "Tiger Rag" being performed over and over by the self-proclaimed creator of jazz itself, Jelly Roll Morton.

Yet the old way reasserted itself, and Simon lifted the battered face of his stepmother into his lap and cradled her on his naked thighs, crooning her assumed name almost soundlessly, over and over: "Charlotte, Charlotte."

Her patrician nose was cocked at an odd angle. Blood coated her upper lip and cheeks, drawing her thin hair into sticky clumps. Air wheezed in and out of her body.

A bloody smear formed on the wall where Simon leaned his head. Blood dripped from his crushed nose.

"We will kill him, Mother," Simon said. "That I promise. Her, too. We will kill them both."

The woman in the clothing store approached him warily, as if she'd just realized she'd made a mistake in not calling the police the instant he'd first walked into the Clothes Rak.

"May I help you?" she asked, but her tone was as if she'd asked him what in the name of our Lord and Savior Jesus Christ he was doing there. She hadn't seen him pull the Ferrari into a distant corner of the lot. She'd never had a

193

"street person" come wandering in out of the heat to check out women's apparel before.

"Sorry about my appearance," he said, giving the clerk a Cyclopean stare, one eye still puffed from the battering Jersey'd given him. "I'm looking for an outfit for my daughter."

She looked him over doubtfully. The brute stank. The daughter ploy stank too, always did. "Daughter" translated to girlfriend, and that meant he was cheating on a wife, except that this troglodyte could hardly be expected to have either. "What did you have in mind, exactly?" She wouldn't, couldn't, address him as sir.

"The works. Pants of some kind, I guess. Blouse, bra, panties. Guess you don't sell shoes here, huh?"

She frowned. Business wasn't usually conducted this way. The gargoyle added nothing to the ambience of the place, which wasn't all that deathlessly swank to begin with. It was just as well that things were usually slow on Monday afternoons.

"How old?"

"Huh?"

"Your daughter. How old is she?"

"Eighteen." He wanted to hurry this along but didn't know how. Suki had told him she'd be all right, but how could he be sure? With dried spit crusted on her chin, she looked like a person on death's doorstep. He had to get her dressed and looking presentable, and soon.

"Size?"

"Uh, I don't know."

They never did. Men had some sort of a disease or lacked a critical portion of their brains that was capable of turning the female figure into the abstraction known as size. Men were so involved with *function*. It wasn't that Eileen Pengelly was a particularly deep or gifted thinker, but she wasn't *unaware*, and she'd seen this kind of thing often enough over the years to have had her awareness congeal into words: men were brutes, period. Glandular heathens who functioned on

194

an entirely different plane from women. And now a new and not unexpected bit of information impressed itself on Eileen: street rabble, like the rest of God's ill-breed creations, came without that necessary refinement in the cortical fold.

But they got past that stumbling block with the usual estimates of height and weight and, the brute's face turning a nice plum color—which served him right—a not very useful description of bust size. Eileen had never before dealt with the descriptor "kind of a good handful each," but what could be more functional than that? A good mouthful? She wordlessly translated this information into a 34B cup. The girl didn't sound very large, and the gargoyle didn't have big hands, so a 34B seemed likely. If this guy was a nascent cross-dresser of some kind he was going to be in for one hell of a surprise, since he was a good 46C. It'd been a while since she'd seen a chest like that on a man; shoulders, too.

Tan pleated slacks, yellow blouse, white cotton panties, white bra. The brute lacked all imagination, but it was only to be expected. What she didn't expect was that so evidently destitute a soul, when presented with a bill for seventy-two dollars and twenty-three cents, would casually reach into one of those grubby voids and produce a hundred-dollar bill that didn't even look counterfeit. She took it from a hand from which part of a finger was missing.

Frank saw her eyes linger. He tried to resist, couldn't. "Lost it in a knife fight down Tijuana way," he said. "Nineteen and fifty-eight it was."

She looked appalled. "Thank you for your business," she said, handing him his change and the packages. But she still couldn't call him sir and she didn't ask him to come back soon, either.

He walked back to the car. Suki was asleep. She'd wiped her mouth and was looking better; not a lot, but some. She roused groggily when he opened the door and got in.

"Get me somethin' pretty?" she asked.

"Christ, I dunno, you tell me."

Frank found a side street that had been abandoned to the blazing heat. Beyond a tall cinderblock wall covered with graffiti, an apartment complex sweltered under the afternoon sun. Countless air conditioners emitted a restless, insectile drone. Frank opened Suki's door and helped her out, unwrapped her from the curtain and held it loosely around her while she stiffly, painfully, climbed into the newly purchased panties.

Two boys on skateboards came rolling toward them, wheels double-clicking on the expansion grooves of the sidewalk.

"Better hurry," Frank suggested.

"Fuck 'em," Suki said, in no mood for modesty. Frank held the curtain around her as the boys tore on by, staring at one long, half-exposed leg, one of them saying to the other, "Oh, man, too cool. You see that?" But they didn't stick around, just kept clacking away; Frank's glowering countenance ensured that.

She couldn't hook her bra. She turned her back to Frank and he fumbled with it, got it connected. Suki hiked up her pants, worked the blouse on over her shoulders, fastened the buttons with trembling fingers.

"Lookin' good," Frank offered.

"Like hell. I feel like a well-dressed stiff."

Frank couldn't argue the point. Her face was still in desperate need of a washcloth and her hair was a wreck.

She sank back onto the seat, wincing.

"Can you walk?" Frank asked.

"A little, I guess. Why?"

"We've got to dump the car somewhere. It'd draw attention if I had to carry you around afterward, though."

"I can walk."

"You sure?"

She gave him a tiny reassuring smile. "Yeah."

He drove to Carson Street. Suki asked him to pull into a supermarket parking lot and buy her a few things: a gallon jug

196

of drinking water, a comb and brush, a pair of thongs, a sack of sugar, a dishcloth.

"Sugar? What for?"

"I'm hungry, Frank. I'm not really in the mood to answer a bunch of questions, okay?"

"Sure, fine."

Frank bought her the items she'd asked for and a few of his own. He sloshed water on the dishcloth for her and she washed her face, rinsed out her mouth. Frank wet his beard and spread shaving cream on it. Using the rearview mirror, he shaved with a pair of Bic razors, using one until it began to pull, finishing with the second.

"Better," she said, looking at him. "Almost human."

"You too."

"Thanks so much, Mr. Limosin."

"Maybe you better just call me Frank."

"Yeah, all right."

As they tooled up Carson Street, she combed out her hair. Frank grew more and more antsy to ditch the Ferrari.

He passed a Denny's restaurant and turned right at the next side street, went up two blocks and turned right again, parked in front of a dirty stucco house with a waist-high Cyclone fence protecting a dried-out lawn overrun with weeds.

They got out. Suki opened the bag of sugar with shaking hands and unscrewed the gas cap and began dumping sugar into the car's tank.

Frank watched, not bothering to say anything. If there was some way to make money off the Ferrari he'd have done it, but his forte was unarmed robbery, not car theft. He'd just get into trouble, trying to unload the car in a strange town. At least she hadn't set the sonofabitch on fire.

She capped the tank and poured what was left of the water over the cap and the car's body to wash away all trace of the sugar.

Frank wiped prints from the car as best he could, and left the key in the ignition. He steadied Suki as she took faltering steps toward the Denny's. She didn't look too bad though, just a little hollow around the eyes. Inside the restaurant, Suki went straight to the ladies' room while Frank called the local Greyhound bus station. Reunited, they sat at a booth in the back. Exhaustion showed in Suki's eyes, but beyond that she was looking almost like her old self.

"Hungry?" Frank asked.

"Ugh, no. Maybe some tea." Suddenly she stared at him. "Jesus Christ, you forgot to get the money, didn't you?"

"Money?"

"My *money*, Frank. The three hundred thousand. It was probably right there in the house somewhere."

He stared back. "I was in a hurry, trying to get you out of there."

"Goddammit." Her eyes flashed. "That bastard's got all the money again."

"Keep your voice down."

"Shit," she said. "I was rich."

"Now all you've got is your skin."

A softer look filled her eyes. "Yeah, thanks. I didn't thank you yet, did I?"

"No hurry. You're still hurting." He leaned back, tired, gestured toward the phones. "Couple of buses a day leave for Vegas. Or Salt Lake City."

"So?"

He gave her a curious look. "So California doesn't appeal to me right now. In case you forgot, I've got trouble there."

"What makes you think I want to go anywhere?"

"Christ, what's that supposed to mean?"

"I'm staying. That plain enough?"

He glowered at her. "What for? The money's not worth it. Hell, you couldn't get it anyway."

"It's not the money. It's Mink."

"You *crazy*?"

A fierce, determined, wounded look came over her face. In a low voice she said, "I *screamed*, Frank. He said I would,

198

he *told* me I would, and I made up my mind I'd never give him the satisfaction, but I did anyway because it was horrible and it hurt so bad I wanted to die. I never hurt like that before in my life. I wanted to die, Frank. Really. He was going to kill me like that. If you hadn't come along, I would've died—him watching, smiling. Her too. I can't just walk away from that like nothing happened."

"No one's asking you to."

"You are. You sure are. If I leave, Mink gets away with it. I want to hurt him, Frank."

"How?"

"I don't know how; I've got to think. Just I know I can't go off somewhere and forget about what he did to me."

"Christ, Suki—"

A waitress came over, slim, flat-chested, with small eyes and stringy, lifeless hair. She cast envious glances at Suki as Frank ordered tea and a toasted cheese sandwich.

After she left, Suki said, "How'd you find me, anyway? I still almost can't believe it."

He gave her a brief account of the dry walk out of the De Baca Mountains, the wild ride with Hooker to Roswell, the Lear flight to Reno. Their waitress arrived with crockery rattling in her pale fingers, left again, mouth pouty.

Frank told Suki how he'd found the neighborhood, how he'd walked its streets since before dawn and then seen Danny leave in the Trans Am and return again later in the Ferrari.

"I take back anything I ever said about you being dumb," Suki said solemnly, dunking her tea bag.

"You said that about me?"

"I think so. Maybe." She sipped her tea and a new spasm took her. Her face drained of color and her body shuddered.

"You all right?"

"I guess. I told you, Frank, that son of a bitch just about killed me. My stomach hurts and my brain still feels all kinda crookedy."

"I'm not surprised."

She wrinkled her nose, gave him a look.

"What?"

"That . . . smell. You don't smell it?"

"It's us. I told you, it's been a bad couple of days for both of us."

"Jesus, I'm surprised they don't throw us out."

"I think our waitress'd like to. Look, messing around with this Mink character is a goddamned lousy idea."

"I know. I'm gonna anyway. I'm too tired to talk about it right now, though. What I really want is a shower. And a place to conk out a while. I don't feel all that good."

He didn't want to argue about it, not here. Time enough later to try talking her out of it. He stood up. "I'll call us a cab, get us a motel somewhere, away from here."

"A motel?" She smiled, actually managing to bat her eyes at him. He couldn't believe it—after all she'd been through, she could still joke around.

"Jesus," he said, wandering away.

23

The drop grew larger. It glistened like a wet, turgid eye, becoming larger and larger, heavier and heavier . . . until . . .

Thip.

Suki screamed.

Frank came out of bed like a derailing Amtrak, tangled in his sheets. Light from streetlamps filtered through the curtains of the Oasis Motel, room 109. Suki was sitting up, shaking; the scream still lingered in the room.

Frank sat on the edge of her bed and put an arm around her shoulders.

"You okay?"

"Yeah, fine. Just a bad dream."

"Musta been a dandy."

"I was back at that house, in the basement, and . . . and ice water was dripping on my stomach."

"Jesus," Frank murmured.

She moved forward, put her arms around him. Her hair had a fresh scent to it, something herbal. She clung to him for a few seconds, then pushed the blankets aside and said, "Get in, okay?" She scooted over, looking at him. "Please."

He crawled in, dressed only in his underwear. She put an arm across his chest and snuggled against him. "Thank you."

"Don't mention it."

Within a minute she was asleep, and Frank was left staring at blobs of light crawling on the ceiling as traffic passed by on Carson Street. Suki wasn't wearing anything, not a stitch, but Frank was almost used to that by now. Fanny, too.

After ten minutes of meandering, clouded philosophy, Frank dropped off again as well, guilt temporarily suspended.

Waking, Frank felt Suki's hand gripping an erection that was almost painful, but she wasn't awake yet so he cautiously extricated himself from her grasp.

She woke up in mid extraction. Smiled sleepily at him and opened her fist. "I was dreaming about this giant boa constrictor," she said.

He was fifty-four years old, going on fifty-five, and he didn't have an answer to that. What Fanny had called it, of all the damnfool things, was his "Henry." "Henry up tonight?" she'd ask, when the kids were young and had eager, questing ears. She sometimes called lovemaking "pokin' Henry," when she was in a frisky mood. Lots of variations on the theme.

"What that is, Frank, is a big snake."

"I know what a goddamn boa constrictor is."

"Hey, look, it's morning already."

"Twelve minutes past seven, to be precise." He swung his legs over the edge of the bed and planted his feet solidly on the floor, fervently wishing that the evidence of his longing for her would depart more quickly than it was.

"I'm starved," Suki said.

"Got no right to be. You haven't eaten in how long now? Day a half, two days?"

She stuck her tongue out at him and crawled slowly off the end of the bed. She stood with a soulful groan. "God, everything's busted."

Didn't look busted to Frank. A red spot on her belly was all, like a rash. Dim orange light came through the curtains, enhancing her tan. She slowly moved her body, arched her back, "ooching" and "aahing" and "eeeping" as she twisted and turned, testing muscles that had been strained to the breaking point by yesterday's ordeal. Whatever internal messages her body was sending her, she still looked good to Frank, a whole lot better than she had yesterday, which wasn't helping him a bit with his immediate problem.

After a long, lazy shower, she eased herself into bra and panties, slacks and blouse, pushed her feet into thongs. Frank wore new jeans and a shirt creased with fold marks where it'd come straight out of a J.C. Penney package. His old clothes were wadded in a dumpster behind the motel.

"Breakfast?" she asked.

"After."

"After what?"

"After you tell me last night's talk was just talk, that you're not thinking about going after this Mink guy anymore."

Her eyes flashed. "No way."

"Jesus. That's a no-win situation there, you know that?"

"All my life I'll remember what he did to me, Frank. It's something I'll never forget, and you want me to just walk away from it."

"Alive, yes. I want that, very much. I'm sorry for being such an asshole about it, though."

"I'm gonna be careful."

"Great. Want to tell me what the big plan is, then?"

"I haven't got one yet. But I will."

"Even greater."

Tears shone in her eyes. She sat on a bed, hands in her lap. "I want to hurt him, Frank. I want to hurt him like he hurt me. I've *got* to."

"You can't." He sat down on the opposite bed, facing her. "Some things just aren't possible."

"Why not?"

"For one thing, I don't think you've got the stomach for it. At least, I hope you don't."

"I've got the stomach."

"You could tie this guy down, torture him, listen to him scream? You could do that?"

She was silent a long time, looking down at her hands. "If someone else did it to him, I'd be glad. Maybe I wouldn't want to watch or anything, but I'd be glad, just knowing."

"That's not the same thing, not by a mile."

A tear rolled down her cheek. "Then *what*, Frank? What'm I supposed to *do*?"

"Call it a learning experience, move on—"

"No! I can't, I *can't*! Don't you understand, he tried to take me apart, he tried to rip apart my goddamn *brain*!"

She began to sob.

"Hey, Jesus, honey, don't . . ." His words dried up. Don't what? Don't cry? No reason to cry, just 'cause this psychotic son of a bitch tied you down, tortured you, almost killed you.

Damn good reason to get out of town, though. Good reason to keep out of his way in the future, too.

"It didn't happen to you," she said, not looking at him. "It didn't happen to you."

"I know, but Jesus, Suki—"

"I didn't tell you everything. He told me . . . he said he was going to use the heat."

"The heat?"

"Boiling oil, Frank. When I couldn't stand the cold any more, he was going to drip hot oil on me. He said he'd use it

204

when I asked him to, not before. He told me it'd hurt an awful lot more than the cold water, but that I'd beg him for it anyway, just to have a change. I thought I'd never ask because that was crazy, but I was about to. I was almost ready. I was going crazy. He was going to drip oil on me till I died. He was going to fucking *cook* me, Frank. The son of a bitch was going to cook my guts, one drop at a time. How long would I have lasted like that? A few days? Maybe a whole goddamn *week*? And I was gonna ask for it. That's what he did to me. If you hadn't come along, that's how I was gonna die."

Christ.

Jesus H. Christ.

Mink was a monster, or worse; his mother, too. Which made the idea of hauling ass all the more sensible, and the sooner the better. Frank told her so.

Suki shook her head. "I can't."

He stood up, fished around in his wallet, handed her five twenties and a hundred, turned away.

"What's this for?"

"You're on your own," he said curtly. "You want to play patty-cake with a rabid dog, do it alone. I'm gone."

She raised her eyes, hurt.

He said, "I'm real sorry this creep hurt you so bad, but I've got enough to worry about without going after some homicidal maniac." He opened the door, walked out.

He stood in the early morning sun. The day was still cool, but cloudless. It was going to be another scorcher. Which damn well figured; this was the goddamned desert.

The door opened behind him. Suki came out and slipped her arm through his.

"Okay, how about we turn him in to the police, Frank? We could just find out stuff about his operation and when we know enough we could turn him in, let the police handle it. That'd be safe, wouldn't it? Huh?"

"Aw, shit."

Layered defense. Every operation in every city they'd been in since the scare they'd had in Louisville had been built around a system of layered defenses.

Take Reno, for example. There was the house, the Citadel, in which Simon and Charlotte lived, and from which the yacks made their calls. It was important to have the men and women who actually made the fraudulent sales pitches in close contact at all times, in the fold. The house had been rented by a Mr. Cyrus Greenwold, acting as a proxy for the New Chance Agency, an aspiring job-placement firm with a newly acquired business license in Washoe County. Daniel Turpin, Mink's right-hand man, had used the Greenwold ID, just one of a dozen he might have used. A bank of eight phones had been installed by Nevada Bell for the New Chance Agency without anyone raising an eyebrow.

New Chance itself would generate no revenue, however. The agency was a shell, a mere name under which property had been leased and phones installed. Employees of J. Alan Morrow & Associates, a second bogus firm, would actually staff the phones and solicit investors. J. Alan Morrow had been created by the ever-capable Daniel Turpin, using the name Frederick W. Lowe. A two-room office in a business complex on Second Street had been leased to J. Alan Morrow for a period of one year. Other than Turpin's moonfaced visage, no connection whatever existed between J. Alan Morrow and New Chance. The judicious use of local law firms acting as subagents for the new firms rendered the connection even more tenuous.

An apartment was rented in the name of Chester Fine, yet another of Turpin's alter egos. Three blocks off Kietzke Lane in the Woodridge complex, the apartment would be the dropping-off point for a "blind" courier, hired locally, whose only job was to load the contents of six private post office boxes into bags, one for each yack employed by J. Alan Morrow & Associates, and take them to the apartment via a meandering, predetermined route. The courier would make the run on Mondays, Wednesdays and Fridays at 4 P.M., followed discreetly by Benny, Isaac, and Jersey, each in his own vehicle. If the courier was tailed by anyone, anyone at all, a radio message would be sent, warning a woman by the name of Elana Lepori to leave the apartment immediately, and causing Mink's entire operation to fold up and be on its way out of town in minutes.

If the courier was clean, the mail, mostly checks made out to J. Alan Morrow & Associates, would arrive at the Woodridge apartment and be scanned immediately by the competent Miss Lepori for electronic bugs that might have found their way into the flow. Upon passing that test, the mail would be taken to the Flint Street house via a circuitous route, passing again through a protective sieve of countersurveillance by Benny, Isaac, and Jersey. At Flint Street, each piece would be opened and each check thoroughly scrutinized, examined under the light of a fluorescent lamp, and judged valid or invalid. It would then all be sorted, placed into one of ten manila folders, and returned to the Woodridge apartment.

The following day, or on Monday, in the case of Friday's take, another locally hired girl would appear at the Woodridge apartment, pick up the manila folders and deliver them to yet another office, leased in the name of Paul R. Kline, civil engineer. The office, however, had no sign out front; it was, in fact, a nameless bin. Its secretary, another local hired by J. Alan Morrow & Associates, knew the name Paul Kline only as the person or entity from whom or from which J. Alan Morrow had sublet the office. Her only job was to answer the phone, read magazines and chew gum, display no imagination whatever, nor show any interest in Morrow's affairs, and lock up the office on Monday, Tuesday, and Thursday afternoons, when she left it to deposit the delivered checks into each of ten accounts maintained by Morrow & Associates at banks all over the city.

Surveillance was maintained at each of these nodes, and during each transition between them. Simon and Charlotte and all the other principals involved monitored radios tuned to a little-used VHF frequency assigned to the U.S. Bureau of Land Management, listening for the single word "Redsnake," which would send them all fleeing to a previously agreed upon location, in this case, a shopping mall in Sacramento, a hundred and twenty miles west of Reno.

This scenario, which Mink and Charlotte had developed and improved over the years, was a finely honed defense; the few strands that led back to the Citadel were tenuous, well guarded, easily severed.

And now, the day after Suki and her rescuer made their escape, the defense came into play, without, however, the dreaded codeword "Redsnake" being uttered, scattering them like so many dropped marbles. Simon and Charlotte were in a suite at Bally's, Reno's largest hotel, registered as Glen and Tilly Eberhard. Before she left Sherman Oaks, California, and flew with her son to Reno for a long-awaited vacation, Tilly had slipped on a wet tile floor and suffered a broken nose, poor thing, but she had elected not to cancel their trip on that account because Glen so desperately needed to escape the rat race for a while. Tilly only told this story once, to a bellhop who feigned interest, but that was sufficient. No one at Bally's was aware that Glen Eberhard was otherwise known as Saul Garrick, founder of the New Chance Agency, or that he also had an apartment in Reno on Lakeside Drive, rented in the name of Reid Farris. This last identity was in fact Simon's "official" identity in Reno, if Simon could be said to have so concrete a thing as an identity. Simon, the "real" Simon, was vapor, as insubstantial as fog. He had a driver's license in the name of Reid Farris, and the new Ferrari that Suki and her champion had taken off in had been purchased in that name.

As Margaret Farris, Reid's mother, Charlotte Voorhees was equally vaporous. The address Reid and Margaret shared, their social security numbers, credit cards, even the modest bank account they held in common, could be used to track these two apparitions only into a gray and featureless void.

The vast web of subterfuge required to create these defenses—the apartments that had to be rented, couriers and secretaries hired, phone services installed, businesses and bank accounts set up—kept Daniel Turpin extremely busy in the six weeks prior to Simon and Charlotte's move to Reno. Into each new city, Danny led the parade, Simon and Charlotte entering securely in his wake. Once things were settled, Danny moved on. Next stop was Tampa, Florida, where Simon's traveling minstrel show would bleed retirees who flocked in droves to the comfort and safety of their Sunbelt condos. Danny's loyalty to the Voorheeses, his penchant for intrigue, his boundless energy and organizational acumen accounted for his salary of $360,000 a year. A mere pittance, in that Simon and Charlotte had grossed something over ten million the previous year and were well on their way to surpassing that total in the current year.

Charlotte stared silently out the west-facing window of their eighteenth-floor suite; her bony fingers explored the bandage that covered her nose. Simon phoned the residence of Reid Farris on Lakeside Drive and punched in the four-digit code to retrieve messages on the apartment's answering machine. There were but two, the first from a drunken woman screaming furiously into the phone, calling him Gus, telling him to get the hell back home *right now* 'cause she *knew* he was with some floozy, and he was the world's all-time rottenest son'vabish. The second message, considerably less addled, was left by Detective John Shroeder of the Washoe County Sheriff's Department. Shroeder informed him that his new Ferrari had been found abandoned in Carson City, blocking traffic on a main street, keys in the ignition, and had been towed to the Carson City Police Department impound yard. And would Mr. Farris please be so kind as to contact Detective Shroeder concerning the incident at his earliest convenience. The detective left a number.

Well, the Ferrari was a loss anyway, had been from the moment Suki and the guy who'd saved her took off in it. Mink had never even set eyes on it. Lost in that same instant was the Reid Farris identity. Already Danny was slipping through the bureaucratic underground, creating yet another "official" identity for Simon, and one for Charlotte. He had a headache but seemed otherwise unhurt by yesterday's events.

Simon left the room, rode the elevator down to the lobby, and called Detective Shroeder on a pay phone. Charlotte was still staring out the window when he returned.

"They went to Carson City," Simon said.

She turned, waiting for more. Stranger, in her own way, than the boy she'd raised.

"Police found the car a few minutes after midnight last night. Lights on, doors open, right in the middle of the main drag. Witnesses say a couple of kids left it there, ran off. The engine was frozen. Sugar in the gas tank."

"Suki's work."

Simon nodded. "Or the old man's. What we may infer from all this is that they ditched the car in Carson, loaded the tank with sugar, and took off. Later, some kids found it and decided to take it for a joyride; not long into their little adventure the engine seized up on them." He paused. "Detective John Shroeder would very much like it if Mr. Farris would come in, file an official report on the stolen car, go through the whole nine yards, and then claim what's left of his vehicle."

Charlotte stared at him.

Simon shrugged. "Reid Farris doesn't exist anymore." He picked up the phone, dialed the Rancho Sierra Motel on Fourth Street, asked for room 22.

Mote lay on the bed nearest the bathroom, shoes off, alleviating his boredom by trying to balance a half-full can of

Coors on his forehead. Jersey stared at the television in a catatonic glaze. Some championship bowling tournament going on in Ohio somewhere, on cable TV; this tall skinny dufe in glasses beating the shit out of last week's PBA champ, 209 to 167 in the eighth frame. New skinny-ass champ this week, looked like. Guy's wife was sitting there in the audience, already spending the first-place prize of $35,000, lips bunched up like little rosebuds, eyes bright.

The phone rang. Mote spasmed, drenching the front of his T-shirt with beer. "Shit, man," he said, lunging off the bed.

Jersey turned down the tube, picked up the phone. "Yeah, this's Jersey."

Mink said, "We've got a lead on the girl."

"Yeah?"

"Carson City."

Mote was still cussing. Jersey threw an ashtray at him, clipped him on the jaw with it. He turned away. "Yeah, okay, what d'you want us to do?"

"I want Benny, Isaac, and Mote on the roads south and east of Carson." A pause; a map rustled in the background. "Put Mote on U.S. Fifty, east. Benny and Isaac south, on Fifty west and Three-ninety-five."

"Yeah, sure. What about me?"

"I'd like you to nose around the bus stations down there, talk to taxi drivers, see if you can get a line on where they might have gone."

"Yeah, okay, right away."

"Mrs. Garrick will coordinate the search from the Woodridge apartment. You've got the phone number, I trust?"

Jersey closed his eyes. Christ, the Bitch again. "Yeah."

"Make sure the others have it, too. And Jersey . . ."

"Yeah?"

"I'm giving a bounty of fifty thousand dollars to the man who brings Suki in; ten thousand more for that guy she's with. Tell the others."

"Sure, okay, Mr. Garrick."

"Get on it." Simon hung up. Kind of like his old lady, but not quite as difficult to talk to. The Bitch had a corncob up her wazoo, no doubt about it.

"That hurt, Jers," Mote said, rubbing his jaw. "Shouldn't throw stuff like that."

"Get your shoes on, bucko. We're rolling."

24

W hatcha looking for?" Suki asked.
"Something cheap, invisible."

"Invisible?"

"The kind of car you see, but you don't see. Something
that wouldn't stand out parked all alone in an empty lot.
What we don't want is a goddamned Edsel."

"An Edsel? What's that?"

Frank shook his head, ran a finger down a column of the
folded newspaper. They sat in a coffee shop in the relative
morning quiet of the Carson Horseshoe Club. Suki stared at
a lighted board with numbers on it, GAME 87 lit up on its
side. A waitress drifted by and filled Frank's coffee cup.
Her eyes snagged momentarily on his finger.

"Lawn mower," he said. "Chicago, Nineteen and sixty-
two." The girl smiled uncertainly, moved away.

Suki nudged him. "What's that?"

"What's what?"

"That." She pointed at the lighted board.

"Keno."

"What's that?"

"Gambling game."

"How's it work?"

"DamnifIknow." He pushed the paper over to her, rubbed his eyes. "Here, see if anything strikes your fancy."

She pushed it back. "Very goddamn hilarious."

"Huh?"

"You think that's funny?"

"Do I think what the hell's funny?"

"I can't read, Frank. You gotta know that by now." She looked away.

He stared at her. "You can't?"

"Pretty much."

He didn't know what to say.

"Don't look at me like that. I'm not a bug or something. I can read 'See Spot run. Run, Spot, run. See Dick ball Jane. Ball Jane, Dick,'—that kinda stuff." Her cheeks were burning with color.

"Look, I didn't mean to—"

"Yeah, I know. It's not your fault." She'd withdrawn into a shell, mouth tight.

Now what? Frank thought. His foot was so far in his mouth he had argyle at the back of his throat. What could he say? C-R-O-K she'd inscribed on Mink's forehead. Crook. Yeah, hell, he should've known. Should've at least guessed. Christ, up in the De Baca Mountains he'd even offered her a book.

"Look, I'm sorry."

"Sure."

"I should've known. I didn't, but I should've, so I'm sorry, okay?"

The intensity of her silence gave off fumes.

"Okay?"

She gave him a sidelong glance. "Think I'm dumb, right?"

"Nope."

"Well, I'm not."

"Jesus, I just said—"

"I can't read, and I can't change flat tires, and there's lots of other things I can't do, but I'm not dumb, Frank."

"Gotcha."

"Just don't ever forget it."

"Never. Look, there's that goddamn keno board over there. I've seen those things for thirty years now, never figured out how they work yet."

"Don't try to make me feel better, Frank. I dropped out of regular school in the sixth grade. They sent me to some kind of special place, but it just didn't work out. There was this old teacher there with gray hair who was always putting his arm around me and squeezing my shoulder in this special reading class, like he was trying to help me out. He tried to feel up all the girls, not just me. You could tell he thought everyone there was a moron, but some of them were smart. Like me. Just . . . I don't know. We got left behind somehow."

"You could take an adult class, learn to read. It's not too late."

"Maybe." She stared off at the keno board again.

He picked up the paper. "How 'bout this? 'Seventy-nine Dodge Omni, great condition, real clean. Sunroof, mags; six hundred dollars."

"Mag wheels, sunroof, six hundred? It's a dog," she said. "Guy's lyin' like a rug."

"Probably. How about an 'eighty-seven Ford Tempo GL, air, fifty-five hundred?"

She sipped her tea. "How much you looking to spend?"

"Not that much." He read another: "Here's a 'seventy-four Chevy Nova, V-six. Eight hundred fifty. A goddamn Nova wouldn't attract attention in a phone booth."

She smiled then. It looked good on her. "Dad had a Nova once," she said. "Piss yellow, Ma called it. Really attractive color. I can't hardly remember what the darn thing looked like now."

"There, you see? That's what I mean by invisible."

"Go for it then."

He went to a bank of phones, sank a quarter, dialed the number.

An elderly woman answered. "Yeah?"

"About that car, the Nov—"

"Bobbiiiee, it's for you. Bob*biiiiiiiiiiiiiie*!"

Frank waited, ear throbbing.

A man came on the line, in his forties by the sound of his voice. "Yeah?"

"Still got that Nova for sale?"

"Yep."

"How's it run?"

"Good. Got eighty-two thousand miles on 'er, but she's a runner."

"What color?"

"Christ, I dunno; kinda faded yellow. Got practically new tires on 'er though. Goodyears."

"Where're you at?"

"Pleasant Valley. South of Reno. Pagni Lane, just westa the fire station."

"Tell you what, Mr . . ."

"Curtis. Bob Curtis."

"I'll give you eleven hundred for it, Bob."

Silence. Then, "I was askin' eight-fifty, what's the deal here?"

"Two things. One, you drive it on down to Carson City, be here inside an hour. Two, you leave the plates on it."

"One, I can do. Two, that's against the law."

"Plates are worth an extra two-fifty. You can tell 'em you forgot. They might fine you twenty bucks."

More silence. Then, "How do I find you?"

"Horseshoe Club, downtown. Know where that is?"

"Course. Lived here mosta my life."

"I'll be around back, holding a newspaper. Hair's kinda gray. I run on the large side, about two-forty."

"I'll be there. Thirty minutes, 'bout."

By noon, Frank and Suki were in Reno, rolling along South Virginia Street in a Chevy Nova the approximate color of a clouded urine specimen. Minor rust damage and a good-sized dent in the passenger-side door, scrapes and dings too numerous to count, but its engine was in good shape, transmission too, and its seat cushions weren't too far gone. The radio was tuned to a country station, KBUL, FM 98; when Frank started up the car after giving Bob Curtis eleven one-hundred-dollar bills, Hank Williams was blowing the carbon out of his lungs singing "Lovesick Blues."

"Ever been to Reno?" Frank asked.

Suki shook her head. "Not before yesterday."

"So you don't actually know where this house of Mink's is, do you?"

"I could find it. Same way you did."

"That's what I'm afraid of. First thing we want to do is find a place to hole up. Then we want to quit looking so much like ourselves."

"Say what?"

"Disguises," Frank said. "Your hair in particular. We've got to do something about the way we look."

She looked at him. "Maybe I could. But how're you gonna hide two hundred and sixty pounds?"

He feigned a hurt look. "Two-forty-five, sugar."

"Whatever."

"I'll think of something."

"Frank?"

"Yeah?"

"I appreciate all this. Really. It's not something you have to do, and it's costing money."

"Yeah? Well I still don't know what the hell we're doing here. There's no goddamn profit in revenge. If things start looking bad, I'll probably tie you up, dump you in the trunk, haul ass, and *keep* you tied up in some out-of-the-way place somewhere until Mink gets himself good and lost."

She gave him a big, bright smile. "You care, don't you?"

He looked over at her and said, "Oh, Jesus Christ."

"No, you really do, huh?"

"Don't go making some big deal out of nothing, okay?"

"Mountains out of molehills."

"Huh?"

"What you say is, 'Don't go making mountains out of mole-hills.' See, I'm not so dumb. Except what you said wasn't a molehill, it was more like . . . like . . . Fuji or something."

"I said I'd tie you the hell up."

"Exactly."

"Might be the best idea I've had since I got out of the army back in fifty-four. A gag might not be such a bad idea either."

"It shows you care, Frank. That's the thing." A smug look appeared on her face.

"I'll be goddamned—"

She put a hand on his arm. "Don't let it worry you, okay? Anyway, we *are* looking for a motel, aren't we?"

"Aw, Jesus."

"How do I look?" Suki did a turn for him, showing off her new outfit.

"Stunning." Frank sat on a bed in the Shamrock Inn Motel on North Center Street, staring at her.

"Bet you tell that to all the dumpy old broads."

"As many as'll listen, sure."

Suki posed for the mirror, fluffing the worn cotton dress, tugging on a shoulder. She turned sideways to examine the way the foam rubber bulged her midsection, adding thirty pounds to her frame and tripling the size of her breasts. The hem of the dress came just below mid calf, revealing nine inches of oversized nylon hose that hung in soft, bagging folds around her ankles. Her feet were wedged into old lumpy shoes they'd found at a thrift shop on Gentry Way. Dark glasses covered her eyes. She squinted at the mirror and adjusted the short gray René of Paris wig they'd picked up at Bellissima's on First Street, near the downtown casino area.

"How old you think I look?" she asked, whirling.

"Ninety-five, minimum."

"Seriously."

"Seriously, maybe sixty, sixty-five; at a distance. Kinda senile, with that hose squirreled down around your ankles like that. Just don't let anyone get too close a look at your face or hands."

"Wait'll I lump on some pancake foundation, lighten my face, rub a little too much rouge on my cheeks, and put some eye shadow under my eyes. You won't recognize me."

"I don't now."

"I mean, it'll make me look even older."

"Hop to it. We've still got things to do today."

"In a minute. This isn't right." She unzipped the back of her dress, shrugged it off and let it fall to the carpet. She stood there in bra and panties and some kind of high-tech spandex horror hacked off at the top and bottom, packed with foam rubber around her middle. "Itches," she said.

"Why am I not surprised?"

She adjusted the foam, retied a tie, bent stiffly and pulled up her dress.

"Zip a gal up?" she said.

"A dotty old broad, you mean."

"Whatever."

He stood with difficulty, zipped her up, caught a glimpse of himself in the mirror. He stopped, fascinated at the sight of this old duffer staring back at him, totally bald, glasses with heavy black rims, blue suit way out of style but who gave a shit? Not the old duffer. Suspenders. Weight about three-fifty, with all the foam padding. If you couldn't get smaller, the only thing left was to get larger. He looked bloated, an oil drum with arms and legs. Still had big shoulders, but they didn't dominate the way they had before.

She rubbed the top of his head. "Miss the fuzz?"

"Yeah. Feels drafty up there."

"Well, you look like such a sweetheart without it. Harmless, too. Probly feed pigeons in the park." She stood up on tiptoe, pulled his head over, kissed him square in the middle of his naked dome.

"Shit," he said.

"Looks deserted," she said, disappointed.

"Looked that way when you were in the basement screaming, too."

"Jesus, Frank!"

He turned to her. "I just don't want you to forget what kind of dangerous slime you're screwing around with here."

"I know what Mink and his mother are."

"Just keep it in mind." He pushed his soiled homburg back a few inches on his head.

They were parked on Ridge Street in front of an architect's office, just west of the intersection of Ridge and Flint. From there they had an oblique view of the clapboard mansion, cooking in the day's heat. Sweat formed on Frank's brow. He mopped it away.

"Think they've skedaddled?" Suki asked.

"Don't go talking to anyone, either. Your voice doesn't jibe with your wrinkles."

"I'll try to remember. So, what do you think?"

"About what?"

She stared at him. "Christ, you gone senile too, Frank? Think they've run off?"

"Oh. Who knows? I would've. Maybe."

"Maybe?"

"From what you told me, this is some expensive operation he's got going here. I guess he'd want to keep it going if he could."

"That's what I thought. Mink wouldn't want to run. He's not the type to—"

"Uh-oh."

"What? Oh, Jesus, Frank."

A taxi pulled up in front of the old house and a man and woman got out. The man was slender; the woman reed-thin, with red hair.

"My God," Suki said, voice quivering. "That's them."

"Okay, okay, calm down."

The two went up the walk, opened the front door, went into the house. The taxi rolled away.

Suki began to tremble. "Jesus, Frank."

"Okay. Here, remember this number. Eight four four, seven one one seven."

"What's that?" she asked.

"Real estate broker."

"Huh? Why?"

"Forgot the number already, have you?"

She hadn't; she reeled it off.

"Good," Frank said. "Old bag's short-term memory's still intact, anyway." He started the engine and drove away.

"Meyer and Dunn Realty," said the voice.

"Yeah," said Frank. "I'm interested in that property on Ridge Street. You got a sign out front. Two-story brick job, wisteria all over the front porch, trim needs paint."

"I'll connect you with Mrs. Meyer. Who may I say is calling, please?"

"Mr. Steven Wiley."

"Thank you. Please hold." Frank got a muted earful of George Gershwin's "I Got Plenty of Nuttin'. "

"What'd they say?" Suki asked.

221

He clamped a hand over the mouthpiece. "I'm on hold. And old ladies don't chew gum. At least they don't snap it like that. Swallow a denture that way, end up in a rest home somewhere, brain damaged."

"You think?"

"This is Gloria Meyer, Mr. Wiley. How may I help you?"

"I'm interested in that place over on Ridge—"

"Oh, yes. The Pratt place. Beautiful, isn't it?"

"Could be."

"Well, yes. It needs a little exterior work, but that's really a minor—"

"What I was wondering, is it available for rent or lease?"

"Yeeeeess." She seemed hesitant. "In a manner of speaking. It depends on the use one intends to make of it."

"How's it zoned?"

"That's quite a complex question, Mr. Wiley. It's never been a place of business, so for residential use the house may be grandfathered in under the old R-five zoning, which was multi-family dwelling and offices. R-five's been superceded, howev—"

"But it's available for residential use?"

"Yeeeeeess. However, the owner is primarily interested in selling the property, not maintaining it as a rental. Therefore, no long-term lease is possible, and it isn't—"

"Wife and I wouldn't be needing a long-term commitment."

"Well, in that case, perhaps something can be worked out."

"We'd like to look it over today," Frank said. "If that could be arranged."

"I've got . . . well, I suppose I could fit you in in, say, half an hour. Either that or tomorrow afternoon some—"

"Half an hour would be dandy."

"Then I'll see you at the property, Mr. Wiley."

"Bring papers," Frank said. "We might work something out this afternoon."

"Is there a reason for all this hurry, Mr. Wiley?"

"Nope. The wife and I just like old places, and the area, that's all. We've had enough of hotels."

Inside, the place was reasonably clean. Hardwood floors, a few scatter rugs here and there. Casement windows with several cracked panes. Fireplace with a massive walnut mantel. The kitchen had a huge double sink, expansive white tile counters, a view of a fenced yard and more flowering wisteria. Catalpa trees with long curving pods rustled in the breeze; honeysuckle grew rampant up one side of the house. A basement, four bedrooms, three baths with old fixtures, big open living room. The place was dusty, battered and worn, but comfortable in spite of its wounds, filled with a palpable sense of history.

Frank stumped through the house on a cane, leaning on it heavily. Suki kept in the background, fingering the curtains; stoop-shouldered, quiet, faking some sort of dumb-ass limp.

A window in one of the rear bedrooms gave a view of the front and side of the clapboard mansion on Flint Street. Suki stood staring at the mansion for a long time.

Two thousand two hundred twenty-two dollars a month, Mrs. Meyer said. The price was not negotiable, by order of the owner, Helen Pratt, an eccentric old biddy without a businesslike bone in her body, who wanted not a penny more than $2222 a month, and not a penny less. Something to do with what a card reader had recently told her.

Frank tried not to wince. "Fine," he said in the grainy voice he was cultivating. "We'll take it."

"I'll need the first month's rent in advance, and a fifty-percent security deposit."

"Fine."

Gloria Meyer filled out a boilerplate rental agreement and gave Frank a startled look at the sight of the cash. She handed Steven Wiley a receipt for $3333.00, a set of keys, and drove off in a charcoal Mercedes 300E before the day had begun to cool off appreciably. It was 4:16 P.M.

"Bought you a house," Frank groused, turning to Suki.

She gave him a kiss that left smudges. "Treat me so good, snookie. Told you you were an old sweetheart, didn't I?"

"Shit," he said.

wo birds with one stone. Simon found the economy of action agreeable.

He sat in the first-class section of United flight 516, bound for JFK airport in New York City with an hour layover in Denver, looking out at the dry brown mountains of Nevada as the 727 rolled along the taxiway toward the south end of the runway. Turn. Spool up, down. Then up again, and the big plane leapt forward, pressing him into the seat, speed building, wingtips beginning to rise, *bump*, and they were up. Reno sprawled below in the hot afternoon sun, the carcass of some eviscerated beast with its arteries and nerves exposed, decaying in the heat.

Bird one: a freebie. Reid Farris was on his way out of Reno. If the Ferrari investigation went anywhere at all, it would go to New York and turn to vapor. A Mr. Carl Sullivan would return, and Sullivan and Farris had nothing whatever in common, including the airlines on which they traveled.

Bird two was the actual reason for the trip: cash was needed. Though the flight east was necessary, it was little hardship; viewing his diamonds always gave Simon great pleasure. Five safe-deposit boxes in five banks under five assumed names. Over forty-one million dollars in diamonds sat in those five boxes, discounting gains in the diamond market in the time since the stones had been purchased. Forty-five million was a conservative estimate of their present worth.

Soon they'd have enough. Simon smiled, closed his eyes. Enough for what? And what was enough? A pleasant, circular dyad to ponder, the basis for an absorbing soliloquy to while away a few unburdened minutes.

The French Riviera; Rio; Macao. No, too common. Skiing the Hohe Tauern in Austria, perhaps; sampling twelve-year-olds in the more enlightened districts of Berlin. Yes, certainly. But what could be better than a quartet of *ten*-year-olds in the rackety, squalid depths of Katmandu, or a similar quartet of goatherders' offspring in the Tibetan city of Qagcaka? Or a death or two, here and there; something slow, exotic, exquisite, unique. The world was a playground, infinite in opportunity for one with imagination and a fondness for experimentation, and the resources to indulge them. Wealth is the universal standard by which men are truly judged. Money, not character, is the key that flings wide the world's doors. How much, though, was enough?

Ten-year-olds in Katmandu. A tremor ran through him. Perhaps another year, if that. He wasn't getting any younger. There was a time for all things, and Katmandu and Qagcaka were the songs of Lorelei in his blood.

Suki, though.

The reverie broke. Suki first. Suki was a loose cannon; she might still be dangerous. For safety's sake they would need money, a generous reserve of ready cash. Danny would soon leave for Florida to set up the Tampa operation; that would take a bundle. Fifty thousand to whoever brought Suki in, and if her saviour was taken too, another ten. Mink would require a new car, and the Reno operation might never bring in a nickel. Moving expenses, new identities, money for bribes.

Trouble, the Suki bitch was. So they needed cash, and all their money was in diamonds. Mink had to go to New York even though his heart, his *soul*, was in Reno tracking Suki.

But he'd be back in just over twenty-four hours. It'd be nice if Jersey and the others had captured her by then.

Because then . . .

Thip.

She screamed, muscles tearing. . . .

Thip.

Screamed again, louder, voice shattering. . . .

Thip.

And her mind was cracking, shrieks rupturing the tissues of her throat, entreating God, screaming at Him, which was a joke because there was no God, was no God, was no God; because if there was, if there was a capital-H Him, loving, benevolent and kind, how did one explain Simon Voorhees?

Now what? Jersey thought.

The bus station hadn't panned out. Dinky little place, and the girl there hadn't seen anyone like Suki or that overgrown son of a bitch she was with, who'd even managed to get the best of Simon Voorhees, alias Saul Garrick; heavy on the *rick* if you please.

Taxis'd come through for him, though. But what the hell did you do with it? This fat old fart, musta been sixty years old, said he'd driven this older fellow and a girl with nice white-blond hair from a Denny's restaurant up on Carson Street to a motel in the southern part of town, the Oasis. Yesterday, about four in the afternoon, maybe five.

So, okay, Jersey'd even taken the same cab, same goddamn driver, Denny's to the Oasis, gotten out, paid the $4.35, and what had it gotten him? Squat, that's what.

Owner of the Oasis remembered them—so what? Room 109; how did you forget a sweet little piece like that, and with a guy could be her father, too? Even showed Jersey the room for five bucks. Nothing. Maid had it cleaned up, and Jersey'd even talked to her, chunky little rag pusher, used the Oasis guy to cut through her Mex, and you think she'd know anything? Fuck no. What, you kiddin'?

No one even saw them leave the place.

Okay, then he'd gotten lucky. And so what? Found this other taxi driver, girl with braids and acne, couldn't've been over twenty-two, said she took them from a gas station a block or two from the Oasis just that morning to the middle of town, left them off on the corner, right by the Carson Nugget, biggest gambling place in town. Good, fine. Think they'd go in?

Hell no. Had to go into the goddamn Horseshoe Club up the street; cost Jersey another hour, tracking them down. But he'd done it, managed to get hold of some skinny waitress who was going off duty, no boobs, pretty fair legs though, pale as new ice, and she'd said, yeah, they were in that morning, saw 'em leave but she didn't see which way, or how, or where.

And that was it. Cold trail after that. A glacier was what it was after that. They walked out of the club and wandered right off the foggy rim of the world. He'd been good, he'd even been lucky, and what it all amounted to was shit.

"Tell me."

Fuck you all to hell and that tell-me shit, too. "It's Jersey. Ma'am."

"Yes, Jersey."

He told her what he'd found. Lots. Nothing.

"What does all that suggest to you, Jersey?"

That they didn't want to walk anywhere, that they got hungry and sleepy, just like other folks. "I don't know."

"Does it suggest to you that they aren't in a big hurry to leave the area, Jersey?"

"Maybe." Yeah, that'd been bugging him. Way back in his mind, of course, but yeah. It was him, he'd've had that frigging Ferrari screaming through Nebraska by now.

"It may mean they're still around. You've done very well so far, Jersey. Will you keep digging a while longer?"

Like she was giving him a choice. Oh, shit, yeah. He'd like nothing better. "Yes, ma'am."

"Now listen carefully to me, Jersey. Are you lis—"

Jersey whacked the phone against the wall.

"Christ, Jersey! What was that?"

"Dropped the phone, Mrs. Voor—Gar*rick*. Sorry."

She coughed, roiling a gummy wad of phlegm in her throat. "Are you listening very carefully to me, Jersey?"

"Yes, ma'am."

"I'm going to send Mote down to help you. I want you to tell me when and where he can meet you."

Jersey made arrangements. Mote would be a big help down here. Mote had roughly the same capacity for intelligent and creative thought as leaf mold. Be one big whopping, goddamn help, yessiree. Send 'im on down.

She hung up. No preamble, just *click*.

Fuck all this chase-after-Suki shit, Jersey thought. He went into a bar downtown, ordered a Wild Turkey, double, and chased that with another. Lots of money for Wild Turkey, and the dough wasn't even his, either.

Job had to be worth something. Right?

26

The lady at the county clerk's office in Reno, fictitious business names division, had a decidedly equine mien, one of those long, thin faces with a stretched jaw. Kind of like a starved Clydesdale, Frank decided, not intending to be unkind. An unfortunate masculine face with mule's eyes, and horn-rimmed bifocals hanging from her neck on a beaded chain. Wisps of gray at her temples. Flat-chested. Gnarled fingers tipped with synthetic heliotrope nails.

You'd think this stolid guardian of the portal of public inquiry would delight in rolling out reams of red tape, revel in trotting out every roadblock available to the superintendent of records of a bloated bureaucracy, relish the all-encompassing "No," point one of those crooked phalanges toward the door and say, "Try corporations, downstairs," where another vessal of the administrative merry-go-round would with secret joy continue the process, ad nauseam.

But, not so, not so.

What she wanted was to please Steven Wiley. Evident in every gesture she made, every word she spoke, was that Miss Evelyn Snoke—*Miss*, not Ms. or Mrs.—wanted to please the portly Steven Wiley in every possible way, such ministrations to include whatever a delicate reddening of the Morgan features might imply.

Her eyes strayed, landed on his finger. "Meat cleaver," he said. "Connecticut, nineteen and fifty-two. Sold it for one twenty-nine a pound. Used to be a butcher, in my younger days."

"Oh, my," Miss Snoke said. Her mouth twitched in an indecisive smile. "Does it hurt?"

"Not in thirty years and more," he assured her. "Although I frequently anticipate rain. What I wonder, Evelyn—if I may be permitted to call you Evelyn?"

But of course. But of *course*. And nothing would do but that she should call him Steven. And lean a little closer on the counter, the better to serve him.

"What I'm wondering, Evelyn, is how a person might obtain a list of businesses that have been granted licenses to operate in the city or county in the past two months."

"Yes," she said. "I mean, that's quite simple, really. Are you certain you mean *all* businesses though? There's no specific one you have in mind? That *would* be simpler." And she did so want to be helpful.

"No, nothing specific. A general listing of some kind is what I'm after. Might that be arranged?"

"Of course, Steven." Her mule eyes searched his face. "Are you in business, then?"

"Thinking of it."

"Would it be, ah, prying to ask what kind of business?"

"Finance," he said vaguely. "Investments."

Another little flare of interest behind those dobbin eyes. She tapped several keys on a computer terminal on the counter, waited a few seconds, tapped a bit more, waited, asked, "What dates are you interested in again?"

"Let's say, middle of May until the first week of July. Something like that."

Tap. Taptaptaptap. Frank turned, looked toward the door, saw Suki lurking about, stoop-shouldered and gimpy. He waved her off, turned back toward Evelyn and her taptaptapping.

"Oh, my," she said. "There's been one hundred sixty-two licenses issued in that time. Are you sure you want a listing of them all?"

"Quite sure," Frank said, and Evelyn taptaptapped, and in a room behind her a dot matrix printer began whining like a forty-pound mosquito. A few minutes later it stopped. Evelyn smiled at Frank and went into the room. She returned a moment later carrying a folded sheaf of paper with track holes on the sides.

She consulted her computer screen and said, "There's a six-dollar-and-eighty-cent charge for this, Steven, but I imagine I could, that is, I'm sure I could just—"

"Certainly not," Frank said. He dug seven dollars out of his wallet, waited as she opened a drawer and handed him two dimes change. He tucked the computer printout under one arm, took his cane in the other, and said, "You've been most helpful, Evelyn. Many thanks."

She wanted to do more, clearly she did, but, alas, it was not to be. Frank stumped toward the door, gave her one last smile before leaving, and then went out.

"What'd you get?" Suki asked.

"Jesus, you sound about eighteen years old, Mrs. Wiley."

"Sorry. No one's listening though, Frank. What'd you get in there? Get her phone number?"

"Thought she was going to stamp it on my hand, but no."

"So, what *did* you get?"

"Keys, roadmaps, ciphers, secrets. Let's go home, have a look."

On a secondhand mattress in an upper bedroom of the "Pratt" place they'd spread a couple of sleeping bags, zipped together at Suki's insistence. A card table and two folding chairs were in a corner, beneath one of the ugliest floor lamps Frank had ever seen.

A Tasco eighty-millimeter refracting telescope stood on a tripod in the northeast corner bedroom, aimed at the Voorhees's mansion; so much power that they could just about see the mesh of the window screens over there, if they wanted. Too much power, so they used the low-power eyepiece, forty times magnification, and supplemented that with 7X40 Zeiss binoculars.

Suki slipped out of her dress and the spandex iron maiden, into something more comfortable: shorts and a halter, little different than the outfit she'd been wearing up in the De Bacas. She kept her face on, however, in case they had to go out without much notice. The contrast between her face and figure was a bit disconcerting.

Frank opened the printout on the card table and sat down, still in his blimp suit. He flipped through the pages idly to get a sense of it while Suki inspected the house, first with the binoculars, then through the Tasco.

"Nothing," she said.

"When it comes," Frank replied, "it'll come fast, be over in an instant."

"When what comes?"

"Whatever. Someone comin' or goin'. These people aren't the types to hold parties on their front lawn."

"You got that right. This's boring, though."

"So I've heard. Over and over."

She made a face at him. "How's that look there?"

Frank turned to the first page. Entries were in chronological order, beginning on May sixteenth.

233

"Clair's Donut Shoppe," he read. "Got a lot of other information here too, but that's the business name."

"Not Mink's style, that one."

"Didn't think so. How about Northern Nevada Urologic?"

"No way."

"Joyner Automotive?"

"It's gotta sound *financial*, Frank. Got anything with 'Associates' or 'Investment Group' or 'Ventures' in it?"

His finger slowly traversed the page. "How 'bout this? Ranier and Son Marketing."

"Could be. Better mark it."

A pause. "Wheeler, Sloan and Dietrich. CPA outfit."

"Mark it."

"J. Alan Morrow and Associates."

"Mark it."

"New Chance Agency."

"What's that?"

"Job placement service of some kind."

"Don't think so."

Pause. "Strauser Investments."

"See, you're catching on."

"Thanks."

In half an hour he had nineteen possibles, another twelve maybes. The house was dim, quiet, airless, hot. Musty too, definitely musty.

"How're you doing?" he asked.

"Bad. Nothing's happening."

"Put your good dress on, Tilly. We're goin' dancing."

She stared at him. "What?"

"I'm done here. Let's start checking out a few of these places, see what we come up with."

It was the only way he could see to unravel Mink's organization. Get a little poop here, a dram of information there, scrounge around until the weight of evidence seemed big enough to send to the district attorney's office—anonymously. That might be a catch, anonymity, but Frank thought they could get around that by writing a reasonably literate letter explaining that if the DA didn't follow up on this information and nail these jokers, the office might find itself up a creek. Tell them about Mink's other operations, where and when. Tell them they had a real tiger by the tail this time if they wanted it, make them look good; national exposure, promotions.

Might work, might not. It was a crapshoot, same as everything else in life, except without a payoff, other than Suki's peace of mind. At times, Frank wondered what he was doing, staying mixed up like this in her problems. But he didn't wonder for long, didn't probe too deeply, because somewhere in those depths an answer lurked, waiting to bite.

So he watched as Suki pulled on her baggy nylons, wrestled into the bodice, wriggled into the gray-green dress, adjusted her wig, and pushed her feet into the old black shoes. She looked at him with a senile simper on her face.

"Terrific," he said. "A real classy dame."

"Sweet-talker. See what it gets ya."

They went outside, into the furnace of the day. The garage stood at the side of the house. He swung open the doors, backed the car out, shoved open the door for her. She got in, moving stiffly.

Two things were certain: one, she made a godawful strange-looking old broad; and two, until they had at least the name of Simon's latest operation, they had nothing. Nothing at all.

Ranier & Son Marketing was five guys in suits and a couple of harried secretaries. A going concern, complete with ulcers.

Wheeler, Sloan, and Dietrich were CPAs, all women: Kathy, Ann, and Celeste. They looked a little hungry when he walked into their office, eager, but their desks weren't empty and a computer was humming quietly in a corner, so Frank thought it unlikely that they were starving. They seemed serious enough, businesslike and subtly aggressive in professionally tailored suits.

On to J. Alan Morrow & Associates, over on Second Street. A weedy-looking row of offices in a dismal green stucco building, dark windows facing an asphalt parking lot that shimmered in the heat. The parking area looked like a tar pit, but Frank pulled the Nova up in a slot anyway. Got out with Suki, looked for suite seven.

It was right next to six, which figured, but it was locked up tight and no sign was out front or on the door. Frank stuck his nose to the glass, cupped his hands around his eyes and peered inside. The room was dark. An empty expanse of beige carpet, blank walls, stray wires snaking along the floor. A cardboard box stood against a wall.

"Nothing," Frank said, backing away.

"Then it's a possible."

"Yeah. Kind of a dead end, though."

"How about we ask around?"

Frank shrugged. "Give it a try, I guess." He went to the door of the next suite over, careful to use his cane and move slowly, like he really was carrying around that extra hundred pounds.

On the door of suite six was the legend: DAVID J. YBARRA, M.S.E.E., M.B.A., B.S. COMP SCI. Frank tried the door. It was locked, but a few seconds later it rattled, opened, and a sallow man with tiny features in the middle of a large face peered out. His forehead was a great curved dome, pale and wrinkled.

"Yes?"

Frank pointed. "I was wondering about your neighbor next door. Thought I'd find J. Alan Morrow there."

"Come in, come in. Too hot outside."

Ybarra ushered them into his cave, piled high with boxes labeled cryptically, slippery stacks of computer magazines, a long table piled high with computer debris. Dishevelment, disorder, dirt. Clutter, confusion, chaos. McDonald's bags, Burger King detritus, Wendy's cups; smoke in the air and butts in an ashtray that served only as a target, having long since overflowed. Something purple had congealed on the carpet in a corner; it looked like a blob of raspberry epoxy.

Ybarra stuck out a pudgy white hand. "Dave. Computers."

"Steve Wiley. Computer illiterate."

Dave the Programmer grinned. "Me too. Just nobody's found out yet. More you know, the more you don't." He dropped into a chair, jiggled unhealthily. Before him was an amber screen, filled with indecipherable nonsense. A pair of jogging shoes were rotting on his feet. His shirttail was pulled out.

"So, you're wondering about my neighbors?" He picked up a Bonnie Hubbard orange juice can with a spoon in it. "Lunch," he explained. "Whole month's vitamin C." The concentrate was still half frozen.

"J. Alan Morrow; you know 'em?"

"Nope. Whadda they do?"

"I don't know, exactly. I was hoping to find out. I find myself in need of an investment counselor."

"Wish I could say the same." Ybarra peered past Frank at Suki, who was looking as senile as ever and not saying a word. "Sorry I can't help you, though. Don't think they've moved in yet, next door."

"No one's been around?"

"Nope."

Dead end, just like he'd thought. Frank couldn't think of anything else to ask. "Well, thanks anyway," he said.

"Hey, no problem. You got a monster in your software, I'm the man who can help. Dave Ybarra. Spread the word."

Frank and Suki went outside.

"Still a possible," she said.

"Yeah, but we still don't know, one way or the other."

237

"Now where'd that sonuvabuck go?" Ybarra asked, pursing his lips. Asked himself because there wasn't anyone else to ask, but it was good to have someone to talk things over with and you always had yourself, right? Never really alone, because you were always right there with you. Computer logic, he'd found, had elements in common with masturbation. He was a fine listener—when he was the one doing the talking. Never knew one better; couldn't ask for more reliable company. . . .

"Ah-hah! There you are. Two hundred bucks, right there." He pulled a Post-it off the side of an empty filing cabinet, which had been stuck there along with a patchwork of other Post-its. The cabinet was empty because he was never able to find the time to organize it, or anything else. One of the reasons Crista'd left him, but only one of hundreds. Too many things Crista wanted, so what was the point in dealing with any of 'em?

He dialed the first number.

It rang.

Rang and rang and rang. "Out to lunch, Davey boy. Everyone's out to lunch."

He took another bite of orange juice and dialed the alternate number. It rang and rang and . . .

"Tell me."

Dave stared at the phone, scrunched his eyebrows. Finally he said, "Peachtree," just like he'd been told. Just that one word. Stupid, James Bondian, but the guy'd said do it and—

"Mr. Ybarra?"

Hey, it goddamn worked; old broad knew it was him. "Yeah," he said. "That's me."

"You have some information for us?"

"I just had a visit, some people looking for that Morrow and Associates outfit."

"What did these people look like, Mr. Ybarra?"

This was one old termagant he didn't want calling him by his first name, he thought. Mr. Ybarra was just fine; forget Dave. "Some old guy, bald, run over three hundred pounds, and an old lady, his wife or mother or something."

"How tall was the woman?"

"Tall. 'Bout as tall as the guy. Five-seven, five-eight, something like that. Kinda stooped-looking."

"They're not still there, are they?"

"No. They drove off."

"What kind of a car were they driving, Mr. Ybarra?"

"Chevy Nova, kinda old and beat-up. Pale yellow; license number seven seven three–XVN."

"Describe the woman further, please."

"Well, she didn't say anything. Just let the old guy do all the talking. Gray hair, old dress, walked with a limp or something. Wore dark glasses. Oh, and her nylons didn't fit. Hung down around her ankles, kinda."

"Did that seem at all strange to you, Mr. Ybarra?"

"Christ, you oughta see my grandmoth—. . . A little, yeah, but I've seen 'em like that before, they get old, start losin' it."

"What color dress?"

"Dishwater, old soup. Kinda gray-green. It was old."

"Did you get a look at her hands?"

What was this? "No. She stayed behind the old guy pretty much."

"And him, what was he like?"

Big, bald, old, round, Dave told the woman. Used a cane. Blue suit, suspenders, a hat. A homburg, maybe. That, or possibly some kind of derby.

"You've been most helpful, Mr. Ybarra."

"This guy told me I'd get two hun–"

"That will be taken care of within twenty-four hours, Mr. Ybarra. In the meantime, will you please continue to keep your eyes open?"

"Yeah, sure."

Click. For a moment Dave the Programmer sat staring at the dead receiver; then he set it back in its cradle.

Weird, he thought. World was a weird goddamn place, fulla weirdos.

Like himself, he thought happily, and went back to spooning slushy orange juice concentrate into his mouth.

27

The phone rang.

"Tell me," Charlotte Voorhees said.

Jersey reported in, telling her he hadn't found anything yet and—

"Listen very carefully to me, Jersey," she broke in. "Are you listening ver—"

Crack!

Damn that clumsy, wretched oaf! "*Jersey!*"

"Yes, ma'am?"

"Do you have a firm grip on the receiver now, Jersey?"

"Yes, ma'am."

"And in addition to your firm grip, are you listening *very* carefully to me, Jersey?"

"Yes, ma'am."

"The girl is in Reno, Jersey. I've just found out—never mind how, it isn't important. The important thing is that you and Mote get up here immediately. Is that perfectly clear?"

"Yes, ma'am."

She stubbed out a cigarette. "I've already told Benny and Isaac. They phoned in from Bridgeport half an hour ago. What I want is for you to come to the house. Is that understood?"

"Yes, ma'am."

She hung up. Whirled, just as her mind seemed to whirl, and pressed her bony fingers unconsciously to the splint that had replaced the bandage and the intranasal packing. The girl was still in Reno. Who would have guessed the creature was so witless? Who would *ever* have guessed?

And, of course, that could mean only one thing, only one. Simon would be so pleased.

She phoned for a taxi, took one final look around before locking up the apartment; she knew this place would never be used as an intermediate drop for the money, as intended. There would be no money now, not from this city—not with the girl still around. The Reno operation was effectively over.

Simon was due back at 6:17 P.M., in not quite two hours. She fidgeted, waiting for the taxi to arrive, and lit up yet another Vantage cigarette with her gold Dunhill lighter.

"How much money you got?" Isaac asked.

"I dunno," Benny said. "Couple thousand, I guess. Why?"

"I've got about the same." Actually he had a good deal more than that, nearly five thousand, but Benny had no idea he had that much and Isaac was no fool. He squinted reflectively up the road, back in the direction of Reno.

"So?" Benny said.

"So, we've got wheels and a little bread. How 'bout we split, man?"

"What for?"

"I've had enough of this shit, haven't you? Anyway, it's

gettin' bad. You don't feel it? This guy comes in, beats the shit outta Mink. Thought nobody could do that."

"Guy had a gun, Izzy."

"Don't matter. What I'm thinking is maybe now's a good time to get out, go on down L.A. way."

"Money's been good," Benny said, conviction ebbing away. Benny was never one to stand firm in a breeze.

"Been good, yeah. How much longer, though?"

Benny shrugged.

Isaac said, "These people're crazy, Ben. Time to move on, check out the action elsewhere."

Benny shrugged again. "You want, I'm in. We gonna call the Bitch, let 'er know?"

"Christ. What d'you think?"

They got in the Malibu and took off, headed south instead of north. L.A. was just seven hours away. Good town, L.A., if you had money. And, Isaac reflected, it shouldn't take him too long to figure out a way to get Benny's cash away from him and strike out on his own.

Mink knew diamonds. It didn't make sense not to know what you were dealing with when you had forty million plus invested in so subtle a commodity; when the tiniest flaw or discoloration could mean thousands of dollars, even hundreds of thousands.

But he hadn't thought that the VVS1 10.17-carat marquise would bring in as much as it had, or that Manny Herrmann would locate a buyer for such a stone so quickly. Manny was one of the best in New York City, however; his contacts in the market were like the root system of a giant sequoia. His partner, a thin, blind Jew named Hillel Weiss, spent virtually his entire existence on the phone in a back corner; the instrument seemed an excrescence of his ear. Questions never ran to the personal with Manny; transactions were invariably hassle free. If they hadn't been, Simon would have taken his money elsewhere. Duane Chafee, Simon's alter ego during his dealings with the diamond broker, was not a minor player in the market.

Simon had been looking to turn an even million, but he would have settled for as little as nine hundred thousand: sorting through stones, mostly in the four-to-six-carat range, lacked the precision of summing bank notes. But Hillel Weiss had made one phone call, only one, and twenty minutes later the big marquise had gone for a pleasantly ridiculous price.

Now Mink was sitting in a Deluxe cab on his way to the Flint Street house with $1,375,000 in a locked briefcase on his lap. All hundred-dollar bills, some new, some used; a little over thirty pounds of paper. With Manny, there was never a problem with money. Manny shuffled a quarter billion dollars' worth of diamonds a year. He could look at a diamond, four and a half carats, and in about ten seconds, no more than twenty, say something like, "Forty-eight five," and then go on to the next. But he'd paused appreciatively at the sight of the big marquise for just a moment, a connoisseur transfixed by the stone's cold beauty. In no time at all, he had a firm offer of $825,000 by the Boston broker of a Mrs. Pendergast. On the transaction, Manny took $20,625, two and a half percent. The rest had ended up in Simon's briefcase, along with what Manny had given him for the other stones.

The taxi pulled up at the Citadel and Simon got out, paid the driver, tipped him two dollars and went into the house.

"She's here," Charlotte said. "In Reno."

A peculiar glow filled Simon's eyes. "Where?"

"Around, Simon. Around. Mr. Ybarra phoned. It appears that the little fool is prying into our affairs."

"Tell me everything."

She told him everything, which wasn't much and which was all the world. Suki was nosing around with this guy she'd picked up somewhere in Texas or New Mexico, the same guy Jersey had kicked the crap out of up in the hills, so the old guy could take some punishment and seemed quite resource-

ful, all things considered. Amazing how he'd found Suki out
here in Reno, and so quickly, too; it told Mink something
about the man. That he'd bothered told Mink even more.

Yellow Chevy Nova, complete with license number. Suki
now wore a gray wig and had been seen in a drab green dress.
The old guy was bald, and very fat.

"You know why she's doing this," Charlotte said.

"Of course. She's trying to find out what she can about our
operation. Evidently she hopes to make trouble, and even
though she cannot, she doesn't know that yet."

"Mote and Jersey are back; Benny and Isaac aren't. It's
been over five hours. They may be gone."

Mink stood at an upstairs window, looking down at the
street through the partly opened curtain. "Perhaps. It has
happened before. I feel her out there, Mother. I *sense* her,
don't you? Don't *you*?" His hands hung quietly at his sides.

"Yes, darling."

"She's so close. So very close."

"I see him," Suki said, unconsciously whispering. "My
God, it's like he's right here in the room, Frank."

She had the Tasco on sixty power. Simon, a hundred and
twenty yards away, appeared to be but six feet from her. The
slanting afternoon sunlight cast shadows across his face.

"Trade you," Frank said.

He handed her the binoculars and then bent over the
telescope, brought the image into focus. "Doesn't look much
like a homicidal maniac, does he?"

"Not at first."

"Makes our job a little harder, though, wouldn't you say?"

"I still want him, Frank."

"Yeah, I know, I know."

Dressed only in an *orosu*, Mink danced. Now fast, now
slow, always in control, always with perfect balance, his feet
in perfect contact with the basement floor. The orosu, a Jap-

anese thong similar to the *mawashi* worn by Sumo wrestlers, was a coarse white cotton cloth that looped between his legs and tied at the waist, clothing his crotch while leaving his buttocks exposed, his movements free.

He lashed out with a foot, landed in a defensive crouch that was utterly without motion, wiry, unassailable.

"She knows about this house," Charlotte said, watching Mink unwind from his trip. "She will come around, don't you think?"

"If she's doing what we think she is, yes. Inevitably."

"Jersey has a new car. And a haircut and suit, off the rack, of course. I've given him instructions to patrol the neighborhood and keep his eyes out for a yellow Nova, or an old man and a woman matching the descriptions given to us by Mr. Ybarra."

Mink's entire body twisted slowly on the floor, his shadows following, fingers curled into a kind of wedge. "I hope the car is something with less visibility this time," he said.

"A Buick Century, I believe. Several years old. I told him never to bring it here to the house."

A blur of motion. Mink's fingers stopped a quarter inch from the light bulb. His body was arched, muscles etched.

"Good," he said.

"Even so, she knows him. If she sees him driving around the neighborhood dressed like that, she might guess that we're on to her."

"We need someone new."

"A precaution I've already considered, darling. Danny is seeking a suitable replacement to take over Jersey's task."

"When that's done, I want to talk to Jersey. And Danny; I have one last task for him before he leaves for Tampa. And I want the yacks to come in tomorrow, Mother. If Suki is watching, we must keep up appearances."

"I'll see that it's done."

"Where's Mote?" A lunge, a deadly flurry of hands, then

an elbow driven into an imagined face, shattering bone, followed by stillness, evaluation.

"Driving around the city, looking. I thought it best to keep him occupied, and even a fool may have luck. He reports in every few hours. I trust even Mote is capable of identifying a yellow Nova and checking license plate numbers."

"Presumably."

"How much longer will you be, dear?"

"Several hours. New York is still with me. It clings."

She turned wordlessly away.

When she left him, he was standing on the toes of one foot, the other foot fully six and a half feet off the floor, hands lifted in a praying-mantis position before his body.

28

The following day, Thursday, Suki looked out the window with the binoculars. "There goes Mote again," she said. "In the Toronado. Keeps comin' and goin'. I wonder where Jersey is."

"My, aren't you a pretty sight?" Frank said, hitching up his suspenders.

She was dumpy, gray, busty, senile again. She followed the Toronado with the binoculars until it disappeared around a corner, then she turned and smiled, face larded with pancake and rouge.

"Really know how to talk it up to the ladies, don'tcha?"

"Comes naturally. Words just bubble up. You gonna put on shoes, or are you adding a new dimension to your act?"

"Damn things hurt, Frank."

"Can't do much about it now. Let's get moving, huh?"

"I'm coming, I'm coming." She tilted her head to one side and looked at him. "Funny. I said the same thing last night, didn't I?"

"Aw, Jesus."

She smiled. "When your face turns red, so does that shiny dome of yours, Frank, you know that?"

"C'mon," he said grumpily. "Crawford and Bell Securities is next on the list. Let's get to it."

The Century could move all right, but not like the Toronado. The Toronado could just get up and haul ass, which is what the road called for, but the Century just sort of rolled along the empty highway through the hot empty desert, which is what cars did in the hands of little old frosty-haired ladies but which was hardly enough to keep Darby Etchemendy, otherwise known as Jersey, awake.

Etchemendy was bad enough, but *Darby?* The name was a horrible joke, the name of a great-grandfather who'd owned a drygoods store up in Vermont, back in the days when Darby wasn't automatic grounds for a fistfight. So he called himself Jersey. Grew up . . . where the fuck else? . . . in Newark.

It was billed as "The Loneliest Highway in America," Highway 50 was. Not until you got east of Fallon, though. Until then it was just a flat and roomy run. East of Fallon, east of Frenchman, really, is where you started to learn what Highway 50 was all about. The ribbon of asphalt cut through a sun-charred expanse of grayish barren wasteland. Thirty-six empty miles beyond Frenchman was Cold Spring, which had been named by someone hallucinating furiously while the sun vulcanized his brain; another forty-nine empty miles to Austin, quaint and useless; then fifty-six even emptier miles to Eureka.

Jersey got a sandwich and a beer at Eureka. Then another beer, and another, and then backtracked a couple miles to the junction of 50 and 278, turned right, and then found that

249

all that talk about Highway 50 was pure bullshit because here was 278, maybe not a real highway but eighty-eight miles of wavy molten desolation that made 50 look good by comparison, and if your car failed you here, Jackson, you were in deep shit.

Jersey got out the topographical maps he'd purchased at Ken's Mountaineering just off Mill Street in Reno. All those contour lines; Mote'd think it was a game, some kinda maze.

Mink had asked Jersey to find him a place where people rarely go, someplace so remote that you could fire a howitzer and no one would hear.

You want desert or trees or what? Jersey'd asked.

Mink thought it over a moment and said he wanted desert, someplace hot.

Out-of-the-way hot, Jersey'd said, and Mink had commended him on his perceptiveness.

Well, just look at the map. West was a joke. West was California, all that mess. South wasn't any good; not if you wanted real desert, open, empty desert. That left north and east, and north wasn't all that bad, really, once you got past Nixon, and it got even better once you got past Gerlach, but when some stretch of asphalt is dubbed "The Loneliest Highway in America" by *Life* magazine, you just had to listen.

Just look at the distance between towns, and then look up north of Eureka, at what was called the Sulphur Spring Range, right next to that alkali flat. That had to be lonely. That had to be out-of-the-way hot.

Was, too. Thirty-two miles up that road and all you could see was nothing at all. A grim and airless drive on the face of the moon. Tinderbox, sage, dried yarrow and gumweed, rocks and rocks and rocks.

Up ahead a kind of pass looped over a low ridge. At the top, a barely visible dirt track wandered along the ridge and dropped out of sight. Jersey slowed the car. He stopped dead, right in the middle of the road, and who gave a shit? Road was as empty as the Sahara for miles in either direction.

He backed up, turned off 278, took the Buick along the

ridge and down a slope. Path didn't look as if it'd been used in twenty years, but the desert changes slowly and it didn't matter if it'd been forty years since anyone'd been down this way, the trail would still remain. Down around the back of a low hill, along a flat, up over another rise, a low place between hills of the Sulpher Spring Range, down again, and there was the southern tip of that alkali flat, a vast, hot, colorless plain. Desolate hot, too.

Jersey stopped the car near the edge of the flat, leery of the sand. Get stuck here and you'd walk out, and maybe if you were lucky the crows wouldn't pluck your carcass clean on that road back there before someone came along. Why anyone would want to drive from Eureka to Carlin was beyond him. Why anyone would want to end up at either of those godforsaken places was as unfathomable a mystery.

Scary place, this.

So empty. Like you were the last one left on a planet razed by nuclear holocaust and you were gonna die because there wasn't any food or water left and this was it, man, just this scoured emptiness and a bunch of bugs waiting to feast on your remains wherever you happened to drop.

No breeze, no nothing. The air was so hot and still that Jersey imagined himself standing in one place and suffocating in his own personal cloud of carbon dioxide.

Howitzer, hell. You could set off a small atomic weapon here and not disturb jack shit.

He located the alkali flat on the map, judged his position in relation to the hills, and marked an X where he stood. He got back into the car and damn near couldn't figure out how to get back to the highway again. Panic popped and sizzled inside his head as he lost the trail, found it, lost it again. Two hours later, with the smell of splintered sage hanging thick in the air around the alkali-crusted Buick, Route 278 appeared ahead. Jersey gazed back at the dusty rolling hills.

It was everything Mink wanted, and more. Jersey found he didn't even want to know why Mink wanted such a place.

Some things were better not to know.

Chase Kohler & Associates was a bust. Chase Kohler himself was a dapper man in his fifties, five foot two, enormous eyebrows, big ears, as tireless and full of energy as a bumble bee. His associates, an eclectic crew of three, were evidently in the business of buying and selling mortgages, working off commissions with some big outfit back east.

"Where now?" Suki asked, looking wilted. Her pancake seemed about to melt right off her face.

"Argosy Planning Group," Frank said. "Financial planners of some kind."

"Super."

"How about we get something to eat, first?"

"Fine, anything. You pick the place, okay? I'm dead."

The streets threw off an acrid smell of asphalt in the heat. Road construction made traversing the city an adventure; major thoroughfares had been cut down to single lanes in which traffic moved haltingly past stinking machines that roared and sprayed oil.

They'd learned to avoid Kietzke Lane, but Kietzke was home to many of the city's fast-food places, so Frank turned off Mill onto Death Row, as he and Suki now called it, and crawled southward, headed toward a Burger King he'd seen earlier.

What to do? What to *do*?

Mote's fingers were sweaty on the wheel. Salt stung his eyes.

What would Jersey do, huh? If Jersey was here Jersey could tell him, but—shit! Did that make any sense, huh? If Jersey was here, Mote wouldn't . . . uh, wouldn't hafta ask, 'cause Jersey'd just do whatever he was gonna do, right?

But do *what*?

Mote switched off the engine. He sat in the hot Toronado in a parking lot behind a Chevron station across Kietzke Lane from the Burger King where that yellow Nova'd gone in, just a few seconds ago.

They hadn't seen him. Couldn'ta seen him, because he was just coming out of Vassar Street when they turned into the BK. So he'd turned right onto Kietzke while they parked, come back around into the parking lot of that fish food place and went behind the Chevron station, and here he was.

Maybe it was them. This old fat dude and a broad got out, went into the BK. Old folks; moved old too. Reminded Mote of his grandfolks, back about ten years ago.

Mink had said they looked old now, but, shit, *that* old?

Green dress. Yeah, Mink said Suki might be wearing a greenish dress. Said the old guy was bald. But the guy over there'd been wearing a hat, so how was he supposed to know if the guy was bald or not, huh?

Still. Might be them anyway, even with the hat.

At the thought of that fifty thousand bucks Mink said he'd give to anyone who found Suki, Mote's hands grew damp. Jesus.

Fifty *Kay*, Jersey'd called it. Why he called it Kay, Mote didn't have any goddamn idea. Grand, he understood; fifty big ones. But fifty *Kay*?

Now what? Jesus.

Dimly, he perceived that he could call the house, get Mink on over here. Except that he wasn't really all that sure where he was, didn't think he could tell Mink exactly how to get to this place, and besides, Mink might not get here in time. And just as dimly, he perceived that following the yellow Nova in his air-scooped Toronado might not work out real good either. All it would take is one look in the rearview mirror and then, poof, they'd know it was him and be gone. Suki had sat in the car all the way from New Mexico.

What to do?

They hadn't come out yet. Good. Maybe they'd sit there a while and eat.

But what to fuckin' *do*?

He flexed his arm, admired the way the muscles bulged his sleeve, the way his veins popped up, just like Arnold's. . . .

253

Didn't help, though. Didn't help at all.

He felt panic building. He had to get out of the car, had to do *something*.

He stood there, looking around. Wheels. He had to have wheels. Had to follow Suki when she left the BK, and couldn't do that in the Olds. Thing was too loud an', an'. . .

Wheels. Where?

Kietzke was clogged, smelly, hot. Traffic moving slow; he could just rip some door open, jerk some pencil-neck asshole out into the street, take his wheels. Like in the movies.

No, couldn't.

And here came along a taxi. Some old broad in back, mouth flapping like crazy, but it gave Mote what he'd had only rarely before in his life and that was an idea, an actual, honest-to-god idea.

He waited at the intersection, using a telephone pole to shield himself from the windows of the Burger King. Waited as the light changed, turned red on Kietzke, green on Vassar, and traffic began to pile up.

Mote ran across the street against the light, across Vassar, and began walking south, looking into cars. Guy in a big brown Caddy, no good. Two broads and kids in a station wagon, no good. Pickup truck with three Mexicans, no good at *all*. A teenage kid in an almost new Mustang, and that was good, that was just about perfect.

He knocked on the window. The kid cut him a look, pimply little pinhead sitting there in his air-conditioning and loud music; Mote could hear it beating through the windows.

The kid ignored him.

"Hey!"

The kid inched the car forward, but there was no place to go.

Another idea. Mote got some money out of his wallet. He had lots of money. He got out three hundreds, pounded on the window again and held the money up.

The music sounds faded. The window slid down an inch.

"Yeah, man, what you want?" the kid said.

"I need a ride. Bad."

The kid stared at the money, licked his lips. "Where to, man?"

"What I gotta do is follow this car."

"What car?"

"Over in the BK over there."

"The what?"

Kid was an idiot. "The BK. Y'know, the Burger King 'cross the street."

The traffic began to move.

"What for?" the kid asked. The Mexicans up ahead began to roll.

"You want the money or not?" Mote shouted. "This here's a lotta money, dude." The car behind them honked.

The kid reached over, unlocked the door. Mote hopped in and the Mustang leaped forward.

The kid looked at him, at his muscles. Mote smiled. He liked it when people looked at him like that, kinda like they were scared of what he might do. It's what he liked best. He flexed his chest, made a muscle for the kid.

"What car?" the kid asked, nervous now.

"In the BK over there. Yellow Nova, beat-up lookin'."

"Okay, I see it."

But there wasn't any way to get over there, not with the street all torn to shit and graders pushing gravel in the next lane over, so the kid hugged the Mexicans' bumper up to Automotive Way, then tore around the block back to Vassar, stopped at the light.

"How much you gonna give me?" the kid asked.

Now Mote wasn't sure. Three hundred? Did he want to give the kid all that? But he wanted the pinhead to stay interested and he wanted him to do it right, not lose Suki or anything.

"Tell you what," he said, handing over one of the bills. "I'll give you a hunnerd now. You stay behind this car as long

255

as it takes, till I say, an' don't lose 'em an' don't let 'em see you followin', I'll give you two hunnerd more."

"These guys you're after, they drive fast, or what?"

"I don't think so. They're just old folks."

"What're you, like some kinda private eye or something?"

Mote liked that idea, liked it a lot. "Yeah, that's right. Like Mannix on TV," he said. "You ever seen Mannix?"

"Never heard of it."

Figured. Figured, the pinhead wouldn't know Mannix. Mote was thirty-three. He'd been fucking *raised* on Mannix. Mannix was the best, him and Peggy.

The light changed. The kid drove across the street. They didn't have Kietzke torn up where Vassar crossed it, so it was easy to cross on over, slip into the parking lot of the Carl's Jr. roast beef place on the corner, right next to the BK, and then park beside a couple of big green dumpsters and look over, see the Nova still sitting there. Thank Jesus.

"I was going to my buddy's house," the kid said.

"Now you're gonna make some money," Mote told him. "Easy money. Which'd you rather do?"

Kid didn't answer.

Pinhead.

By 3:48 Danny Turpin was on a United flight to San Francisco with $175,000 in his bag; good, untraceable cash. In Turpin's line of work it wasn't advisable to leave a paper trail; cash was clean, especially when you had your choice of aliases. If William G. Ridgeway's plan, Bold $troke, ever came to fruition, they'd be out of business—fast. But there was blessed little chance of that. Right-wingers'd all scream bloody murder about some communist plot; Ku Klux Klan'd dynamite the White House and the Mafia would blow away half of Congress.

From Frisco he'd go to Atlanta, and from there he'd catch a flight to Tampa. In a month, possibly a little more, Tampa would be ready for Mink and the yacks to move in, begin making a little money. Too bad the Reno thing hadn't worked out. He had done some of his cleanest work in Reno.

Last order of business before he left was buying that nice little Jamboree motor home for Mink. He'd paid cash, $42,575.28, bought it at Camino Camper in the name of Carl Sullivan, Mink's latest Reno identity. Mink didn't say what he wanted it for, just that he wanted a nice one, comfortable, but not too big.

Other than unloading bank accounts, you never really had to shut a town down. What you did when you left was you just looked in all the closets and then took off. Like he was doing now. Catch a plane or get in your car and go, let the rental properties, leases, post office boxes and all the bureaucratic bullshit sort itself out. It always did, somehow, although at times Danny imagined the municipal wheels locking up and tossing dozens of pale drones through the municipal windshield.

One thing Danny didn't do was think too long or hard about the sounds that had come from the cellar of the big old house. Do that and you'd just feel bad, and if you got to feeling too bad you could end up blowing over a third of a million dollars a year doing something about it. Mink had his life and Danny had his. If Danny didn't approve . . . well, he didn't have to approve, did he? It wasn't his job to approve or disapprove of anything Mink did.

He was just the setup man, nothing more, flying off to Tampa to set things up. Again.

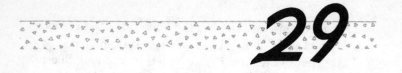

29

Jesus," Mote said. "Lookit that."

"Look at what?" the kid asked.

"No, don't stop!" Mote yelled. "Keep on goin'!"

The kid gunned it and the Mustang shot down Ridge Street, past Flint.

"Go around the block," Mote said. "Go on past where they just went in. Fast."

The kid, Rick Bonoli, did as he was told, and they roared south on Hill, back around to Arlington, then cruised up Ridge again.

The old guy and the old woman—Mote still couldn't see her as Suki—were just going into the house on the corner. The yellow car was nowhere in sight.

"Okay," Mote said. "Take me back to where we first met an' I'll give you the rest of the money."

He didn't want to, knew he could scare the shit out of the kid easy, but he gave him the two bills anyway after they got back to Kietzke and Vassar. All the thinking he'd done that day had stimulated his brain, made him craftier, and the idea occurred to him, still dimly, that if he cheated this kid the kid might come nosing around the last place that guy and Suki had gone, back at that house, and that Mink might not be real happy if he did. So Rick drove off rich and Mote got back in the Toronado and made his way across town to the Citadel. The first thing the Bitch said when he walked in was "Where've you *been*, Mote? It's been hours since you last reported in." Her and Mink both standing there, looking at him. And Mote, heart pounding, said, "I found 'em, Mink. I found Suki."

The two just stared at him.

It was frustrating in the extreme. There was the house over there—the Citadel, Mink called it—and still she and Frank didn't know the name of Mink's business, didn't really have much of anything they could go to the district attorney with. The yacks had all come in that morning, casually dressed young men and women that Suki knew from Louisiana and before, but it wasn't likely that any money was rolling in yet. Probably no crimes had been committed thus far, nothing prosecutable, and they didn't have the name of Mink's business, so this cat-and-mouse game was going to have to continue a while longer.

J. Alan Morrow & Associates and Silver Sage Investment Group; those were the two most likely, and still she and Frank hadn't checked them all out. Tomorrow was Saturday, though, so they could rest a couple days, even if they didn't particularly want to.

Suki lay flat on her back on the sleeping bag, sweaty in her bra and panties, the miserable layer of pancake freshly scrubbed from her face.

She could feel the house over there, Mink and Charlotte roaming its hallways, Mink doing that scary killing dance of his, silently breaking imaginary bones. More than that though, she felt the terrible malevolence of his spirit, like noxious gas venting from a bloated corpse. The Devil had his implements, and Mink was one of his worst.

Maybe this wasn't so smart, staying here in Reno, but what else could she do?

Frank wandered into the room. "Cheer up."

"What's to cheer up about?"

"You're young, alive, beautiful. That's not so bad. Once this is over, you've got your whole life ahead of you."

She rose up on an elbow. "Doing what?"

"Doing whatever." He sat down at the card table, began to flip through the computer printout again.

"What about you, Frank?"

"I've got my own load to haul."

"That trucker talk?" She sat up. "Why'd you do it? You never said. I can't imagine you ripping off a whole truck like that. I can't imagine you stealing anything."

"It's sort of complicated."

"We've got time. Tell me."

He sighed. "You really want to hear?"

"Yeah, and I'd like a shower, too. How about we do both, together."

"Christ, give my heart a break, huh?"

"C'mon." She stood up, long muscles rippling in the washed-out light coming through the curtained windows. She took his hand. "You're not that frail."

"Who says?"

"Me." She slipped off her bra and stepped out of her panties. "I say."

Mote pointed out the window. "That house, right over there."

"Are you sure, Mote?" Charlotte asked, eyes narrow. "Are you very, *very* sure?"

"Sure, I'm sure. I followed 'em all day. Got a look at their license up close lotsa times. Seven seven three–XVN. I seen 'em park at that house there, seen 'em go inside an' every-thin'."

"It has a certain daring logic," Mink said, and Mote cast him a hopeful look.

"Of course it does," Charlotte agreed. "But there simply cannot be any mistake about this, Simon. None at all."

"So bold," Mink said softly. "So marvelously angry."

"So foolish," Charlotte said.

Mink turned to Mote. "You did very well today."

"Do I get that, uh, fifty Kay?"

"What we'll do is check out the house. If Suki is there, you'll get the fifty thousand."

"What about the guy?"

"What about him?"

"I found him too, din't I? I get the money for him, too, like you said?"

"Yes, Mote," Mink said. "You get the money for him, too. Now why don't you go on back to the motel, take a shower and a nap or something?"

"Uh, I hadta give that kid three hunnerd bucks."

Mink peeled off five hundred dollars and handed it to him. Mote left, humming happily.

"It's coming together," Mink said. "It's happening."

"As we knew it would, in time," Charlotte responded. "But what I find incredible is that Mote, of all people, is the one who found her. Do you really intend to give that—that hopeless *churl*, sixty thousand dollars?"

"He's had his moment in the sun, Mother. I rather think not."

"I positively shudder to think what that dimwit would do with so much money."

Jersey knocked on the back door and came in, interrupting them. "That Mote I seen leavin'?" he asked.

"Yes," Mink said. "Did you find us a place?"

"The best." Jersey spread his maps out on a table and

explained the dotted lines, told Mink what it looked like out there, 288 miles east of Reno.

It was good, Mink saw. It was very, very good indeed.

"I knew this secretary at J. K. Lomax," Frank said. "JKL, we called the company."

"Yeah? How well'd you know her?" Suki lathered his chest with soap, giving him one of those smiles of hers.

"Not *that* well. And you don't have to do that, I'm perfectly capable of washing myself."

"I want to. That all right? So you knew a secretary at this company. That's pretty exciting, Frank. After that, what happened next?"

Water drummed down on his shoulders. Suki stood eye to eye with him in the big shower stall, one of the finer features of the house, caressing him with soapy hands.

"Maddy Newton. Guess her name is Madeline or something. Anyway, she's about sixty years old and what you would call a bit hippy, maybe more than just hippy, always into chocolates and whatever else came through the office."

"What you're saying is, you weren't interested."

"Maddy was one of the good ones," Frank said. "Still is. Always pleasant to be around, good-humored. Anyway, she's got an inside track at Lomax and she doesn't always agree with the way they do business."

"What? They're crooked?" Her hands drifted lower.

"Um, no. Not to their customers. They turn out a damn good product. What they sometimes do though, is they lay off employees who're older, like me, people who're getting close to having their retirement vested. I didn't start working for Lomax until a little over five years ago."

"Is that legal, them doin' that?"

"No, but legal considerations have never stopped a crook yet. At JKL, what happens is they fire you for something that doesn't have anything to do with your age. In my case, Maddy said a dock foreman by the name of Tug Winders was all set to testify that I'd knowingly signed a manifest for a long load."

"What's that?"

"A truckload of stock that's bigger than what shows on the shipping manifest. In my case, long by about thirty-six hundred dollars."

"So you could sell the extra somewhere, right?"

"That's the general idea."

"Did you?"

"Hell no. Tell you what did happen though, about half a year back. I caught Winders—*oof!*"

She smiled. He was aroused and she'd just jangled his circuits with firm, slippery hands.

"Jesus," he said.

"You were saying?"

"Winders," he said hoarsely.

"What about Winders, Frank?"

"Christ, girl!"

"We're having trouble getting this Winders thing out." She crouched and began lathering his legs. He took a deep breath.

"I got to work late one day. Ran out of gas on the goddamn freeway, which isn't any fun, lemme tell you. I went out on the loading dock at midmorning and didn't see anyone, so I went around back and caught Winders loading this box into the back of a pickup. Small ID roller bearings. Driver looked nervous as hell, but Winders just looked at me, told me to go on back to the dispatch office and he'd be with me in a minute. When he got back his eyes had a look in them, like what did I think I'd seen and how much did I know and was I likely to say anything. That kind of look.

"He was stealing, of course. Must've been seven, eight thousand dollars' worth of bearings, and the son of a bitch was going to accuse me of taking off with a long load. No doubt he could back it up with paperwork, too—dock and weight records, everything. Winder's a sly sonofabitch."

She stood up, handed him the soap. "Here, make yourself

263

useful." He lathered his hands and began soaping her breasts.

"Very nice," she said.

"So . . . Maddy took me aside one day and said they were gonna can me, said it would probably happen in about two weeks. The bastards weren't going to formally accuse me of anything, just let me go quietly. She said she thought it was a rotten deal, that she didn't believe for a minute I'd done what they said I did, but that it was gonna happen anyway. Funny, though, that they didn't do it right off, if they were so certain then that I'd stolen from the company.

"But of course they knew I hadn't. Just that by getting rid of me before I was vested, the bottom line looked better for some of the front-office hotshots—are you listening to any of this?" Her nipples were turgid, eyes closed.

"Sure, Frank. Just don't stop, okay?"

"Jesus. Anyway, that's why I did it. Wasn't right, I know, but Fanny was dead and I was all alone, kids grown up, if you could call 'em that, and these college boys in the front office were about to trash my retirement with Lomax. I've been stepped on before, but never before by such cowardly slime, so I decided to fix up my own goddamn retirement."

"You coulda gone to prison, Frank." Her eyes were still closed.

"Maybe it wasn't the brightest thing I've ever done, but I didn't want to fight it in court. It would've taken years, and there wasn't anything to fight anyway. They would've just said they fired me for stealing. Can't fight that. Like fighting vapor, just these suited slimes behind their walnut desks in their paneled boardrooms. I was just a liability to them, a greasy trucker who had a few years of hauling left in him and then a lot of years of bleeding them, drawing his pension.

"So Maddy told me what they were planning, and I started visiting a bunch of these sleazy places, bars mostly, and—"

Suki pressed herself against him, moving slowly, the soap making their bodies slick.

". . . And I talked to this one scroungy character who put

264

me in touch with another one who knew this guy who was willing to deal. I deliver a truck and he'd give me two thousand dollars plus twenty percent of the manifest value of the small general-purpose bearings and three percent on the special-order stuff. Hard to unload turbine bearings, things like that.

"This guy and I were on a run up to Sacramento, to a distribution center up there. I'd been on trips with him before. Cliff Tabert, thirty-three years old. We stopped at a truck stop near Bakersfield, a hundred or so miles north of L.A., went in for coffee. I told Cliff I was going to the head, and then I slipped out, climbed in the truck and took off west, through Greenacres and then up north to Shafter, where this other guy was waiting for me. Drove the truck into a big shed south of town and we figured out what he owed me according to the manifest. Then I caught a bus to L.A. and another one out to Palmdale, just in case, bought the truck and the camper, and headed east."

"To New Mexico."

"Yeah."

"Lucky for me. I'd probably still be stuck out there if you hadn't come along."

"Probably."

"Are we clean enough now?"

"For what?"

She smiled at him. "What d'you think?"

"Jesus."

"And afterward I want dinner, Frank. A real dinner somewhere. I'm hungry."

"Christ."

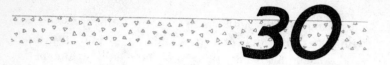

30

This was where they would come out, if they came out at all: a door at the side of the house nearest the garage, just off the kitchen. It wouldn't be too bad a place to go in either, if it came to that.

Night had come. Mink stood in the shadow of an enormous juniper bush, dressed in a BDU SWAT uniform, a flat-black cotton utility suit with a vaguely martial-arts look to it that blended invisibly with the darkness. Black T-shirt, bare feet. Around his waist was an Airborne belt with a buckle that was also a three-inch carbon steel knife. He had several lengths of nylon cord in his pockets.

Lights were on in the house; several upstairs windows were pale luminous rectangles. No sound came from within.

Would they come out?

The question had suprisingly little relevance. It was a Westerner's question, blunt, without subtlety. A grasping at assurance. It denied flexibility. It denied *capability*.

If they came out, he would take them here. If they stayed inside, he would take them there. Either way he would take them. The where didn't matter, so the question had no meaning.

Very Zen, it was.

Spider's mind. Empty, patient, asleep-alert.

Waiting for the inevitable.

Waiting.

Waiting.

"C'mon," she said. "Get up."

"I'm whupped."

"I know, I whupped you. But now I'm hungry and you oughta respect that."

"I'm having trouble breathing."

She pulled him to a sitting position. "It's that bald head of yours, isn't it? Makes you think you're old."

"I *am* old," he groaned. "I am very, very old."

"Bull-oney." She pulled harder, got him standing upright.

"Is that English?"

"Sort of. We'll begin with your shorts. Here, put these on. Legs go through these holes here. That's right. Now the other leg. Very good, Frank."

"I'm dying, you're laughing."

"You'll feel better with food in you."

He clung to a wall for support. "We're not dressing up in our bladder suits again, are we?"

"I'm sick of that. Let's go someplace out of town where it's safe. Like regular people for a change."

"Father and daughter, huh?"

"Not *that* regular."

"Think I oughta shave my head again before we go?"

"Let's just let 'em think you're a punker, okay? All that fuzz growing crazy wild up there."

"Yeah, let's."

Waiting was not unpleasant. Waiting was a state in which one merely *was*. Inert, but ready. Coiled, cocked . . . waiting.

Waiting.

Deadly—knowing he was deadly. Invincible, and knowing that too. Knowing the advantage was all his for this next encounter: surprise, eyes adjusted to the darkness, and, most of all, technique and training, terms that did little justice to what he had become. Much more than a collection of techniques, his training was an entire philosophy, every muscle and neuron of his body responsive to inner commands that resulted in specific effects on the outer world. Those who did not understand found those effects irresistible, deadly. His thoughtways were focused and calm, ready. He was a weapon.

And what this weapon wanted was Suki.

Suki beneath the boiling-oil drip.

Suki pleading.

Suki screaming.

Suki dying.

From the old house came a thump. Someone coming. The spider grew awake-alert.

Voices. A light. More voices, from within. And then the scrape of a doorknob turning, the whispery rasp of a door just beginning to open and now the question that had no meaning had its inconsequential answer.

"Still warm out," Suki said, voice hushed.

"Got some clouds up there tonight," the man said. "Clouds keep the heat in."

"Funny, I thought clouds made it cold."

"Not in the desert, not in summer."

The door closed: *click.* The spider tensed.

Two steps down to a concrete walk that led past the side of the house, past the juniper bushes. Shadows moving.

Simon glided forward, out.

"Boo," he said softly.

They turned, eyes wide, staring at the empty nothingness of the night, and Simon spun effortlessly, in control, and the nothingness took the old guy first, clipped him under the chin with a foot like a blade and the guy didn't make a sound, not a grunt, just fell back and landed on the ground as the girl stared, stared, didn't know what was going on, it'd happened so fast. Then she began to scream. The spider took her in the solar plexus with the same foot, so easy, so easy, and she couldn't scream, couldn't even breathe, blind agony in her eyes, and then he had her by the hair, forcing her head up and back, and he said, whispering in her ear, "Remember the heat, Suki. You've felt the cold, now you will feel the heat."

She tried to scream, tried to empty her paralyzed lungs in one final effort, but he flicked his fingers against the side of her head, just so, and she crumpled next to the man.

So easy it was. Didn't take ten seconds. These were not people who understood the essential nature of violence, that at its very best it really wasn't violent at all. These were not people who commanded respect.

These were flies.

And now they would die. Slowly, slowly, slowly.

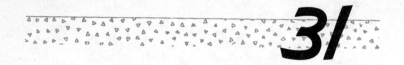

atching Mote, Jersey smiled. As Jersey turned from Court Street onto Flint, Mote kept his eyes averted from the house on the corner where Suki was holed up. Didn't even want to look, as if he thought something bad would happen if he just glanced at it. Jersey couldn't hardly believe that Mote had found the girl. Mote, of all people. Like a caveman banging two rocks together and, *boom*, there's a bust of Lincoln or something. Worse, if Mote's happy burbling had any merit, Mink had told Mote he was going to give him sixty thousand goddamned dollars and, worst of all, it looked as if Jersey, who'd been out running around in the desert on one of Mink's useless errands at the time, wasn't going to see squat from it, not one lousy, freaking nickel.

Morning sun fell on the corner house, an old place that needed paint, like most of the houses in the neighborhood.

"Right over there," Mote whispered, pointing—like they could hear him from a hundred yards away, right through the windows of the car.

Jersey smiled. Imagine, Suki holed up right there under their noses! Under Mink's nose, especially. Girl had balls, he had to give her that.

He pulled the Toronado into the drive at the Citadel, went around back and parked. He and Mote clumped up the stairs and went into the house though the kitchen door.

The place was deserted. Eight o'clock, and it was like a tomb or something. Empty. Jersey's skin prickled.

They went through the house. Nothing. Mink and his crazy Bitch-mother were gone. All their clothing was gone too, so it looked as if they'd cleared out, weren't coming back.

"Jesus Christ," Jersey breathed.

"Now what? Think I'm gonna get my sixty Kay, Jers?"

"Shut up, Mote."

On a kitchen counter, Jersey found two manila envelopes, one labeled MOTE, the other JERSEY.

He tore open the one with his name on it and read the note inside, ignoring the money that fell out in his hand:

Jersey:

Your services, and those of Mote, will no longer be required. In gratitude for services rendered, here is $10,000. Consider it termination pay. Mote has been given $5,000. Calm him, Jersey. Make him see that this way is better than any other.

And do not make the mistake of thinking that any of your future continues to lie with us.

Mink

"What's this mean?" Mote asked, handing his note to Jersey. It was similar, but shorter.

271

"It means we're unemployed." Jersey stuffed his money into a jacket pocket.

"Five Kay. All I got was five lousy Kay, Jers. How 'bout you?"

"Same."

"He said he was gonna gimme sixty Kay."

"Forget it, Mote." Jersey turned away. He went out the door into the morning heat, telling Mote how lucky he was it had ended this way, this simply, all things considered. It'd been one hell of a ride while it lasted, though. Trouble was, nothing lasts forever.

Finally, he and the Bitch were quits.

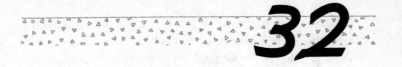

A delicate purple-blue translucency limned the mountains, first sign of the approaching dawn. Pretty, Frank thought. Spectacular, in its own quiet way. Just when you're sure the desert is beyond redemption, it surprises you, puts on a show like this. The world was alive with unexpected beauty. He hadn't seen enough of it, not yet. He didn't want to die.

Overhead, stars still twinkled, just beginning to fade. In the dim light, Frank couldn't see for great distances, but he sensed a vast openness around them.

"Sit," Mink commanded.

Frank sat. His hands were tied behind his back, and resistance was simply met with pain, directed against Suki. It had happened once that night already, and once had been enough.

Frank's jaw ached where Mink had kicked him, eight hours earlier. Even though he'd slept for a few hours in the motor home, he felt exhausted, eyes grainy.

Before leaving Reno, Mink had tied a single loop of tough nylon cord around Frank's neck, knotted in back at the base of his skull. Now Mink secured the trailing ends of this line to a canopy strut at the east side of the motor home. Mink was good with knots, knew just what he was doing, and Frank wasn't any Harry Houdini. His hands were held immobile at his waist, his wrists tied to a belt of nylon rope. After Mink went back inside the motor home, Frank explored the knots, couldn't get hold of a single one, found no weaknesses in the bonds at all. He finally gave it up when his fingers began to cramp.

The sky brightened from purple-blue to royal blue. No lights moved out there in the desert, no sound reached Frank's ears. He had never seen such an expanse of nothingness. Miles and miles of it.

Mink came outside, stood beside Frank and sipped a cup of something that threw off tendrils of steam. A patch of light shone on the ground from a window of the RV.

Frank shivered.

Charlotte Voorhees moved about inside, clattering dishes. From time to time Frank caught a whiff of tobacco smoke. Suki was in there too, also bound, but Simon had gagged her to keep her from spitting. Charlotte had objected to Suki's method of showing disrespect.

"Restful, isn't it?" Simon said softly.

Frank didn't say anything.

"Pity to disturb all this with screams." Simon gazed out at the emptiness. "But that's life, isn't it? This world was never meant to be a happy place."

The sun climbed above the hills; the air warmed. Simon went down to the alkali flat and wandered about for half an hour. He strolled a quarter mile north along the edge of the flat and then returned. A tracery of pink lines on his forehead stood out where Suki had tattooed her word on him.

Mink untied Frank from the motor home, told him to stand. Frank's wrists remained tied; the ends of the nylon cord trailed from his neck.

"Can I trust you?" Simon asked.

"What do you mean?"

"I'm going to move the RV over there." Mink pointed. "If you want, you can walk on over, meet us there. How would that suit you?"

"You gotta be nuts."

Mink smiled. "It'd save me some trouble. I thought maybe you'd like to stretch your legs a bit."

Frank didn't bother asking what would happen if he tried to run. Suki'd get hurt, and Frank wouldn't make it a quarter mile before Mink would be on him.

"Why move? What's over there?"

"Anthill," Mink replied. "Big one. I'm going to feed you to it."

Frank felt the color wash out of his face. "Jesus, you're really certifiable, aren't you?"

"Merely curious," Mink said mildly. "Anthills have always fascinated me. All that instinctual, genetically encoded activity. This is a wonderful opportunity to watch a big hill at work. Start walking."

Frank moved off a few paces. Simon watched, then climbed up into the cab of the Jamboree and started the engine. Frank kept walking, trying to think, trying to keep his mind from shutting down entirely. It was important to continue exploring options, but under the circumstances it was difficult, forcing his legs to carry him downslope through scraggly sage toward the inhuman fate that awaited him.

I'm going to feed you to it.

So cold-blooded a statement, said in so matter-of-fact a manner. It didn't seem possible that Mink had a soul. Mink was a monstrous void in the universe.

Frank felt like a prisoner who'd been told to aid his own executioner. If only he could start a fire, perhaps it would flare out of control and attract attention. But he had no way of starting one, and the sage was too thinly distributed for a fire to spread effectively. He could run, of course, but the gently sloping plain was empty—there was no place to run to, no place to hide. And even if he could somehow save himself, Suki was still in Mink's hands.

Other options? Very few. He could try to bite Mink; if he got close enough, he'd give it a try.

The Jamboree swayed through the sage, down toward the edge of the vast, shimmering alkali flat, heat mirages already obscuring its far northern extremity.

Frank followed, flexing the muscles in his legs. They were going to die anyway, so what he could do is try to kick Simon in the groin or knee, then kick him to death. What difference did it make now if Simon threatened to hurt Suki, or hurt him? Quick deaths were preferable to the horrors Simon had chosen for them. Simon was rapidly losing his leverage.

Ants. Frank remembered that anthill he'd seen while walking out of the De Baca Mountains. Hungry, swarming little bastards. It wasn't the thought of being bitten that made his knees feel powdery, but the idea of being carted, bit by tiny bit, into the ground. He'd come across that anthill in the De Bacas how long ago? Just last Sunday, five days ago. Jesus. The Monday before that he'd stolen the truck. Curious, how life moved along so damn fast.

His ribs still weren't a hundred percent, but they didn't bother him too much anymore. Just a twinge now and then. He could maybe get off a fair kick at Simon. It was worth a try. Just about anything was worth a try at this point.

The motor home halted at the edge of the playa. Mink and Charlotte climbed out, and Mink unfurled the canopy to provide a shady place overlooking the miles-long flat. He stood up as Frank drew near.

"Nice walk?" he asked conversationally.

"Very."

Frank swung a foot at Simon's groin, hard. Simon twisted sideways and, almost gently, lifted Frank's leg. Frank landed on his back in the dirt. His ribs flared.

"Telegraphed it," Simon said, backing off a few steps. "Eyes, everything. Too slow, too clumsy, but I can't say I blame you, so we'll let that one go. Look over there, old man. That's what I'm going to feed you to."

A mound almost two feet high and eight feet across stood twenty yards away, out beyond the edge of the flat. Its crown was somehow blurry, a shifting, dusty-raspberry color. It took Frank a moment to realize that he was seeing a vast swarm of ants, already beginning to move.

The skin stirred on the back of his neck.

"First things first, though," Simon said. "Move over here by the RV and sit down like you did before. I've got things to do and I don't want to have to worry about you."

Frank was still on his back. "How about you make me?"

Simon smiled. An almost sleepy look came over his face. "As you wish."

He took a step closer and Frank raised his legs defensively. Another step and Mink was within range. Frank kicked out at him, trying for a kneecap, and Simon easily caught his foot in both hands, heel and toe, and twisted. Frank cried out and flipped over on his stomach, hands still behind his back. Mink leapt on him and grabbed the loose ends of the cord still tied around Frank's neck. He pulled Frank's head up.

The noose cut off Frank's wind.

"Let that be the end of your foolishness, old man," Simon said softly in Frank's ear. "If you persist, I will tie ropes so tightly around your ankles that your feet will gangrene. I have heard that the process is most unpleasant. If you like, we can delay your burial a day or two while you rot."

Simon stood up and said, "Sit over there."

Frank got to his feet awkwardly and sat down where Simon indicated. There was no point in further resistance, not yet. Simon tied Frank to the canopy strut as before, using the neck noose, and then checked the bonds at his wrists.

"Preparations," he said. He gave Frank a wink. "So much to do and, happily, so much time in which to do it."

He gathered four steel stakes, thirty inches long; one end of each was formed into a loop. He pounded them into the sand of the alkali flat in an approximate square, eight feet apart. As he worked, Charlotte came out and watched silently, drawing on a cigarette, arms folded across her skinny chest. Her nose was discolored by a bruise.

Simon returned and went into the Jamboree. He came out with Suki in his arms, bound hand and foot, still gagged. He placed her on her feet in the shade of the canopy.

"Soon you will feel the heat, darling," he said. "Do you remember our previous discussion?"

Charlotte turned, watched as Simon used a pair of scissors to cut Suki's clothing from her body. Snip, snip, right up the front of the blouse she'd put on to go out to dinner the night before with Frank. He didn't bother with the buttons. Suki's eyes were wide, staring. The scissors slashed, and the blouse opened at the throat, fell open in front. Mink began cutting her sleeves; he started low and moved up over her shoulders to her neck. Suki's wrists had been bound in the same manner as Frank's, held firmly at her waist by a rope around her middle. Simon pulled the shredded blouse off her. Suki stood there in jeans and a bra, shivering, lips puffed around the heavy gag.

Simon cut the bra off her, threw it aside, and then began shearing the heavy material of her jeans, cutting upward from her ankles. As he did this, Charlotte took hold of one of her arms to help keep her from falling.

Snip, and the waistband parted. Simon crouched before her and started on the other leg. Suki fell suddenly, landed hard on her back and kicked Simon in the face. He twisted sideways and rolled as Suki kicked Charlotte in the shins.

The old woman shrieked and fell howling to the ground.

Frank watched, but there was nothing he could do, no way to help Suki take advantage of the situation.

And anyway, it was already over.

Simon grabbed Suki's feet, flipped her on her belly like he'd done to Frank. He grabbed her hair, lifted her head and pressed his fingers into the sides of her throat. Within seconds, her body went limp.

Simon stared at Frank, an angry scrape on his left cheekbone, dirt and blood. He touched it, smiled. "Ornery little barbwire bitch, isn't she?"

Simon helped Charlotte to her feet and up into the motor home. He came back out and cut away the remainder of Suki's clothing. He picked her up. She regained consciousness as he began carrying her out toward the stakes he'd pounded into the sand. She bucked with all her strength, bending at the waist, lunging madly in his arms. Simon dropped her, pressed on her carotid artery again, cutting off blood to her brain, then picked her up and carried her the rest of the way to the stakes.

He tied her spread-eagled and naked on the ground, out in the sun, thirty or so feet from the anthill. She came to as he tied her arms, and she fought him again, still gagged, but he overpowered her with little trouble and lashed her to the sand, stretched tightly between the stakes.

He removed her gag.

"You *fucker!*" Suki screamed. "You slimy sick sonofabitch! You're gonna rot in hell! You're gonna *rot!*"

"Do tell," he said. He turned away.

Huge red ants roamed the sand, a few whose random foraging took them as far away as Suki. Mink poured a full gallon of Quaker State motor oil in a ring around her. Ants reached the noxious barrier and turned away. Mink stepped on the few that had been trapped inside the perimeter, crushing them into the sand.

Frank was suddenly aware that the idea of the anthill was

no spur-of-the-moment decision. Simon had planned it; the oil barrier was proof of that. The anthill was meant for him, not Suki. For her, Simon intended to use the hot-oil drip.

Simon returned to the motor home and crouched in front of Frank. "Now things get interesting," he said. "You see, you're going to dig a hole for me—well, it's for you, actually, but it means I'll have to untie your hands and give you a shovel, and that means you'll have a wealth of ideas about how to use the opportunity to attack me."

"Never," Frank said.

Simon smiled, went inside the Jamboree, came out with a .22 revolver in his hands. "I may be wrong, but I've gotten the impression that you and Suki care for one another. I understand your feelings for her; she's young and beautiful and relatively witless, a rather nice combination. But any reciprocal feelings on her part seem quite preposterous." He shrugged. "But that's irrelevant, isn't it? What's important is that I'm not certain to what extent you can be trusted to care about her welfare under these conditions. So here's how it'll work: you pull any stunts while you're digging and I'll remove her nipples with a razor. Shall I show you the razor, old man, or do you believe I've got one?"

"I believe you."

"Very good. In fact, I have several. And do you believe I'd use it in the manner specified?"

"I believe you're capable of anything, yes."

"Yes, very good again. I am. Anyway, as I said, I can't rely on you to care about Suki's pain, so the gun is a form of additional insurance. If you try anything, I'll gut-shoot you low in your intestines. It's only twenty-two caliber, so it's quite unlikely to kill you, but the pain would be tremendous. Do you understand?"

Frank said nothing.

Simon's fingers lashed out, struck a nerve in Frank's arm that drew an involuntary cry of pain from his throat. He had never felt pain like that before, couldn't believe that a mere

280

tap near his elbow could do that to him. His vision blurred as his eyes filled with tears.

"Do you understand, old man? Answer."

"Yes."

"Very good. We may never become friends, but I guarantee you that before this day is done we will understand one other perfectly. When I ask questions, you *will* answer."

Charlotte came out, looking old and frail. She had a glass of orange juice in one hand. Simon unfolded a lawn chair for her and she sat down slowly. She was silent and evil; the air around her seemed miasmic, almost chilled. She didn't look at Frank as she sipped her drink.

"Now," Simon said, "here's the drill. I'm going to tie your feet, leaving six inches of slack between them. Then I'll untie your neck and we'll walk down to the anthill. When we get there, I'll free your hands. Think we can manage all that without Suki losing her nipples, old man?"

"Yes."

"Very good. Let's give it a try, shall we?"

Simon tied his ankles using a stout length of nylon cord, untied his neck, and ordered him to stand. Frank got to his feet and Simon picked up the shovel. He motioned Frank forward.

Frank could manage nothing more than a shuffle. The temperature was already in the eighties. It would be a hundred before the day was through; where Suki lay on the sand the air temperature would rise to a hundred and forty.

"Stop," Mink commanded.

Frank stopped, twelve feet from the central hole in the top of the anthill. It was teeming with mindless, scurrying scavengers. Forty feet away lay the bleached skeleton of a bird, picked clean, along with the scattered, empty shells of countless insects.

Simon stood behind him. He cut the bonds at Frank's wrists and stepped back. He dropped the shovel at Frank's feet, pulled his gun and backed away twenty feet.

"Don't forget what I told you, old man."

Frank bent over stiffly and picked up the shovel.

"Begin," Simon said. "Not too wide. Two feet in diameter, shall we say, and about five feet deep." His dead eyes gazed at Frank. "Do you wonder why, old man?"

"Not particularly."

"When it's finished, I'll stand you up in it with your hands tied at your waist, and bury you to your chin. When the ants find you, well, we'll just see what happens. They ought to go wild, finding a big hunk of meat like you within reach."

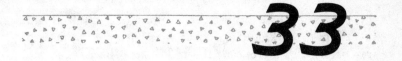

ig red ants stumbled about. As Frank worked, he dumped
sand on those that came nearest. Mink had warned him
not to throw his tailings on the central hill. Doing so didn't
seem like a terrific idea to Frank anyway—all it could do is
stir up the nest, maybe get the ants hungrier, worked up,
aware of him in some way—

Foolishness. His mind was simply churning, trying to
deny the awful thing that Mink had planned for him. When
Mink put him in the hole, the ants would do what they were
going to do, and it wouldn't matter very much what he did or
didn't do now to provoke them.

He tried not to think about it, tried not to visualize his
head resting on the sand as if decapitated, easy prey for the
scavenging ants, Mink watching with clinical detachment as

the little army first explored this miraculous intrusion and then went to work, perhaps covering his head until the flesh was barely visible beneath the red swarm, burrowing into him like tiny miners with their tough, scissoring mandibles. . . .

He looked over at Suki. The sun was hot, blazing down on her. She lay ten yards away with her eyes closed, not saying anything, not moving. Sweat glistened on her body. She looked so horribly vulnerable.

Hell, she *was* vulnerable.

Simon and Charlotte sat in the shade of the motor home on lawn chairs with drinks in their hands. Certainly they were creatures less than human. Nothing Suki had told Frank about them had prepared him for these black, suppurating horrors.

A foot beneath the surface the sand was dark, still damp from June thunderstorms; the sides of the hole held firm as he dug. Too bad. Mink had even given him a piece of plywood on which to stand to keep his weight from collapsing the sides of the hole as he worked. Mink had planned this bleak insanity with care.

A salty rivulet of sweat ran into Frank's eye. He blinked it away. The sun beat down on his shaven head. His scalp was already beginning to burn. If it blistered, it would give the ants a place to start. . . .

Jesus, quit with that, will you?

The hole was waist deep. He'd had to get in it to dig. About two feet left to go.

Simon walked over, carrying the gun. When he was twenty-five feet away they went through their charade again.

"Toss the shovel behind you, old man."

Frank judged the distance between himself and Simon. Too far. Reluctantly, he did as he was told.

"Get out of the hole and step away, to your right."

Frank shuffled away. Mink came closer and peered down.

"I think you're not working as fast as you might," he said softly.

There wasn't anything Frank could say. It was true. He had no desire to hurry this along. He'd hoped the hole would collapse, but the sand had just the right moisture content to keep from falling in on itself. It was hard-packed, having sat and settled where it was for countless years. Left undisturbed for another forty million years or so, it would turn to sedimentary rock.

"Continue," Mink said, backing away.

Frank retrieved the shovel and stood again over the hole, his own grave. When the ants were done, his bones would collapse into the hole. Sand would blow over the plain and bury him. In only a few years, this would all look exactly as it had before he'd begun to dig.

Mink crouched on his heels in the sand, observing Frank's labors.

"Know how much this is costing, old man?" he said.

"How much what is costing?"

"This." He swept a hand at the desert, including Frank and Suki in the gesture.

"Twenty bucks?"

Simon chuckled. "Man's got a sense of humor. I like that. You're tough, old guy, I'll give you that."

"Maybe you'd like to try your luck. Just the two of us, one on one."

Simon flicked away an intruding ant. "Actually, that's just what I've got in mind. Before I put you in the ground, I want you softened up a bit, not too much, but a little. But I digress. What these experiments are costing, in round numbers, is about two and half million dollars."

"Too bad."

"Isn't it though? The amazing thing is, not only can I afford it, but it's worth it to me. I haven't had a real vacation in years. Certainly not one as interesting as this. You see, my line of work involves a great deal of stress."

"Running scams on old people. You're a real hardworking guy, just full of that old-fashioned Protestant work ethic."

Simon smiled. "Suki's been telling tales, I see."

Suki spoke up. "Until forever, Mink, worms will crawl in and out of your brain and your rotten, horrible heart."

Mink's eyes never left Frank. "In your own way, Suki girl, you're as bad as I."

"Nothing on earth is as bad as you," she said.

"So," Mink said to Frank, "this is costing a lot. Not many people can visualize so much money, so let me put it into perspective for you. Two and a half million dollars, arranged as a stack of one-dollar bills, would make a pile over a thousand feet high. How about that?"

Frank kept on digging. There was nothing to say, nothing to be gained by exchanging madness with a madman.

"As you're being consumed, old man, I wonder if you'll spare a moment to appreciate the cost."

If not for Suki, and the hope that Simon might yet leave some tiny opening for counteraction, Frank would have already thrown the shovel in a futile attempt to split Simon's skull. Then, failing that, he would charge him in what amounted to a hopeless shuffle, see if he couldn't take a bullet in a place that would prove fatal quickly and deny Simon the pleasure of watching him die beneath that voracious, churning swarm.

But he couldn't. Not yet. And what had Simon said about softening him up a bit before putting him in the ground? Was there any hope in that? Exactly what had he meant by it?

"Where'd the money come from, old man?"

"Huh?"

"Sixty-six thousand dollars, give or take. It was in the house where I found you two."

"Know how you empty out your pockets when you get home, accumulate a bunch of spare change? Well, after thirty years of that I ended up with quite a pile."

Simon chuckled again. "Doesn't really matter, does it?" He sent another ant scurrying away with a flick of his finger. "Sixty-six thousand is a rather insignificant sum, isn't it?"

He stood up, began circling the anthill from a distance of perhaps fifteen feet, observing it, keeping an eye on Frank as he moved along.

"Fascinating, isn't it?" he said. "Consider, if you will, this coming exercise from the ants' perspective. Word is somehow passed that a large quantity of raw material has been discovered not far from the nest." He stopped, on the other side of the hill from Frank, still out of reach. "It's alive, still moving, this raw material is, and perhaps that's a consideration, but it's essentially defenseless. So, alive or not, the workers begin to hack away at it, because it's important to get as much of it as possible into the nest in as short a time as possible. No doubt that's one of nature's gentle axioms of survival out here.

"This raw material eventually quits moving and becomes an inert, decomposing mass, infinitely intriguing to our little friends. A vast pile of drying tubes and gristle and meat all waiting to be nipped into tiny portions and hustled down into the nest, and every so often a pocket of something particularly savory is discovered—thyroid, liver, pancreas—and a renewed flurry of excitement ripples through the nest. . . ."

Frank tried not to listen to the pustulant conversation, but it was hard—impossible, really. The image was too real, too awful to be denied. It would happen as Mink described it, if not in its particulars then in its broad outline. It would not be in anger that the colony would eat him, but as a simple matter of survival and applied economics. Without a doubt, he would be the greatest discovery in the history of the nest—

Mink had said something and was looking at him.

"What?" Frank said.

"I asked if you'd care to estimate your approximate value in dollars per pound at this moment."

Jesus, don't listen. Mink was just trying to get to him, trying to play with his mind. What he could maybe do is use the shovel to cut the rope that held his feet together, try to get an edge on Mink in case he got careless and moved closer.

"Five thousand dollars a pound," Mink said. "Assuming, that is, you are worth half of the two and a half million you and Suki are costing us, but I think that's fair, don't you? After all"—Frank rammed the shovel down edgewise between his feet, almost losing his balance as the ropes jerked his ankles inward—"this is a most interesting experiment, and you did interrupt my previous session with Suki. And if you try one more time to cut that rope with the shovel, Suki will lose her tits, understood?"

Frank held the shovel motionless before him.

"Dig," Mink commanded.

Frank took another scoop. The hole was deeper now, deep enough that it was difficult to remove more than a third of a shovelful at a time. The dark sand came out heavy with moisture, drying quickly in the heat where he slung it out onto the ground.

Mink moved around the anthill, now crossing over to where Suki lay. He said a few words that Frank couldn't make out.

"Fuck you." Suki's response rang out clear and strong.

She was still fighting. Frank's heart felt heavy, filled with a terrible sadness.

Another partial shovelful.

And another.

The day was cloudless, the air still. Heat refractions corrugated the desert, causing it to shimmer in the distance. Ants lurched across the sand.

Could he risk another assault on the rope at his ankles? The first blow had frayed it, but only slightly, and it was unlikely that he could hit it twice in exactly the same spot. If Mink caught him at it, would he do to Suki what he'd said he'd do? Perhaps. Certainly he was crazy enough.

Risk it?

No, not yet.

He tossed another few pounds of damp sand onto the alkali and glanced back at the motor home. Mink was watching him; his mother too. Crazy old bitch, silent and sullen and crazy as a loon, but she wasn't raving crazy, just crazy crazy. How had God managed to pair up two such as that, assuming He had anything to do with that kind of thing? What a colossal, cosmic blunder that had been. The two of them made Manson look like a guy with vaguely antisocial tendencies, nothing serious.

"I'm sorry, Frank," Suki called out to him.

"It's all right," he answered. What else could he say?

"God will punish him."

"I know."

Simon chuckled. Frank heard the sound from all the way out by the anthill, felt its darkness.

Twenty minutes later the hole was completed, deep enough for Mink's purpose. Things started to happen faster then.

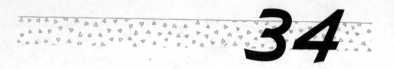

imon knelt beside her. Ice clinked against the sides of the glass as he lifted it to her lips. Even though Suki knew it would be better not to drink, knew that whatever Simon had in store for her would be easier to endure if she were dehydrated, she lifted her head and drank thirstily.

She wasn't ready yet to die.

She turned her head. Frank sat in the shade of the motor home. He'd been tied by his neck to something at the side of the vehicle, hands bound again.

"More?" Simon asked her.

"No."

"We'll see." He strode back to the Jamboree, returned with another glass.

She drank all of that one too.

"See," Simon said. "You didn't mean no."

Her eyes hated him, loathed him, stared at him venomously, tried to kill him. Please, God, split open the earth and drag this worm back down to hell!

"Soon we will begin," Simon said. He crouched beside her, stroking her hair. "Do you remember what I told you about the heat, Suki?"

She arched upward and spat into his face.

He wiped his cheek. "Extremely hot oil," he said. "The outcome of this experiment will be twofold. First, the physical impact of each drop will be much greater than it was with the cold, no doubt accelerating the destruction of your mind. The second result will be less interesting, but unavoidable. The oil will cook you, darling. Just your guts, of course. To tell the truth, I don't know which will ultimately cause your death, but we will find out, won't we?"

"My God, Simon, how can you *do* such horrible things?" She hadn't wanted to say it, hadn't wanted to say anything, but it just came blurting out.

He smiled. "Ask any quack psychologist, Suki, dear. I was scarred by an unhappy childhood. I wasn't permitted to play, to become skilled at social interactions. I was laughed at, introverted, shy. I'm seething with latent hostility, acting out feelings of aggression against a father who gave me none of the love I so desperately needed, and then deserted me at a tender age. Girls didn't like me as an adolescent. I didn't date and I had no real friends. I was lonely, frustrated, and made the butt of cruel jokes. Choose one or several."

He stood up.

"Please," she said. "Please . . . don't."

"If at any time you have the urge to scream, darling, do not hesitate to do so. I chose this place with you in mind." He walked away.

She trembled, told herself she would never scream—but this time she knew she would. She pulled at her bonds, felt no give in them. The stakes were driven too deeply.

Simon returned, carrying a medieval-looking apparatus: a wooden arm connected to a heavy plank base; at the end of the arm were a pair of metal hooks. He set it on the sand beside her, the arm suspended about a foot above her midsection. A bucket of sand held the base firmly in place.

"See what I made for you, Suki."

She didn't want to look, couldn't help it though. Mink's face was calm as he worked, tranquil insanity and empty death moving around inside his eyes.

"Please don't do this, Mink, please."

As if he hadn't heard her, he adjusted the arm of the contrivance to a position almost directly above her navel.

And then he went away.

Simon emerged from the motor home dressed only in some kind of a loincloth. Frank stared at him. Simon's feet were bare, his buttocks naked. Sinewy muscles rippled in his legs. His rib cage showed. The coarsely woven cloth, knotted at either side of his waist, covered only his groin.

"It's called an orosu," Simon said. "Any number of garments worn throughout the world are similar in appearance, but the orosu is unique. It originated in sixteenth-century Japan, specifically in the Oki Gunto archipelago in the Sea of Japan, off Honshu. Only those skilled in hand-to-hand combat were permitted to wear it, and then only within the walls of the temple-schools known as *kishoki*. My use of it is a bit of a bastardization though. You see, my specific discipline is an offshoot of kung fu practiced only in the mountainous Xinjiang Province of China. It's quite exotic, nothing at all like the form of self-defense that evolved in the Oki Guntos of Japan."

"You look very sweet in it anyway," Frank said. "Quite the fashionably dressed child molester."

Simon smiled. "I will enjoy tearing you down, Frank. May I call you Frank? You're just a bit overly self-righteous for my taste. You and I are going to engage in that hand-to-hand you expressed such an interest in a short while ago. It's been a while since I've had an opportunity to practice my art. And, as I said earlier, I'd like to soften you up a little before I put you in the ground."

"Try it, asshole. Nothing'd suit me better."

"Good. Bravado; I like that. You know what's in store for you, of course, and you have some idea of how Suki will die if you should lose. I went into detail about how the ants would strip your husk for a specific reason, Frank: I want you to do your best to win. I like a challenge, and I especially like it that you challenged *me*. I trust you won't disappoint me and make things too easy."

"Just so long as you untie me, asshole."

"Oh, I will, Frank. After Suki's punishment has begun. I want to be certain you're properly motivated."

Charlotte came out of the motor home, smoking a cigarette, wearing black silk slacks and a blouse with short sleeves and a high collar. Dark glasses covered her eyes.

"When?" she asked. Her voice shook. It sounded empty to Frank; hollow, as if she were in pain.

"Soon, Mother. Very soon now."

"I want the gun, Simon, just in case."

"There's no need."

"All the same, I intend to keep it with me."

Simon and Charlotte came toward her. Simon carried a thermos encircled by wire bands with loops formed in them. A curious attachment was at the top. Suki trembled.

Simon crouched beside her and placed the thermos upside down on the hooks of the wooden arm cantilevered above her.

"You will note," he said, "that I have positioned you in such a way that you will be able to observe Frank over there as the ants consume him. You might find that an interesting diversion from your own troubles. It will help."

"You . . . bastard."

293

"Making fun of my unhappy childhood, darling?"

"There is a God, Mink. You'll see. You can't do this."

"I'll believe in God when He stops me. Until then, all there is is what happens."

He placed a sponge on her belly. "Don't move, Suki." He twisted a tiny glass valve attached to the cap of the thermos. Pale yellow oil dripped onto the sponge. Slower. Slower.

Thip. . . . *Thip*. . . .

Thip. . . .

Thip.

Simon packed a bit of fiberglass insulation around the valve and stem, then stuck the back of his hand into the drip. The next drop landed on his flesh, and he closed his eyes and shivered, the muscles in his arm and shoulder standing out.

"It's ready, Suki. Are you?"

"My *God*, Mink. Please, please, don't. Please, I'm sorry I hurt you, I didn't mean—"

Simon took his hand away. And the sponge.

Thip.

Her body tensed when the fiery drop hit her belly. Lean muscles stood out everywhere like rawhide strips.

"Oh, God," she breathed.

"Yes, Suki. Yes, darling," Mink said. "Tell me of your pain."

No. She *wouldn't* scream, not ever. The insulation hid the drop as it formed. This time she couldn't see it, couldn't tell when the next one hung bloated and—

Thip.

"Ahhhhgg." She writhed on the sand.

Mink stood up. "Mother will keep you company for a while, Suki. Tell Mother of your pain." He walked away. Charlotte Voorhees stood above her with a gun in her hand.

Please, God, kill him, kill her. . . .

Thip.

Simon cut the noose from around his neck. Frank got slowly to his feet.

"Walk," Simon said. "Out there."

Feet still loosely bound, Frank shuffled out to the sandy area between Suki and the motor home.

"Stop."

Frank obeyed. Charlotte stood on the far side of Suki; the gun dangled from her fist. Suki moaned.

Blind rage threatened to overwhelm him, and blind rage was not what he needed now. He took a few deep breaths.

Mink moved behind him with a knife, and suddenly the ropes that held his wrists came free. Frank massaged his wrists and arms, pulled off remnants of the rope.

"I'll leave it to you to untie your ankles, old man. Then we'll see how motivated you are." Simon moved off a dozen feet and began to dance around, loosening up.

Suki cried out.

Crazy, Frank thought. Madness.

He had to win, had to. He outweighed this skinny fucker by at least a hundred pounds, and that Bruce Lee kung fu shit was just that, shit.

The guy was limber, though, standing on one leg, the other stuck damn near straight up in the air.

He remembered what Suki had told him about Mink, how the guy was fast, real fast. Frank wondered how fast he'd be with his eyes full of this alkaline grit.

He sat on the ground and untied the rope at his ankles. A weak feeling spilled through him as Suki groaned again, louder this time. Frank's belly was empty, hollowed out. Charlotte's eyes watched him. Simon spun gracefully, without effort, hands doing weird things—all just shit. In a real down-home brawl, kung fu was just a bunch of crap.

The rope came free. Frank got slowly to his feet. In his clenched right fist he had a handful of sand.

"Ready?" Mink said.

Frank nodded. Could he reach Charlotte before Mink took him down, or before she put a bullet into him? Would it do any good if he did? Maybe . . . if he could get his hands on that gun of hers.

"Your move, old man," Mink said. "You're the one with the gripe, remember."

No good. Mink was nearer to Charlotte than Frank was. He would never make it.

He tried circling.

Still no good. As Frank moved, Mink shifted with him. His muscles were stringy but well defined, tough-looking; the orosu was a considerably less ridiculous garment now than when Mink had first appeared in it.

Mink smiled, hands swaying. Frank took a step closer.

Another step. He threw a fist experimentally. Not close enough. Mink didn't duck, didn't flinch, didn't even lose his predatory little smile.

Frank threw the fist again, whipping the sand into Mink's face. Suddenly Mink pinwheeled, a spinning blur, and a naked foot caught Frank beside the ear. A single bright light exploded inside his head.

He was on the ground, on his face before he was aware of having fallen. Bitter sand flecked his lips. He was dazed, the sand close, blurred in his vision.

Frank rolled suddenly, panicked at the thought of Mink pouncing on him. But Mink was near Suki, dancing, not coming for him, waiting for him to get up again.

Frank took his time.

Suki sobbed. Not loud, but it got Frank to his feet. He couldn't reach her. Mink was right there, in the way again.

"What this is," Mink said, "is *kha xih*. Kung fu is really just a distant relative, and nowhere near as interesting. I doubt that half a dozen in the West practice kha xih with any regularity."

Frank approached cautiously.

"Now I'm going to break your nose, old man," Mink said. "See if you can stop me."

Frank covered up, guarding his face. But Mink might also be setting him up, so Frank was wary for an attack elsewhere. Mink glided up and Frank dropped way down and lunged for him, trying for a shot to his groin or to get an arm around Mink's waist. Mink danced to one side and grabbed Frank's wrist, gave it a gentle twist; pain shot up Frank's left forearm all the way to his shoulder. He almost screamed. He rolled in the sand, and again the foot came out of nowhere and cracked against the side of his nose.

The pain was excruciating. Frank landed on his back. His eyes watered and suddenly there were several Minks, fractured, drifting around.

"The wrist hold is called *chong jhu xih*," Mink said. "The broken nose is painful, is it not?"

It was, very. Blood bubbled down his throat.

Suki cried out. Frank staggered again to his feet, blood from his nose drenching the front of his shirt.

Thip.

She heaved against her bonds. The pain was all-encompassing, like nothing she'd ever experienced before.

Charlotte stood impassively above her, to her left, watching her boy battle Frank beneath the hot desert sun.

That was just hopeless. Mink was too good. Frank was on his feet again, but his nose was bleeding badly and he looked stunned.

Thip.

Suki sobbed thickly. Such an ugly, sick, demented way to die.

Please God, Jesus, help me, help Frank. *Help us!*

Her body gleamed with sweat, every fiber standing out as she strained at her bonds—and the stake that held her right leg in place moved, a quarter of an inch.

"Next," Simon said, "I will break one of your ribs. Unlike the wrist hold I used to defend against that barroom stunt of yours, you should expect a blow. *Kwan du xih*, this is called. There are many variations, however."

Frank's wrist still hurt; his nose was seething agony. It

seemed loose, the cartilage torn. But what seemed the biggest hurt of all was that Mink had told him he was going to break a rib, and Frank felt utterly powerless to stop him.

Still, he had to try. If only he could somehow get his hands on the bastard's skinny neck. Mink was fast and strong, but he wasn't what you'd call powerful.

Mink glided forward, danced, spun, and Frank expected the foot again. He threw his hands up to block it but the foot didn't come. A hand slapped his face—so fast he never saw it coming—and then his balance was gone and he stumbled forward. Mink's elbow cracked viciously into a lower rib on his left side. Frank felt it go.

He fell to the ground on his side, barely able to draw a breath. Five seconds. Mink had told him he was going to break a rib, and five seconds later it was done. Maybe this wasn't just a bunch of shit after all.

"You disappoint me, old man. I expected better from you than this," Mink said.

Suki cried out again, a terrible sound, full of agony. It took all Frank had to get his knees under him and push himself partway up with his hands.

This was no good. He couldn't touch the guy, couldn't so much as lay a finger on him.

"Last demonstration," Mink said. "Get up. You're going to like this one."

Slowly, Frank got his feet under him.

"It's called *xian jian xih*, a paralyzing strike to a specific nerve in the thigh. Quite difficult to do properly, I might add. You will be unable to use that leg for some time afterward, I'm sorry to say, so this will conclude our little session, old man. The nerve is in the center of the thigh, a few inches above the knee. I will strike your right leg, so be prepared to defend in that area."

Frank could draw only shallow breaths. There was no hope in this, but he gathered himself to meet Mink's attack as best he could.

*   *   *

Thip.

Suki's entire body tightened in agony, tendons creaking, and the stake that held her right leg gave another inch. She had a few precious inches of freedom now.

Her scalded belly was on fire. She lunged one more time against her restraints, felt the stake give another half inch. She pushed it outward with her ankle, then tried to work it from one side to the other. Some freedom there, but not much. Charlotte stood close to her, inside the oil barrier that was keeping the ants away; the gun hung from her thin, blue-veined hand. Her eyes shone as she watched Mink. Her boy was in no danger from Frank.

Thip.

Suki cried out involuntarily. Her muscles went rigid. The stake that held her right leg moved inward another half inch. She pushed outward, then tried to lift up. It wouldn't budge. She pulled the stake toward her body and then hammered it out, in and out, in and out, working it, using her other limbs for leverage.

She tried to lift again—and the stake slid upward a quarter of an inch.

Thip.

The pain filled her and she sobbed again, tears coursing down her cheeks. In, out, in, out. Now up, and the stake was looser now. It came up several inches. In, out. Now up, and suddenly the stake ripped free and without thinking Suki threw her leg upward in a slashing arc, body twisting, the metal rod whipping awkwardly at her ankle. Charlotte glanced down, surprise just beginning to contort the features of her face, when the stake smashed into her shoulder and slammed against the side of her head.

Charlotte went down. Her legs caught on the apparatus that held the thermos over Suki's body. Pinwheeling, shrieking, red hair flying in her face, Charlotte fell beside Suki's left hand and Suki's fingers closed on her hair.

Her grip tightened like iron.

Mink closed with him. Out of the corner of his eye, Frank saw movement where Suki lay on the sand.

Charlotte shrieked.

Mink's hands were already in motion, too late to stop. One hand, the right, grazed Frank's face; the left, fingers held together forming a blade, knifed into Frank's thigh but then faltered as Charlotte's howl reached a sudden crescendo. Frank's fingers closed on Mink's wrist.

Frank squeezed. His right leg collapsed and he slumped to one knee, but his grip tightened, strengthened by years of squeezing tennis balls while traveling the highways. In all those years, he had never clutched anything with such savage, blind intensity. Ropy muscles stood out in his forearm.

Mink's bones popped. Where the radius and the ulna joined the wrist, the radius tore loose and ground against the ulna. Mink screamed. Frank caught the same wrist in his other hand and dropped to the ground and rolled, twisting the joint as he yanked with all his strength. Mink's shoulder came apart; the humerus ripped loose from its socket. In an instant the arm was useless, limp, an appendage attached to the beast whose flesh was consumed in blind, screaming agony.

Charlotte thrashed. Suki's grip tightened. The gun lay on the ground a foot from Suki's face, pointed directly at her eyes, but that didn't matter; all that mattered was that her fingers were knotted into Charlotte's hair and the bitch was face down in the sand.

Like a hydraulic ram, Suki's wrist crushed downward. The stake still holding her wrist gave her the leverage she needed to shove the deadly harridan's face into the earth.

Charlotte screamed, inhaled. Alkaline grit rattled down her throat and into her lungs. Her skinny arms hammered the sand. Her fingers, formed into claws, tore at Suki's arms as she tried desperately to crawl forward and rip at Suki's eyes. Her left hand landed on the gun, knocked it away a few inches, and her fingers scrabbled for it, groping blindly.

Frank rolled over and over on the sand, holding tightly to Mink's arm. A gagging wail came from Mink's throat, and still Frank rolled, destroying the arm, paralyzing Mink's brain with pain. Mink flopped in the sand as Frank dragged him by his mutilated arm. Mink's brain was a raw, white cauldron of pain as his tendons ripped, blood vessels burst. The mad dog clung fast to his arm and rolled and rolled, until nothing remained—no pounding, grinding movement; no scintillating horror of agony—and Mink's world was a place of soft and silky dark.

Charlotte screeched, inhaled. She coughed, hacked dryly, abjectly. Suki shoved her face deep into the alkali. Tendons stood out on her arms; her face flushed with effort. Down and down and down and down, kill the bitch and kill the bitch and—

"Die," she breathed. "Die, you fucking witch!"

Charlotte's hand found the gun again. Suki shifted her elbow and mashed the muzzle into the sand.

Down and down and down. Strands of hair popped. Bury her, *crush* her, down and down and down. Charlotte's nose filled. Sand crusted her lips, coated her tongue, clogged her throat, drifted into her lungs. With all her old strength she tried to lift her head.

"Simon!" she cried, but it was an inhuman, gritty sound, a pathetic cough, muffled by sand. Her finger found the trigger of the gun, jerked, and a dull explosion blew sand over Suki's face. Charlotte's chest heaved. A spasm shook her, and then, weakly, another. Her nails raked furrows in the sand and her arms went slack and then her fingers began to twitch.

Down and down and down, the muscles in Suki's arms burned like they were on fire and now the burn was good, pure, and if she had to do this until eternity she would this was good this was God's fire, clean and honest, her fingers like steel wires burning, burning as she forced the viper's head down and down and down and down and—

"Enough."

She didn't hear, couldn't hear; there was nothing in the universe but her wrist and her fingers in the viper's stringy hair, her muscles burning, burning, burning—

"Christ, Suki, enough."

Something forced her fingers apart, pried them one by one from the loathsome thing in her grasp.

Her fingers tightened. *"No!"* she screamed.

"She's dead, Suki." The voice, coming to her from some unimaginable height, wasn't Charlotte's, wasn't Mink's. Her eyes opened. Frank was there, on his side beside her. Frank, with blood oozing from his nose, eyes bloodshot. Frank, not Mink. Frank. Mink was crumpled on the ground nearby, lying very, very still.

"Oh, God," Suki wailed. She opened her fingers, turned her head away and began to cry.

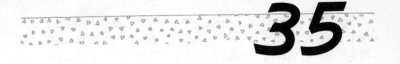

35

V i," Mink sobbed. "Oh, Vi . . ."

He lay on the sand, ankles bound, his one good arm lashed securely to his waist and thigh. Frank had rigged up a lawn chair and a bedsheet, providing him with a small amount of shade. Charlotte still lay face down on the ground where Suki had suffocated her ninety minutes earlier.

"Mother," Mink wailed. *"I'll have you killed!"* he shrieked suddenly. "Both of you. I've got money." His voice drilled through the quiet of the afternoon. The windows and doors of the motor home were open, allowing a faint breeze to drift through.

Outside, Mink started sobbing again.

Suki wore nothing but a towel wrapped around her hips. Mink had ruined her clothing and she couldn't bear the

303

thought of wearing anything that had belonged to either him or Charlotte. A red blister several inches in diameter covered her belly. Frank had rummaged through the motor home and found a first-aid kit. He'd rubbed some ointment onto a piece of gauze and gently taped it in place over her wound. She sat with her feet up now, nursing a bottle of mineral water.

Frank's nose throbbed and his broken rib pulsed with every beat of his heart. He'd removed his bloody shirt.

"I need a doctor for this arm!" Mink yelled.

Frank's right leg was able to support his full weight now, though it was still shaky. Charlotte's gun lay on a table within easy reach.

While hobbling about looking for a first-aid kit, Frank had found a sturdy black-enameled safe hidden away in a closet next to the toilet. A Fidelity model 40, probably the same one Suki'd opened in Louisiana. No telling what was in it. Maybe later, when she felt up to it, she could give it a try.

A map on the driver's console gave Frank a good idea where they were: central Nevada, Sulphur Spring Range, thirty miles north of Eureka.

"Vi," Mink moaned. "Vi." With sudden fury he shouted, "You killed my mother! I'll hunt you both to the ends of the earth!"

"We gotta listen to that?" Suki asked.

"How's the stomach?"

"It's been better. Guess I'll live, though."

"I'll carve out your eyes!" Mink screamed. *"If it takes all the money I've got and all the rest of my life, I'll find you!"*

Frank looked at Suki. He felt sick. "He means it."

"Shit, Frank, I know that. When Mink gets to talking about hurting people or killing, he means it."

Frank got slowly to his feet. Dark folds of skin sagged beneath his eyes. "Stay put a while."

"Why, where're you going?"

His voice was suddenly angry, fists white. "Just stay the hell inside, all right?"

"Jesus, all right!"

Frank went outside. He trudged over to Charlotte's body. Mink watched him. Frank took hold of Charlotte's arms.

"Hey!" Mink said. "What're you doing?"

Frank dragged her toward the pit he'd dug earlier, the hole that was to have been his grave—no, much worse than a grave. His broken rib ached miserably.

"What're you doing? Put her *down!*"

Charlotte's heels dug shallow grooves in the alkali. She weighed no more than ninety-five pounds. Her flesh was hot and dry, almost scaly. Rigor mortis had already begun to set in.

Frank stood at the edge of the hole, staring down. Head first or feet first? The hole was little more than a shaft.

"*No!*" Simon screamed. "*The ants'll get her in there!*"

"At least they'll get her dead, not alive." Frank grabbed her ankles, dumped her in head first.

Simon went crazy. "*Whatever it takes!*" he screamed. "*No matter where you go, I'll track you down!*"

Now the sadness filled Frank to overflowing, an emotional sludge of immeasurable bitterness. He didn't want the responsibility, didn't want to be the one to do it, but there was no one else to shoulder the burden. He wouldn't let Suki do it, not even if she wanted to. And she would. No way he could allow that to happen, or even to give her a say in the matter.

Hugging his ribs, he walked over to Simon and looked down at him. Simon's arm was dark, discolored, well on its way to becoming gangrenous. The flesh was bloated, horribly twisted at the shoulder, the artery kinked shut. Simon was on his back, breathing shallowly. His eyes were pits.

"Whatever it takes," he hissed.

Frank grabbed the ends of the nylon cord he'd tied around Simon's ankles.

"What're you doing?" Simon asked.

Frank pulled. Simon slid across the sand, his ruined arm

305

trailing uselessly. Simon screamed in agony and Frank willed himself not to hear, not to feel, not to think.

It didn't work. Simon's shrieks reverberated through a black horror that filled Frank's brain. It would have been a blessing if Mink had simply passed out, but he didn't.

They approached the hole.

"What're you *doing!*" Simon cried. "Oh, Jesus Christ, no, *you can't! You can't!*"

Frank hurried now, not wanting this, not knowing what else to do. If it was just him, he'd probably risk it—but it was Suki too.

It had to be done. Had to.

"*NO!*" Simon screamed.

Into the hole, head first. Simon lay crumpled against Charlotte, neck bent forward, chin on his chest, legs reaching three-quarters of the way to the surface. His ruined arm was sprawled across Charlotte's livid face.

Frank picked up the shovel.

"No," Simon Voorhees said, staring up at him. "I don't want to die." His eyes were shiny.

"Neither does anyone else, pal. Too bad you never understood that."

He threw in a shovelful of sand.

Simon sputtered. "Don't, please *don't*—"

Another shovelful.

Simon coughed.

Another. Frank didn't look. Another, another, working quickly now, and Frank didn't see Simon's legs begin to kick, thrashing against the sides of the hole, his body bucking as his head went under and the ancient sand filled his nostrils and poured into his gaping mouth.

Frank began shoveling madly, scooping sand into the hole, sweat pouring off his body beneath the hot sun, ribs burning, the sand gritty, landing in the hole with heavy plops, Frank's breath coming in hoarse gasps, ants stumbling about, Mink's feet gone now, only Charlotte's still showing, and then it was

306

done and nothing was left but a place in the empty shimmering desert where the sand had been disturbed, not far from a giant thriving anthill.

"God keep you both," Frank whispered over the grave. The words seemed ambiguous enough.

36

Sun sparkled on the water, glittering on the sand across the road, Avenida Vieira Souto, and reflecting off bodies lying lotioned on the beach. Ever-present samba music filled the tropical air around the café.

The beautiful mulata waitress, her skin the color of café au lait, leaned forward and said something in Portugese, then paused at the sight of Frank's missing fingertip.

"Tell her I lost it in an elevator in London," Frank said. "Nineteen and sixty-one. Door closed on my finger and took it straight up to the fourteenth floor. Back then they had lousy safety devices on some of those old lifts over there."

Suki glanced up from the book she was studying. "Christ, Frank, she doesn't want to know what happened to that old finger of yours."

"Course she does."

"What she asked was if you want another *chopinho*."

Cold draft beer. "Tell her no, I want a *batida*, and tell her about the finger, too."

Suki hesitated.

"Go on, tell her."

In halting Portugese, Suki spoke to the girl, a native of the city, known as a Carioca.

The girl smiled, went away.

"See, what'd I tell you?" Frank said.

"What I told her was they let you out the first Tuesday of every month and that you're harmless and mostly sweet in spite of the way you look."

"Jesus." He shook his head.

It was March, hot. They'd survived Rio's famous Carnival, barely, and now the city's *avenidas* were merely raucous. Suki sat across the tiny table from him, dressed in a batik print dress, beneath which Frank knew she was wearing some sort of a thong bikini that wasn't much better than wearing nothing at all. Possibly worse.

Ipanema beach, right next to the Garden of Allah beside the canal separating Ipanema from Leblon. To their left was a stretch of sand where many of the women were lying topless in the sun, not a bad view, Copacabana beach beyond that, past Ponta do Arpoador, while to the right, two kilometers away and rising fifteen hundred feet above them, was Pedra Dois Irmãos, with its shantytown debris visible among the trees.

No bugs, that was the amazing thing. Well, a few, but none that really bothered him. He'd taken to Rio like a duck to lingonberry sauce. Rio was different, exotic even, but nothing he couldn't get used to. Except for the damn Portugese, which was just screwed-up Spanish. Suki was acting as interpreter, picking up the lingo like a champ. Learning to read English, too, and Frank was finding he wasn't too bad a teacher.

309

She'd opened Mink's safe in the Jamboree and there'd been $1,363,900 in there. Even now, just thinking about the sight of all that money made his scalp tingle. So they'd used some of it to set him up properly as Frank Wiley—social security, driver's license, passport; the whole shebang—and then they'd flown to Georgetown on the Cayman Islands where they'd set up his-and-hers accounts, $650,000 each, and then gone on to Rio with almost $50,000 still jingling in their jeans.

At an interest rate of 6.18 percent, each of them was making $40,170 a year. Frank didn't know how they were going to spend that much, and they weren't, of course, living practically like natives as they were, so the money was already growing. For now they lived dutch, in a nice white apartment off Rua Barata Ribeiro, and Frank still hadn't asked her how long she was going to stick around before getting on with the rest of her life, and really didn't want to know.

What to do, that was each day's question. But there was always something. One thing he was going to try someday was deep-sea fishing. Tuna, marlin, maybe dorado—but for that you had to go out about forty miles, out near the continental shelf. That could wait a while. The fish weren't going anywhere. . . .

Suki stood up, let her dress slip down around her ankles. The swimsuit was even smaller than Frank had remembered.

"Christ, you're gonna cause a riot," he said.

"Sweet-talker. I'm just gonna get my feet wet. Watch my stuff, okay?"

"I'm watching your stuff right now. So's everyone else."

She made a face at him, turned away and then turned back. "How the hell *did* you lose that goddamn finger, Frank? You've told so many stories, my head is spinning."

"Korea," he said. "Nineteen and fifty-two. I stepped out of this helicopter just north of Pyongyang, when I felt this tremendous draft. So I wet my finger and stuck it up to see which way the wind was blowing, and, *pow!* off the sonofa-bitch came. Turns out the draft was a goddamned downdraft, and—"

"Jesus." Suki turned, walked away toward the water.

He watched her go. It was quite a sight.

Pretty terrific book!
(★★★½) 8/2/91